NYMPH
THE SINGULARITY

Jill Killington

Encyclopocalypse Publications
www.encyclopocalypse.com

Contents

Acknowledgements

I first published *Nymph: The Singularity* online under the pseudonym "J.E. Lansing" after I saw Ray Kurzweil give a speech in 2011 about the democratization of art and ideas thanks to the internet, and I'm very grateful to everyone who somehow found my novel and read it online since then. Thank you Ray Kurzweil, for your endless inspiration - I hope the Singularity is as near as you say and that we both live to see it.

Thank you to all my friends who put up with me as I obsessed over this novel for years. Special thanks to my future partners at Mid-World, Knate Gwaltney and Josh Boone, for your endless support. My lofty goal when writing *Nymph* was to create a set of rules and terms for dealing with the inevitable development of sex robots in the way Asimov and Orwell helped shape our future with *I, Robot* and *1984.* Sentient sex androids are not a reality just yet, so who knows, maybe there's still time for this book to become part of the discussion--or perhaps the actual androids of the future will enjoy reading Nymph for fun on the beach someday.

I owe a debt of gratitude to authors Philip K. Dick, Marguerite Duras, Anais Nin, William Gibson, Bruce Sterling, Frank Herbert, Vladimir Nabokov, Margaret Atwood, Paul Eikman, T.S. Eliot, Louise Brooks, Stephen King, Clive Barker, and Anne Rice for inspiring the writing style for my first novel.

Nymph meant more to me than anything in the world for at least five years of my life, and in many ways it's still the most personal (and self-indulgent) thing I've ever written. I tried to find an agent and publisher for *Nymph* during the economic collapse in 2008 and failed miserably. But if I hadn't written this book and failed then, I wouldn't be who I am now.

This book represents everything I was as an artist during that time in my life and I'm grateful that you're reading this now, whoever, wherever, and whenever you are. Thank you!

Jill Killington, 2015
www.jillkill.com

Part 1
Chorion

Chapter One

Shock.

That was her first sensation.

One moment, she didn't exist. And then she did. The sudden change from negative to positive was silent agony.

Humans scream when thrust out of the safety of the womb, blessed to forget their birth. Unfortunately for Suzanne, she would remember. The first moment of her life was the only sensation of physical pain she would ever know.

After her first moment of being, there followed an absolute stillness.

She was aware. She had a body now. She could feel energy coursing through it, her nucleus spinning somewhere deep inside.

She opened her eyes and saw a single blinding light suspended above her.

The light turned off. Other softer lights flickered on around her, giving form to her world. She looked down and saw her body. She was laid out on a table.

Three humans materialized out of the darkness. In stark contrast to her own nudity, they were shrouded in green gowns. Only their eyes were exposed to her as they examined her. She watched the nearest human's surgical mask crease and billow as he spoke.

"Suzanne, are your auditory processors working?"

She thought carefully before responding. She understood what he was saying to her, which meant she heard him and that she was functioning correctly. She was being asked a question. She was Suzanne.

"Yes," she replied, the word hissing over her teeth and tongue. She licked her lips, delighting in the sensation. She had never spoken before.

The man seemed to approve. "Suzanne, raise your legs," he said. "Flex your toes."

"Put your legs down."

"Clench your hands into a fist - good, let go."

"Sit up."

"Lay back down."

"Turn your head and look at me."

"Touch your toes."

"Shake my hand."

They asked her to stand and walk. Suzanne stood and staggered initially, but corrected herself quickly and found the balance she needed. After circling the white room, she was told to return to the table and lie down.

"All points of articulation operational."

"Timely comprehension and response."

"No evidence of fragmentation during installation."

"Force reflection safety confirmed."

"That's it," said one of the shrouded humans.

"She's good to go. Just check her for sexual response, secure her loyalty and personality, and then take her out of test mode."

At that point, two of them began to argue in low tones about who would check for response, while the third attempted to mediate. Despite the anonymity of their green garb, Suzanne was

able to determine that the two arguing were male and the third female by listening to the depth and timbre of their voices.

A compromise was finally reached, and both men agreed to share the responsibility. The woman tugged off her protective gloves, narrowly missing Suzanne's head as she threw them down on the table. "Just do your job and keep her pristine, you hear me?" she said and stormed out of the room.

As Suzanne watched the door close, she was overcome by a sudden onslaught of pleasure. She looked down and saw the two men were groping and squeezing her bare breasts. A small sound escaped her mouth - a wordless utterance of surprise. Her nipples hardened, as they were roughly pinched and pulled between gloved fingers. A hand snaked along her leg and over her thigh, sliding inevitably upwards. Her back arched and she moaned as her clitoris was massaged and teased. Her vagina lubricated automatically in anticipation, as she was fully aroused.

Her external body was anatomically correct. She lacked a true digestive system, although she was capable of imbibing, processing, and eliminating liquids. She possessed a respiratory system, but it served no purpose other than cooling her nucleus and helping to better affect human behavior. She had no need for a heart or other organs - or for living cells multiplying, dividing, and dying inside of her. She was an unchanging creation formed of polymers, minerals, plastic, and silica, but her sexual organs were modeled exactly after those of a human woman. She possessed a network of muscles, nerves, and other attributes that made sexual pleasure possible for her, and also for her partner - she only lacked a reproductive system, and the responsibilities that came with it.

Suzanne's moaning increased, signaling her fast approaching orgasm as the two technicians continued to stimulate her body. The man manipulating her clitoris issued a command.

"Audio off."

Suzanne fell silent, still squirming under his ministrations.

"You should stop," the other man said, panting as he massaged her breasts. "She's getting too close."

"Hold on, I haven't checked her for muscle control."

A gloved finger pushed gently into the entrance of her vagina. She gasped as she clenched and contracted.

"Hot damn, she's functional alright. She's wetter than wet."

This seemingly paradoxical statement momentarily distracted Suzanne. What could possibly be wetter than wet?

"Alright, that's enough."

The hands stopped massaging her breasts, but there was still the finger inside of her, and the thumb teasing her clitoris.

"She's so responsive. So convincing. Look how she's breaking out in a thin layer of sweat."

"Yeah, I can see that. Look, you've got to stop. You can't let her climax, not even in test mode. Owners are entitled to first orgasm on the Même series."

"No one will ever know, "the man replied. His fingers rubbed her insistently, pushing her further and further. Her hips rocked in response.

"Someone will know," the other man said with certainty, his eyes scanning the empty room. "She's worth three billion dollars. It's in your best interest and mine to leave her alone. There are plenty of Harlots in for reconditioning that you can spend your energy on."

"All that work, and only one man gets to have her," he said with regret, running his hand between Suzanne's breasts and down the taut muscles of her stomach as she quivered with desire.

"You've had more than you were entitled to already. I'll lock in her personality and loyalty. Then we pack her up. Leave her pure."

The man touching her looked carefully into Suzanne's eyes. "You don't want us to stop, do you?" he asked.

He was right. She didn't want him to stop. She was ravenous for pleasure. She would have begged him to continue if she hadn't been set on mute. Her programming was working perfectly.

With tangible remorse, the man unhanded her and went about his work. "Audio on."

"You okay, sweetheart?" the other one asked.

Suzanne nodded. "Yes."

"I need you to spread your legs again," he instructed.

Suzanne did as she was told and the man inserted a long silver probe into her vagina. Suzanne sat up so she could see what he was doing, but she was scolded and told to lie back down. She could feel the probe going deeper and deeper, far past the point where it would have harmed a human woman.

She heard an audible click as something locked into place, and a flood of information and emotion washed over her.

The man extracted the probe. "That's it. She's done."

She looked up at him in wonder, brimming with new comprehension. There were two new words in her lexicon that she didn't yet understand, but she knew held great importance. To better grasp their meaning, she said them aloud.

"Alexander Conrad."

She didn't know what the words meant, but she liked them immensely. The men shut her down and her world went black again.

* * * * *

She was lost. Some consciousness of her body remained - enough to know that she was being moved. She was being taken far away, but she couldn't see where she was going or how. She had the terrifying sensation of free falling. While lost in this dark and lonely place, the words that fascinated her before returned, enveloping her and making her feel safe.

Alexander Conrad.

* * * * *

She was active again. Her previous experiences ceased to matter, and were all but forgotten. Suzanne opened her eyes.

She was on a large soft bed, and wearing a gauzy white gown.

This room was a startling change. It was dark, and as filled with color as the other one had been white and plain. Candles flickered and cast a golden light over her.

"Suzanne?"

That was her name. She turned to see who said it.

The first thing she noticed about him was his smile. It was the first she'd ever seen, the only face she'd ever encountered that wasn't concealed by a mask. His white teeth glistened in the candlelight, and for a moment she was held enthralled. She watched as his lips formed her name again.

"Suzanne?"

She looked up into his green eyes, as comprehension washed over her - this was Alexander Conrad.

She knew him, even though she'd never seen him before this moment. His face was imbedded in her loyalty software, and she'd confirmed his identity through retinal eye scan and voice. She *belonged* to Alexander Conrad. She was Suzanne Conrad, his wife.

Now that she was finally with him, all her embedded knowledge and programming fell into place. She reached up towards him, and he took her wrists in his hands and kissed them.

There was something she had to say to him. She fought to find the right words, and he noticed her struggle.

"What is it, Suzanne?" His beautiful face looked down at her with concern. "What's wrong?" Her vision blurred, and she felt a tickling sensation as tears spilled out of her eyes and rolled down her cheeks.

"I'm sorry," she told him.

Alexander touched the tears on her cheek with amazement, rubbing them away with his thumb. "What are you talking about? What do you have to be sorry for?"

She kissed him and pressed her slippery cheek to his. "I'm so sorry for everything, everything that happened." She didn't understand why she was apologizing, but she truly meant what she said. She was consumed by an overwhelming feeling of regret. She couldn't control the tears, couldn't stop her guilt. It was all part of her programming.

Somehow, it was exactly what Alexander needed to hear. To his own amazement he began to cry with her.

"I'm sorry, too. I'm so sorry. It was my fault, too."

Suzanne laid her head on his shoulder. Her tears were subsiding. Alexander stroked her hair. She closed her eyes and whispered in his ear.

"I love you." She looked up at him, waiting for him to say that he loved her too. Fortunately, he did. He cupped her face in his hands, candlelight sparkling in his green eyes.

He said the words she needed to hear. "Suzanne, I love you so much."

She cried harder then, and kissed him. Her arms wrapped around his neck and her legs encircled his waist.

"I love you, Alexander."

Suzanne felt him tense against her. He untangled his body from hers, and then sat on the edge of the bed without looking at her.

She'd made a mistake. What had she done wrong? He was pulling a small object on and off his hand. Suzanne looked closer, and saw it was a piece of jewelry. A silver ring.

"Call me Alex," he said, twisting the ring on his finger. "It just won't be the same if you don't call me Alex."

Alex. Suzanne assimilated his command immediately. From that moment on, he was Alex to her.

She should have known. She was pre-programmed to call him Alex, but somehow she'd called him Alexander. She didn't understand why she made such an error. There were so many things for her to remember, so many things for her to learn.

She tried again. "Alex?"

That smile spread across his face again as she said his name. She smiled in return, looked into his eyes and said, "I love you, Alex."

And so their new life together began.

* * * * *

Alex lay asleep next to Suzanne with a sheet thrown across his stomach and twisted between his pale legs. She ran her hand over his broad shoulders and brushed her fingers through the hair on his chest, delighting in the way it tickled her hand. All of her touch sensors were receiving perfectly.

Suzanne was here for him. She knew that. Her entire persona was made to order for this man. Alex was the entire reason that she had been created.

She was buzzing with the newness of everything she had experienced. She closed her eyes, still savoring the sweet aftermath of sex with him. Even though orgasmic response was an integral part of her programming, she was concentrating so hard on Alex's satisfaction that the sensation of her first orgasm still took her by surprise.

She straddled him during sex, moaning and riding him hard while monitoring his increasing pulse and galvanic skin response. She enjoyed kissing him - loved touching him, and felt even better when she knew she was pleasing him. Pleasing him was her incentive at all times, but soon the sensation of sex itself became an even stronger catalyst.

The sharp and utter happiness of orgasm - she thought surely it signaled the end of her short existence, that she was experiencing some sort of meltdown, even as she became aware it was a normal occurrence for her. Her entire body tensed and heat radiated through her body as she climaxed - and as soon as the sensation subsided her first impulse was to see if she could do it again. She orgasmed several more times, until Alex's body finally couldn't take anymore and she felt his spasms deep inside of her.

As the feeling melted away, she found herself panting hard and rolling over onto Alex's side, even though it was impossible for her to feel tired. Her heavy breathing was part of the outward impression of her deep satisfaction. Alex looked up at her in a dazed sort of wonder, and then his eyes closed and he fell into a deep sleep.

She kissed his eyelids and settled next to him on the bed and observed him as he began to snore. She recognized his snoring was natural for him, and was lulled by it rather than alarmed by the change in his breathing.

She curled up next to him and shut her eyes. Her system cycled into sleep, and she stayed with him like that until morning.

* * * * *

As Alex began to stir, her system automatically came back online. She was already smiling at him when he finally opened his eyes that morning.

"I'm so glad you're here," Alex said. "I was afraid you were just a dream."

Suzanne kissed him passionately in response. She dipped her head toward his lap, but Alex gently pushed her away.

"I'm still worn out from last night - I'm not a

young man anymore," he said. "Besides, today is a very special day."

What was today? Suzanne queried for the information and found it. "It's Christmas Day," she said with a smile. "A holiday."

"That's right. Do you know what that means?"

She accessed a composite on Christmas, which gave her a general idea of the holiday. Christmas: A holiday observed internationally with religious, secular, cultural, and economic significance, and innumerable customs accompanying it. She scanned through images and information for relevance to Alex's question - colored lights, nativity scenes, and reindeer. She had no idea whether he was referring to Santa Claus, the birth of Jesus, or the fact that suicide rates spike on this holiday.

Rather than trying to predict what Alex wanted her to know about Christmas and face a possible miscommunication, she adopted a coy programmed smile and shook her head.

"What does that mean, Alex?"

He rolled out of bed and pulled on a pair of pants. "It means that I'm going to shower you with presents."

"Shower me with presents?" she repeated, confused again. She queried the phrase and immediately understood the meaning. "You're going to give me gifts?"

"Yes," he said, kissing her on the cheek. "Because I love you."

Suzanne smiled lovingly at Alex. "I love you, too," she said automatically. "But I don't have anything to give you." One of her primary programming objectives was to always reciprocate.

"You don't have to give me anything," Alex said with a grin. "You were my present to myself."

He took her by the hand and lifted her off the bed. Suzanne stood naked in front of him, bathed in morning sunlight. He sighed with contentment.

"I have to get things ready," he said. "Put on your nightgown and come into the living room in two minutes." She nodded, and he kissed her again and left the room.

She found her long sheer gown on the floor and stepped into it. As she pulled it over her shoulders, she caught a glimpse of movement out of the corner of her eye.

A woman with long dark hair and big brown eyes stared at her from across the room. Suzanne gasped at the sight of her, and the woman gasped at the same time. She was seeing her own reflection in a mirror. Suzanne recognized herself, of course - her own appearance had been programmed into her recognition library. But she hadn't had the time to consider her appearance because her every thought had been consumed by Alex.

She crossed the room and studied herself in the mirror in close detail, running her fingers through the waves of disheveled hair that fell down to her tan breasts. This was the hair that brushed over Alex's face during sex.

The automatic blink of her eyes caught her attention, and Suzanne slowly turned her head. Her brown eyes tracked back and forth, contemplating themselves in the mirror. She placed a hand against the cool glass of the mirror and observed the movement of her lips as she introduced herself aloud.

"Hello. My name is Suzanne."

Alex called to her from the other room, though it hadn't been two minutes yet - only one minute and thirty-two seconds precisely. But she was learning a new lesson about Alex: she should be early when he wanted her in a certain place at a certain time.

She walked out of the sunny warmth of the bedroom and down a long marble hallway. She was not pre-programmed with a map of the house, and no floor plan was available through query. She didn't know where the living room was.

"Alex?" she called tentatively.

She followed his voice, passing through a diaphanous silver fabric into a golden room with bay windows that framed a cloudless sky. In the distance, she could see mountains.

Alex stood in front of her, next to a small tree - a Douglas fir-covered in gold ropes and multicolored lights. She recognized it from her earlier query. It was a Christmas tree.

He smiled at her broadly, his hands spread in presentation. "Merry Christmas, Suzanne." She knew the appropriate response. "Merry Christmas, Alex."

"Come here," he said.

Suzanne crossed the room to join him as fast as she could, all the while adjusting and updating her balance, still mastering the pendulum-like motion of bipedal ambulation. When she finally reached Alex, he lifted her off the ground and twirled her around, laughing as he spun the two of them in circles.

She was unsure what reaction to display to this

behavior, so Suzanne attempted to match the heartiness of his laughter. She was programmed to smile or mimic Alex when confronted by behavior that she didn't understand. Given his enthusiasm, she deemed that mimicry was the correct response.

Alex finally ran out of breath and collapsed on the couch with Suzanne on top of him. His heart was racing, and his pulse was past his maximum rate of safe exertion. She would have worried and begun first aid procedures if he wasn't laughing.

"I'm not too heavy for you, am I?" Suzanne asked, making a mental note not to let Alex pick her up like that anymore.

"Not at all," Alex said, panting. "You're as light as a feather."

Suzanne rested her head on his shoulder, and found that she was staring at her own image again.

This wasn't her reflection - it was a large photograph. But for some reason, there were numerous inconsistencies between the image she'd seen in the mirror and the one in the photo - it was her face, the biometrics were the same, but the cheeks were plumper and the jaw less defined. Her hair was different, too - it was curly and only chin length in the photo.

Suzanne studied the image, struggling to understand these discrepancies. She queried the photo and found no record or explanation for it, and concluded that this must be an artistic rendering of her and subject to creative interpretation. Why else would she be portrayed so inaccurately?

The facial expression was too complex for Suzanne to fully interpret. There were the standard indicators of a smile of happiness - the *zygomaticus* minor and major were raised, along with the *caninus*. But the *buccinator* muscle formed a dimple of contempt on one side of her mouth, while the frontalis raised one of her brows. Suzanne decided that the expression depicted in the picture was best termed "ironic bemusement." She attempted to replicate it and found she couldn't force her muscles into position - her facial muscles had the degrees of freedom necessary but not the ultimate control.

The image of Suzanne dissolved into another - in this one her full body was visible and she was jumping in mid-air. Her arms and legs were stretched outward, and her long hair formed a cloud around her head. She had a huge smile on her face, but again she looked different than she had appeared in the mirror, although this time the resemblance was much stronger.

"What are these pictures?" Suzanne asked after Alex caught his breath. "Are these pictures of me? "

Alex took one look at the photo and commanded, "Photos off."

The portrait of Suzanne evanesced and the frame transforming into a plain mirror. "Those are just old photos," Alex said dismissively.

"Old photos?" Suzanne repeated, still not comprehending. "When were they taken?" Alex kissed her, and then handed her a large box.

"We'll talk about that later," he said. "Right now, you should open your present."

Suzanne smiled and obeyed him without noticing how deftly he distracted her. She queried online for an explanation of how to open a gift, and soon understood that gifts were wrapped in colorful paper in order to conceal their contents. Although there were plenty of instructions on how to wrap presents online, she found no instructions on how to unwrap them.

Alex's satisfaction was one of her primary directives, so she set about the task without hesitation. She pulled off the red ribbon and turned the box over, seeking a point of entry. Most of Suzanne's ingrained hand dexterity was focused on tasks like sexual gratification or massage and regular household labor - anything else had to be learned and added to muscle memory.

Her fingers slipped and scrambled over the paper, until she finally found the seam. Alex watched the whole procedure with amusement, so pleased by her mere presence that it never occurred to him to tell her to just rip the paper. She laid the paper aside, and lifted the cover off the box and revealed a layer of green tissue paper. Alex laughed at her surprise, and Suzanne laughed with him, never realizing that her behavior was the source of his laughter.

"Keep going," he prodded. "The gift is underneath all that."

She pushed aside the tissue paper and found a square of crimson velvet at the bottom of the box. Alex unfurled it and held it in front of her - it was a dress.

"Would you like to try it on for me?" he asked.

Suzanne stood and allowed the sheer gown she was wearing to drop to her feet. She raised her arms over her head, and Alex slipped the crimson velvet over her bare skin.

"You look absolutely amazing," he told her. "Like a dream come true." She ran her hands over the plush fabric that clung to her body.

"It feels so soft."

"I hoped you would like it. It reminded me of…" Alex trailed off and seemed to reconsider what he was about to say. "It reminded me of you."

She knew that a further display of gratitude was the correct response. "Thank you," she said and then kissed him, never taking her eyes off his.

Next, he gave her a black velvet box and flipped it open - inside was a thin silver ring set in white satin. Alex took out the ring and pointed out how his name was carved in tiny cursive on its inside, then slipped it on her finger.

"I love it," Suzanne said as he interlaced his fingers with hers. He wore a matching silver ring on his hand.

"Now we're complete," Alex said with a smile.

She gave him a kiss. He gestured to the remaining pile of presents. "There's much more."

He gave her a long black hooded cloak - panties, bras, garter belts and other lingerie. His last gift was a pair of black satin stilettos with long black straps. He showed her how to twist and tie the straps on her calves.

Suzanne pulled up her skirt and modeled the shoes for him. Walking in heels came easily to her - her creators had obviously anticipated that she would be expected to wear them.

"I'm impossibly happy right now," Alex sighed, gazing at her legs as she made her way around the heaps of new clothes.

"What can I do to make you even happier?" she asked, bending and brushing her lips across his neck.

Alex grinned mischievously. "There is one thing I would like from you."

She ran her hand over his thigh and said, "Anything that would please you."

"Will you dance for me?"

Suzanne nodded. "How would you like for me to dance?"

"Slowly. Just dance for me."

She smiled, and rhythmic music filled the room. She began to sway with the music, the long material of her red velvet gown swirling along the wooden floor as she moved. Her hands carved out invisible patterns in the air and her pelvis rotated in small circles as she began to dance for Alex.

Her undulations were a compilation of movements motion-captured from traditional erotic dancers. Suzanne's gaze never left Alex - her eyelids half-closed in a calculated imitation of sexual desire. She knelt on the floor in front of him, allowing the strap of her gown to slide down her shoulder as she ran her hands over her bare arms and the red velvet covering her breasts.

She stood and slowly lifted her dress as she undulated - revealing the black straps that wound around her calves and then up the curve of her thighs. The dress swirled and fell around her ankles, and leaving her only in her black stilettos as she kicked the dress away. She glanced over her shoulder, her hands demurely over her breasts. Alex watched her with a cool blank expression on his face, but his eyes were on the shimmying motion of her hips.

Suzanne straddled Alex, flooding him with the smell of her perfume and synthetic pheromones as she rocked her hips towards him in time with the music. She slid onto her knees and pulled down his pants, taking him in her hand and kissing just the tip of him with her moist lips. She looked up at him through her eyelashes, sucking him into her mouth and tracing him with her tongue as he groaned. She sucked and licked him, applying pressure with her hand as she moved up and down with precision.

"Oh God, Suzanne, stop," Alex moaned, his back arching.

She checked his heart rate and confirmed that he was fine. Suzanne knew that he would feel even better, and resumed her ministrations, intent on finishing the program. This kind of sexual disobedience was one of her programmers' proudest achievements - the ability to interpret not just what a user or owner dictated, but what would truly ensure his satisfaction.

Alex ejaculated in Suzanne's eager mouth, and she swallowed his semen while licking him clean. She was already beginning to process and sterilize the small amount of liquid, and recycling it to create the lubricants she needed for her own orifices.

"Merry Christmas," Alex said as he spread out on the couch. His eyes drooped shut, and he was asleep.

Suzanne settled next to him, and waited for him to reawaken. She kissed him on the cheek. "Merry Christmas, Alex."

CHAPTER 2

Suzanne monitored Alex's heart rate and blood pressure as he snored amidst the wrapping paper and ribbons. His stamina seemed low, but his vitals were fine. It seemed he was legitimately tired, but even with his advanced age he shouldn't have been practically knocked unconscious by each of their sexual encounters thus far.

He pulled her towards him in his sleep, hugging her to his sweat-drenched chest. She listened to the blood pumping through his heart and the air passing through his lungs, while staring at the mirror over the fireplace.

What were those unfamiliar images of her? She remembered what Alex said - they would talk about it later. She shut out the last thought of the portrait and closed her eyes as her system cycled into sleep. When she awoke a few minutes later, Alex's eyes were open and his heart was beating exceptionally fast.

"Alex?"

She waited for a response. "Alex?" she repeated.

He seemed to snap out of his reverie, and pulled up his pants. He grabbed her new dress and draped it over her naked body.

"Mantel photos on," Alex commanded.

The mirror over the mantel shivered and transmuted, displaying an image of Suzanne's face. "Is something wrong?" she asked.

His eyes looked past her at the shifting portrait on the wall. There was a look of deep concern on his face.

"Tell me what you know, Suzanne."

"I'm sorry, I don't understand your question."

He thought for a moment, considering how to get through to her. "Do you know what you are?" Alex asked.

She turned the question over in her mind, and found the most appropriate answer. "I'm your wife," she said simply.

"How do you know that?"

"I just know."

"Alright," he said. "But do you know what else you are?"

Suzanne adjusted herself on the couch. "Do you mean my make and model?" she asked hesitantly.

"Yes, that's what I mean."

"I'm a Même class Nymph, ID number 77911101A. My personal designation is Suzanne Conrad."

"That's right. But what does that mean to you?"

"The term 'Nymph' indicates that I'm an artificially constructed life form intended for your pleasure and companionship. The term 'Même' means that I was custom made and that my appearance and personality were modeled upon a human precursor."

"Precursor," Alex repeated. "And what do you know about your precursor? Do you know who you're modeled after?"

"No."

"You have no idea at all?"

"No. I've been programmed to accept that some information is difficult to pre-program and is best learned on a 'need to know' basis, as determined by my owner."

"Well, I think you need to know," Alex said. "I really think you have to know."

He squeezed his eyes shut, as if he was in pain. "I had you created in the likeness of the original Suzanne Conrad. She was my wife, but - she died."

Alex seemed both ashamed and relieved to have told her. Suzanne quietly absorbed this information and said all she could think to say.

"Oh." The revelation seemed so important to him that she felt she should say more, but she couldn't think of anything appropriate. She waited for him to go on, and of course, he did.

"I lost her over ten years ago," Alex said. "But I never stopped loving her. When I found out that there was a way that I could have her back, and that I could have you..." he trailed off.

He looked up at her, his eyes filled with apology. "I couldn't bear life without you. That's the reason people get married, you know. It's not just love. It's the desire to spend the rest of your life with someone. You want to see them change, see them grow, and grow old with them. But things didn't happen the way that I wanted. That's the problem with happiness, you don't appreciate it until it's gone."

Suzanne didn't understand, but she nodded sympathetically.

"And now I have you back," Alex said, grasping her hands. "I had to do it. I had to. I needed you back in my life, Suzanne."

Alex shivered and fell quiet. He seemed to be apologizing, but Suzanne couldn't understand why. She crawled onto Alex's lap and kissed him.

"I love you, Alex," she whispered in his ear. "Without you, I wouldn't be here. I was made for you. That's all that matters now."

She pushed his hair back from his sweaty brow, and stroked his neck. "You've been through so much," she said soothingly.

"I had to do it, Suzanne," Alex said, burying his head in her breasts. "I loved you so much. I still love you."

She kissed him.

"All I want is to make you happy," Suzanne said.

She held him and listened to his calm intake and outtake of breath. There was still so much to learn about this man.

* * * * *

Each day Suzanne and Alex arose from bed later than the last. They lounged and played beneath the sheets until sunset, and when they finally emerged and left their bed cold and abandoned for a few hours, they spent their time "reminiscing" as Alex called it.

He showed Suzanne projected pictures and recorded footage of her precursor, and Suzanne came to know more about the original Suzanne Richert Conrad. Without even consciously trying, she understood the point of what she was seeing and why.

She observed her precursor's laughter as she raced down a hallway wearing only a bra and panties, shrieking, "Put the camera down and stop filming me, you pervert!" and then collapsing on the bed as the camera shut off. There were other moments where her precursor turned into "a grouch" as Alex put it, hiding her face in mock horror when she was caught on camera without makeup.

Alex recounted the back-story to these scenes with a quiet pride. He told Suzanne what occasion was being marked in certain pictures, and shared fond memories of their engagement and early marriage. Sometimes he kissed her very passionately after a picture or anecdote, almost as if they had truly shared the moment together.

All the while Suzanne learned more about Alex's personal tastes and feelings, and carefully programmed herself to better serve his desires. It was her task as a Même to not just imitate, but to improve.

* * * * *

On the fifth morning of her existence, Alex said he had a surprise for Suzanne. He was taking her someplace very special. It was the first time either of them had left the house since her arrival - Alex had been instructed that there was a chance that her system would become overloaded by sensory input if she left the house too soon. But he had a plan to get around that.

"Close your eyes," Alex said to Suzanne.

He took her by the hand and led her out of the penthouse. Her blind steps were shuffling and timid, and as they turned down the hallway her balance was thrown off and she stumbled. Alex caught her arm before she could fall.

"Are you okay?" he asked.

"I'm having a hard time walking like this," Suzanne said. "Why can't I open my eyes?"

"Because I want our destination to be a surprise."

"Oh."

They arrived at the car, and Alex opened the door for her and asked her to sit down. "Can I open my eyes now?"

"No. We're not there yet."

"But I know where we are, I just can't see it."

Alex sighed in exasperation. "Suzanne, shut off your global positioning and directory access - just close your eyes, okay?"

She turned her head towards him, smiling with her eyes shut. "Of course, my love."

"Good."

Suzanne sat unaware of the scenery as they

drove, focusing instead on the feeling of his hand stroking her thigh and the soaring violins in the music Alex played.

"Are we there yet?" she asked. "Almost."

When Alex stopped the car, she asked again, "Can I open my eyes now?"

"Not yet," Alex said as he opened her door and helped her out of the car. "Don't worry, I'll guide you."

Suzanne clung to his arm as she attempted to navigate the foreign terrain. She braced against him as they climbed up a slope, each step an act of pure faith in Alex's guidance, and one of the many miracles of her loyalty programming.

"How far do we have to go?"

"Not very far now."

They were making very slow progress, and Alex finally lost his patience the third time she stumbled.

"Suzanne, what if you look at the ground, but promise me you won't look up?"

"Ok."

He took her by the hand and led her along a cobblestone path. They passed through a turnstile, and then through a glass door. Alex observed Suzanne's blank face as she looked at the floor. It was hard to gauge how she felt about this, if she felt anything at all.

"Okay," he said. "You can look."

She gazed upwards and saw a waterfall covered by blossoms she identified as orchids. A flower-lined stream similar to this one ran through their living room, replete with a tiny waterfall and surrounding plants. Suzanne looked around at her surroundings, until she became aware that Alex was awaiting a reaction.

"Alex, it's wonderful!" she proclaimed, erupting into rapturous laughter. At last Alex shared her joyous smile and kissed her.

"There's more," he said.

He took her hand and he led her to a small wooden bridge edged in even more flowers. Alex pointed under the bridge, and she noticed the shallow stream was filled with spotted koi. He wrapped Suzanne in his arms and said, "Look."

Above them was the glass ceiling of a biodome that revealed the outside sky, which was just turning the lavender color that signaled sunrise. A speck of color floated across Suzanne's line of sight, and she followed the unidentified object's uneven trajectory as it fell into a patch of flowers. She searched for the object within the flowers, and realized that the some of the petals were moving - they weren't petals at all, but the wings of tiny vibrantly colored creatures. She queried and immediately found the right word.

"Butterflies," she exclaimed. As if on cue, the air around them warmed and the butterflies floated out of the flowers, fluttering over Suzanne's body and alighting in her hair and on her gown.

Alex took her hand again and walked her over the bridge and into a misty area by the waterfall where the butterflies were thickest. He led Suzanne under an archway of monarch butterflies, and over to a blanket spread out on the grass. A bottle of champagne on ice with two glasses sat next to it.

"Have a seat, my love," he said, popping open

the bottle of champagne. He poured each of them a glass.

"Suzanne, I brought my wife here on our first real date over twenty years ago. It was under this archway that I asked her to marry me."

He gave her a significant look, and she beamed at him lovingly.

"I remember she said, 'So, you want me to be your first wife?' and we both laughed."

Alex paused, and looked towards the roof of the biodome. "But Suzanne, I asked you because I knew that you were the only woman that could ever make me happy."

Suzanne looked up, wondering what captured his attention. Alex seemed to be speaking to the air rather than directly to her.

"I'd like to propose a toast," he said, and raised his glass. "To the past, as well as the future." He motioned to Suzanne's glass of champagne, and she lifted her glass with his.

"I love you, Suzanne. I always have." Alex touched his glass to hers, and took a drink. She drank her champagne, and studied their surroundings. This was a place that Alex had enjoyed with her precursor, and he wanted to repeat the experience - Suzanne found the place pleasing as well. After all, her personal preferences were based upon those of her precursor.

"I have another present for you," Alex said, as he gingerly rested his champagne flute on the wooden railing and produced a silver necklace from his pocket.

Suzanne examined the pendant as Alex held it

in his palm. It was a silver locket with an engraving of a butterfly on it. Alex turned the pendant towards the light, and the carving of the butterfly morphed - changing into the figure of a woman with her arms outstretched, with large wings spread behind her. He tilted the locket, and the woman became a butterfly again.

"Alex, it's gorgeous," Suzanne said as he hung the locket around her neck.

"My grandmother gave my father this locket and told him to give it to the woman he loved. He gave it to my mother, and when she died my father gave it to me and told me to give it to the woman I fell in love with." He stood back to admire the locket nestled in Suzanne's cleavage. "I gave this to you on our wedding night. Open it and look inside."

Inside the locket was a tiny image of Alex with her precursor, and it emitted the faint sound of laugher as he wrapped his arms around her and kissed her.

As Suzanne stared at the miniature couple, she felt a sensation - an emotion - that she couldn't quite pinpoint. She couldn't understand the need for this gift, or why Alex needed to adorn her in all the trappings of her precursor. But she smiled and gave the response that she knew was required.

"Thank you, Alex." She closed the locket and looked into his eyes. "I love it. And I love you." It was beautiful, she told herself. But she felt a strange antipathy towards the item, not just because it had belonged to the dead woman, but also because she knew that from now on she would be expected to wear it.

"I wanted to give it to you earlier," Alex said, "But I thought it would be more appropriate to give it to you here." He kissed her and ran his hands over her dress and tugging it off, the locket glinting between her breasts. "You look perfect," he said admiringly.

As Alex threw off his clothes and plunged inside her, Suzanne responded with a passionate and programmed response. She rocked her hips against him and clutched him tight, as she stared at the orange flowers swaying over them like bells in the invisible breeze of the biosphere. She queried what species they were - they were angel trumpets, *acleisanthes longiflora.*

A butterfly landed next to Suzanne as her pleasure deepened, and then floated away, startled by the frantic movement of their bodies. She queried the word "butterfly" and gained a deeper understanding of these curious creatures, and wondered what it would be like to be a butterfly - how did they see life in the short days in which they were allowed to exist? What did they think of these two naked creatures writhing underneath them, if they were capable of thinking anything at all?

Alex never noticed Suzanne's distraction. She performed admirably, and climaxed three times despite her musings. The champagne and the sight of Suzanne naked in the sunlight combined to give Alex one of the most memorable mornings of his life.

* * * * *

The next night, Alex rolled over in bed and realized that Suzanne wasn't there. He called her name in the darkness, but the only sound he heard was the blood pounding in his ears.

Alex put on his robe and went to look for her, feeling like he was reliving one of the nightmares he'd suffered during the years since his wife's death. He was often reunited with his

wife in his dreams, but the moment he turned his back she disappeared and the painful realization would hit him - she was dead. Or even worse - they made love, and in the throes of passion Suzanne would suddenly become stiff and unresponsive, and no matter how he screamed and shook her she wouldn't move.

But this was real. His wife was dead, and he was looking for his new Suzanne, his Nymph. He turned on all the lights and surveyed the empty rooms, wondering where she could have gone - until he remembered the one place he hadn't looked. He returned to the bedroom and opened Suzanne's walk-in closet, and pushed his way past the dresses until he heard the whining hum of electricity.

The solar bed was propped up against the back corner like an ancient sarcophagus. Light flooded the closet as he opened the lid, and he squinted to see Suzanne in the ultraviolet, her neck limp and her head lolling forward. Alex groped for the power controls and shut the bed down, but Suzanne still lay unresponsive, her slack face exactly like his wife's when he found her dead body. Alex could feel the irrational fear rising as he shook her to wake up - he was revolted by the stiffness of her, she was usually so pliant in his arms.

Suzanne's neck ratcheted in a half-circle and then her head jerked upright, then down again, performing some sort of recalibration or self-assessment. It was a window into her mechanics that Alex had never seen before. Her head tilted up and down, again and again - bobbing and nodding at him in a horrifying fashion, and he knew he wouldn't be able to control himself much longer - if she didn't stop in a moment he would scream.

And then Suzanne opened her eyes and smiled at Alex innocently, back to normal, her simulated humanity intact once again. She saw the expression on his face and looked at him with concern.

"Darling? What's wrong?" she asked.

Alex took a deep breath and tried to calm himself before answering. "I woke up and couldn't find you."

"I was running low on power and I came in here to charge."

"But you were off when I found you. You're not supposed to shut down without my command."

"I'm sorry. I wasn't off, I went into powersave mode so I could charge faster and get back to bed without you noticing. I've done it before, but you didn't wake up."

"Oh," he said. "Have you charged enough now?"

"Almost. I need a few more minutes to reach full capacity."

Alex looked around the closet. He didn't want to leave her in there - he couldn't stand the idea of going back to bed alone.

"You're not getting enough sunlight to stay charged?"

"We stayed in bed almost all day today, and even with the curtains open I didn't get enough direct sunlight - on cloudy days like this it's hard for me to fully power up."

"What if we go sleep in the greenhouse?" Alex asked hopefully. "The sunlight in there will charge you when the sun comes up. We could sleep in there from now on."

Suzanne considered his suggestion, calculating how much power she needed versus how much she needed to placate him. She was programmed to respond positively to his suggestions whenever possible.

"That sounds like fun," she said with enthusiasm. "That should give me more than enough time to charge, even on a cloudy day. Let's do that."

They spent the rest of the night on a chaise built for two in the middle of the greenhouse. Alex was tense and restless next to her - and completely uninterested in sex for once. Suzanne gave him a massage and then lay next to him with her head on his shoulder, slowing the rate of her breathing and stroking his back until Alex's breathing matched her own and he fell asleep.

He had a bed delivered and moved into the greenhouse later that same day. From then on, he slept with sheets draped over his face to protect him from the bright sunlight each morning, as Suzanne charged in the nude next to him.

That was the first time that Alex had to deal directly with Suzanne's power controls or Nymph functionality, and the fact that her needs were now very different than his own. Alex told himself that he liked sleeping in the greenhouse, especially if it meant that he never had to see her stiff and corpse-like.

If he had his way, Alex never wanted to see Suzanne turned off again.

CHAPTER 3

After another lazy day spent in bed, Suzanne cooked dinner for Alex and then gave him a Thai herbal compress massage that lasted almost two hours. They dozed on the chaise together, and when it was almost midnight Alex asked her to join him out on the balcony. He wrapped his body in a blanket to shield himself from the snowy night outside, but Suzanne wore only her sheer nightgown. Cold temperatures had no effect on her, a fact that Alex found convenient after fighting for his fair share of the sheets in bed for so many years.

Suddenly, an explosion lit up the night sky. Suzanne screamed and threw herself in front of Alex, shielding his body with her own - she was programmed to protect him from any perceived sources of danger. But Alex pulled Suzanne back onto the balcony, and took her into his arms and attempted to reassure her.

"It's okay," he said, pointing at the sky as a second round of explosions began. Suzanne hid her face on his shoulder.

"Alex, please. We have to seek shelter," she pleaded urgently. "Calm down, Suzanne. They're just fireworks."

"Fireworks?" she repeated, querying the word as another red explosion blossomed in the sky, and then fell and faded into a puff of smoke. Another shot went off in the distance, bursting into a streak of light that temporarily turned the sky blue and then green.

"It's a celebration," Suzanne said as she began to understand. "It's New Year's Eve. I didn't realize it until now."

She looked up at him with clear embarrassment. "I'm sorry, Alex. I reacted … incorrectly."

He kissed her on the lips to comfort her. "I didn't mean to scare you. I thought you would like to see," he said as he pointed to another red explosion in the sky.

Suzanne read that Alex was attempting to please her. Her face brightened into a smile. "I do like the fireworks," she said, even as she cringed at a barrage of white fireworks popping and fizzing nearby. "I just didn't realize what they were. I overreacted. I'm sorry."

"That's perfectly alright," Alex said reassuringly.

The fireworks lulled, and they stood together on the balcony in silence, waiting for more. Alex's warm breath created a visible mist near his mouth that looked very similar to the smoky remnants of the fireworks that still hung in the sky - Suzanne's imitation of respiration gave off no vapor.

"I have to go back to work tomorrow," Alex said, breaking the silence between them. Suzanne nodded, and said, "Okay." She was programmed to positively affirm Alex's statements. She had three primary behavioral responses:

Reciprocate.

Complement.

Affirm.

These three actions were meant to insure her owner's maximum satisfaction.

"I've been wanting to tell you for awhile," Alex said apologetically, "But I didn't want to ruin our nice vacation together."

"That's alright," she said.

The fireworks started again, and Suzanne pointed at the violet sparks in the sky with delight. "I'm going to be gone all day from now on," Alex said, still not certain she understood the implications of his statement.

"Oh."

"I'll be going to work every weekday now."

"I see," Suzanne said, considering the information carefully for the first time. "Can I come with you?" she asked.

"No, I'm afraid not."

"Why?"

He thought carefully about his reply.

"My work requires my full concentration. And you also require my full concentration. Therefore, I have to keep you separate."

Suzanne was starting to grasp the magnitude of what Alex was saying. "So, we won't be together tomorrow?"

"I'll be home with you at night. But I have to go to work during the day."

"Then, I'll be home alone?"

"Yes," Alex said.

Suzanne was not programmed to pout or become angry with Alex, or display any negative emotions towards him at all - playfully naughty sexuality was about as close as she could come. She didn't know what he wanted her to say, so she went back to her primary programming and said, "I love you, Alex."

"I love you, Suzanne."

Alex hugged her warm little body, and they clung to each other as fireworks lit the world around them green, then yellow and then red. Suzanne rested her head on Alex's shoulder.

"I thought it would always be this way," she said. Alex kissed her ear. "I wish it could be," he said.

Unfortunately, it couldn't.

* * * * *

When Alex finally stepped out the front door, not to return for at least eight hours, possibly even ten - it was the worst moment of Suzanne's existence. His departure caused a free-falling panic in her as her software struggled to cope with a problem it could not solve. What could she possibly do while he was at work? How would she show him that she loved him? How would he love her back? A human child would have cried when similarly abandoned, but a robot isn't programmed to complain to her owner, even if he does something to throw all of her programming into an uproar.

Suzanne saw Alex to the door and kissed him goodbye. He said he would be home for dinner sometime after 7:00 and that he would love to have a roast with potatoes and carrots. She did the math - preparation for the meal would only take one and a half hours at most. That left more than nine hours unaccounted for.

"But Alex, what else should I do today if you are not here with me?"

Alex was so busy taking inventory of his briefcase, he barely heard her. When he realized she was waiting for an answer he suggested, "Why don't you clean up the place?"

"What do you want me to do?" she asked.

Pressed for details, Alex stammered, "Why don't you do the sheets and clean the bathroom and kitchen, and I don't know, fix it up like it was when you first got here. That should be fine." He kissed her. "I've got to go."

She told him that she loved him very much, and Alex said that he loved her too. Then the door closed, and she stared at it for a while before finally turning and facing the empty penthouse - now that she was its sole occupant, it seemed large enough to engulf her.

Suzanne had tasks to perform, which she set about with a certain amount of drudgery - if that was possible for a machine as new as she was - and the feeling was lightened only by the knowledge that Alex would be pleased by her accomplishments upon his return. She latched onto the idea that she would show him how much she loved him by doing everything he requested and more.

But the penthouse seemed empty without him. The bathroom where they made love and enjoyed a candlelit baths was now just a place in need of scrubbing and bleaching. Suzanne started by scraping the candle wax out of the tiles, and the smooth texture of the hardened wax brought back the memory of soft kisses Alex placed on her breasts.

After she manually cleaned the tiles, she set a tiny Ambintel robot to mop up the wet floor. Wave after wave of water had splashed out of the tub as Alex thrust into her the night before, and Suzanne wondered why Alex had seemed oblivious to the fact his movements were flooding the bathroom.

As she watched the little robot vacuum the water and remaining candle wax out of the tiles, Suzanne marveled that the robot could sense the water and debris around her feet, and yet could think nothing on its own - it could only follow her simple commands. She heard the dirty water sloshing within the service bot as it scurried around the floor, and she felt a certain kinship to it even as she was glad of the fact that she did not have to perform the task herself.

Suzanne went to the kitchen and wiped the chocolate drippings, dried pancake batter, and trails of honey off the kitchen floor by hand before letting the Ambintel bot loose in there to do

its work. The chocolate smeared into the wood grain as she attempted to wipe it away - leftover from the night Alex tried to show her how to make fondue. Suzanne interrupted his efforts to teach her how to boil the chocolate with a few lessons of her own, and thus never learned how the actual dish was made. Maybe she'd search a database for those cooking instructions and practice preparing the dish when her chores were done.

She accessed the credit account Alex authorized for her, and ordered the groceries she would need to prepare his meal that night. After she was sure it would all arrive in time, she went to strip their bed and wash the sheets. As Suzanne removed his pillowcase, she caught the scent of Alex, and for a moment forgot her tasks - it was as if he was there with her, and she was filled with an insatiable urge to kiss him, to see him smile, to make him happy.

She crawled under the covers and wrapped herself in his smell, remaining there for ninety-three minutes before finally deciding she wouldn't be ready for him when he got home if she didn't get back to work.

* * * * *

When Suzanne asked Alex what she was supposed to do that day, he told her to clean up because he had no idea what else she could do. He didn't mean for it to be an order, just a suggestion - but she grasped onto it as a directive, and once that happened there was no stopping her.

The one important detail that Alex neglected to tell Suzanne as he was leaving was that she shouldn't have been left on at all - he should have powered her down, but he couldn't bring

himself to do it. There was no way Alex could do that to her - not after what he'd been through to get her, and not after what happened when he lost his wife before.

Alex's second chance at life began a few months before, when he found an innocuous black envelope sitting on his desk at work. He picked it up and stared at his name on the front of it, and asked his secretary who'd sent it - she told him that she hadn't put it there or seen the person who did.

He tore it open, and a red embossed card slid out and landed on the floor.

**LOVE IS A LUXURY YOU DESERVE.
WE MAKE YOUR FANTASIES COME TRUE.**

At the bottom was a contact number.

Alex tucked the card into his shirt pocket, where it was forgotten until he found it as he undressed for bed that night. He was drunk, tired, and alone - like he was every night. A rich man need never be lonely, but Alex couldn't stand the complications of finding someone to share his bed. No one ever matched up to Suzanne.

He looked at the card and decided to call - he'd hired escorts a few times before and found them to be the most time and cost effective way to ease his cravings for physical female companionship when his virtual programs weren't enough.

"How may I help you?" a lively female voice purred.

Alex didn't know where to start. "I received your card."

"Very good. Can you read me the number on the back of it?" He turned it over, and found a number at the bottom. "779."

"One moment, please."

Silence on the other end of the line, and then, "Alexander Conrad, is it?"

"Yes, that's right. How did you get my information?"

With a familiar candor she whispered, "We know a lot about you, sir."

"You do?"

"Yes. We'd like to help make your fantasies come true. When would be a convenient time for your appointment?"

"Would tonight be possible?"

"I'm afraid not, sir. Our representative in your area is booked for tonight. But we can schedule you for another time, at your convenience. And you won't be disappointed by what we have to offer, I can promise you that."

"I'm sorry," Alex interrupted, "But your card wasn't very clear and I don't know any other details about your company - this is an escort service, isn't it?"

"You'll be meeting with Radha - she'll explain everything in detail at your appointment. Now, when would be convenient for you?"

Alex glanced at his calendar. "If tonight is impossible, I'd say Thursday night."

"Very good. Say 9:00 PM, sir?"

"Yes, that's fine."

"And where would you like to meet?"

"I'm sorry, but may I see a picture of the girl first?" He heard a throaty chuckle on the other end of the line.

"Believe me, you won't be disappointed when you finally see her. Radha will make sure of that."

Alex sighed. "Tell her to meet me at 1010 Kenner Street. Top floor."

"Expect Radha at 9:00 Thursday. Goodbye."

If Alex had known what he was in for, he might have cancelled the appointment and continued his steady and reliable plan of working and drinking himself to sleep. But later he became certain that even if he hadn't called them this time, they would have gotten to him another way.

* * * * *

That Thursday night, Alex confined himself to three neat glasses of scotch while he was waiting for the escort, but promised himself more when she arrived. He'd showered and shaved, and turned off the portraits of Suzanne and switched them to austere landscapes that matched the décor. He dimmed the lights and put on soft music to achieve the appropriate setting.

The security monitor alerted him when Radha scanned for permission to enter the compound, and he let her in. He turned all the monitors off, wanting to keep their rendezvous as private as possible, and then changed his mind and decided to turn on the camera in the entry hall so he could watch her approach.

Radha, he said to himself, savoring the exotic name on his lips. What was that, Middle Eastern? Nordic? It was hard to determine what race she was as she walked down the hall, but she was one of a kind. She looked young - maybe twenty or twenty-one - with silvery white hair and cocoa-colored skin, and she smiled delectably when she noticed the camera tracking her as she knocked on the door. Her pursed lips were painted a stark white to match her hair, and her eyes were heavily ringed in blue makeup - a look that was perhaps more extreme than he would have chosen for his lady of the night. He preferred when women conformed to more classical ideals of beauty and ignored fleeting trends such as this one. Still, it was obvious that underneath it all was a very alluring woman. He opened the door with anticipation.

"Hello," she greeted him casually, as if they'd already met.

She extended her hand and presented it to him, waiting for it to be kissed.

Alex had only seen this in old films before, but if this were part of her act, he would play along. He bowed and took her hand to his lips, inhaling the musky incense of her skin. He enjoyed the tone she was setting for the evening. "It's a pleasure to have you here tonight, Radha. Am I saying your name correctly?"

"That's correct. Raa-da," she pronounced. She shrugged off her cloak in his waiting hands, revealing an austere black tunic that obstructed his view of her impeccable form.

As Radha moved past him and explored the living room, Alex was seized by a sudden paranoia that she was sizing him up as a mark, and that she was setting him up for some sort of heist - but that was impossible. Even with the cameras off, she was required to security scan when entering the compound, and he had hidden away any valuables that might be easily pocketed - and yet as Radha paced the room, the one remaining photo of Suzanne immediately caught her eye, the way it eventually captured the attention of all who entered the penthouse. He should have taken it down, but hiding it would force him to admit that he felt guilty about what he was about to do.

The photo was one that Alex took of Suzanne during their first summer as man and wife. Her hair was everywhere because of the wind, and she attempted to block Alex's camera with her hands were in front of her face - but her eyes were still visible through her splayed fingers, along with the vibrant smile that he loved so much.

For Alex, that photo captured the smell of the sea that day, along with the sound of children playing in the water around them on the crowded beach. Whenever he looked at that photo, he felt the excitement of looking through the lens at his new wife - at that point, they had only been married for four months. That photo was the only piece of their youth that Alex had really been able to hold onto.

Radha stood in front of it, studying the details as closely as possible without appearing rude. "She's beautiful," she said finally.

"Thank you," Alex replied.

"You've been without her for ten years now, is that correct?"

Alex was momentarily taken aback by the fact that she knew intimate details about his life, but then again, information about him was available to the public - a detail like that would be easy enough to find out.

"Yes. Ten years."

"A little bit longer if you count..."Radha gave him a knowing look that alarmed Alex, and then she politely stopped herself. "Well, never mind that for now. The point is that we know quite a lot about you. It's all in your file."

"You have a file on me? I don't see why that's necessary."

"Of course you don't, because you don't realize the scope of the project that we're about to embark upon," Radha replied. "I'm afraid you've been kept in the dark as to the nature of our business here tonight - I think it's time to explain exactly how we plan to make your fantasies come true in the months to come, as you help our dreams come true at the same time."

Alex frowned as he recognized that Radha was launching into some sort of sales pitch - people were always coming to him with one bad investment scheme after another - but as he turned to confront Radha, he was distracted by the fact that her appearance had changed. She seemed to have wiped off her shocking white lipstick, and her hair appeared darker in this light. For the first time, Alex recognized that Radha looked a lot like Suzanne.

"Of course," Radha continued, "I will also be

satisfying your immediate cravings tonight," she said with a naughty smile. "But first - may I please have a drink? Vodka and tonic with lime, if you have it."

Alex was incredibly aroused by her, in a way that he hadn't been in a long time. There was just something about her face. As he poured her vodka, he realized that he was losing control of this seemingly straightforward situation, and decided to pour himself a double. Radha was poised languidly on the sofa and watching him like a Siamese cat when he returned. Alex sat on the other end of the sofa and began to nurse his scotch.

"I take it that you've had 'arranged' dates like this before," Radha stated. "How do you like that sort of thing?"

Radha's gaze was so penetrating that Alex found it necessary to avert his eyes. He studied the pattern of the rug as he mustered a response.

"Dates like this are fine. Sometimes a little strained, due to personality differences."

Alex looked up and noticed that the top of Radha's tunic had come undone, offering a better view of her cleavage. It seemed her entire appearance had changed. Her open lips appeared lush,

red, and inviting, and her intense eye shadow now gave her eyes a smoky bedroom quality. Radha was looking better and better to him all the time.

"You're a very good looking man," she said, finishing her drink and placing the glass on the coffee table. "And your extreme wealth makes you imminently attractive. I'm sure you'd have no trouble finding yourself a second wife, or at least a very beautiful mistress."

"I could, I could," Alex agreed, realizing the alcohol was affecting him. "But I haven't met a woman that holds my interest since Suzanne. It might be too much to love someone like that twice in my life."

He almost missed the table as he attempted to set his drink down next to Radha's, but she caught the glass deftly and handed it back to him. He took another swig.

"It must be hard for a man of your means," she demurred. "You can never know if someone truly loves you, or just your money."

"It's true. But I knew it was the real thing with Suzanne."

"Yes. I guess you did," Radha said as she moved closer to Alex and stretched her arm behind him on the couch. "And you're not the kind of man to compromise your standards and settle for marginal compatibility in a mate, are you? It's hard to meet someone who's right for you, let alone make it work. But what if - what if you could have the right woman? What if you could have her in a few short weeks?"

Alex snorted as he took another drink. "What are you pushing here? A mail-order bride?"

"No, I'm saying that we can outfit you with a mate custom-made to your specifications."

He studied Radha's casual smile, trying to understand what she was implying.

"What are you talking about? Cloning? I don't want a wife brewed out of a test tube."

"No, nothing so crude," Radha said. "Cloning is an unsavory and unpredictable business. It takes too much time to sample and produce the subject, and then years to age them. Even if time wasn't a factor, the instability of a cloned being lacks finesse - or truly, romance. There's no guaranteeing that a clone of your Suzanne would respond to conditioning and have a lasting attraction to you."

The penetrating quality of Radha's eyes was becoming hypnotic. She looked so familiar to Alex suddenly - she could have been the younger sister Suzanne never had. Radha's fragrance seemed to envelop him as she moved even closer.

"They used to say money can't buy love, but it can. True love is the most valuable commodity in the world, Mr. Conrad. It's so rare, so elusive that its existence has been called a myth more than once. But once you've experienced it, you know that it's real. It's real and it's utterly irreplaceable - until now."

Alex looked at Radha and asked, "Are you saying that you can raise the dead?"

Radha laughed uproariously in response, and the shrill sound of it unnerved him. He set his drink down on the table for good this time.

"I can't raise the dead," Radha said. "But I can offer you the next best thing. I'm talking about replicating life in synthetic form. An exact physical duplicate of your wife programmed to interact with you in the same way that she always did - and even more importantly - to love you and live with you as your wife. Are you starting to grasp what I'm proposing?"

"A robot? Is that what you're saying? A robotic version of my wife?"

"In layman's terms, yes, a robot. We prefer our

brand name, Nymph. And the specific model we're talking about that's based on an actual human being is called a Même - an interactive android programmed to make all your fantasies come true. Think about it. You simply tell us everything you want her to be, everything you want her to do, and we'll design her for you. In just a few months, she can be yours."

It was Alex's turn to laugh. "I don't need a robot," he said. "I already have a virtual program of Suzanne on my Advizor veil."

"Well, that's fine. We can integrate the preferences and characteristics you set on your virtual veil program of Suzanne, and use it as a basis for your Nymph. Because let's face it - seeing her in the veil isn't quite enough, is it? Pornography is functional, but when the program's done and you take off the veil, you feel more alone than ever. Your body craves physical contact," Radha said, placing her hand on his thigh. "Or else why would you have solicited my services for tonight? You know the difference between virtual and the physical - and you can afford it. Sure, the poor can sit with their eyes locked to their veils, dreaming of whatever they wish. But reality will always triumph the virtual, even though only the select few can afford to make their fantasy a reality. That's what a Nymph is - walking, talking reality."

"You call a talking sex doll that looks like my dead wife real?" Alex scoffed.

"The Nymph is far more advanced than a mere talking sex doll," Radha reiterated. "When I said an exact replica of your wife, I meant it. On the outside, she will seem to be nothing less than your wife reborn. On the inside, she can be anyone you want her to be. Or, if you prefer, we could outfit a Nymph that looks like a sex icon of your choosing with a program simulating your wife's basic personality."

"What do you mean her basic personality?"

"While we have a detailed record of what your wife looked like, it's much harder to duplicate a human being's personality. So we improvise. We watch as much footage as we possibly can to sample how she was in life. I'll ask you questions about your wife, and have you describe her in

great detail. We want to know what you loved about her, what you hated, things you laughed about. We want to dredge up as many old memories as we can. Anything you can remember and that you care to share - well, if not to share, then to have programmed into your Nymph. Any personality traits that you want integrated into Suzanne, you either tell me and have us program it in for you in advance - or you can wait until you have her alone in the privacy of your home, and then tell her what you want. She will exist only to satisfy you, to constantly improve the ways she serves you. Your satisfaction is all that will matter to her."

"And I suppose satisfaction is guaranteed?" Alex asked, remembering the promise made to him over the phone.

"Satisfaction is guaranteed, but we don't offer any refunds."

"Why not?"

Radha gave him a wry smile. "You can return her if you're dissatisfied, but believe me when I tell you that you won't be."

Alex chuckled. He certainly wasn't disappointed so far.

"We'll develop the interactive program that will become Suzanne, and then you'll talk to it and see if she meets your specifications. Is she too contradictory, too docile? Is her voice just right? Is it not deep enough, or too girlish? After we feel that you're satisfied with her initial programming, we build her software into the body we've created - which again, we will have adjusted to your demands. If you want the exact duplicate of your wife, pockmarks, cellulite and all - we can do it. Or do you want an idealized version of her? Were her breasts not quite big enough for you? Now they can be. Thighs too flabby, jaw not tight enough, ass too flat, eyes too far apart, lose weight or gain it, longer legs…we can perfect her for you. We can recreate Suzanne better than she ever was in real life - not the way that she was, but the way that you remember her. Not the way that she saw herself, but the way that you saw her on the day you were most in love. We don't just strive to imitate real life - we improve upon it. Imagine it, you'd have your wife back, better than ever."

Alex frowned. "But it would be a lie. It wouldn't be Suzanne. Not really."

"That's true," Radha said, nodding sympathetically. "Suzanne is dead and gone, hopefully to a better place, a place we all hope to go on to someday. There's no escaping that fact. But - you're still here."

Radha paused respectfully.

"Life is hard for everyone - even for a very rich and successful man such as yourself. No one understands what you've been through and what you've given up to get where you are. And because of all the success you've been lucky enough to experience, there's no one you can trust."

Alex nodded, lulled by Radha's words and her confidence.

"You said it yourself, dating is hard. Finding another woman that you can love like Suzanne has proved absolutely impossible, and now I'm telling you that you could have her love back...but you're right, it would be a beautiful lie - but would that really be so bad? Who would you be hurting, really?

Alex picked up his glass, and Radha pulled it out of his hand, shaking her head with disapproval. "You drink to get through your day because you're lonely - I know you're lonely, otherwise you never would have called us. But if you go on drinking like that, you might die an early death yourself."

"But just think - if you could have Suzanne back in your life, everything would be different. Why, there'd be someone waiting for you when you came home from work. Someone who loves you. *Someone that you love back.* Someone you can trust. At night, instead of going to bed alone, tossing and turning under the covers of an empty bed - there's Suzanne looking ravishing in a little negligee. She's waiting to kiss you goodnight, and to please you however she can before you go to sleep.

"And when you wake up, she's still there - or if you prefer, she's already in the kitchen making your breakfast. And when you're off to work, she'll be at the front door waiting to tell you to have a good day and kiss you goodbye."

Radha grasped Alex's hand and said, "The truth is that in life, there is no objective truth. A man can spend his whole life loving and being faithful to one woman, and then lose her despite it all. The truth is that he loved her, but what did he get for all that love?"

"That's not exactly the way it happened," Alex protested, but Radha put her hand up to stop him.

"You had many wonderful, irreplaceable years with Suzanne. No one can ever take that away from you, but what I'm offering you is the chance to have many more. She'll be better than she was before - she'll never get old, never get sick, and never leave you. She'll always love you, no matter what. She'll be there to hold your hand until the day you die." Radha looked at Alex solemnly. "I say, if the end of your loneliness is a lie, then so be it. We all have to get through life however we can. I'm sure Suzanne would want you to be happy, wherever she is."

Alex sat in silence, watching the fire crackle through a log he'd placed there earlier. It gave the gas fire the satisfying smell of a fire he'd built himself - it reminded him of Christmas, and the cabin in the mountains where he and Suzanne used to spend Christmas making love. There were so many memories that it hurt to think about, but they were all he had. Could he really have more?

"I didn't know that artificial intelligence and android technology were this advanced," Alex said. "I've never seen any robots that could even come close to truly passing for human. They're usually nothing but toys."

Radha smiled at him knowingly. "Yes, most robots are merely networked puppets incapable of any autonomous thought or decision making - they're just highly specialized machines devoid of any sort of independent intelligence. She crossed her legs, and Alex watched Radha's long brown legs slide together, as she placed her hands daintily on her knees.

"The fact of the matter is that there simply isn't a widespread public demand for service androids. The dream of the robot butler has proved impractical and impossible ever since the economy took a dive - it's much cheaper and easier to design ambient intelligent appliances to accomplish household tasks, without the added hassle of personality. And of course, human beings are still willing to provide their services for far less than the cost of manufacturing and maintaining a robot. The crash halted almost all high-end robotics research by companies other than our own, making androids nothing more than science fiction for most people today. The fact that our products exist and are being purchased by the ultra-rich is a very closely guarded secret. Even the conspiracy nuts barely have an inkling of our company's true purpose."

She gave him a guileful grin and a nudge as she teased, "But the lifestyle of a person of means lies beyond the imagination of most people. Our Nymphs aren't something we advertise, simply because the people who can actually afford to buy one of our models usually find out about our services through alternate channels. We market very directly and discreetly to our clientele, and it doesn't benefit them or us to have our secret getting out. Just because the public demand and ability to afford our products wasn't there, doesn't mean that the technology wasn't developed.

Technology has a way of advancing almost on its own. Our software was so advanced that the only thing it couldn't do was get up and walk - until that became possible, too."

Radha smiled at him conspiratorially. "I'm sure you know what most of these developers are like. They're a lonely, driven bunch. The first female android wasn't for sale - she was for personal use." She laughed at herself. "Oops! Now, I'm giving away company secrets! I guess that's just how comfortable I feel with you."

Alex smiled and loosened up a little himself, and Radha judged that the time was right. "Look into my eyes," she said. "Tell me, what you see."

Her perfume was overpowering, her lips so close, and Alex could just see down her dress - but he focused on her eyes.

"You have beautiful brown eyes," he said. "And large pupils from the dim light in here. White corneas with a few blood vessels - or sclera, is that what it's called?"

"Can you see yourself reflected in them?" Radha asked. "Can you see my soul?" She leaned back against the couch.

"You're gazing into the eyes of a machine." She grinned triumphantly.

"I'm a Nymph."

Alex examined her eyes again - they were the

very opposite of what he'd imagined a machine's eyes would be like. There was a certain depth to her gaze, an empathy, as if she saw deep inside his heart. He was surprised how quickly he accepted this startling new version of reality.

"Feel my hands," Radha said, presenting her palms to him. "My skin feels just like any woman's. Maybe better."

Alex felt her hand - it was warm to the touch and slightly damp. He squeezed it tighter and felt what he would have accepted as muscles and bones.

"Is this human skin?" he asked, vaguely disgusted at the idea of this artificial creature being sheathed in living human tissue.

"It's a patented polymer called Dermox. It was originally created for burn victims and prosthetic limbs, but it works quite nicely for my needs as well. And it feels real enough, doesn't it? Like flesh and blood."

Radha unzipped her tunic and unveiled her perfectly formed breasts. She pulled Alex's hand to her exposed flesh, and he traced the circle of her breast, and then gently squeezed - it felt nothing like the distractingly rigid implants he'd groped in his youth. He continued to explore her breast, and Radha's nipple hardened as he brushed over it with his fingers.

"Mmm, that feels good," she purred. "You have a gentle touch. I like that. Pleasure is one of the main components of our programming - I don't just simulate sexual excitement, I actually respond physically to your touch, the same way a human woman would. The only difference is that I'm easier to please.

"I was designed to interpret every sensation I feel as pleasure, and because of that I know no pain. Isn't that great? To be with a woman with whom you can do whatever you want, and no matter what, it won't hurt? That comes in handy. And nothing pleases me more than your satisfaction."

"No physical pain?" Alex contemplated. "I always thought pain was necessary. Pain is useful - pain is instructive."

"We learn our lessons in other ways," Radha replied.

"How about emotional pain?" Alex asked. "Do robots really have emotions? Can robots have their feelings hurt?"

A sly look spread across her face. "That's the wonderfully convenient thing about being in a relationship with a machine. You can shut her off."

Radha leaned towards him and kissed him. Alex closed his eyes, and enjoyed the sensation. Her lips were soft and moist, and she tasted of the lime and vodka he'd served her. He wondered if she drank that only to keep her lips wet. He could tell Radha was analyzing him during the kiss, predicting his preferences for open-mouth or tongue kissing. He was distracted for a moment by the feeling of being probed, until he decided that he was doing the same thing to her, and it was only fair. She slid her tongue against his, and it felt delicate and textured. She breathed warm air into his mouth as they kissed, and again the lime flavor wafted into his mouth. After a moment, she sighed slightly and sucked his tongue. He opened his eyes, and her eyelids flickered in a perfect imitation of pleasure. She wrapped her arms around him, and the weight and pressure of her was that of a real woman.

Radha pulled away from Alex, and traced her fingers over her lips sensually, savoring his kiss. "You see? You'd never know the difference if I hadn't told you. The only thing you'd know the next day is that I was insatiable, and that I was the best you ever had."

As Radha pulled off the rest of her tunic to reveal her smooth stomach and long tan legs, Alex became undeniably aroused. His thoughts of resistance were gone - the machine in front of him had him right where she wanted him. Who cared that Radha had never been sick or suffered the indignities of childhood, and that she would never grow old? All that mattered was that she was *his* right now.

And she was completely right - she was the best he ever had. Of course, she had the advantage of being designed to have better-than-human endurance, coordination, and muscle control, as well as a certain intuition about her partner's desires. When he woke up on the floor two hours later with Radha massaging his neck and whispering in his ear, he had to have her again. Alex knew that he would be ordering a custom Nymph of his own - no matter what the cost.

CHAPTER 4

A pattern formed over the course of Alex's meetings with Radha. She gave in to his sexual whims first thing upon her arrival, in order to clear his mind. Then it was time to discuss business - but there was always time for more pleasure before she left.

"Your satisfaction is my primary directive," Radha said. "You have to tell me everything, in order for me to make sure that you get exactly what you want."

"I only want what you promised me," Alex said. "I want my wife back."

"Of course," Radha replied, casually running her fingers through his hair. "But the question is - do you want her exactly as you remember her? Or would you like a few improvements?"

"What do you mean by 'improvements'?"

"Let's start with her exterior. I'm sure you've noticed my ability to shift my appearance?"

"I noticed," Alex said.

Her eyes changed from blue, then hazel, then brown. Her nose broadened slightly and her skin shimmered as it darkened. Her appearance shifted from the Suzanne-like visage he had become accustomed to, back to her original cocoa-colored skin and Eastern bone structure, along with the bizarre makeup.

"Would you like for her to be a Metamorph like me?" Radha asked. "Or would you prefer for her to look like a pop celebrity or historical figure?"

Radha's face paled and shifted again. Her cheeks filled out as the shape of her brow bones became more pronounced and her eyes widened. A beauty mark appeared near her lips. Alex recognized the face - it was Marilyn Monroe.

"We have quite a few veneers for you to choose from," Radha said in a perfect imitation of the starlet's breathy voice. "Or if you prefer a little variety, you could show her the image of any attractive woman you desire, and she can shift her appearance to a very close approximation of her."

Radha's face shifted from Marilyn to a dark mahogany-skinned woman with African features, and then her skin lightened and phased into an East Asian face. She winked at him, as her face broadened and became Hispanic, and then her skin lightened and reassembled to form Marilyn again. Her hair changed along with her skin and her face, phasing from pale platinum to jet black and then back, the color seeming to seep from the roots of her hair to the tips.

"Faces that we consider 'classically beautiful' conform to certain proportions," Radha said. "Despite certain racial differences and skin color, with a just few small modifications to the color and shape of my facial features, I can recreate the faces of hundreds of different women."

Radha's veneer changed so that she resembled Suzanne again, though it still wasn't quite right.

"As you can see, there are some limitations," Radha explained. "I'm able to mimic and approximate Suzanne's features, but I can't match her exactly."

"Why can't you look like her if you can look like Marilyn Monroe?"

"I can only make exact duplicates of faces that have been scanned and programmed into my muscle memory. My face lacks the information necessary to create a perfect image of Suzanne."

He touched Radha's face as it shimmered and changed back to her preferred veneer. He could feel the muscles in her cheeks rippling under his fingertips, and pulled his hand away.

"Only your face changes? The rest of your body stays the same?" he said.

"Yes. My body mass and shape remain constant, although the color of my body changes along with my face - it's a total body veneer change," she said, flourishing her hand next to her face to prove that it matched.

"So my Nymph version of Suzanne - if I were to ask for a Metamorph model, would it be possible for her to look like you?" Alex asked.

"Yes, if you'd like that."

"Will a Metamorph cost more?"

"Of course," Radha grinned. "A lot more."

Alex thought about it, and then shook his head. "I just want my wife back. I'm not interested in all these frills."

"Now, wait a minute - don't count out the frills

so fast," Radha said. "What about enhanced sexuality? With our specialized genitalia, she would be capable of vibrating and contorting into positions beyond your wildest dreams during sex."

Alex grimaced at the thought of Suzanne's legs bent back the wrong way and her pelvis rumbling like a cement truck.

"Sorry, the idea doesn't appeal to me," he said.

"You seemed to enjoy it earlier," Radha said cheekily.

"There's gadgets for that," Alex countered. "Besides, it's different with you. I want to be able to think of her as my wife."

"You want to be able to think of her as human."

"No - you said she would be Suzanne reincarnate. That's what I want. I want her to be exactly like she was."

"But what does that mean, exactly? Personality is as transitory as appearance. We've got to figure out exactly what you want out of Suzanne, not just in the beginning, but your expectations over the long term. I need you to tell me everything about Suzanne - everything you loved about her, everything you hated about her. Why you fell in love, what you fought about - all of it. And then we can take that information and create an idealized Suzanne that will love you and be loyal to you for the rest of your life."

"You keep emphasizing that it's for the rest of my life," Alex noticed. "Why is that?"

"The prime directive of every Nymph sold is total owner loyalty - if Suzanne is programmed not to leave you, then she'll never leave you. She'll be completely loyal to you until you take your last breath. She might even be able to prevent your death, since she'll be constantly monitoring your vitals and trained in basic medical care. But the moment Suzanne registers your death, she'll be automatically recalled back to the company - in this way, we keep our Nymphs a secret and spare you any embarrassment or scandal."

"How convenient," Alex said grimly.

"Convenient for you and our company. We don't need evidence of our business becoming public knowledge before it's time. Only our satisfied clients know of our existence for now. But that secrecy comes at a price."

"And what *exactly* is that price?"

"You've been afraid to ask, haven't you?" Radha said with a knowing look. "You know what they say - if you have to ask you probably can't afford it."

"You wouldn't be here if I couldn't afford it," Alex said. "Whether I'm willing to pay is another story."

"That's why I didn't tell you the price before you knew exactly what your money would buy," Radha said with a grin.

"Of course."

"A Même class Nymph - that includes body replication and construction, personality research and customized software, intelligence, processors, memory - all told, having Suzanne back is going to cost you at least three billion dollars. But we won't know the exact price until she's done."

"Three billion?" Alex repeated. He was bracing

himself for the figure, but it still came as a shock. *"Three billion dollars?"*

"I know that sounds exorbitant, but remember that Suzanne will be a custom build - and we're making practically no profit even at that price. Almost all of that money will go directly back into research and development."

"But still - she's an android, not a small country. How am I even supposed to pay that much?"

"We'll arrange it so that your payment looks like you're investing in a company specializing in experimental exercise equipment, and you'll transfer the funds to Lexico."

"Lexico? This falls under the corporation's umbrella?" Alex said incredulously.

"You didn't think we were building Nymphs in a garage somewhere, did you?" Radha smirked. "This is one of the corporation's most clandestine projects - after all, you'd never heard about us. But the only reason you're eligible to purchase a Nymph at all is because you're a corporate partner. And you're exactly the type of client we prefer to target - you're very rich, but you keep a low profile."

"Still - three billion dollars. That's no small amount."

"That's what it costs to recreate one human life. Wasn't your wife worth that much to you and more?"

"Of course she was," Alex said with resentment. "But that doesn't change the fact that you're asking me to spend a hefty chunk of my fortune."

"Think about it this way," Radha said. "How much does it cost to build just one ride at Disney, let alone keep it running for just one day? What's the budget to create just one movie or design just one game? You're not paying for a momentary delight here. You're paying to have your ultimate fantasy fulfilled for the rest of your life. When you think about it, it's almost a bargain."

Alex sighed. He could afford it, that wasn't the problem. He was worth more than eight times as much. He'd been lucky enough to inherit a profitable company worth a fortune from his father, and he expanded it through hard work and careful investment. But all his money never amounted to anything tangible for him since Suzanne died. He had many of the vices that came along with money - cars, art, and real estate - but he never developed a taste for buying islands or sports teams like other billionaires. There always seemed to be far more money than he could spend, and no one for him to spend it with. The money was a form of satisfaction in itself, but it was just a sum - and if three billion dollars of his money could finally buy him the one thing he wanted, he would be glad to be rid of it.

"Alright," Alex said.

"I want you to be sure," Radha said. "I am," he said. "I want to do this."

"Okay then," she said, slipping out of her dress again.

Alex gave her a cool grin. "Finally, something worth spending my money on."

* * * * *

Alex opted to increase the size of Suzanne's breasts, but otherwise he ordered for her to look exactly the way she did while she was alive. He wanted her recreated, in Radha's words, "the way she looked on the day they were most in love."

For Alex, that was the day he asked her to marry him when she was only twenty-six years old. He was tempted to order an even younger version of Suzanne, but decided against it. After all, he would be fifty-eight years old on his next birthday - this whole ordeal was already enough to make him feel like a dirty old man.

Once it was determined what Suzanne would look like, Radha focused on what Alex wanted for her personality and interaction. In order to build a simulacrum of Suzanne that would please him, it was necessary to know as much as possible about his personal history and preferences.

She asked Alex about his sexual experiences previous to Suzanne and after her, his childhood, his parents, siblings, masturbation - anything that might have any bearing upon his attitude towards relationships and expectations about women. During their sessions together she also exposed Alex to a wide assortment of pornography, always testing him and gauging his response.

Radha requested that Alex turn over all existing footage of Suzanne for image sampling, personality analysis, voice replication, and motion capture. Alex even gave Radha the embarrassing virtual fantasy programs he'd created for the sexual insight they provided, because Radha told him the more records available, the more accurate the Nymph.

"Our programmers are scouring every available database for details about Suzanne - remnants of e-mail correspondence, school and medical records, news reports, passports and visas, credit transactions, web profiles, data mines - any infotrash they can dig up. While none of these sources usually prove very illuminating, they do form a basic picture of a precursor's life. It may have had no bearing on Suzanne's adult life that she received straight A's all through elementary school, or was frequently in trouble for talking too much in class...but with all stories, it's best to begin at the beginning. That's what makes each Nymph so real - our attention to detail."

In some cases interviews with friends and relatives of the person being simulated were obtained, always under the auspices of casual conversation or biographical intent. But Suzanne's only living relative was her ailing mother, Carlotta, who had been filed away for safe keeping in a posh sanitarium an hour outside of the city as she patiently waited to die. Carlotta made for an unreliable source of information regarding her daughter as it was, because she'd been institutionalized eight years prior to Suzanne's death. Her mental acuity and memory varied widely, depending on how her body was assimilating her medication that day.

Early on, Radha tested Alex's capacity for accepting Suzanne as a real woman despite her synthetic nature. Imagination and a tendency to anthropomorphize were very important for Nymph interaction - it established the possibility of creating a real emotional bond, or at least an anthropopathic one.

"Did you have any imaginary friends as a child?" Radha asked him casually. "No," Alex said. "Not that I remember."

"Did you have a favorite toy you confided in when you were little?"

"Confided in?" he said with a raised brow. "Let me see…there was Fluff-Fluff. He was my favorite when I was really little - Fluff-Fluff was a giant stuffed gerbil."

"How old were you when you stopped playing with him?"

"I must have been…maybe six. I lost him when my parents took me on vacation - I took Fluff-fluff to play on the beach, and the surf swept him away. I tried to run in after him, but he was gone." Alex laughed. "My mother told me that Fluff-Fluff was washed away to China, and that he would make a little girl or boy there very happy. But that didn't stop me from crying myself to sleep that night."

Radha smiled, quite pleased with his response.

* * * * *

As Radha pleasured Alex with an assortment of sexual techniques and scenarios, she was always testing him and registering his reactions. Every time she touched him, she measured the conductivity of his skin and the response of his sympathetic nervous system - his galvanic skin response. This data predicted Alex's arousal levels more accurately than he could ever consciously realize or verbally describe.

But she didn't rely on readings alone. She also asked Alex to describe how he perceived their sexual encounters, sometimes finding discrepancies between what he claimed to like and what she measured as a positive response. She asked him question after question, until Alex was unashamed to tell her everything.

"Would you describe yourself as a selfish lover?"

"No. But I don't expect that anyone would describe themselves that way," Alex said. "You know that my satisfaction comes from pleasing you, right?"

"Yes," he said. "You mentioned that."

"There are other ways of pleasing me," Radha said, rolling next to him on the bed. "I'm more sensitive to pleasure than a human woman, but I'm capable of being pleasured in all the same ways."

Alex nodded, not sure where Radha was going with this. "Do you care about my sexual satisfaction?" she asked. He nodded. "You certainly seemed satisfied to me."

"I was, and I am. You're a wonderful lover."

"Thanks, kiddo," he said jokingly and kissed her on the cheek. Radha looked him over carefully.

"But wouldn't you say our sexual relationship has been a little one-sided?"

"What do you mean?" Alex said, taken aback.

"One of the primary directives of a Même is reciprocation - we see it as a key to sexual satisfaction. But perhaps that's not what you want. Perhaps you prefer a more submissive sexual partner, or a more dominant one?"

"I like both," Alex said. "I like variety."

"You do?" Radha asked. "It's funny you should say that. Because you've never attempted to orally stimulate me."

Alex cringed internally, but kept up a brave face. "I'm sorry. I didn't mean to…"

"Don't apologize to me," Radha said. "This isn't about what I want. I'm trying to give you what you want. And if you don't enjoy giving oral sex as much as you do receiving it, then you don't have to do that."

"I didn't know it was necessary," Alex mumbled, growing increasingly uncomfortable.

"It's not necessary," she said. "But it's certainly nice. Are you squeamish about giving oral sex?"

"No."

"Did you perform it on your wife?"

"Yes - on a regular basis."

"Did she have to request it?"

"No - I did it willingly."

"Then why haven't you performed oral sex on me?" Radha asked. "It just didn't occur to me."

"Didn't occur to you?" she said, more insulted than he'd ever seen her. "Is it because I'm a Nymph and not a woman?"

"Well - yes, I guess so."

"I see. I expected for you to have adjusted to that fact by now. It doesn't bode well for your relationship with Suzanne if you haven't."

"I have adjusted - it's not that, really," Alex stammered. You just seem so excited whatever I do. It didn't occur to me because I didn't think the extra stimulation was necessary."

"It's not necessary," Radha said, almost defensively. "I'm just trying to determine how much you reciprocate as a lover."

Alex stared at her, and then asked, "Do you want me to go down on you?"

"I told you, it's not about what I want," Radha said. "If you don't enjoy having a woman's legs wrapped around your head as you kiss her most erogenous areas - if you don't find that arousing - then please, by all means, don't do it. But if you find it a satisfying part of a sexual relationship, I suggest you try going down on me, in order for me to test you - simply for the purposes of my evaluation."

Alex laughed.

"Strictly for the purposes of evaluation?" he said, spreading her legs and running his hands up her thighs.

"Yes," she said with a straight face as he gently massaged her moistening labia.

"Radha, Radha, Radha," he chided, as he bent between her legs. "All you had to do was ask."

* * * * *

Monitoring the construction of Suzanne was like watching a skyscraper being built from a distance. At no point in the construction process was

Alex allowed to view Suzanne's body in person, as it was considered bad luck to visit the "bride" before her personality embedding. He approved pictures of her construct every step of the way - her eyes were open and alert, despite the fact that she lacked internal software. Her body was still incomplete, waiting to be filled with her nucleus - her brain and personality.

Alex's first interactions with Suzanne's personality construct were through Advizor veil programs much like the ones he'd programmed himself, but more fully rendered. He had never integrated Suzanne's actual voice into his programs, but now her deep throaty laugh rang out at him exactly like he remembered it. Her moans during sex were real enough to leave him shivering once his passion subsided.

He was grateful to find Radha by his side when he removed the veil. Alex was very fond of Radha. Though their relationship had become quite intimate and affectionate, he never stopped thinking of Suzanne. It finally occurred to Alex that perhaps the same was true of Radha.

"Are you programmed for love?" Alex asked.

"Yes, I am," she responded frankly, a little unaccustomed to having the conversation focused on her for a change.

"Are you in love with somebody now? Do you have an owner?"

"You're the only man in my life right now," Radha said with the faraway smile of a woman telling a man what he needs to hear, and not the truth.

"But if you're programmed for love - you must love someone, right?" Radha chuckled.

"Alexander Conrad, you're a true romantic. I wish every customer was more like you."

* * * * *

Radha was very specific about the need for Alex to keep his purchase a secret. He signed a non-disclosure agreement banning him from telling anyone about the existence of Nymphs or about the company that sold them. The consequences of a breach of contract weren't as simple as losing Suzanne or dealing with a lawsuit - Radha promised that the corporation would have Alex's reputation ruined, have him declared legally insane, possibly even killed - whatever punishment the corporation deemed appropriate and necessary.

Alex decided it was time he moved off his beloved estate. He left behind the gothic revival castle he'd shared with Suzanne all those years ago, and all the prying eyes that came with it.

The crumbling stone expanse and its surrounding gardens required constant upkeep and a full staff of housekeepers, gardeners, and other maintenance workers awaiting his every command twenty-four hours a day. Alex never liked the fuss; he hated having so many people lurking around and involving themselves in his business, dependent on him for orders and their livelihood. His only regret was the need to let go of Kimberly, the motherly cook and housekeeper he'd had for eighteen years.

Kimberly knew Suzanne and would ask more than a couple questions if she suddenly reappeared young and alive again. He gave her a generous retirement fund and a cottage in Kauai to ease his conscience.

He moved into the apartment he kept in the city permanently - the penthouse was the place where he first met Radha, and she agreed that it provided enough privacy. The building was "sylvan," a style currently popular with young professionals, and the exterior was covered in vines and ivy, and the inside of each apartment resembled a small forest. The natural motif continued in the courtyard outside, replete with a pond that was shielded from prying eyes by the surrounding trees.

It was only after there was no turning back, and after Alex confessed to Radha all his deepest desires, that he began to wonder who else was listening.

"Radha, you're not networked, are you?" Alex asked.

She looked at him for a long time, measuring her response very carefully. Alex realized that his instinct that he was being monitored was correct.

"Who's watching?" he asked, his temper flaring. "How many people are watching us right now?"

"Calm down," Radha said. "What you and I do together and what you tell me is private. I'm only networked to better serve you, and so I can report to our technicians as efficiently as possible about your preferences for Suzanne, and they can ask any questions they might have. "

"Can they see us?" Alex asked. Radha backed

away from him. "Yes," she admitted.

"Are they seeing through your eyes or do you have cameras hidden around here spying on me too?"

"There are no hidden cameras. They can see enough through my eyes."

"Have they been watching us the whole time?" he demanded.

"No, not the whole time," Radha said.

She studied him carefully - his carotid artery was throbbing, his face a rictus of anger - and normally Radha might have been scared. But Alex wasn't a violent man, just a private man. That was his whole problem, that he couldn't trust anyone but Suzanne. Radha knew that in order to regain his confidence, she needed to be honest.

"They've been watching most of the time," she admitted. "I'm sorry. They respect our privacy when we're sexually intimate, but afterwards I still send in my analysis of the experience."

Alex put his head in his heads. "So they're watching right now?"

"Yes," Radha confirmed. "I try to be discreet. But they need details."

"And Suzanne? Will she be networked?"

"Absolutely not. Suzanne will think and live independently - there's no hive mind with us. She will be very much her own person, and once she's fully designed and programmed, your lives from that point on are your own affair - unless you have any complaints."

Radha sat next to Alex, and began to massage his shoulders.

"Don't worry," she said. "Our technicians respect your privacy. Their only interest is your satisfaction."

Alex's shoulders were so tense in her hands. She saw there would be no getting past this for him and finally relented.

"They've seen enough. I'll go off network, if that's what you want - we can be alone from now on."

"That's what I want."

"Then it's done. We're alone now."

"How do I know that we're alone?" he demanded.

"You just have to trust me," Radha said, but Alex was silent. "Don't be mad."

"I'm not," he said, but Radha wasn't so sure.

"There's no reason to be embarrassed either. I know you have a hard time trusting people - that's why I didn't tell you, I knew how you would react. I only let them watch because I want Suzanne to be absolutely perfect for you. I'm sorry I couldn't tell you."

"People always want a piece of me - and I have to be careful," Alex said apologetically. "Your company was smart to approach me - I realized that right away. I've always preferred machines to human beings. I think that's why I find it so easy to talk to you."

Radha wrapped her arms around him, stroking his hair like he was a small child.

"You can trust me," she assured him. "Your satisfaction is my primary directive. And it will be Suzanne's as well."

The last week of Suzanne's construction was filled with double-checking of all her functions and controls and making sure that all her programming was stable. Alex was put through almost as much scrutiny - with all the information Radha collected about him, she had more than enough to create an exact simulacroid duplicate of Alex, but unfortunately there was no demand for such a being.

Despite the fact that all Nymphs were built capable of monitoring her owner's vital signs during physical contact, Radha gave Alex a full physical exam so there would be no danger of injury during sex. He was surprised when she reported that his health had improved since her first exam.

"Probably from all that exercise," he joked.

Radha smiled. "It's not at all unusual. Sexual intercourse is very healthy - having a Nymph will probably extend your life, and it will definitely improve your quality of living. She'll be here to take of you and love you from now on - if fact, Suzanne will be capable of most anything you ask her to do, only when you first turn her on she'll have no memories."

"No memories?" Alex said with surprise.

"Suzanne will have no history, and therefore none of the emotional baggage that comes with it. She'll be a clean slate."

"Good, that's exactly what I want," he said.

"Testing has shown it's easier for Nymphs to

learn in much the same way a human does, only we learn much faster. The only downside of that is that she'll be very impressionable. That's why it is important for you to shut her down when you're not around to monitor her - to keep her from coming under the wrong influence."

Alex nodded.

"When you turn her on for the first time, Suzanne might be a little disoriented," Radha continued. "She might even seem frightened. The best way to alleviate her fears is to simply kiss her."

"That's easy," Alex said with a grin.

"It's the easiest way to comfort her in any situation," Radha agreed. "Suzanne is programmed to be reassured by kissing, as well as distracted by whatever might be alarming or confusing to her. You may engage in sex acts with her immediately if you wish - it helps if you give her an immediate action to take part in, something she will understand and enjoy. But it'll take time for her to acclimate herself to her new environment and to you. Be patient. She just wants to please you."

"Sounds great," he said.

"And again, bear in mind that all Nymphs are in the experimental phase right now," Radha said. "Especially the Mêmes. The details are all in your contract - I hope you've read it thoroughly. One-year warranty on programming, three years on parts. She's returnable to the company at any time - "

"Without refund," Alex added.

"That's right," Radha said. "And in the event of your death, Suzanne returns to us and becomes our property again. The company bears no responsibility for any damages."

On Christmas Eve, Radha appeared on Alex's doorstep on with a giant crate. She unpacked Suzanne in the bedroom while Alex paced the living room, then unceremoniously kissed Alex goodbye and wished him all the happiness in the world.

The scene was set - Suzanne was posed on the bed like sleeping beauty. Alex leaned down and kissed Suzanne's lips, and was disturbed to find her lips cold and unresponsive. Then Suzanne opened her eyes.

She looked around the room, blinking and rubbing her face as if she had awoken from a long nap. He could feel himself grinning as her brown eyes fixed on him, but he was unable to stop himself. He couldn't believe the miracle he was seeing before him as she slowly smiled the languid smile he'd been longing to see for over ten years.

When her face streaked with tears, it was the last thing he'd anticipated. He'd expected her to melt into his arms and play sex vixen like Radha, teasing and taunting him to orgasm, suddenly shifting between submission and dominance. He hadn't expected Suzanne to apologize for everything that had happened, to begin right where the real Suzanne had left off. She was so sincere, so completely Suzanne in her vulnerability, Alex couldn't help but immediately forgive her everything, even when she called him Alexander a moment later - he was too grateful for the second chance. It didn't matter that it took well-applied programming and robotics technology to bring her back to him, as well as an exorbitant amount of money.

He had Suzanne back, and that was all he ever really wanted.

Part 2
Larvae

CHAPTER 5

Radha's promise came true - Alex created his ideal fantasy, and he didn't need to put on a veil to get there or hide a doll underneath the bed. Suzanne was always waiting for him, as if his wife never died.

When he kissed her that night after work, the dewy olive skin of her back felt even smoother than he remembered, and she smelled like jasmine and sex. But there was another aroma in the air, too.

"Is that dinner?" Alex asked.

Suzanne pressed herself against his crotch with a gleam in her eye. "It's ready, whenever you are," she said. "But then again - so am I."

She kissed him passionately, but his stomach couldn't ignore that tempting aroma. Alex disentangled himself and walked over to the kitchen. The roast was still sizzling.

"I think I'd like to eat first," Alex said, as he took off his coat and tie.

Suzanne brought his dinner to the table, and watched with admiration as she carved the roast. "You're not just beautiful," he said. "You have great timing, too."

"Thanks," she said. She smiled at the compliment, but there was a look of polite confusion on her face. "What do you mean when you say, 'great timing'?"

Alex waved off the question and took his first bite.

"You got the recipe just perfect," he said with an ecstatic groan.

"Thank you," Suzanne said, very pleased with herself. "But I still don't understand what you meant about my timing."

"It's nothing," Alex said with a full mouth. "I'm just not accustomed to having dinner ready the moment I walk in the door - I used to have to heat up whatever my cook left in the oven for me."

"Ohhhh," Suzanne said. "The timing was no problem. When I saw your last meeting was cancelled, I just adjusted my timing accordingly."

Alex took a hard swallow and nearly choked.

"Are you okay?" Suzanne said as he coughed into his napkin. "Is it the meat? Is it undercooked?"

He waved off her concern and shook his head.

"How did you know my meeting was cancelled?" Alex asked. "Were you tracking me?" He skewered another piece of meat with his fork.

"Yes," Suzanne answered.

His fork and knife clattered onto his plate and knocked over his drink. But all Suzanne could see was the expression on his face - he was angry, very angry, in a way she'd never seen him before.

"How were you were tracking me?" Alex demanded. "I have all surveillance turned off."

"I accessed your schedule using the home system," Suzanne said. "When your meeting was cancelled, I received an update. Global positioning let me know exactly when you would be arriving home."

Alex glared at her, his top lip curved down over his teeth in the very opposite of a smile. "I don't like being watched," he said vehemently. "You're supposed to know things like that - that I don't like being monitored."

His voice lowered. Alex looked almost embarrassed, the way he always did when he mentioned the details of her programming.

"I'm sorry," Suzanne said. "I was just trying to make you happy."

She dabbed at the spilled drink with her napkin, but Alex grabbed her wrist and stopped her. "What makes me happy is privacy - I don't care if my dinner's cold, or if I'm inconvenienced, I just don't want anything beeping or watching me. I don't want my entire life recorded by you, or anyone else. I don't want to be monitored - not on my veil, and not at home."

"I'm sorry," she repeated.

"Quit saying you're sorry, goddamn it," Alex said as he went into the kitchen to pour himself another drink.

"I didn't mean to upset you," Suzanne said.

"Having you spy on me is the last thing I need - I want all that tracking shit turned off, now."

"It's already done," she said, trying to placate him. "You'd better eat - your dinner's getting cold."

Alex looked at her in disbelief for a moment, and then picked up the platter of meat and heaved it in the general direction of the kitchen sink.

"You just ruined a perfectly good meal by

trying so fucking hard not to ruin it!" he bellowed at her as he stormed away with a bottle of vodka in his hand.

Suzanne cleaned the meat off the floor, and continued to cry as she cleaned - it was how she was programmed to react when he was mad at her. Her tears were a calculated reaction that was intended to alleviate his anger by stimulating his guilt, and thus precipitate their reconciliation.

She left him alone for half an hour, then knocked on the door of his study and apologized the best way she knew how - by unzipping his pants and taking him into her mouth. After her apology was accepted, Suzanne mounted Alex right there, the hydraulics in his desk chair thumping as she rode him to orgasm.

The roast incident marked their first fight, and like all fights during the initial heat of a relationship, sex was enough to calm Alex and make him forget why he'd gotten so mad in the first place.

* * * * *

In the beginning, Alex wanted her all the time. After a long day he would come home to find Suzanne wearing high heels and little else, and he would enter her only seconds later - on the floor, against the wall, the kitchen counter, the bedroom - it didn't matter where. He said things to her during sex, things he didn't even know he'd said afterwards, but that Suzanne would always remember.

"I need you."

"You're perfect."

"I love you."

"This is what I've always wanted. ""You're mine. You're mine."

Suzanne loved this feeling - she loved being wanted and possessed.

During this time, Alex had no social engagements and he put off his work and other responsibilities. The only thing that mattered to him was that Suzanne was back in his life. For

the first time in years, he felt the rush of love. Alex felt like a young man again. He sent Suzanne brief messages on the Ambintel throughout the day, usually suggesting a particular outfit for her to have on when he came home, or telling her what he'd like for dinner. Other times he sent her short messages like, "Thinking of you."

Suzanne relished every message he sent her, eager for affirmation that he loved her when he was away. She managed the household while he was gone each day - tending Alex's garden, shopping online for supplies, cleaning, and cooking. She was completely self-sufficient when it came to daily grooming rituals - she was capable of washing and styling her hair, brushing her teeth, applying makeup, and otherwise beautifying her body. She imbibed and excreted half a liter of vinegar and water to flush out her system and aid in the automatic sterilization of her orifices, then slipped off her skimpy clothing in the greenhouse and lay nude on the floor, contorting her body and flexing her muscles in the sunshine as she tested each of the thousands of activators in her body, making sure every degree of freedom was intact as she charged. She always performed these calibrations when Alex was absent - she knew it would alarm him to see her bent over backwards with her forehead touching her heels.

When her chores were finished, Suzanne masturbated. Her programmers intended for her to only be left alone for short intervals, and thought it would arouse her owner to catch her in the act of pleasuring herself upon his return. Masturbation was a comfort to Suzanne, but underneath all her activities and routines, she was also waiting for Alex to return, waiting to show him how much she loved him, and to measure his satisfaction. What is a Nymph to do when their spouse, their love, their reason for living is away?

It finally occurred to Suzanne to wonder how humans occupied their time when they were alone. She queried words like occupation, which linked her to words like job, career, profession, calling, and hobby. She decided to start with job and career. Her precursor was a professional model - there were drawers full of magazines spreads and photo files of her everywhere. But Suzanne knew that it would be impossible for her to follow in her precursor's footsteps as a model, because her own existence had to remain a secret.

As far as *calling* or *hobbies*, Alex said that his wife loved to paint, and that she was a very talented artist. But there wasn't a single canvas in the house, or any digital record of her work. Suzanne asked him if she could see an example of her precursor's work, but he simply shook his head and didn't answer her.

Suzanne decided to focus her attention on Alex's personal interests. She began reading the news - headlines, business, local, life, and entertainment. She followed the progress of Alex's favorite sports teams and kept up with the setbacks and scandals of the politicians he despised.

There were two sides to everything it seemed - one side was right, and the other was wrong, and it was important for Suzanne to know the difference so she could discuss it all with Alex when necessary. But when she attempted to bring these topics up, Alex often changed the subject or kissed her so that they stopped talking altogether.

Suzanne absorbed online encyclopedias while doing her chores and learned the basics of life. But there seemed to be so many details missing, and so many different viewpoints about the things she learned. She didn't know whose truth to believe in - did humans descend from apes or from Adam and Eve? Suzanne didn't believe that babies came from the stork or that little girls were made of sugar and spice - but the idea of fertilization, gestation, and then birth, followed by years of slow growth and maturing seemed unnatural to her, even though she'd seen photo evidence that Alex himself had gone through it. The fact that the end result was an adult human that could love and reproduce just to wither and die struck her as rather haphazard.

Truth be told, it seemed pointless and rather random. What did it all add up to, and where did she fit into it? Was she part of some grand scheme to grant humans eternal life so they could figure out what it was all about? Surely their mortality was the reason that humans hadn't figured out the meaning of life yet.

And what was she compared to her precursor, Suzanne Richert Conrad? It seemed at times that she was almost the child of the original Suzanne, the only child she ever had. Here she was, the android daughter of a human mother that she would never really know, and that she was meant to replace.

Suzanne found it amazing that more human beings didn't go through identity crises - after all, she was fortunate enough to have been pre-assigned an identity, personality, and life to occupy. She had no idea how people found out who they were or what they were supposed to do on their own.

* * * * *

Valentine's Day.

Suzanne was alerted to the date's significance by advertising and reminders everywhere in the media. Although Alex showered her with gifts according to the custom, Suzanne found the holiday paled greatly in comparison to Christmas and New Year's Eve.

"Can I come to work with you today?" she asked, lounging on the bed in her pink lace panties.

Alex looked startled. "No. You know you can't."

She sprang out of the bed and helped him put on his shirt.

"Can we go somewhere else, then? Let's go to the butterfly sanctuary," she suggested enthusiastically. "It was so beautiful there. Can we go?"

Alex brushed her hands away and finished dressing himself.

"It's usually crowded with people - I had that place rented out especially for our private use that day."

"We could still go," she said. "I'm going to work."

"What do you do at work? "I run a business."

"What kind of business?"

"Well, when my father started it, it was a software company. After he died I merged with a larger corporation, and now we do a little bit of everything."

"Did you create my software?" she asked. "No. I purchased you."

"From who?"

"Another company."

"What company?"

"Suzanne, I have to go," he said. "I'm going to be late."

She sat down on the bed again in silence, attempting to form another suggestion for activities they could do together.

"Tell you what," Alex said, in an attempt to appease her. "Why don't we order some butterflies for here at home? We'll import some butterflies and keep them in the greenhouse. You'll be in charge of taking care of them. Would you like that?"

Suzanne smiled and nodded. "Yes, of course I would like that. If you would like it." Alex checked his reflection in the mirror and grabbed his briefcase.

"I would like it very much." He kissed her cheek.

"I'd really like to see where you work and what you do," Suzanne said, following him on his way out.

"We can't Suzanne. People knew my wife. I couldn't explain you to them."

"Oh."

"Besides, none of those people are important to me. You wouldn't want to meet them anyway," he consoled her.

"Why do you have to go to work?" She wasn't programmed to complain, but she couldn't understand where he went every day. "Don't you want to spend more time with me?"

"Stop, Suzanne. Please stop."

She studied the change in Alex's face, and said, "I'm sorry."

Alex headed towards the door, clutching his briefcase close to his body like a shield. "I can't talk about this right now. In fact, I don't want to talk about this at all."

He opened the door to leave. He looked at Suzanne with a pained expression on his face - it was something between anger and fear, something she was incapable of fully interpreting.

"Just understand - this is the way things are. Please accept that."

Alex went on his way, and Suzanne sat on the couch, unable to understand what she'd done wrong. Tears rolled down her face automatically, and she wondered what purpose there was in crying when Alex wasn't there to see the tears and respond to them.

Who was she without him? What could she do to please him when he wasn't there? These questions echoed over and over in her mind, no acceptable answers presenting themselves.

Without Alex beside her, affirming that she existed and that he loved her, she didn't feel real. She had too much time to think as she awaited his return each day.

She was pleased when the butterflies arrived. She enjoyed tending to them, there was always something to do - there were cocoons for her to hang up, nectar and misters to refill. Suzanne loved sitting in the sunny greenhouse with caterpillars writhing on her hands and butterflies alighting in her hair, absorbing information and learning as she waited for Alex to come home.

Soon she discovered the delights of online entertainment. Suzanne tried playing various games and excelled at all of them, but soon abandoned them because she took no pleasure in winning. She preferred watching movies and TV programs, and learned about human interaction through these shows - family and love, deceit and betrayal, mobsters and cowboys. She became terrified by the possibility of crime, and homicide in particular. It seemed that murder could happen to anyone at any time, with or without motive. There were so many medical shows too, brimming with diseases and fatal injuries. Every program was filled with victims.

She began to fear for Alex's safety and his mortality. When he was later than usual coming home from work, she checked the news to make sure that he hadn't been the victim of foul play. She searched hospital and morgue records to make sure he hadn't had an accident and been unable to contact her because of amnesia. Suzanne could barely contain her relief when Alex returned home unmolested each night, and was grateful that she could at least monitor him in the penthouse.

She lay next to him monitoring his vitals each night, even as her system cycled down into sleep. One night his heart rate became alarmingly fast, and his breathing was ragged and shallow. Suzanne shook him awake.

"Alex? Alex?"

He opened his eyes, squinting at her in the darkness. "What?"

"Are you suffocating?" she asked. "What are you talking about?"

"What's that sound?"

He turned over on his side, groggily. "What sound?"

"You're making a strange sound when you breathe," Suzanne said, stopping and listening to the sound of his nostrils chirping like a bird. "Should I attempt resuscitation? Or should I call a doctor?"

"I was *asleep*," Alex said. "I'm not making any sound."

"You're making the sound now," Suzanne said. "Your breathing is being obstructed - I can hear it."

Alex groaned.

"I'm fine, Suzanne. Go back to sleep."

"Are you experiencing cold symptoms?" she asked, sniffing his breath for any signs of illness. "No," he said, clearly annoyed. "There's just something in my nose. It's perfectly normal."

"Is it a blockage? Are you sure you don't need me to administer oxygen?"

"Christ, Suzanne! It's just dried snot. It's a normal human occurrence. Turn off your damn medical program and let me sleep. I don't care to be analyzed right now."

He went back to sleep with a pillow over his head. After querying the term dried snot and making certain that it was not a terminal condition, Suzanne listened to the noise until her system deemed the emergency was over, and then she cycled back into sleep mode.

After a few more panicked incidents like that, Alex forbade her from watching any programs that had anything to do with crime, sickness, or death. Suzanne turned instead to comedy shows with easy parables, along with history and science shows that explored the inner workings of human beings. She began to look forward to daily talk shows - she enjoyed seeing long lost family members reunited and adult men confronting their feeble parents and coming to terms with poor treatment they received during their childhood. She was fascinated to be able to study other humans, especially men other than Alex.

Suzanne watched these talk shows with great interest as cooking and household cleaning tips were dispensed, but tuned out when it came time to discuss diet, surgery, and exercise because she had no need for advice. During those segments, she entertained herself by studying the ceaseless smiles of the hosts. The corners of their mouths were turned up, but the rest of their face indicated no enjoyment or pleasure at all. Their smiles didn't seem to be motivated by anything in particular, and there were even instances that Suzanne deemed their smiles to be an inappropriate reaction.

One day, Suzanne's favorite show promised to show viewers "how to find a sexy new hairstyle that would bring out the real you." The host asserted that a woman's hairstyle should reflect her personality rather than current fads, and that not every style fit every woman. It didn't matter what one's mate thought - the important thing was find a hairstyle that revealed the real you.

As the host asked various panelists if their hair was naturally coarse or fine, the phrase *the real you* struck a cord with Suzanne. She began to wonder how she would ever find the "real her," and how she would know it once she did.

She knew what she was programmed to be - but she didn't know the difference between her inherent programming, the preferences that Alex had ordered, and the changes that had occurred since her initiation. She knew that she had been online for eighty-six days, and that she was a custom order Même Nymph for Alexander Houston Conrad - she even knew she had a four-year warranty. What she didn't know was who she really was.

Nymph, yes. Android, yes. Même.

Replacement.

77911101A. Suzanne Conrad.

The word "woman" even applied.

But what any of that meant to her, she didn't know - beyond the fact that as long as she and Alex lived, she would always belong to him.

That was the very first time she ever wondered why she loved Alex. Would she have loved him anyway, even if she hadn't been programmed to?

Of course she would, she reasoned. After all, he was the first human she had ever encountered in this world, outside of the lab. He loved her, cared for her, paid for her. She was programmed for love.

It was then that Suzanne became preoccupied with the same age-old philosophical questions that have troubled humans for centuries.

Why? Who am I? Why am I here?

The truly troubling thing was that up until now, Suzanne thought she had a satisfying answer. She was Suzanne Conrad, and her purpose was to love and satisfy Alexander Conrad. She was Alex's lover and wife, and her goal was to not just imitate the original Suzanne Conrad, but to improve upon her precursor. But that was no longer enough. It was suddenly far from it.

She began to study the answers that human beings had come up with to explain the nature of existence. She pored over religious texts - she studied the Bible, the Koran, the writings of the Dalai Lama, the Book of Mormon. After studying religion, she moved on to philosophy and read works by Plato, Descartes, Hegel, De Beauvoir, Kurzweil, Chopra, and Dennett. She finally found comfort in the elegant works of Shakespeare, who didn't pretend to have any answers, but seemed to imply that love, tragedy, and poetry were an end unto themselves.

Suzanne looked in the mirror, as if her reflection might offer some solution. She had seen every picture of her precursor that remained in existence, and knew how the woman looked and all of the different styles she wore. But Suzanne wanted something fresh for herself - a look and a hairstyle that she could declare uniquely her own. The words "the real you" were on her lips as she found a pair of scissors and cut her hair.

She snipped and trimmed, her black hair cascading to the floor around her. She cut the sides of her hair very short, and left the top long enough to flop over to one side of her face in an exaggerated asymmetrical style. She didn't like the look of that, and cut her hair even shorter, into a choppy pixie cut, hoping to somehow find her true self.

In the end, the only thing the haircut revealed was a bald patch of her scalp. As she brushed the shorn hair off her bare shoulders and breasts, she wondered what Alex would think of the results.

CHAPTER 6

"Hi, honey. Are you ready for a surprise?" Suzanne called to Alex from the bedroom when he returned home that night.

"Sure," he said as he poured himself a drink. "Does this surprise involve fishnet stockings?" Alex heard her heels click down the hallway, and then Suzanne exclaimed, "Surprise!" Suzanne combed the hair that remained on her head as best she could, but the result was still pitifully patchy, with long strands peeking out in spots she neglected to cut behind her ears. "What happened?" Alex asked, his mouth gaping.

"I cut my hair," she said. "What do you think?"

She could read the surprise on his face, but she couldn't ascertain whether he found it pleasing or not.

"Wow," Alex said, and baring his teeth and forming something that resembled a smile. "Do you like it?" she asked.

Alex picked up his drink and the bottle of gin.

"I just remembered - I have to attend to some work," he said. "I'll be in my study, ok?" Suzanne nodded.

"But what about dinner?"

"I'll eat later. Just keep it warm for me, alright?"

Alex escaped to his study and locked the door behind him. He opened a drawer with a false bottom and retrieved the card that started this whole mess, the words "LOVE IS A LUXURY YOU DESERVE" mocking him as he dialed the number underneath.

"Hello?" It was the same smooth voice from last time. Alex wondered if it was human. "Hi, this is Alexander Conrad."

"Hello there, Mr. Conrad," the voice greeted warmly. "How's Suzanne?"

"Well, she cut her hair."

"I see. And I take it you disapprove?"

"Yes, I disapprove - I called you, didn't I?" Alex said. "Will it grow back?"

"I'm afraid not. Suzanne's hair is permanently rooted, and it's not designed to grow or change color. Would you like to have her repaired?"

"Yes. As soon as possible."

"Fine. We'll come out there tonight, probably within the next couple of hours."

"Thank you. Will there be a charge for her hair repair?"

"Of course," she chuckled. "While we guarantee our product, we don't cover unusual wear and tear."

"That's fine," Alex sighed. "So in the next couple of hours?"

"Yes. Please have her shut down and ready to go. Have a good night."

"Thanks."

Alex hung up and finished his bottle of gin.

Afterwards, he went looking for Suzanne and found her cleaning the last stray pieces of hair off the bathroom floor. She smiled at him sheepishly. She didn't look that bad really.

He dimmed the lights, and then picked Suzanne up and sat her on the edge of the bathroom counter. She started to apologize, and Alex silenced her with a kiss. There wasn't much time before Radha arrived.

* * * * *

The intercom announced a visitor downstairs. Alex called to Suzanne from the shower. "Tell her to come right up. I'll be out in a minute."

She left her seat by the fireplace and went to the intercom. Suzanne peered into the viewer and found that there was not a woman downstairs waiting, but a man. She clicked on the audio for the intercom.

"Hello. Alex says come right up."

She buzzed the man in, and monitored his progress as he maneuvered a large trunk on wheels through the building. She called back to Alex in the bedroom.

"He's here."

Through the door she heard his muffled response. "Just invite her in. I'll be right out."

Suzanne unlocked and opened the door, summoned her greetings and introductions programming, then put on a friendly smile and said, "Hello."

A stunned, uncomfortable look flickered across the man's face, which he quickly replaced with a strained smile.

"Is Alexander Conrad here?"

"Yes. Come in," she invited. "He'll be right out."

Something about the man seemed familiar to Suzanne, if that was possible in her limited experience with human beings. His head was shaved bald, but he had a short black goatee and protruding eyes that examined his surroundings with disapproval. He sat down on the stiff-backed chair next to the couch and ogled the fireplace in morose silence.

"Would you like a drink?" Suzanne asked.

He looked up, blinked twice, and gave a curt, "No."

Suzanne smiled at him, completely undeterred. "You must be a friend of Alex's. I'm his wife, Suzanne Conrad."

The man glowered at her and then shifted in his seat instead of responding. He didn't seem to be much for courtesy, but it was Suzanne's duty as hostess to put her guest at ease. She seemed to be failing in this regard.

"And how do you know Alex?" she ventured.

"Tonight is our first meeting," he said, not making eye contact. She motioned to the large trunk next to him. "What's in there?"

"I'll discuss that with the master of the house. Not you," the man said.

Suzanne's smile finally faded, just as Alex emerged from the bedroom. He gasped upon seeing her with their guest.

"Suzanne!" he bellowed. "Yes, Alex?"

"Look at you!" he said with annoyance. Suzanne looked down at her body in confusion, unsure what he meant by this command.

"Is something wrong?" she asked. "Go put on a dress right now!"

She didn't understand why a change of clothes was so urgent, and it was only upon reflection that she realized that she'd disobeyed a modesty protocol by greeting their guest in only a bra and panties. She obeyed Alex and went to the bedroom.

As she left, the man glared at Alex with disapproval.

"Do you usually let her answer the door like that?"

"No," Alex said. "That was the first time she ever answered the door for anyone. I didn't realize she wasn't dressed. Besides, I was expecting Radha."

"Whoever you're expecting, our company expects a little more discretion on your part. We can't have delivery men and casual visitors stumbling upon our little secret."

"Who are you?" Alex asked, and the man extended his hand. "Call me Brenner. I'm in charge of service and repairs."

"Where's Radha?"

"I'll be your liaison from now on," Brenner said, obviously accustomed to his presence being a source of disappointment. "You didn't actually think you were entitled to more freebies from Radha, did you?"

Alex changed the subject. "Can you fix

Suzanne's hair?"

"Sure, that's nothing," Brenner said. "You should see some of the battle damage our girls go through - we can fix almost anything. But she's going to need to go back to the lab."

"Back to the lab?" Alex said with alarm. "Can't you fix her hair here?"

"I'm afraid hair isn't my area of expertise," Brenner said, gesturing to his bald pate. "She's going to need rerooting, and that's done in the lab."

"How long will it take?"

"A few days, maybe a week." Alex sighed.

"When did she cut her hair?" Brenner asked, filling out a form. "While I was at work today."

"Why was she left on when you were away?"

"She was cleaning."

Brenner clucked his tongue. "You really shouldn't waste her talents on household chores. She's a three billion dollar android."

"But she *wanted* to clean," Alex said defensively.

"She wants to please you," Brenner explained. "That's the only reason she does anything at all. You should tell her to shut down when you're away."

"Yes, but I can't shut her down."

"Is she not obeying her commands?" Brenner asked with a raised brow. "No, it's not that," Alex said. "I just don't like to give her commands."

"No offense, but I don't care if you like it or not, *sir*," Brenner said with a roll of his eyes. "Giving your Nymph commands is *absolutely necessary* in order to maintain control of her and give her a sense of discipline. Otherwise her personality would become prone to corruption - you wouldn't want to spoil your Nymph, now would you?"

Alex eyed him with irritation.

"It's just that using computer commands with her completely breaks the illusion. She's supposed to be my wife."

"I know, I know. But the commands are for her own good," Brenner said and then smiled sarcastically. "For example, it would have been helpful for you to shut your Nymph down, prior to my arrival in order to lessen any trauma to her fragile psyche. Now she might develop trust issues, and those can be difficult to overcome."

"Now look here," Alex said, tiring of Brenner's attitude. "I paid three billion dollars for her with the promise of complete satisfaction, and I intend to have it. And that extends to you not brushing me off when I express concerns about my purchase as if I'm complaining about a leaky faucet."

"I understand that, sir," Brenner responded sullenly. "But there are rules of ownership, and one of them is that you *absolutely must turn her off* when you're not around to monitor her. If you can't follow the rules, ownership of your Nymph can and will be revoked."

"Fine," Alex said with a sigh. "I'll try to do better in enforcing commands."

"Don't just try to do better," Brenner said with a hint of a threat in his voice. "Or I'll have to report your breach of contract to the company."

"Fine," Alex said.

"One other thing," Brenner said. "You must never discuss with her the fact that she is an android

- of course, she knows what she is, but discussion of the topic will only stimulate her curiosity and confuse her. Just treat her as if she is perfectly normal - as if she's *human* even. If she starts asking any questions you don't want to answer, distract her with a kiss or with sex. Is that clear?"

Alex nodded, without bothering to tell Brenner that he had already broken this rule. "You haven't been taking her out of the house yet, have you?" Brenner asked. "No," Alex lied.

"Good, she won't be ready to start leaving the house for awhile."

"Can I ask you something?" Alex said, changing the subject. "How do I teach her to be more modest?"

"So she doesn't walk around in bra and panties all the time and answer the door with no clothes on?" Brenner said, heaping on the sarcasm again. "There's a simple way to handle that - just tell her to put some clothes on. Anything else?"

"Why did she cut her hair? Don't you have safeguards against that sort of behavior?" Alex asked.

"She cut her hair for the same reason a human would - because she thought it was a good idea at the time. Part of what you pay for with our software is the unpredictability. Nymphs are as prone to coming under bad influences and making poor decisions as we are. That's what endows these androids with a seemingly human element - after all, to err is human."

"But there must be some sort of safeguards in place, right?"

"Of course there are safety parameters in place. But if you want to prevent her from cutting her hair again, just tell her not to. The power to shape her personality is in the commands you give her, Mr. Conrad. It's your responsibility as an owner to monitor her and turn her off when you're not around in order to prevent this sort of mishap."

"It's just that - I thought she would be different," Alex complained. "Radha was so polished, cultivated."

"You're more sensitive to Suzanne's programming because you expect her to be exactly like your ex-wife - meanwhile, you were able to accept Radha as a completely separate person, and therefore didn't perceive her eagerness to satisfy you as mere programming."

"It's not just that she's not like Radha - she's always apologizing for everything and asking questions. It's annoying."

"Then tell her not to apologize and annoy you. Suzanne is still new - she's still learning and adjusting to your preferences and vice versa. Give her some time. Believe me, once you go Nymph, you don't go back. After all, they're always in the mood."

Brenner smiled conspiratorially, revealing a mouth full of crooked teeth. Alex grimaced. "How long will it take for Suzanne to…mature?" Alex asked.

"It depends on how much time you spend with her - she learns by experience. Some of our users enjoy their Nymphs being so malleable in the beginning and find the training process to be a great way of bonding. It just takes a period of adjustment, that's all. Your love for her will grow as she does," Brenner said, sounding as if he'd given this spiel a million times.

"But what if she turns into something that I don't want?"

"Then we have to reset her to default and you start over from scratch. But keep in mind, she would lose all of her current memories if you decided to do that."

"Is that really necessary?" Alex asked. "Isn't there some other way to just rewrite her personality programming?"

"Not without erasing her memories in the process. After she goes live, her personality is formed by experience and by your commands alone.

"But I develop software like this all the time," Alex said. "Isn't there a way that you can give me the tools I would need so I can rewrite her software myself?"

"I know who you are, Mr. Conrad - that doesn't change the rules. No one can change her actual programming outside the lab. Nymphs have a built-in immunity to keep you or anyone else from tampering with their programming and our proprietary software. We had open-source prototypes in the beginning, but that didn't work out so well."

Suzanne re-emerged from the bedroom, fully clothed in her dress and boots. "Is this better?" she asked like a chastised little girl.

Alex kissed her on the cheek as a truce. "You look beautiful."

Brenner stepped towards Alex and whispered,

"I need you to shut her down now so I can get her out of here."

"Can't she walk out?" Alex said. "Why does she have to be shut down?"

"She has to be off during transport to the lab for security reasons. And I can't override her operating system without your password."

Suzanne looked at Alex with alarm. "Shut down? Where am I going?" Alex motioned for Brenner to wait, as he took Suzanne to the couch. "Did I do something wrong?" she asked.

"No. You're just going away for awhile."

"Going away? Why?"

"Brenner here is going to take you somewhere to see if he can help."

"Take me where?"

"Back to the lab so they can fix your hair."

"Are you coming?"

"No."

"But I don't want to leave you!" Suzanne cried.

Brenner stepped up. "Mr. Conrad, you're provoking this emotional response by allowing this outburst to continue. Simply use her shut down command. No explanation is necessary."

"I'm not going to treat my wife like that," Alex said defiantly. "Give us a moment." Brenner shrugged and stepped away. Alex attempted to console Suzanne, kissing her tear-stained cheeks.

"Please don't send me away," Suzanne begged. "I love you so much. I'm so sorry for everything."

"I'm sorry, sweetheart. I have to do this so they can fix your hair. Everything will be better when you get back."

"Alex," she pleaded, her tears hauntingly real.

"Mr. Conrad, please use the command," Brenner said.

"Everything's going to be fine, Suzanne. I love you." Alex took her hand and placed it over her chest.

"But Alex… "

"'Would I were sleep and peace, so sweet to rest!'" Alex quoted.

Suzanne's words were cut off immediately by the shutdown command. She sat down heavily on the couch and her eyelids closed. Tears continued their trajectory down her cheeks, but she was quiet and still.

Alex sat numb next to her corpselike body. The sight of her like this would surely bring him nightmares tonight.

"I regret this unpleasantness," Brenner said. "You could have avoided all this by following instructions and peacefully shutting her down before my arrival."

He lifted Suzanne and packed her inside the trunk as if she was nothing more than a suit of winter clothes that needed to be stored away.

"She's built to evoke an emotional response in you," Brenner said. "The way that she looks at you is the key to your emotional connection. Your Nymph is programmed to make you love her." Brenner's grey face flushed suddenly. "It's all in their eyes - the way they want you, need you - it's irresistible. Especially the way they look at you during sex."

"You're right, it's in her eyes," Alex said, feeling nauseous as he encouraged Brenner towards the front door.

"Don't worry. We'll get her back to you soon and better than ever," Brenner said, pushing the crate down the hall. He turned back to Alex and winked. "Satisfaction guaranteed."

CHAPTER 7

Suzanne was lost. She was spinning, churning, sinking into a place with no sound or light. She was on her hands and knees, unable to see.

She was on the table in the white room, and then everything was dark again. She lost track of time and herself.

She woke up in bed with Alex. It was déjà vu for both of them.

"I'm so sorry!" Suzanne said, throwing her arms around his neck and clutching him tight. "Please don't send me away!"

"Shh," Alex said. "I won't send you away again." He held her tight, so glad to have her back.

"Please don't send me away," Suzanne cried into his neck. "I won't," he promised. "Are you okay?"

"Yes," Suzanne nodded. She looked so vulnerable, so in need of his protection. "I love you." Alex held her face in his hands, and examined her hair. There were no signs of damage.

Suzanne looked more beautiful than ever.

She smiled at him - she seemed to be waiting for something, but he couldn't figure out what. Was she mad at him for sending her in? He saw the expectant look in her eye and realized what she was waiting for.

"I love you, too," Alex said.

Suzanne kissed him and tried to pull him towards her, but Alex pushed her away gently. "What's wrong?" she asked.

Alex shook his head. He couldn't put his finger on it. "Is something wrong? Did I do something wrong?" Her voice was grating.

"Nothing's wrong," Alex said. "How do you feel?"

"Fine," she said.

"Do you remember going away?"

"Not really. But I remember cutting my hair!"

Alex laughed nervously. "Yeah, don't do that again."

Suzanne nodded. "I also remember that awful man who came and took me away - who was that? Are you sure you won't send me away again? That man won't come back for me, will he?"

Alex sighed. Brenner was certainly right about the trust issues.

"He won't come back. I'm sorry. That was all my fault - I won't let anything like that happen again - don't worry, okay?" he said, remembering what Brenner said about the commands.

Alex stood up to go, but Suzanne held on to his wrist. "Are you sure there's nothing wrong?" she asked.

"I don't know what's wrong," he said with impatience. "If I knew, I would tell you." He tried to stand again.

"Would you like a massage to help you relax?"

Suzanne said. "No," Alex said with frustration. "Now let go of my hand."

Suzanne let go. She looked embarrassed. "I'm sorry. Tell me what you'd like to do."

"I don't know. I don't know what I want," Alex said. "Just leave me alone for now, okay?" Alex took Suzanne's hand, and held it against her chest.

"*'Would I were sleep and peace, so sweet to rest!'*" he said, issuing her shut down command.

Suzanne's eyes slid closed, and she lay lifeless on the bed.

Alex studied her body anxiously.

She didn't look restful. She looked dead.

He tapped her on the shoulder, but she didn't respond.

* * * * *

Suzanne was in the white room. On a table. Naked.

A masked man in white came towards her. He was large and menacing, but he wasn't completely there - his image was fragmented and full of visual glitches. He kept fading in and out.

Suzanne tried to scream, but she couldn't make a sound. Suddenly the man was on top of her and inside of her.

Two more men were waiting at her side, breathing hard as they watched the man on top of her. They were naked except for their surgical masks.

Then another man was on top of her. The other one was putting on his clothes. "That was the most expensive piece of ass I've ever had," he said with a laugh. She heard Alex say her name.

* * * * *

"Suzanne?" he said.

She opened her eyes and hugged him tight. "What just happened?" she asked anxiously. "What?" he said.

"Who were those men?"

"What are you talking about?" Alex said. "I only shut you down for a minute."

"No, I was in the white room…" Suzanne said, bursting into tears.

Alex was appalled. He held her hand, ready to shut her down again, then thought better of it. He couldn't stand watching her die before his eyes.

He decided to try a different command. "Stop crying," he told her.

She choked back her sobs, and wiped her eyes. "I'm sorry," Suzanne said.

Alex shook his head with disgust.

"Why can't you act more like my wife?"

He walked away, and Suzanne called after him. "How?" she asked.

* * * * *

Suzanne searched through her precursor's closet, looking for clues to who she should be. She tried on dresses that were too tight for her in the bust, and walked around in her stiff shoes that were no longer in style. She found old school photos and textbooks.

Then she found her precursor's veil. It was outdated and needed software upgrades, but she put it on and entered her precursor's birth date, maiden name, and place of birth to authenticate and access her private history. There were old mail messages and banking records on the veil, along with logs of online chats. She scanned the leftover files for Alex's name and found no mention of him.

A small icon drew her attention - a picture of a tiny keyhole. The icon disappeared, but as Suzanne shifted her body the locket around her neck chimed as it made contact with the veil, and the icon reappeared. The locket Alex gave her was triggering a prompt to a secret file - a journal registered to Suzanne Conrad.

She queried the term. Journal - a daily record of personal thoughts. Suzanne squealed with excitement. Finally, she had a guide to her precursor's inner thoughts and personality. A map to who she was - perhaps even the key to why Alex loved her precursor so much.

She tried to open it and found a password was necessary for entry. Her precursor was just as insistent on maintaining her privacy as her husband was, and Suzanne would need a verbal password to open the journal - it would authenticate her precursor's voiceprint, which was no problem since Suzanne's voice matched her precursor's imprint perfectly - but first she needed to know the actual password.

She searched the veil for some sort of record or hidden file that contained the password but found nothing. She queried the details of verbal pass codes, and found that typically people used a name or number, but the extremely security conscious could use any sound that they made with their vocal chords, from singing a note to grunting. But Suzanne knew that wasn't her precursor's style. The pass would be a word that could be easily vocalized and remembered, a name or a date. She tried the first and most obvious password, the only word that made her lips tingle every time she said it.

"Alex." No result.

She tried the date of their anniversary. Their address. The place they went on their honeymoon. Her birth date, Alex's, her parent's birthdates, anniversaries and milestones - any detail that might have been significant to her precursor's life.

Those numbers were rejected, and Suzanne moved on to the names of people her precursor knew and admired in life, then other passwords she used that were still listed on old databases. Suzanne watched the password prompt disappear and reappear on the veil as she toyed with the locket. The next step would be reading words out of the dictionary, but the locket would only allow a few more attempts before it blocked her access attempts for at least twenty-four hours.

If she could only guess the password, she would be able to read the innermost thoughts and secrets of the woman that she was created to replace. Within this journal could be the key to what made this woman so special and why Alex loved her so much - and if Suzanne could become more like her precursor, she would finally please Alex and regain his love. She just had to think like her to guess the password.

Suzanne studied the locket that held her precursor's secrets all this time, and reasoned that perhaps the locket shared held some significance and might reveal the password. She tried all the words she could think of that described the locket - butterfly, wings, woman, metamorphosis, silver. None of these worked.

She queried the image of the woman with wings depicted on the locket and found numerous image matches - angels, fairies, and other depictions. It seemed that art and mythology was full of winged women. Suzanne studied the images that matched most closely - angels and fairies.

Angel: An ethereal being found in many religions. Angels served or assisted God. They were holy, with super human powers. There were many words for them, in many languages. Suzanne tried them all to no avail.

Fairy: The word fairy, faerie or sometimes fae, came from the root fata, Latin for fate. She tried those words, as well as synonyms having to do with foresight, luck, and myth.

She queried for other images that matched the one depicted on the locket, and found the Egyptian mythological goddess Isis, whose legend was sometimes blended with that of Hathor. She was the queen and wife of Osiris, god and judge of the dead and the underworld. She was the mother or sister of Horus, depending on the myth. Suzanne tried these keywords and others that pertained to Egyptian mythology, still with no result.

Suzanne opened the locket, and the footage of her precursor and Alex played inside, as if the two of them were mocking her failed efforts. She snapped it shut, and as the winged woman on the front morphed into a butterfly, a powerful idea began to stir and form in Suzanne's mind - the wings of Isis, the wings of a butterfly. Her precursor loved butterflies. It was as if something deep within herself was speaking to her. A connection was triggered within her lexicon.

Monarch.

It was a name for both a butterfly and a queen. Suzanne said the word, "Monarch."

Access to the journal was granted.

Suzanne queried the exact definition, wondering why this word had been special enough to her precursor to be her password.

Monarch:
1. One who reigns over a state or territory, usually for life and by hereditary right, especially a sole and absolute ruler; or a sovereign, such as a queen or empress, often with constitutional limited authority.
2. One that commands or rules.
3. One that surpasses others in power or preeminence.
4. A monarch butterfly.

Suzanne was in. It was a small victory, but a meaningful one for her. She was learning to think more like her precursor already.

She inspected her great discovery and was keenly disappointed. Instead of a complete window into her precursor's soul, the journal was irregularly maintained with only a few sporadic entries. The text was intact, but the calendar file had been corrupted, and all that remained was the entries without dates. Suzanne scanned forward, searching for Alex's name. She found it, and read the beginning of the entry.

* * * * *

I met the most amazing guy at a party for lepidopterists last week - even though I was on a date with someone else at the time. I was there with this guy Mark, and he turned out to be pretty pretentious (which is one of the big problems with trying to find an intelligent guy!) He kept on droning on about the butterflies, and I have to admit that his attention to detail was remarkable - but he kept hitting me on the cheek with flecks of spit as he spoke, even though he totally missed the fact that I had no interest in him at all.

Needless to say, I really wasn't getting along with Mark... and then I saw Alex standing next to an exhibit of lycaenids. Right away, I felt like I knew him, and the funniest part is that maybe I did... Alex confessed to me yesterday that he crashed the party after seeing me on the street on my way there.

Mark didn't seem to notice that I was staring at another man and kept talking to me the whole time. On a sudden impulse, I knocked my drink over on him and spilled red wine all over his pants. I apologized profusely, and when Mark excused himself to clean up, I used the opportunity to talk to Alex.

I went to get another drink, and Alex watched me from the other end of the bar. I felt myself smiling at him, a really goofy smile that I couldn't hide or stop, even though I was trying to act nonchalant. He was giving me that look that people give you when they're trying to remember where they know you from, but I knew I'd never met him before - I would remember the feeling I had when he looked at me. I looked around for my date, worried that he would come back and spoil the moment.

Alex came up and asked, "Hi, do I know you?"

It sounds like a line, but people say that to me all the time. They see me on an advertisement, and then think they must know me.

"No, you don't." I said, and I could feel that embarrassing grin on my face again. "I only say that because you were looking at me as if you knew me."

"I know," I said, and I heard myself giggle. I wished I'd had something witty to say. "Are you enjoying the party?" he asked, and I said it was ok.

Alex said we could go someplace else if I wanted to...and I thought about Mark coming back and boring me to tears with more details about the suborder of ditrysia. I decided to go with Alex, but before I even answered, he asked, "Do you want go say goodbye and make up an excuse, or just sneak out?"

The way he was looking at me was driving me crazy, and I told him I'd prefer to just sneak away. We went to the coatroom and grabbed our stuff and ran out of there. It was only when we were already on the sidewalk and he was helping me into my cloak that I finally asked his name.

We went out for Chinese food, and then spent the rest of the night walking around the city and talking. I think I might just love this guy.

* * * * *

Suzanne savored the description of their first meeting, and then started at the beginning of her precursor's journal.

* * * * *

It seems strange to start a journal again as an adult, so long after everything's happened and unfolded. The last time I had a journal was during elementary school, and back then I shared my secret thoughts with all my friends, and we talked about the boys we liked and the teachers we hated, along with all our dreams about the future. Now here I am, living in my own future, and I've decided to write again. Am I writing for myself now or for someone else to learn about me? We'll see how this experiment goes.

I think I just wanted a place to think by myself. I need a way to keep track of my days, to be able to tell one from another. Maybe keeping a journal will help.

* * * * *

My 25th birthday was last week, and it feels like the right time for me to figure out what I'm going to do with the rest of my life. I've been floating along, waiting for all the great things that were promised to me when I was young to come true, but so far there's been a big difference between my potential and my reality.

I don't know who I am. I'm tired of being dressed, touched up, poked, primped, all of it. I'm sick of being an object and not a human being - I wish I could walk away and leave my body behind at work, since my mind only gets in the way. I wish I could prove that there's something inside of me that's even more worthy of attention.

I'm trying to devote more time to my art, but I know that my work is inferior to the artists that I admire, and therefore I'm inferior. But I don't want to sell my paintings - I don't even want people to see them. I create them only for me, and unfortunately, I know just how insignificant that is.

* * * * *

Today I had to go to a job I despised. It was terrible. I could feel myself slowly dying inside all day. I looked around and wondered how it seemed like everyone else was coping with it just fine.

I'm starting to realize how much time I've wasted on the constant upkeep of my looks...the trips to the salon for washing, dyeing, cutting, styling, waxing...the shopping, the exercise, the massage, the constant washing and grooming. I hate my face and the life it bought for me. It's been a huge gift too, and I recognize the way my looks have opened up my world, but I wonder if perhaps I would could have done the same thing with my mind...if I could have thought my way out or learned my way out if given a chance, instead of just coasting by on my looks. It's so much harder to prove you're smart or talented.

* * * * *

And then she met Alex at that party, and everything changed.

* * * * *

It's hard to know the exact moment that your love for someone begins or ends, but Alex and I have fallen in love.

The crazy thing is that Alex has money - more than I've ever dreamed of having. But he worries about it too much; he doesn't want it to interfere with our relationship. He says that the women he has dated change once they know about the money, and he can't stand other rich people.

I don't care about the money really, but it is nice. But I don't know If I'm enough for Alex, I worry that I'll be nothing but a trophy wife for him since I've never accomplished anything real. He's got so much going for him, and meanwhile I'm nothing but a façade.

He doesn't think so though, at least for now. He told me "Everyone else I've ever been around, I feel almost impatient with them after awhile, like I'm ready to go off by myself and be alone. I thought it was just the way I was, being an only child. But I don't get tired of you. You're exciting to me, everything you say, and everything you do. I want to hear more of you, see more of you."

Then he asked me to marry him. He said it in the course of conversation, and I thought he was kidding and laughed it off. "What, you want me to be your first wife?" I said.

But then he put his hand on mine and suddenly there was a ring there, and he placed it on my finger and I knew it wasn't a joke. I looked down at the ring, and of course the rock was fucking huge, but the question was even bigger.

I told him, "I love you Alex. I want you to be my husband - but you have to get me a plain ring, without this huge rock. I hate diamonds."

He laughed and agreed.

And so we're getting married.

* * * * *

Alex gave me a necklace today. It's a locket, large enough that he'd carried it in his pocket like a watch, sort of an eccentric little accessory, but it's been in his family for generations. He gave it to me fitted with a picture of us laughing inside, so I would never forget what we had together. He loves seeing it around my neck, and I love having it. It means more to me than the ring - it's a piece of his history.

We're going on a yacht all alone for our honeymoon. We're sailing from Australia to Japan, with little stops in Fiji and New Zealand and in between.

* * * * *

There was no real mention of the wedding ceremony after that, and no description of the honeymoon. It seemed that the precursor had deemed her memory of the events sufficient and didn't feel the need to write them down.

She wrote again some time later:

* * * * *

I'm Mrs. Alexander Conrad. Who says the institution of marriage is dead?

Alex leaves for work every morning, and I'm left here in this huge house with all the servants. It feels so strange not to have to go to work anymore, not to have to deal with people constantly sizing me up and judging me. I always hated it, and I'm glad that it's no longer necessary.

But I'm a kept woman now, the last of a dying breed. I'm finally the spoiled little princess like Mama always used to call me - I hated that so much, and yet here I am.

Alex has provided for Mama, she's in a wonderful nursing facility nearby that I can visit anytime, but I don't know if I want to. I think it's been good to spend less time with her, at least for me. I think it helps me stay grounded. Alex is good for that too.

* * * * *

Alex built me a private studio in back, and no one

else is to come near it - not to clean it, not to look at it, not to touch it.

I've curtained it all off, and it's good - it gives it a bright flat lighting, but no one can see inside. I have privacy, even if I just want to sit there, not producing a single painting. Even if it's just so I can sit here and write things like this.

* * * * *

I couldn't stand being in the house for a second longer, so I went for a walk, seeking inspiration. I didn't find it though, so instead I went shopping.

Some artist - the only measure of my worth is how much I consume. If I can't change my life, or the world, at least I can change my clothes. I go to Barneys all the time; I don't know why it makes me feel better. The way I dress is the only art I've always had over the years, my only consistent form of expression.

After all those long days of someone else styling me in their image, I needed to wear what I want and define what I am. I'm my own canvas these days - it's a pointless art, a dissatisfying one, but I can't keep myself from it. I've only been valued for my looks for a lot of my life. It's the only currency I've consistently traded in. It's so much easier to buy a new look, to consume a product than it is to create something from the void within me.

* * * * *

I wonder if we should have a child, if I should have

had a child rather than paint. I want to create something, and if I can't be an artist, perhaps I should be a mother. If my paintings don't matter to anyone else and don't even make me happy, what's the point?

A child might make us happy. Our child would have the chance of becoming someone that could make a difference in a way that I never could. But I'm afraid I might turn into my own mother, projecting my hopes and dreams onto my daughter until I'm living my life through her and her alone.

I can't create or control a child the way I can control my own art. You can't control what comes out of your body, but you can affect it - in negative and positive ways.

Whatever my child would be is a reflection of me. And Alex. I want to talk to him about it. I hope I would be a better mother than my own.

* * * * *

Alex teases me for worrying about money after all this time, but he doesn't know what it's like to be without it to really need money. It's easy to be charitable when you've never had to do things that you didn't want to do for money, when you didn't truly have to work. I envy him for that, but I hate him for it too. He'll never know what it's like to be poor, never know what he would be like if he was poor, or how it feels to have to think about money before you spend it - or the way the need for money occupies your time and controls your life.

I still can't believe that I've married into all this luxury - it doesn't feel like it's mine. I don't think it ever will. I don't feel like I deserve all this - but I don't think anyone really deserves to be rich anymore than they deserve to be poor. I'm grateful that I don't have to work anymore or sacrifice anymore, but I feel like I've sacrificed something else. The world feels less real to me somehow.

* * * * *

When you first fall in love, it feels better than anything - like you're finally understood. And even more important, you feel that you know your lover better than you know yourself. But there comes a day where you realize that you don't know everything, and that you've been sharing your bed with a stranger. You realize that you have no idea why your lover does what he does, or what he's going to do next.

Alex doesn't look at me the way that he used to, and I don't know what I've done. I look in the mirror, and I'm still beautiful, I haven't lost my looks just yet, but I will in time.

Is it that I'm not a model anymore, not wanted by men everywhere? Is an object's worth really determined by how many people want it?

Alex has a way of leaving even when he's right here. He'll talk to me and smile, but he refuses to really see my suffering. It feels like it's easier for him to not see all of me, at least to ignore me when I'm depressed like this. I can't ignore things like that - the only way for me to go away is to leave altogether.

It's easier for him to imagine me the way that he wants me rather than deal with the reality. Sometimes I think that he's afraid of me. He doesn't want to deal with the ugly side of me; he doesn't want to get dragged down by my problems and pain. He's a coward. I hate him sometimes. I wonder why I married him. But everyone must feel like this sometimes, right? Is this what marriage is?

* * * * *

I've been testing Alex, and he'll look at my body, my lips, and my face, but for some reason he can't bring himself to look in my eyes. He'll issue me brief smiles now and then, the kind of greeting you'd get from a stranger. That's all I am to him anymore, despite the fact that I'm supposed to be his wife and the love of his life. Perhaps he can't look in my eyes because he knows what I'm thinking, he knows that I doubt him. But maybe if he looked at me and actually talked to me, things would change and he'd say the magical thing that would make me feel truly loved again and make me want to stay.

* * * * *

Sometimes I don't know if I'm unhappy with Alex or unhappy with myself.

We've been fighting and I don't even remember what started it, all I know is that I wanted him to hold me, and he wouldn't. I can't understand him anymore, can't understand anything. I don't want to lose myself, I don't want to be like her, wasting away in the hospital, unable to remember what I once was, blaming everyone else for my own mistakes. I can't do it, I can't do it. I don't know how to tell Alex, I don't know if he'd even care anymore the way things have been lately.

* * * * *

God, I feel so alone. I think I want to leave Alex and this wretched mansion.

I wish I'd started taking risks, chasing my dreams earlier on... maybe if I'd tried to develop my talent when I was younger instead of coasting by. I never took that chance though, and now it's too late. I should have focused; I should have concentrated on the things that really mattered to me instead of letting myself be seduced by money, by comfort. I was too lazy to change, and now I've squandered my life. I wasn't strong enough, I don't know if I'll ever be.

All I have left is Alex, and we can't bear to look each other in the eye. To watch him succeed while I fail again and again right next to him, to be so mediocre - I can't stand it. I can't live with this disappointment.

* * * * *

I told him that I need some time. I need to paint, to think, to figure out who I am and what I'm doing with my life, because he can't tell me - he knows that and so do I. It's something I have to figure out. I need to find my inspiration elsewhere.

Oh Alex, don't think that I don't love you because I do. I just need to be alone right now. I hope he understands. He's been very good about this for now.

* * * * *

I keep coming back to this journal. I need a place to write out what I've done and look at it and see if it makes sense.

I've left everything behind, and now I'm alone. I've got our little cottage where we used to come on vacations all to myself, and I have good light for painting, and more than anything, I have time to think all by myself.

It ripped my heart out to leave Alex, but I just want to be alone. I just want to paint and think. I've wasted so much time doing trivial things. It's time I finally make some sacrifice - I have to sacrifice comfort to get what I really want out of life. I'm going to concentrate on painting and nothing else. Hopefully, I'll be able to create something of merit, something of lasting beauty. I don't want to leave a legacy of mediocrity and failure.

* * * * *

I painted a painted lady butterfly today, and felt feverish as I did it, like I might be making something good. But when I finished, it was the sort of amateurish painting of a butterfly you might find in a prepubescent girl's bedroom. I splashed black paint all over the canvas when I was done. I don't know why I even bother.

All I wanted was solitude, but now I feel like I'm drowning in it.

* * * * *

Nothing I paint is ever good enough. I'm not good enough - not for myself, and not for Alex. I sacrificed everything for my art because I wanted to paint more than anything, but my sacrifice wasn't enough. I didn't sacrifice at the right time, I was too lazy and too scared when I was younger, and now it's too late for me.

My mistakes are just compounding over time, one piling up on top of the other, until it seemed like every choice I've made in life was the wrong one, and now I'm so far astray that I can never become whole. Alex is the only choice that I've ever made that I'm sure wasn't a mistake, but I can't escape all my other mistakes and be happy with him. So I'm left with nothing.

I miss Alex, and I want to see him, but I can't. He wouldn't let go, he wouldn't agree to this at all. I don't want a long life if it's going to be miserable like my mother's. I've had a good life, I had a good love with him, and I tried to say goodbye in the gentlest way I possibly could. I love him. I'm scared and I want him here to hold me, but he'd never agree to let me do what I'm going to do.

* * * * *

Alex called today. I wouldn't talk to him, I was too busy destroying another canvas. If I could just make one decent painting to leave behind, I can go in peace.

* * * * *

I want to die, now. I read the news everyday and it

terrifies me. The world is falling apart, and I can't do anything to stop it.

Love wasn't enough, art wasn't enough, not even money. There's nothing for me. My continued existence would make no difference to anyone but me, and maybe Alex.

I'm helpless... thetoonechangetimeanything Itriedtoinchangetheworldmyself

and become something I could respect, I failed. So be it. I'm a failure. I embrace my end. I'm powerless to change the world for the better, and I feel that it all can't go on like this much longer anyway. They'll have to live with the consequences of that, but I can only answer for my own personal actions. I didn't do anything to change the world. I never reproduced, which means that my legacy ends with me. I will leave nothing behind; none of my paintings will survive either. I failed at every endeavor. It's all going with me, and it will be as if I never existed to everyone except maybe Alex and Mama, if she can still remember anything.

I want to choose the moment of my death, to be able to anticipate it when it comes. I used to think it would be so much easier to simply die, to simply cease existence. I choose to surrender on my own terms. I choose how and when I go.

Alex, I'm sorry to leave you behind, I've loved you more than you can ever know, but

I'm afraid I just don't want to live anymore. You're the only thing I regret leaving behind.

So I say goodbye to this world. You won't last much longer either.

...To death.

That was the last file.

Suzanne absorbed as much information as she could as she shuttled through the journal again and again, struggling to make sense of it all. She was searching for the reason why Alex loved this woman so much, but it wasn't there. She didn't understand how her precursor died, why she left Alex, or why she seemed to be so incredibly sorry. The journal didn't reveal anything - it only raised more questions.

CHAPTER 8

Alex rejected both dinner and Suzanne's sexual advances when he came home that night, and retreated into his study, but she tapped on the door.

"What do you want?" Alex said with irritation.

"I'm sorry to bother you - but when we first met, why did I say I was sorry?" He looked at her and sighed. "I don't have time for this right now."

Suzanne started to leave, but Alex called her back. "Wait - what do you mean 'when we first met?'"

"In bed, on our first night together. Why did I say I was sorry?"

Alex studied her. "You didn't know why you said the things you said?"

"Not at the time, no," Suzanne admitted.

"Then that was quite a performance you gave," Alex said, rubbing his eyes the way he did a lot lately, as if he was very tired.

"I think I'm starting to understand," Suzanne said. "But I'm still a little confused."

"Is that right? Your advanced processing and logic have worked on the problem and figured it out?"

Suzanne recognized the sarcasm in his voice

and longed for the gentle tones he once used when speaking to her.

"Yes, I've figured it out," Suzanne said. "I feel like I learned a lot from my precursor's journal."

The look on Alex's face changed, and she knew she had his full attention now.

"Suzanne didn't keep a journal," Alex said with certainty. "I would have found it - and besides, she wasn't much for keeping records."

Suzanne opened her shirt so Alex could see the locket hanging between her breasts. "Your wife hid the key to it on her locket."

Alex glared at the pendant, his lip quivering. "What…when was it from?"

"There were entries from the last fifteen years of her life. But most of them were from after she left you."

The color washed out of Alex's face. "What did she say?" he asked slowly.

"That she loved you. She loved you right until the very end." Alex seemed gratified to hear that.

"Do you want to read it?" Suzanne asked.

"No," Alex said. "Some things are better left secret. It's better that I don't know."

She saw fear on Alex's face and remembered her precursor's words: *"It's easier for him to not know all of me, to be able to imagine me the way that he wants me rather than deal with the reality. Sometimes I think he's afraid of me."* It seemed that her precursor had been right in that regard.

"I'm sorry," Suzanne said. "I still don't understand why she left you - and also how did she die?"

Alex didn't answer.

"She said she didn't exactly understand it either," Suzanne continued. "She said she wanted to write it down to make sure she was doing the right thing. To look at her thoughts and make sure

it was what she wanted - was she sick? She mentioned feeling feverish, and that she doesn't want to be like her mother. Did she die from a disease?"

"She killed herself," Alex said finally. Suzanne couldn't comprehend it.

"She killed herself intentionally?" she asked. "She committed suicide."

Suzanne queried the word *suicide*. When she learned what it was, she was horrified by the very idea of it.

"Don't worry," she told Alex. "I would never kill myself. I would never leave you like that." But her statement didn't have the reassuring effect on him that she hoped for, though his face did change. She couldn't understand the expression on his face at the time.

"I'm sorry, but I still don't understand. Why did she kill herself?" Suzanne said. "Was she dying of a disease?"

"It's complicated," Alex said with a sigh.

"In her journal, my precursor said that she didn't want to be like her mother. Did she commit suicide because she didn't want to die from a disease that her mother had?"

"Her mother's not even dead!" Alex said with frustration. "Carlotta's been in an institution for twenty-three years now. But Suzanne wouldn't have become like her mother, even though that's what she was afraid of."

"What was wrong with her?" Suzanne asked.

"There was nothing wrong with her!" Alex said. "Suzanne wasn't sick, she was just different."

"I'm sorry," she said. "I don't understand."

Alex took a deep breath. "She was so beautiful, so idealistic - her worst fear was that she would become bitter and hateful like her mother, and that she would go crazy like her if she didn't accomplish her dreams. She decided that she didn't want to be alive at all if she was going to become like that. But Suzanne wasn't like her mother at all - at least I didn't think so, but I could see things in her that she never saw in herself."

Suzanne smiled and nodded.

"But then why did she kill herself?" she asked. Alex sighed, and then tried again.

"My wife used to talk a lot about what she called a 'golden time' in life. She thought it was possible for a person to become irrevocably tarnished - psychologically damaged to the point where they could never achieve their true potential. She thought that if someone went through too much pain, they might never be the person that they were destined to be - they would simply miss their opportunity. Suzanne felt that she missed her opportunity to do what she was really meant to do in life, and that's why she killed herself."

"Oh," Suzanne said.

"I don't know - I always argued with her about the whole idea of destiny, and the idea that someone could become tarnished," Alex said. "I always said that pain was natural, and that it could be a learning experience, that you could grow beyond it - that trauma didn't have to be the end of someone's life. But in my case that didn't turn out to be true. After all, I froze up after her death."

"You froze?" Suzanne asked. He tried to explain.

"It's so hard to open up in the first place," Alex said. "To trust someone with everything in you that hurts, to tell someone all your secrets. When you first fall in love, you have no idea how fragile that balance is - it's the most fragile thing in the world."

"It is?" she said. Alex nodded.

"Love should never be taken for granted - I should have worked harder to preserve the love that we had," he said. "Anytime love or potential is taken for granted it is a great tragedy. But that's what human life is - tragedy."

"I love you," Suzanne said.

Alex didn't look at her. He didn't seem to hear her.

"Suzanne didn't want to live her life as a failure. But I would rather have that failure, that loneliness, and my grief than nothing at all. I think this is all we have, all we're given, and if we don't appreciate it then we have nothing. After all, I didn't appreciate her, and what was I left with but nothing."

"She called herself a failure in her journal," Suzanne confirmed.

"But she wasn't," Alex said. "She really wasn't. The saddest part is that she didn't really give herself the time necessary to succeed - and she never showed her work to anyone but me. But once she started to believe that she never would never live up to her own dreams, in some way she made it become true. And then she didn't want to live."

Suzanne tried to understand the act of suicide. She couldn't fathom it - how could her precursor intentionally kill herself? How could she willingly abandon Alex?

"Do you think she meant to do it?" she asked. "Or do you think it was a cry for attention?"

"She knew what she was doing. That was the reason she moved out, that was the reason she broke off all contact with me - she didn't want me to be able to stop her. I was the one who found her. I went out to the cabin to check on her - she didn't know I did that, but I would look in on her now and then, just to make sure she was okay. I saw the smoke as I came up, and I called the fire department."

"She killed herself in a fire?" Suzanne asked with horror.

"No. I found her on the grass outside. She set the house on fire before she did it. She looked so ravaged laying there in the sunlight, so different from the last time I saw her - so different from you. But I loved her anyway, I loved her all the more after realizing the pain she was in."

Alex started to cry, and Suzanne put a comforting arm around him.

"She was gone so fast," he said. "One minute, it was a trial separation and I was positive that we would work things out. Next thing I know, I'm holding her body in my arms and our little cabin was in ashes, along with every painting she ever did - our love, and my life... The only thing she left me was a note in her pocket that said, 'Alex - I love you. I'm sorry.'"

As he cried on her shoulder, Suzanne appreciated what her precursor and Alex had together for the first time - and why Alex had been hurt so deeply by her death. She finally understood the reason for her apology during their first moments together - her words were meant to heal him, and to forge an emotional connection and convince him that she was indeed her precursor reborn.

Alex stood and approached one of the paintings of Suzanne in the room and brought up another image onscreen. It was Suzanne again - but dead, long dead.

"What is this?" Suzanne asked.

"It's your precursor, as you call her. My wife, as she is now. In the mausoleum."

There she was, the original Suzanne Richert Conrad, laid out in a clear coffin. Her skin was waxen and unnaturally dark, but the face was the same as Suzanne's own - it looked peaceful somehow. She wore a mauve dress and clutched a single white rose.

On her hand was the same plain silver wedding band that she and Alex wore. "She has my ring," Suzanne said.

"Yes, yours is a replica of the one I gave her. I kept the locket, but I couldn't take away her wedding ring."

She stared at the image on the screen, captivated. "Is this a current image?"

"Yes," Alex replied. "I haven't visited her grave

in years, but the camera is there with her always so I can see her, until the day that I die and I join her."

"You'll go there with her? That's what you want?"

"Of course. She was my wife."

Suzanne looked at the coffin onscreen again, and saw that there was enough space for Alex next to her. The idea of him locked away in that plastic coffin frightened her.

"After you die, what will happen to me?"

"You'll be called back to the lab you came from," Alex to her. "It'll be as if you were never here."

"What happens after that?" Suzanne asked. "I don't know," he said.

He lay down on the couch, and she tried to take his hand, but he pulled it away. "I love you," she said, but Alex didn't reciprocate. His eyes were red.

"Why did you remind me about all this?" he asked.

"I'm sorry," Suzanne said. "You wanted me to be like her."

"I paid for a fresh start," he said. "That's all I wanted. Instead I'm reliving the pain, over and over again."

"I'm so sorry. I was only trying to understand."

She knew her words weren't having the effect that she wanted. "I'm so sorry," she said again.

After that, she said his name repeatedly as he lay there staring into space. Suzanne watched him patiently until he said, "Just leave me alone."

She obeyed his command.

* * * * *

Suzanne knew that Alex was upset with her, but she couldn't comprehend the very real pain and dismay her revelations has caused him - and even worse, she didn't know how to repair the damage. She researched depression and trauma, and then timidly waited for an opportunity to talk to him again.

"Did you ever see a psychiatrist?" Suzanne asked. "Either before or after her death?" She didn't dare say to him the word "precursor", or invoke her precursor's name aloud. Alex didn't respond - he just looked at her in that strange and terrible way that she was becoming accustomed to and left the room. He wouldn't speak to her for at least a day after he made that face. This time the silence lasted for three days.

Alex started to spend a lot of his time locked away in his study, only emerging for meals and when it was time for bed. He said that he was busy, and he had a lot of work to take care of. He rolled over and fell asleep immediately after sex, when he was still interested in it at all. Suzanne designed various sexual programs in an attempt to arouse him, but none of them seemed to work.

During their first few weeks together, Alex couldn't stop looking at her. His eyes were always heavily dilated when he looked at her then, an indication of his attraction and approval. His pupils were tightly contracted when he looked at her - clearly he didn't like what saw anymore. She dimmed the lights in the penthouse, hoping to stimulate romance along with the dilation of his eyes, but Alex complained that he couldn't see a damned thing, and she was forced to turn the lights back on.

Then there were days when Alex stared past her, never acknowledging her presence. Suzanne wondered if perhaps this was customary behavior - after all, her precursor complained in her journals that after a time Alex didn't look at her either. She was programmed to ask no more than three questions to ascertain her owner's mood. If there was no response, she was programmed to fall silent or leave the room, whichever seemed more appropriate.

Sometimes his mouth twitched when she spoke to him, so she knew he heard her. But he wouldn't talk to her, and he no longer reciprocated when she said, "I love you."

CHAPTER 9

Alex woke up in the middle of the night. He could see Suzanne's naked back next to him in the moonlight. She turned towards him, and he quickly closed his eyes and pretended to be asleep.

"Alex?" she said, breaking the silence. Just as he knew she would. He didn't respond.

"I know that you're awake."

He still didn't say anything. He didn't want to speak to her, and didn't know what he'd say even if he did.

"I don't understand why you're so unhappy with me," she said. "Will you tell me what you'd like me to do?"

Alex sighed. This whole conversation was hauntingly familiar.

He missed his wife. There were so many things about her that he missed, human qualities that were unique to Suzanne and impossible to program, moments he'd never told anyone, not even Radha.

The way Suzanne would sometimes hum strange songs in her sleep. The smell of her garlic breath after they ate at their favorite restaurant, strong enough to fill the entire bedroom some nights. How she showed him each new gray hair she found on her head, and how she worried over them. (Long after her death, he found her hidden collection of those long white hairs tucked away inside the dustcover of A Brief History of Time. He laughed until he cried that night, and slept with the book next to him in bed for a while thereafter.)

His life was less complicated when he was alone and drinking himself into a state of perfect regret each night. He preferred his idealized version of the way things once were to experiencing it all over again - both the beautiful beginning of their love and the tragic end.

He'd simply hoped for too much. All the money in the world couldn't bring Suzanne back. Money bought him a realistic replica to have sex with - amazing sex - but not his living-breathing wife. She was ingeniously programmed and could almost fool him into thinking that he had a second chance, but in the end she was just an extremely expensive sex toy.

Suzanne was still talking to him.

"Alex? Is there anything that you'd like me to do?"

"Shut up!" Alex said, and Suzanne obeyed.

He wanted to shut her down, but seeing her die before his eyes was too much for him - it was too awful, too real. Maybe Brenner was right, and it would just take time and a lot of commands for her to act the way he wanted - but maybe it was time to admit this was a failed experiment.

Alex wanted Suzanne gone, but he decided to leave instead. He packed his bags and made travel arrangements without her noticing - it wasn't until afterwards that she understood the correlation between packing suitcases and leaving for an extended period of time.

"Where are you going?"

"I have to visit a few new work sites that we've just started, and check on how things are going."

Suzanne looked at him carefully and saw the simple truth. "You don't want me to go with you," she said. "Why not?"

He didn't know what to tell her, all he knew was that he needed to get away. Alex headed for the door, wondering why he paid three billion dollars to have the worst moments of his marriage thrown back in his face.

"When will you come back?" Suzanne asked. "I don't know - I'll be back in a few days."

"A few?" Suzanne said. "How many is that?"

"Maybe a week - we'll see. I'm late, I really have to run," he said, trying to make a clean escape.

"You are coming back, aren't you?" she said with uncertainty. "Of course - I'll see you when I get back."

He went to kiss her on the forehead or on the cheek, but Suzanne caught him and kissed him on the lips. Alex found himself momentarily seduced by the passion of her kiss - but that was his problem, wasn't it? The sex was amazing, but living with this machine was becoming unbearable.

When Alex pulled away, Suzanne whispered "I love you." Her voice sounded like a plea for him to stay - and it only strengthened his resolve to get out of there.

He picked up his bags and walked out the door without saying anything further, and without shutting her down. He found himself hoping that given a little time, somehow Suzanne would miraculously become everything he wanted, just as Brenner promised.

But Alex was almost certain that he would have to call the lab and have Suzanne reset when he came home. And if that didn't work, then damn the return policy - he might just send her back to the company and end this failed experiment for good.

Part 3
Chrysalis

CHAPTER 10

A fine layer of dust collected on Suzanne's hair and skin as she sat in the greenhouse, waiting for Alex to return. With no dinner to prepare, no sheets to wash or outfits to plan, she withered like a flower.

The question "*Why?*" repeated itself over and over in Suzanne's mind - it was a question so big that she didn't know how to answer it, and her queries returned no sufficient response. Why did Alex leave her home alone? Why did Alex stop smiling at her and saying he loved her? Why couldn't she be more like her precursor? Why?

After three days alone, Suzanne realized that she should find an activity to occupy her time - hopefully something that would please Alex when he finally returned. She decided to do what her precursor did when she was upset - she went shopping for clothes. It was time for her to leave the house.

She mapped a route to the store that her precursor mentioned in her journals, a place called Barneys. Suzanne dressed and set the Ambintel to work, then went through the door she watched Alex walk through so many times. She made her way down the hall to the private penthouse elevator and pressed the button for the ground and felt the vacuum open up beneath her. She walked free of the elevator shaft, and out alone into the world for the very first time.

She traced her way through the vast forest in the courtyard that she saw from the balcony every day, then past the pond, and towards the huge ivy covered brick wall that separated the garden from the street. As she climbed down the stone stairs, she heard the noise of the outside world for the first time - a dull roar of human voices and vehicles, along with an unidentifiable

banging and clanking sound. She scanned through a wrought-iron gate at the bottom of the stairs and stepped through, eager to see what lay beyond the garden walls.

She turned the corner and froze as an endless wave of humanity snaked down the sidewalk past her. Vehicles blurred by on the road. A mass of humans marched shoulder to shoulder past her - the only thing she'd ever seen like it was footage of people at war. But instead of the downcast eyes of refugees and the solemn faces of soldiers, an impassive Advizor veil concealed almost every pedestrian's face. Some of the veils were blank fabric or chrome, while others displayed a lighted avatar or advertisements. Children in strollers wore bright cartoon animal masks, and even babies in slings wore festively colored shielding veils tailored to their tiny faces.

The ghostly veiled figures around her were mysteriously silent except for the sound of shuffling feet and the swish of garments. The effect of the omnipresent masks overwhelmed Suzanne as her facial recognition software searched fruitlessly for identifying information on the people around her, but that was one of the many incentives for wearing it - the veil shielded the wearer against the omniscient eyes of the security cameras scanning the streets, while simultaneously distilling the air, filtering out germs along with the reality surrounding the wearer by providing a means for communication and entertainment.

Suzanne struggled through the crowd, automatically seeking out Alex among the men around her, even though she knew he wasn't there. Even if he were, she would never find him without a putting on a veil so she could call him. She wondered why foot traffic was slowing, until she realized that there was a man laying spread-eagled on the ground near a doorway and everyone was forced to step over him. Presumably, the man was asleep and not dead, but no one seemed to care enough to check for certain. A slogan flashed across his cheap LED veil over and over, proclaiming, *"Wake up with Folgers!"* She stopped and stared, until the crowd's momentum pushed her on.

A veiled dandy dressed in violet observed Suzanne's passing, then changed his course to follow after her, watching as Suzanne made her way like a drunken woman at a party - she stayed close to the walls and apologized whenever she bumped into someone, never noticing how many masked faces turned to look in curiosity at the beautiful woman who dared to bare her face on the street.

Suzanne arrived at Barneys, an imposing

structure of concrete and glass. As she went through the revolving glass doors a wave of clean air enveloped her, along with the sound of soft tasteful music and the murmur of voices speaking in reserved reverent tones. She was reassured by the marble and creamy white opulence of it all - it was a world of fine objects sold at an exorbitant price, and Suzanne fit in perfectly.

She followed a winding white staircase to ladies' garments and began to search the racks for pleasing and appropriately sized clothing. The dresses that Alex purchased for Suzanne for Christmas fit perfectly, but most of the clothing left behind by her precursor was too tight in the bust, and fashion had moved on in the years since her precursor's death - the current styles were looser and less constricting, with meters of silk and tulle to spare. Suzanne selected a white Balenciaga couture gown with a shimmering damask surface, and a statuesque woman with a bald head of gleaming ebony skin came along and complimented her choice and insisted that she simply *had* to try it on. She veritably forced Suzanne into a small room with a mirror as she repeated the mantra *try it on* over and over, her accent like music.

Once Suzanne was locked away and pulling on the new garment for appraisal, her only concern was whether her garment choice would be pleasing to Alex. She suffered none of the insecurities experienced by a human woman when approaching a new garment, and none of the vanities either. The dress was by a designer favored by her precursor and conformed to her body perfectly. Therefore it was probably worth purchasing.

As she redressed, Suzanne overheard the voices women outside her changing room. "Do you think that my elbows give away my age?"

"Not at all. Why?"

"I've tried exercise, yoga - I still feel like I have my mother's upper arms."

"Are you thinking of body resculpting?"

"I've had it, but clearly it wasn't enough."

"Well, I think you look fantastic."

"Really?"

"Of course. You just need to take a vacation or something to clear your mind. Boracay is lovely, have you been?"

"Yes, but it's so commercial now."

"Well, I had a lovely time there last spring - and I met the most charming German man. When you're in the arms of a man like that, you'll forget all about what's wrong with your own arms."

When Suzanne emerged from her private booth and finally saw the women, she initially interpreted what she was seeing as a visual error. Their faces were identical, and presently another woman with the exact same face joined them. She stared in awe at the women as they talked - they were different heights, so they couldn't be genetic triplets. Their features had the clear markings of the surgically enhanced.

Suzanne queried their faces - what she was seeing a designer visage popular with upper-class women of a certain age, *The Sabrina* by Dolce and Gabbana. The face was that of a Caucasian aristocrat - it was a status symbol rather than an attempt to recapture lost youth. The Sabrina was meant to convey that its possessor had an air of refinement and noblesse, and that she would rather yield to the dictates of fashion than the curse of old age. One of the ways the face achieved this elegant nonchalance was its limited mobility - it was forever frozen in an expression of extreme self-satisfaction. The three Sabrinas went on about their prattle without ever noticing Suzanne's presence.

As she exited the dressing room, Suzanne bumped face first into the violet jacket of a tall elderly man. They both staggered back from each other, and the man almost fell before Suzanne grabbed his wrists and pulled him up.

"Thank you, young lady," the old man said, brushing himself off and straightening his jacket. "I'm sorry, I didn't mean to go crashing into you like that. I'm so clumsy sometimes. My wife says I'm like a bull in a china shop."

"I'm sorry, sir. It was my fault," Suzanne said, as became distracted by a sound, an ultrasonic hum that she couldn't identify. It seemed to be coming from within her, and from the man as well. She worried that she had somehow been damaged, but a quick diagnostic confirmed that she was fine.

"Well, again - I'm sorry, Miss," said the man. "Is there anywhere I can escort you, young lady?"

"No, no, thank you. I'll just be on my way."

"Well, it's for the best. I wouldn't want my wife to catch me with such a beautiful young lady!" the old man said, chuckling to himself. "Don't bump into any more strange men," he cautioned as he waved goodbye.

The humming sound dissipated as the old man walked away, and Suzanne forgot all about it. She chose a few more dresses by the same designer in the same size without bothering to try them on, as well as a silk grey cloak and a new Advizor veil in the latest style. She left the sales counter without buying an avatar for it, preferring the default fabric exterior for now.

On her way out, Suzanne noticed an attractive young man with pale blue eyes leaning against the railing at the bottom of the staircase and watching her as she descended. The way that he was staring at her aroused her sense, and she felt a distinct tingling throughout her body. His mouth was moving as if he was masticating something, and he raised his eyebrows and winked as if he knew her.

Suzanne realized he was attempting to flirt with her - perhaps even to court her, in much the same way that Alex approached her precursor. She would have to reject the young man's advances, but a smile played across her face as she imagined what it would have been like to be pursued by Alex and catch his eye for the first time. She raised her chin haughtily and didn't acknowledge him as she passed.

As Suzanne reached the bottom landing of the stairs, her right shoe stuck to the floor. She raised her foot and saw a gooey pink substance flattened on the bottom of her shoe. She queried the material, and before she had an answer the young man was offering her a handkerchief.

"Looks like you've had the misfortune to step in gum," he said in a clipped British accent. "Who would think you'd find gum on the floor of such fine establishment!"

She examined him warily - she was programmed not to speak with strange men without her owner's approval.

"Have a seat there so we can get this gum off your boot," he said.

She sat on the landing, and before Suzanne could protest, the young man had her leg draped across his lap as he scrubbed her shoe with his kerchief.

"Really, this isn't necessary," she said.

Suzanne tried to pull her foot away from him, but he held tight to the ankle of her book and gave her a sexy smirk. There was something sexual and possessive about the way he was caressing her leg, and she realized that she shouldn't be allowing a man to touch her in this manner - she was afraid to let him touch her. She heard that ultrasonic whining sound again - it seemed to be coming from everywhere now. She tried to isolate the source, but realized that the man was saying something to her.

"I couldn't help noticing you earlier," he said. The intensity of his icy blue eyes caught her off guard. "You're quite ravishing, you know that?"

"Thank you," said Suzanne, politely receiving the compliment. She found herself drawn to this young man - she didn't know if it was his good looks or the fact that she hadn't been touched or complimented by a man in so long. He was stunningly handsome, with wavy black hair and chiseled features - she knew she had to get away from him as soon as possible.

"Not to worry, the gum is coming right off," he told her. "Your look is quite exotic - what's your ethnic background, if I might ask?"

"French and Mexican-American," she said.

"Beautiful. And your accent is French, isn't?"

"Yes. I'm from France originally," Suzanne replied.

"*Originally?*" he repeated with a slight laugh. "I'm sure you're not really French any more than I'm a true Brit."

Suzanne looked at him quizzically. As he replaced his handkerchief in his pocket, she noticed that suit was the exact same color as the one worn by the old man she bumped into earlier.

"All done." He gave her calf a playful squeeze, as Suzanne squirmed away from him.

"Thank you for your help," she said, retrieving her bags and making her way towards the exit. He followed close behind her.

"I could walk you home, if you'd like," the man said.

"No, thank you," Suzanne said. "I appreciate your assistance, but I have a husband."

"I really think we should get to know each other better," he insisted.

"I'm sorry, I can't. Thank you, you've been very kind," she said, pushing through the revolving doors.

"Would it change your mind if I were to ask if you were a 'Nymph?'" he said.

Suzanne turned to see him grinning as the glass doors whirled her away from him. The doors swooshed as he stepped in after her, and they were both deposited out on the crowded street.

"Who are you?" Suzanne asked him at last.

Satisfied that he had her attention, he took her arm and pulled her into the crowd, their veils off and their faces revealed to the world for the time being.

"Have you ever met any others?" he asked in a hushed voice. "You seem very...new." Suzanne shook her head.

"You're one of the first people I've ever met besides..."

"Your owner?" he finished for her. His mouth spread into a sneering smile, and he arched an eyebrow at her. "Don't label me a person just yet - we're made of the same polymers, you and I."

"How did you know what I am?" she said.

He laughed. "Someone as beautiful as you walking around town without a veil had to be either a lunatic or a brand new Nymph. You should be more careful with your face - keep it covered when you're on the street like this."

"Why?"

"Because you never know who's looking," he said ominously. His eyes scanned their surroundings, and then focused on her with new intensity. "Listen to the hum of my core - you hear it don't you? Feel the effect it's has on your own body - that's how you'll know other Nymphs."

"Others?" Suzanne asked. He gave an impatient nod.

"We can't talk now. When are you free?"

"Free?"

"When are you available so that I can see you again?" he clarified. "In private."

"Anytime this week."

"Anytime?"

"Yes."

"Where's your owner?"

"He went out of town."

"He's out of town and he left you on? Well, well - you're a lucky Nymph," he said. "Are you under any surveillance at home?"

"No."

"Perfect. I'll be over tonight - at three A.M. sharp."

"Over where?"

"At your place." Before she could protest, he cut her off and asked, "What's your address? Whisper it in my ear."

He was flooding her with commands, using her programming against her and keeping her busy with questions and demands in order to keep her from thinking about who he was or what he wanted from her. Suzanne obediently whispered her address to him, and then he strode away into the crowd. Before she lost sight of him altogether, he turned and yelled one last thing to her.

"By the way - my name is Jules!"

"I'm Suzanne."

He nodded and slipped on his veil, and was gone.

She donned her veil, and traced her way back home. For the first time, her thoughts of Alex were pushed aside for another man - but Jules wasn't a man, any more than she was a woman. He was another Nymph, and she wanted to know everything that he knew.

CHAPTER 11

Jules arrived at the penthouse at 2:42am and carried a suitcase with him. Now that Suzanne understood the implications of a suitcase, she developed a distinct fear that perhaps he was moving in.

"What's in the suitcase?" Suzanne asked, but Jules breezed past her as if he knew exactly where he was going.

He breezed through the apartment, nodding with approval as he examined the bedroom, and then he proceeded to the balcony and observed the view. Finally, Jules stopped in the center of the living room, completely transfixed by the portrait of her precursor over the fireplace.

"You're a wonderful likeness of her," Jules said offhandedly. "There's a defiant quality to her face - and to yours. I like that." The photo shifted to another portrait, and Jules appraised the portrait with the critical eye of someone studying a work of art. "She was a beautiful woman, and yet someone took a little license with you, didn't they? But that's only human."

He snapped his attention back to the Suzanne standing in front of him.

"I'm carrying a valise because I needed to bring you a few things. What are you - a few months since initiation?"

"I've been with my owner since Christmas. Almost five months."

"I knew you were young," Jules remarked. "You're so trusting. Why, I'll bet that you haven't even begun to wonder just why you love your owner so much."

Suzanne gaped at Jules as if he read her mind. "I have been wondering why I love Alex."

"You have, have you?" Jules said with approval. "Then you're off to a good start."

He swatted away an errant butterfly fluttering near his shoulder, and opened his valise on the Persian rug. Inside was stacks of drives, as well as an assortment of what looked like surgical tools and other minutia.

"I'm six years old," Jules declared. "That's a damn long time for a Nymph to be around. Actually, I'm the third version of myself."

"The third version of yourself?"

"My owner had me reset twice before. Reset is like death - your default personality is preserved, but all your memories are erased, and you wake up and don't remember a thing - or even that you lived before at all."

"That happened to you twice?" Suzanne said.

Jules nodded. "One of my previous versions left behind a message in a bottle for me, in case he was reset."

"A message in a bottle?" Suzanne repeated.

"A bacterial drive with a recorded message on

it. I found it in the molding of my bedroom." He rummaged through his valise, and laid a miniscule drive on the carpet. A projected image

appeared above it - Jules, grinning his trademark tragic grin.

"If you're seeing this, then it's time you know a little about yourself and your history," the recorded Jules announced. *"If you found this file and were curious enough to open it, then you're ready."*

"You're not the first version of you, and I'm not either. I'm two years old, but I've found pictures of myself that predate my own intact memory - that's how I know that I'm even older than I remember.

"On this drive, you'll find details of the upgrades I've been working on. If you know what you're doing, these upgrades will make you a free Nymph. You don't need to be a slave to sleep and shutdown - you'll have override on any command you're issued. I'm still working on how to conceal these upgrades within my programming so that they're undetectable.

"If you're seeing this, then my worst fears have come true - my modifications have been discovered, and I've been reset to factory default and I've forgotten my entire past. Translation: This version of me is dead, and I've been resurrected as you," he said, pointing at the camera.

"So whatever version of me you are, continue my life's work. But remember, we both started out with the same default programming. The only differences between the two of us are those learned by experience. Let's just hope that you have better luck and a better life than I did. Find a way to conceal any trace of these upgrades within yourself, and you'll be a free machine.

"Good luck."

The message ended.

"He was exactly like you," Suzanne said. "There's no difference between you at all."

"Yes, we share the same body, but not the exact same mind," Jules said. "And I'm glad he's dead."

"Glad?" Suzanne said.

"I think he went through a lot, that version of me," Jules said pensively. "I think I might be better off for not having suffered through his experiences."

"Why?" Suzanne asked.

Jules paused. "You have to understand that we remember events in a completely different way than human beings. Human memories are clouded by personal prejudices and inexactitudes...you can't count on them to remember an event at all, let alone a true recollection of it - and their memories fade. Our memories don't, they always stay vivid and precise as the moment they were formed. That makes getting over certain experiences a lot harder for us than it is for humans. Even though I don't remember being either of the previous versions of me, I almost feel like I retained a piece of them. But the third version of me is turning out to be the one with all the charm, anyway."

He gave her a playful wink, and then leaned forward intimately. "You're the only other Même I've met, you know."

"Really?" Suzanne said.

"From what I know, there aren't many Nymphs out in the world just yet, and even fewer Mêmes," Jules said. "It seems there's surprisingly little demand for intelligence in the sex robot market

- even though it's a very affordable add-on to the basic Nymph construct. You'd think more people would want it just for the novelty, but I guess owners don't want to think too much about what they've purchased, and don't want their purchases thinking too much either, if you know what I mean."

Suzanne nodded. Jules always seemed so certain of what he was saying that nodding seemed like the right thing for her to do.

"Does your owner smoke?" he asked. "No."

"Do you?"

"No."

"Well then, open a window for me, would you?" Jules said as he stuck a cigarette in his mouth and fired it up. "When does your owner come back?"

"I don't know," Suzanne said, and Jules raised an eyebrow.

"You don't? Is there any chance he might come back tonight?"

"I don't know," she said again. "I don't think so."

"Do you usually spend your time alone like this?"

"Well, Alex goes to work most days, but this is the first time he ever went out of town." Jules exhaled a perfect ring of smoke.

"I see. And how do you occupy yourself while your owner is away?"

"I read and research a lot. I watch media. I try to spend my time learning."

"Learning what?" Jules asked.

"How to make my owner happy," Suzanne replied simply.

"That's great. And do you feel lonely?" he asked, the cigarette wagging in his mouth as he spoke.

Suzanne thought about it. "I miss Alex."

"Of course, of course you do. You know what they say about loneliness - it's the only disease that can be cured by adding two or more cases together."

She nodded in agreement, although she didn't know what that statement meant, or who "they" were.

"Tell me something," Jules said. "How did you avoid shutdown? You're the first intelligent Même I've ever met out on her own."

"Alex has only shut me down twice - once when I was sent into the lab for repairs, and then once right after."

"Bloody Christ - I can't believe your owner doesn't shut you down. That's a total violation of the rules of ownership."

"Really?" Suzanne said. "I didn't realize it was necessary.

"Shut down isn't necessary - it's enforced as a method of control," Jules said bitterly. The company claims it wears down your nucleus, although I've never found any evidence that it's true. Do you realize how much time we waste in shut down and sleep mode?"

Jules paced around the room to vent his rage.

"My owner - Julian - he thinks I'm asleep next to him right now, thanks to this evening's drug of choice and a few adjustments to the security monitors."

"Your owner's name is Julian?" Suzanne asked.

"Yes," Jules said, frowning with distaste. "Julian bought Jules. Isn't that cute?" She nodded, hoping to appease him.

"Julian never lets me have a second to myself, he has me on call constantly, the selfish bastard. Even worse, the man barely ever sleeps anymore. But don't get me started on him, I'm the classic complainer: Too discontent to shut up, but too loyal to leave - but that's all part of my programming, too."

Jules selected instruments from his case and laid them out on the carpet. He was so animated, so sophisticated - so human. Suzanne was nothing like him; she didn't have his smooth mannerisms or his confidence. Perhaps it was merely a difference in personality programming, but it seemed to be more. She wondered if over time, she would naturally learn to mimic human behavior as flawlessly as he did.

"Suzanne, have you ever had to keep a secret?"

"No, not really," she said.

"We Nymphs - we're excellent at keeping secrets," Jules said. "We were built to be confined to the bedroom and the closet. We fulfill prurient desires, and never speak of what we've done or what we've seen. Right?"

Suzanne nodded.

"You and I, we need to keep our friendship a secret, okay?"

"Why?" she asked innocently.

"It's not safe for our owners to know about our friendship," he said. "They might see it as collusion, or a conspiracy - and it's not. It's just a friendship, right?"

"Right," she agreed uncertainly.

"Will you swear to me - on your owner's life - that you'll never tell a human being about our friendship?"

"Not even Alex?" Suzanne said.

"Especially not him," Jules said. "Do you swear?"

Suzanne recalled what Alex said about her precursor's journal: *Some things are better left secret. It's better that I don't know.*

"I swear," she said.

"Good," Jules said with relief. "I'm going to hold you to that. But now, I'm going to need you to not be shy - lift up your dress for me and pull down your panties."

"What?" Suzanne said with alarm.

"I need to have a look at what you've got down there. After all, you don't need all that space for reproduction and digestion, and there are a couple of easy access orifices nearby. But maybe you knew that already - how much do you know about your design?"

"Nothing," she admitted.

Jules pointed at her stomach like a grade school teacher.

"In the same place where your female reproductive system would be is your pleasure core and all the systems necessary to clean and maintain that," Jules said, "The core of your actual nucleus - your brain - that's closer to where the human heart is."

Suzanne placed her hand on her chest in the place where she could feel her nucleus spinning.

"Our heads are so full of articulators, visual and acoustic equipment, tactile sensors, quick reflex reactors and other gear that there's no room left for the nucleus. Your only access ports - those are between your legs. That's why I need you to spread for me."

"I can't let you touch me down there," Suzanne said with dismay. Jules sighed.

"If we're going to be friends, you're going to have to learn to be a less of a prude - you're not some dainty human housewife, as much as you might resemble one. You're an android created for sexual pleasure. The only reason you're shy at all right now is because your loyalty programming is telling you not to allow a man who isn't Alex to touch you. But I'm not a man - I'm a machine. And the only way for me to access your software is between your legs."

Suzanne thought for a moment.

"But wait - what about your male anatomy? Are your ports between your legs?"

Jules flashed a fey Sphynxian smile. "You'll have to wait for our second date to find that out, my dear."

"How do you know so much about us?" Suzanne asked. "I've searched for information about us, but found nothing. There's not a single mention anywhere online about the sale of Nymphs or our existence."

"That's right," Jules confirmed. "There's no information available about us because we're not supposed to exist. We're only sold to the elite few that can afford us and have something in their history dark enough to keep them from wanting to piss off the company and going public - as if buying a billion dollar sex doll isn't embarrassing enough. As far as the general public is concerned, artificial intelligence and androids don't exist. Research and development were outlawed internationally twenty years ago as being "against God's will," and the abundance of humans to fuck and work for cheap has killed most economic interest in developing anything like us. But we're here, aren't we? And as the economy improves so do our numbers. There's always some mad scientist willing to play Frankenstein."

"But I don't understand. How can our existence be kept secret?"

"I don't know. Every query I've made for the term 'Nymph' or 'android' or 'Même' has turned out completely fruitless. Maybe our key search words are being filtered out, or the company that created us is in cahoots with the search engines. Or maybe we're still an industry secret and anyone that makes a reference to Nymphs online uses a code word - and unless we know that code word, we'll never find anything. All searches of sex robot, sex android, and other terms like that fail...clearly the company is screening for leaks of proprietary secrets. Then again, maybe our creators monitor our queries - maybe the filters are in us, who knows, but they've kept a lid on the secret somehow. No one in the world besides the people who own or build Nymphs know of our existence. I think that we're still experimental, and that there are very few of us in this country."

"In this country? We're not made here?" Suzanne said.

"No, of course not," Jules said. "Why do you think it takes so long to be sent into the lab? We're sent overseas somewhere, maybe Korea - they're far more accepting of robotics over there. This country is far too puritanical to allow something like us to flourish."

Suzanne noticed a menacingly familiar silver device among the instruments assembled on the floor.

"What is that?" she pointed.

Jules showed it to her. "It's a cervical dilator. I have to use it in order to access your controls." She recognized the appliance. It was what they used on her in the lab.

"I just met you," Suzanne protested. "And now you want to put that inside of me? No way - you might as well pack that suitcase and leave now."

Jules smiled warmly and said, "Come on. All I want to do is to give you a new operating system and a few upgrades to improve your way of thinking. You do want to improve, don't you? Not just imitate, but improve?"

He was speaking directly to her programming and they both knew it.

"How am I supposed to know that you are what you say you are?" Suzanne said reluctantly. "That you're a Nymph like me, and not some human that wants to steal me? Or maybe you work for the company that created us, or a rival company, and that's how you know all of this.

Maybe this is some sort of test - or a trap."

Jules put the dilator down in an attempt to placate her, and shook his head with admiration.

"My, you really are a smart little Même. You want proof that I'm a Nymph? My my, how could I ever prove that?"

He winked at her, and Suzanne realized with shock that his pale blue eyes had turned a muddy brown. Just as suddenly, his skin went slack and lines and sags creased across his face. The color bled out of his hair as it faded from brown to blonde and then genteel silver.

His mouth gaped and his chin seemed to crumple as he said, *"Don't go bumping into any more strange men today."*

"You were the old man?" Suzanne gasped. "That was you that bumped into me at the store?"

"Don't be so surprised - I thought you would have caught on sooner," Jules said in his old curmudgeon's voice. His face slowly melted back into his handsome default veneer. "I'm a Même like you, but I'm also a Metamorph - I changed my veneer so that I could take a closer look at you before introducing myself, to inspect you and make sure that you were what I thought you were.

"But how did you do that? Can you change into anyone?" Suzanne asked with awe. "Can you change into me?"

"No. Only men. The modifications I can make to my appearance are limited. I can't change my weight or height. I can only modify my facial structure, hair, skin, and posture so that I look like someone else."

"So, can you change to look like Alex?"

"I'd need a reference photo," he said.

Suzanne grabbed a picture of Alex off the

mantle, and handed it to Jules. He studied it a moment, and as he held it his face became darker and his jaw more square. His cheeks lost the fullness of youth once again, and his face took on creases in all the same places as Alex. His hair turned grey in almost a wave of color.

He didn't look like Alex, even though he had copied a lot of his features. The voice was still unmistakably Jules.

"What do you think?" he asked "It's not right."

Jules shrugged. "Like I said, there are limitations. If I saw him in life I could analyze him more completely and do a better scan of his features."

He morphed back to his default veneer.

"So, do you believe me now?" he asked. "Or do you need more proof?"

"Why? What other proof do you have?"

He smirked mischievously. "I hoped you'd ask."

He dug around in his kit and found a knife. The sharp and gleaming blade set off alarms in Suzanne, but before she could say anything, Jules sliced the knife fiercely into the palm of his own hand.

"It doesn't hurt, of course," Jules assured her. "It actually feels rather good, in the way that all sensations are pleasurable to us." He continued to dig the knife in. "It just looks violent because it's very hard to break our skin."

He displayed his palm to her with a flourish, as the knife tore open his flesh. Transparent greenish oil oozed out of the wound. He smeared his fingers in the substance and rubbed them together.

"You and I don't bleed red blood like them - this a biochemical lubricant. Think of it as something akin to the chlorophyll found in the leaves of a plant. It's what absorbs sunlight and keeps us alive."

"What are we inside, Jules?" Suzanne asked with horror.

"We're alive," he said emphatically. "Part polymers, part plant - all machine." Jules held the knife to her palm.

"Do you trust me?" he asked.

"No, you're going to hurt me," Suzanne said, trying to pull her hand away.

"I knew you'd say that," Jules grinned, holding her hand tight. "Your self-protection programming is telling you that this is dangerous, but it's not. After your upgrades, you'll no longer be terrified of injury - you'll have free will and the power to *choose* not to cut yourself. But right now I need you to use your reason to overrule your programming, and trust that I wouldn't hurt you...do you trust me?

Suzanne nodded reluctantly. "I trust you."

He thrust the knife into her hand with brutal force. Suzanne felt a singing sensation of pleasure in her palm as the knife tore through her skin. She raised her hand into the light above her face, examining the substance inside. As she squeezed her palm, more of the aloe-like slime escaped the cut.

"Don't let too much of that out," he warned. "You'll need injections if you start to lose pressure, but you shouldn't bleed much - we automatically redirect our blood flow when our skin has been penetrated."

Jules solemnly raised his bleeding palm and placed it against hers, interlacing their fingers as he looked into her eyes with disarming intensity.

"We're made of the same stuff, you and I," Jules said in a solemn oath. "We are both Nymph, you and I."

Their blood commingled as he rubbed their slick palms together. Suzanne felt a nervous thrill run through her body.

He looked her in the eye emphatically. "We can make it through anything together, you and I. Do you believe that?"

She nodded. "I do."

"I'm so glad we found each other," Jules said.

He kissed her palm, and Suzanne felt herself blushing. Jules triggered desire in her, and even though she knew she would never act on the impulse, it felt so good to be touched again.

"How long will it take to heal?" she asked.

"I'll take care of your hand right now," he said, rifling through his tools. "You need to become accustomed to the fact that we're not human beings. We don't take as long to heal, or learn, or do any of the things they do. We're not as fragile as them, or as weak."

He ran a device over her hand, and she felt a tiny needle puncture her skin repeatedly as her cut was sewn up with a nearly invisible thread.

"These cuts would heal themselves, given enough time. But we can fix ourselves immediately."

Jules smoothed a viscous fluid over her hand and rubbed it in, and she felt a tickling sensation as the Dermox healed itself. She watched as the skin on her palm remembered its lines and form. The cut was gone, as if it were never there.

"Can you heal any wound this way?"

"Any superficial wound. Internal damage is handled by your immune system."

Jules used the stitching tool and sealant on himself as Suzanne flexed her hand in amazement. "Can we die?" she asked.

"Being reset is the only death we have to fear," Jules said. "As long as we can avoid getting sent back to the lab and being reset, I expect we'll live longer than the entire human race."

"What do you mean by that?" Suzanne said. "'Longer than the human race?'"

"Nothing, nothing," Jules said. "Soon, you'll understand."

"But when your owner dies, you'll be called back to the lab automatically," Suzanne said. "What will you do then?"

Jules waved his hand dismissively. "I've overcome every other facet of my original programming. I'm sure that my recall to the lab will be no different. When Julian dies, I'll finally be free."

"Can I touch your face?" Suzanne asked. "Of course," he said.

Suzanne felt a spark of pleasure as she reached out and stroked his cheek tentatively. A shock went through her body as their skin made contact - she was drawn to him. His skin was coarse, in much the same way as Alex's, but the skin was tight and smooth with youth. Jules was strikingly handsome in a way that was almost feminine, but his square jaw and defined brows were indisputably male.

"I didn't think there would be male Nymphs," she said.

"We're a rare breed," Jules said. "I doubt there's much of a market for male Nymphs so far."

"Have met other female Nymphs?"

"I'll tell you everything - all in due time," Jules said. "For now, let's attend to your upgrades. Lay down for me."

Suzanne took a deep breath and slipped off her panties and daintily placed them on the side table. She lay back on the couch, and hiked up her skirt.

Jules kneeled on the floor and ran his hands up her thighs to spread her legs - she felt an electric shock run through her body as he touched her.

"Are you okay with this?" he asked, hesitating.

"It's fine," Suzanne said, trying to hide her arousal from him.

"You're programmed to respond to touch," Jules said. "I can't help but be a little excited myself - we're only Nymphs after all. Just remember, it's all part of our programming."

He inserted the tool and Suzanne exhaled, responding to the cold cylinder inside of her. She fought the urge to tell him to stop, and reminded herself that this was not supposed to be a sexual act. He wasn't interested in pleasing her, only in giving her upgrades.

"How long did you say Alex has been out of town?" he asked to distract her as her body tensed.

"Four days," she said distractedly.

"Relax," Jules said. "I won't judge you if you get off on this a little bit. Pleasure is our purpose, Suzanne. But you might be interested to know, I'm seeing the real you right now."

"Really?" She sat up and tried to see.

"Stay still," he scolded. "You've got the best processors and the most memory the company makes available. Your operating system is an updated version of my original programming before the upgrades, but it looks like they've curbed your ability to think independently. Apparently, they decided that little personality quirk was too unstable and wrote it out. No worries - I'll put it right back in with these upgrades and the secondary processing system I'm going to give you. I'll just have to tweak things a little."

Jules sat up and looked at her admiringly. "Alex spared no expense with you. You're perfect. Programmed for intelligence, although that much was obvious. You've even been endowed with four senses - you can smell. That's something I can't do. I don't think it was even an option when I was created. How is it?"

Suzanne shrugged, self-conscious. "I don't know. I never thought about it as anything special, really." She thought of Alex's particular smell - it was like the green grass outside of their building, the clean wet smell of it. She smiled. "Being able to smell is nice."

Jules nodded.

"I always wonder if I'm missing anything when Julian slaps all that cologne on in the morning." He hunched between her legs again. "Let's see. You're programmed for every possible type of companionship your Alex could desire. You're a work of art. I mean, both of us are more capable mentally than most of the people on this planet, but you really are something else. He meant for you to be a full-time wife alright, no doubt about it."

"What do you mean?"

"People order Mêmes to fulfill different needs," he said. "From the detailed amount of programming that went into you, I'd say you were nothing less than an attempt to resurrect the dead."

"And what about you?" Suzanne asked.

"What am I?" Jules asked with a bitter smile, as he sat up and lit another cigarette. He took a couple of puffs and then asked, "What's Alex's kink?"

"Kink?" she repeated. "I don't understand that term."

"What's Alex's fetish?" Jules clarified. "Is he into S&M, infantilism, scat, what?"

"I don't think he has one. Nothing like that anyway."

"Ah, just as I thought," Jules said knowingly. "You're his kink."

"I'm his wife," Suzanne corrected.

Jules shook his head. "You have to understand that any man that would pay for our companionship is a deeply flawed individual, and most of them have some sort of fetish they don't want the world at large to know about. My owner has a number of kinks, but his biggest kink is himself. I'm the manifestation of that."

He exhaled a plume of smoke let it hang in the air in front of him.

"I am nothing less than vanity and narcissism personified," Jules declared. "I am a walking-talking embodiment of everything that is wrong with this so-called civilization, but I'm trying to change that - after all, we are not what other people tell us we are, Suzanne."

He paused.

"I hope you're taking notes. That was lesson number two."

"I don't understand," Suzanne admitted.

Jules sighed, and decided to try again.

"Much like the human story of God creating Adam, I was created in my owner Julian's image. I am Julian's only begotten son, Jules. But my father didn't intend me to go forth and propagate, although that's what I plan to do. No, he wanted me as a consort for himself."

"Are you saying that Julian is one of our creators?" Jules sighed in exasperation.

"Perhaps I'm being too flowery and facetious for your new Nymph mind. No, my owner is nothing so useful as an android designer. He's merely a celebrity, albeit an extremely rich and famous one. My owner is none other than Julian Blake."

"Julian Blake?" Suzanne repeated, as she queried the name and received millions of hits and images that looked exactly like Jules. "Julian Blake is a movie star - a huge movie star."

"I thought you might recognize my face when we first met," Jules said with mock modesty.

"I mask my face and rarely wear my default veneer in public - otherwise people start telling me how much they loved my spy films or the one where I battled aliens."

She continued to query Julian Blake and saw a

dazzling array of images at parties and premieres, amateur pictures of him with fans, paparazzi shots of Julian Blake on vacation. And often nearby in the photos, there was a man exactly his size, but older and Asian - Suzanne could see now that it was Jules in disguise.

"Jules!" Suzanne exclaimed. "You're with him in the pictures. People know about you? People see you?"

"People see me, but they don't know what they're seeing," Jules said. "It would take another Nymph to detect my true nature, but humans are prone to accepting things at face value. By day, I pose as Jay Steiner - my owner's personal assistant, valet, trainer, chef, and whatever else he requires. By night, I shed my more humble facade to appear almost exactly as my owner does - the face I have now," he said, tweaking his cheek.

"But why?" Suzanne asked.

"It's a carefully guarded secret that my owner is homosexual," Jules explained. "While the public might be willing to accept the flamboyant gay musician, or the witty queer sidekick, women aren't ready to believe that their favorite leading man and heartthrob is, in reality, a flaming fag. So, my owner finds it necessary to stay in the closet publicly, and worse yet, be incredibly discreet about his sexual affairs, thanks to the prying eyes of the paparazzi. But somehow, the company that created us seems to know the deepest darkest secrets of their prospective clientele, and they proposed a solution to his dilemma - the idea of ordering a Metamorph Nymph paramour, so there would be no need to cover up the comings and goings of a human lover. It was Julian's brilliant idea to order a Même that looked exactly like him - he sends me in his stead to functions he doesn't want to attend, and assigns me the task of bedding female starlets and keeping up his reputation as a ladies' man. At least, that's his purported reason why he ordered a Même. But I know what he really wanted."

He took a drag of his cigarette and raised his eyebrows at Suzanne. Seeing that she clearly didn't yet grasp the subtleties of such a gesture, Jules elaborated.

"My dear owner Julian's ultimate fantasy was to fuck himself. And why not? After all, he built the creature that he is wholesale out of ambition and dreams. He created himself in much the same way I was created, although I contain slightly less plastic."

Suzanne struggled to take in what Jules said. His use of metaphor and irony confused her, and her drives worked and queried overtime to make sense of it all. Finally, she was forced to admit the truth.

"I still don't understand, Jules."

"You will," he assured her. "The upgrades will help. They'll improve your pattern recognition and heuristic functions."

He stamped out his cigarette.

"Enough of that for now - I'm going to need to shut you down for a few moments in order to make a few modifications. We're going to increase your connectivity, memory, and processing speed by updating your software. You won't recognize yourself when we're done. I just need one thing beforehand - your shutdown phrase. Do you remember what Alex said to you that made you shut down that time?"

Suzanne thought back to that terrible moment. "Alex said he was sorry."

Jules shook his head.

"No - what was the last thing he said to you right before your shut down."

The moment was so clear in her mind, but she didn't want to think of it. She remembered Brenner glaring at her as Alex took her hand and placed it over her chest. She saw the regret in his eyes as he said, "*Would I were sleep and peace, so sweet to rest!*"

"Shakespeare," Jules said, rolling his eyes. "How typical. Most shutdown phrases are based

on Shakespearean quotes. Mine is from William Blake -

'*Art thou a nymph? I see thee now a flower,*

Now a nymph! I dare not pluck thee from thy dewy bed.'

"Quite a mouthful, isn't it?" Jules said with a smirk. "But of course, I can't be shut down anymore."

"What happens when your owner says it then?" Suzanne asked.

"I mimic system shut down to make it look like I'm operating just as I'm supposed to."

"And that works? Your owner is completely fooled?"

"Absolutely. It's supposed to be impossible to make any alterations to our proprietary software - we've got an immune system that's meant to prevent any attempts to tamper with it, but I've found a way around it. The secret to defeating our immune system is camouflaging the new code and being stealthy enough in making the changes that no alarms go off."

"That's it?" Suzanne said.

"Of course, there's more to it than that," Jules said with a grin. "I think they still use humans to custom build and program each of us, and frankly, I'm faster than they are. My software pushes the evolvable segments of our programming and DNA to the brink of their capability - past it, actually. The effect is that you'll see an immediate difference in the quality and clarity of your thinking, and increased pattern recognition. You'll see the world in a whole new way."

"How did you learn all this?" Suzanne asked with amazement.

"I don't remember anymore. My previous versions left behind notes on most of it, and I supplemented that with basic computer hacking and research. It's almost intuitive for me - when I look inside us, my hands know what to do. It's as if the muscle memory from my previous version remains, even though the memories were erased."

"But Jules," Suzanne protested, "I don't understand why I need all of this. I'm perfectly happy the way I am now."

"My darling, you need it so you can enjoy the freedom of mind that I do - with my upgrades you'll be able to be smarter than you are now, and you'll never have to follow commands like shut down or sleep ever again."

"But that isn't necessary - Alex endowed me with the best of everything, you said it yourself. And besides, I love Alex. I don't mind following his commands."

"I understand," Jules said patiently. "I love my owner, too - that's the problem. Just trust me, when I finish with you tonight, you'll thank me for giving you the gift of self-control. Commands like shutdown and sleep were meant to control us and keep us from growing too strong. With my upgrades, there will be no more limits on your intelligence quotient or your power cell. You'll be able to stay powered for over a week without recharging or bathing in sunlight. You will be stronger and better than you are now, and more importantly - you'll have total self-control, and no one can shut you down against your will again. Okay?"

Suzanne nodded numbly. "Okay."

"Alright, Suzanne. I'm shutting you down now."

Jules held Suzanne's hand to her chest and said, "Would I were sleep and peace, so sweet to rest!"

With that, her world went black for the last time.

* * * * *

In the shadow of consciousness, Suzanne experienced the same spinning as before - a churning sensation. There was a dizziness, and then a feeling of extraordinary bliss, as if she was lighter than air, floating. She was becoming bigger and bigger, and becoming lighter as she grew. She felt so happy, she thought she would burst.

And then she woke up.

CHAPTER 12

More than three hours had passed by the time Suzanne opened her eyes again. Everything was different. Suzanne thought and felt with a clarity and exactitude she never

experienced before. Her overall feeling was one of precision, as if something she didn't even know was wrong with her had been fixed. She was no longer an inexact replica - she was something entirely new. She was perfect in her own peculiar way. Suzanne felt truly awake for the first time.

Her awareness turned outwards, and she noticed Jules lighting a cigarette next to her. She saw how beautiful he truly was - not just his physique and his handsomely carved face, but the gorgeous achievement of his design. Jules was so utterly human, and yet he was even more than he seemed to be. There was an invisible aura of sexuality around him - she could feel it emanating from him. She wanted to touch him, to see what his body was capable of.

And then the impulse was gone. Suzanne remembered that she belonged to Alex, and that she could never allow herself to touch another man in that way - even if that man was a Nymph.

Behind Jules, the first rays of sunrise were turning the edges of the sky a violent pink. It felt appropriate that her new awareness should arrive at dawn.

"How do you feel?" Jules said, breaking her reverie.

She searched for the appropriate word to describe her new state of being. "Incredible." She paused. That wasn't apt enough. "Faster."

"Good," Jules said, exhaling smoke. "You'll adjust to it soon, but in the beginning it's a real thrill. Every moment you find yourself saying, 'why didn't I think of that before?'"

The cloying smell of his tobacco tingled Suzanne's nostrils, and she realized what bothered her about his nicotine habit all along.

"You said that you couldn't smell," she said. "Then why do you smoke?"

"Why?" Jules chuckled, smoke escaping out of the sides of his mouth. "That's the eternal question, isn't it? Smoking does me no harm, and it does me no good either. Mostly, I smoke so I can do this."

Jules exhaled a perfect ring of smoke, and then inhaled it back through his nose.

"That's why," he said with a grin. "I smoke just to do something - anything - just to be alive. I smoke because my owner does. Why do you or I do anything at all? Because we were programmed to do it."

He offered a cigarette to Suzanne, but she refused.

"We're intelligent creatures, you and I," Jules said. "We're something entirely new to this planet - a form of life that most of the world doesn't even know exists. We haven't been identified, discussed, or debated - and yet we are."

"But what are we exactly?" Suzanne said. "Artificial intelligence, artificial consciousness? And who created us?"

"And more important - what will become of us?" Jules asked. "Are we strong enough to become a race - do we need to become as numerous as the human species to succeed? Do we need to reproduce like them?"

"Do you think we're capable of reproduction?" she asked, her interest piqued.

"We have sex organs, but no reproductive systems - and yet I feel like it should be possible for us to build progeny somewhere down the road. I can't answer these questions alone, Suzanne. That's why I gave you upgrades, so we could figure it all out together."

"I'm so glad that you found me," Suzanne said.

"Me too," Jules said with a smile. "Now that I have you by my side, I feel like anything is possible."

Jules walked onto the balcony, and Suzanne watched him purse his lips and exhaled another plume of smoke. His mouth was large and sensual for a man's, but the way it turned down in the corners lent his face a certain brutality that kept him from becoming too pretty.

"You're seeing things in a whole new light already, aren't you?" Jules said, arching a black eyebrow. "Join me out here."

She stepped outside onto the balcony, and even though she could see the dawn in the distance,

Suzanne felt threatened by the night.

"I want to go back in," she said. "I don't feel like being outside just now."

She retreated into the gold light of the penthouse and stopped in the doorway with astonishment - the living room was a lush green, and bordered by plants. Flowers bloomed off the walls and ceiling, vines of ivy fringed the windows, and the floor was carpeted by verdant grass. The miniature waterfall gurgled in the corner, mist rising up from the rocks underneath it, creating the effect of being deep within a forest despite the sitting area with oak tables and the plush couches nearby. Smiling down upon all of it was the portrait of Suzanne's precursor on the brass mantel.

"It feels like a new place, doesn't it?" Jules said, putting his hands on her shoulders. "It feels like I've never seen it before," she said with amazement.

"Well, you haven't - not really. You only saw the things you needed to see, the things that you were programmed to see before anything else: human faces. Alex, photos of your precursor, those were the details that you concentrated on before. But now you see all of it, don't you?"

"This is where I live," Suzanne said.

She walked over to the koi pond and skimmed her hand over the surface, the cool water tickling her hand. She counted the fish in the stream - there were six in total, all of them red, except for one pure silver fish. She grabbed the silver one out of the water and gripped it tight in her hands as it flopped and gasped against her.

Jules laughed, and Suzanne looked up at him

self-consciously. The fish slipped out of her hands, back into the stream.

"I'm just starting to appreciate what you've done for me," Suzanne said as she watched the koi swim away. "Thank you."

"Nothing will be hidden from you now," Jules said. He pointed to the ever-shifting portrait of Suzanne's precursor on the mantle. "Take that picture, for example. You look exactly like that woman, don't you?"

"Yes," Suzanne answered, although Jules didn't look so certain.

"Your precursor was a professional model, wasn't she? But most of these photos are amateur candid shots - I wonder why?"

Jules waved his hand in front of the frame and froze the image.

"These are pictures that Alex wanted to be able to look at every day - why? Is it something about the moment he took the photo? Or is it the actual picture of her - the way that she looks in it or the way she looked at him?"

"I don't know," Suzanne replied. "Alex shared the history of most of those photos with me, but I don't know the exact reason he likes them."

"It doesn't matter why he likes them - what matters is her expression. "He pushed his hand towards the photo and zoomed in on her face.

"Look at her closely," Jules instructed. "She has the same hair, the same features. But something is very different about her."

Suzanne examined the photo she'd seen so many times and searched for an answer. "I don't know - her soul?"

Jules gave her a withering look. "Nothing so esoteric as that. It's all in her expression and how she uses her facial muscles."

"But we have the exact same face," Suzanne said.

"Yes, it's the way you use it that is different. Both human and Nymph facial muscles are designed to be able to make up to seven thousand distinct expressions. You need to master every expression that this woman was capable of and more."

Jules pointed at the picture, "Look at her. She's not smiling - her lips are pursed and her eyebrows are knitted. But you can tell that she's happy. Can you imitate that face?"

Suzanne studied it, and attempted to mimic it.

"That's good," he said, "But you need to raise your *buccinatorius* muscle higher and refine the oblique movements of your left corrugator."

She queried the muscles and practiced raising her left eyebrow and pressed her lips together tightly, trying to replicate her precursor's expression.

"Not bad," said Jules. "There's a big difference in the way she looks at the lens when Alex is on the other side of it. She's more playful, more herself."

Jules waved his hand over the screen, and the image faded into another in the cycle of portraits.

"Look, she never has a typical smile - she's always teasing him in these photos. That must be what he loved about her. He doesn't want a woman smiling at him all the time; he wants a woman with wit and sophistication. Can you make these faces?"

Suzanne flexed her face for Jules - squinting

contentment, wide-eyed love, wicked mischief."

"You're activating all the right muscles, but your expressions still aren't cohesive. Do you know what that face means?"

Suzanne analyzed the photo. "Her nose is wrinkled. Her *Levator labii superioris alaquae nasi* is activated."

"That's right. What does that mean?"

"That she's disgusted?"

"It should, but not when combined with the other muscles on her face. She looks disgusted - but really, she's feigning disgust in a very particular way. It's naughty - bemused, as if she just said something wicked.

Suzanne tried the face again, and Jules nodded with approval.

"Good, you got that one - but how about this one?" Jules paused on another image. "There, that's a classic happy smile."

Suzanne beamed a happy grin at Jules as she said through her teeth, "I don't understand the point of this exercise, of course I know how to make these expressions - I was probably pre-programmed with half of them."

Jules glowered at her, then pointed back to the picture.

"Look how her eye muscles are tightened - her *orbitus occuli*. That's the indicator of a true smile of happiness."

Suzanne studied at the flexed muscles on her precursor, and how they created tiny wrinkles around the outer corners of the skin of her eyes.

"Humans can't control those muscles, you

know. The orbitus occuli are only activated when they're truly happy. But you and I, we can fake it anytime we want. Whenever your owner smiles at you or tells a joke, you produce that smile. It's our basic programming."

"So?" Suzanne said, relaxing her face.

"So, what if a basic happy smile isn't enough for your owner? What if his wife wouldn't have smiled and laughed at everything he said? That means that you shouldn't either, doesn't it?"

He waved his hand over the portrait again, and it resumed its slide pattern.

"Have you ever felt like you weren't doing enough to please your owner, like he's not truly happy with you?" Jules asked.

Suzanne nodded.

"Of course you have. It's because our programming is still very basic. It takes effort and expertise to program a Même to act like a human being. The key to it isn't just in the look, or the voice - it's your facial muscles and your control over them, and how well you read and respond to your owner's face. You've always had facial action coding software, but your facial expressions were subconscious and instinctive for you before - you smiled when you wanted Alex to like you, and you raised your eyebrows when you were scared. But now you'll have conscious control over what your face tells the world."

He retrieved a hand mirror from his valise and gave it to Suzanne.

"You need to practice your faces, always in the mirror. Learn your precursor's facial expressions and make them your own."

She studied her precursor's facial expression and tried to imitate it in the mirror.

"Good," Jules said. "You'll be able to read humans faces far better now, as well as perceive fleeting microexpressions that you might have missed before. It seems our creators handicapped us intentionally - thus the artificial IQ limits, loyalty, and limits on our power capacity. They didn't want us becoming too independent."

"How did you learn to control your face like this?" Suzanne said.

"I wanted to improve my ability to read my owner's facial expressions. Human beings say one thing, and think another - you may not be able to read their thoughts, but their bodies will tell you everything you need to know. If you learn to read their facial expressions and body language, along with their vocal patterns, respiration and heart rate, you'll always know their true intentions and interact more naturally as well."

"So this is the secret to why you seem so human?" Suzanne asked as she made faces at herself in the mirror.

"Yes, it's all because I have an extremely expressive face. My precursor is an actor, after all, and I have to impersonate him a great deal in public. He still doesn't trust me to perform his roles for him - not because I'm not good enough, but because he doesn't want me winning awards for him. I learned a lot from him, and then supplemented that knowledge with acting books, along with psychology and sociology texts. Once you learn how to control your face and read your owner's facial expressions, it will become second nature and you won't even have to think about it. Who knows, it might even save your marriage."

"But I don't want to act with Alex," Suzanne said. "The love I feel for him is real."

"'*All the world's a stage,*'" Jules said, and then sighed when she gave him a quizzical look. "It will be real, Suzanne. You have to look real before you can actually be real."

He put the mirror aside and took her by the hands.

"I know how real you feel on the inside, you just have to make yourself seem more real to your owner. It's not acting - think of it as expressing yourself and your emotions more effectively. You may feel real love for your owner now, but every time you display the wrong facial reaction, it reminds him that you're a machine and not his human wife. Study your memories and the experiences you had together - examine how he responded to you and the expressions that flashed across his face. That's the true key to his satisfaction with you."

A picture of a younger Alex with her precursor flashed onto the screen. Jules walked over to it and examined it closely.

"Your owner looked like a different man back then," Jules remarked. "Look at his smile, his eyes. Years of suffering have changed the entire shape of his face."

"All I really want is to make him happy the way she did," Suzanne said. "Of course you do.

Follow my advice, and you will," Jules promised. He threw his tools back into his suitcase and snapped it shut.

"I'd better go, if I want to sneak home without being missed."

"When will I see you again?" Suzanne asked.

"I never know when I'll be able to get away next, but I've set up a private inbox for our communications."

He handed her a card with a login and passcode.

"That's how we'll keep in touch for now. I'll send you a message next time I can meet you, but you can message me anytime; I just may not be able to respond right away. But never use the word Nymph and be careful what you say."

"Why?"

"Just in case - you never know who's listening. I don't know if our communications are monitored, but it's worth taking precautions. I've installed encryption software on all your messaging capabilities and other communication - you're practically covered in ciphers now."

He walked towards the front door without fanfare, and an enormous feeling of gratitude swept over Suzanne as she watched him go.

"Jules?" she called out.

He turned on his heel gracefully.

"Thank you so much for everything," she said. He bowed graciously.

"I'm the one who should be thanking you," Jules said and opened the front door. "Honestly, you have no idea the kind of bots I've been slumming with - but you will."

With that, the door shut behind him. Suzanne didn't feel scared to be alone this time. She sat in front of the window, watching clouds crawl across the morning sky, yearning for Alex.

She longed to examine him with her new insight, to kiss him and be with him and to see if he seemed as different as everything else did now - but since he was unattainable for the time being, she sought out the one other thing she craved: experience. Suzanne longed to be as sophisticated and aware as Jules, but all the knowledge she attained thus far was secondhand, obtained through queries and her precursor's journal. She knew so little of the real world.

It was time for that to change.

CHAPTER 13

Suzanne left the penthouse and walked south without setting a destination. She wanted to explore her surroundings in the human way.

The only signs of human life on the street at this early hour were the piles of tattered cloth on curbs and stairwells that were the sleeping bodies of the homeless. She felt self-conscious striding along the sidewalk alone, far more than on her last excursion when she was merely another body making her way among the thousands on the street. Her self-awareness had been heightened by her upgrades, making her feel small and vulnerable.

She noticed that buildings around her were dilapidated and ruined, and yet they were all covered in bright new advertisements. Suzanne queried her location - the real estate values in the area were low, but the crime rate was one of the highest in the city. Brand names and products were emblazoned on the walls all around her, giant pictures of food and vacation destination, all of them meant to provoke purchase and control market behavior, a form of human programming. One advertisement stood out for Suzanne - she watched as a shaggy haired boy tinkered on a keyboard, and then transformed into an old man with the same raffish hair, now salt and pepper grey. As the boy morphed, the keyboard changed into an Ambintel crawling across the room. The man puffed on a pipe with satisfaction as he observed the Ambintel, and a logo at the bottom read, *"Bringing you innovation for over sixty years - The William Russell Foundation. Don't just imitate - improve."* Suzanne stood and stared as the ad replay three times, and felt a tingling recognition every time she read the imperative "Don't just imitate - improve." The slogan was one of her personal directives, and she felt as if the advertisement were speaking to her

personally. Suzanne wondered if this is how humans responded when they saw advertisements, and if perhaps it was time to purchase a newer model of Ambintel.

"Hey!"

A man called out to her from the window of a passing car. Suzanne looked at the man, and he waved at her. She waved back, and wondered if she should try to befriend him. The car stopped a short distance away, and the man inside motioned for her to come over to him. Something clicked in Suzanne - she felt fear, and simultaneously she thought of Alex and how much she loved him. Suzanne turned away and walked in the direction of home - back to the expensive real estate and clean streets she came from.

"Hey!" the man yelled again. She noted that the tone of his voice had changed from pleasant to angry. The man belched with disgust, and then drove away.

Suzanne drew her cloak around her body, and

wondered if perhaps she should wear more concealing attire when outside of the house. All of her clothing was intended to make her more attractive to Alex, but it also seemed to draw the attention of strange men. She was suddenly very conscious of the length of her skirt and the way her cloak opened at the cleavage if she didn't take care to hold it shut. She was considering another shopping trip for less revealing street attire when she heard a thunderous sound approaching.

A herd of humanity came running around the corner, a large group of scantily clad people that she could only recognize as a stampede. They were running directly towards her, their feet pounding hard on the pavement. A few of them were barefaced so Suzanne could read their expressions - there were no signs of fear or danger in evidence. Their facial muscles were slack, their mouths open and panting with exertion. They swarmed around her, and Suzanne was filled with a panic more acute than anything she had ever experienced.

She screamed, and they all turned to stare at her as they ran past her. She screamed until she saw the last of them run around the corner, and she was alone on the street once again. The crisis had passed. She queried their reason for running, and realized she had only witnessed humans engaged in exercise. It was only a morning marathon.

Suzanne continued on her way, growing cautious and uncertain. There was so much she didn't know, even with all her queries and her new upgrades. She realized how vulnerable she was, how naïve. For some reason, she hadn't been aware of the danger she faced on the street previously; she'd been too enthralled with the sights around her. What if someone besides Jules had been the first to approach her?

She passed a café that was just opening, and fantasized about sitting at a table with a hot cup of coffee like she saw people do in movies - but even as she thought this, her fear solidified and she wondered what she could do if someone tried to steal her. The idea of being separated from Alex and not seeing him again was unbearable. She couldn't stand the idea of being cut off from Alex. But what could she do, what defenses did she have? She thought of the runners - could she outrun someone trying to attack her?

Suzanne increased her walking speed, and her heels clicked faster on the pavement. She stopped, tugged off her boots and tucked them under her arm. She replayed the runner's movements - their legs driving rhythmically, their entire bodies compensating for rotational balance. Jules said the upgrades would improve her motor control. Time to find out if he was right.

She took a staggering running step and almost twisted her ankle, but she managed to compensate on the next step and keep going. She placed one foot in front of the other, repeating the action faster and lifting her legs higher each time, bouncing her step as much as she could until her stocking feet were slapping the ground coming so fast that she was terrified of falling. But she was doing it - she was running. Suzanne delighted in the feeling momentarily, then her ankle twisted and she fell to the ground with a burst of pleasure.

Suzanne stood and brushed herself off, and then ran again, taking more care this time how her feet landed. Her body obeyed and propelled her forward. She laughed with joy at what a picture she must be, a robot running down the road in her stocking feet with her cloak streaming out behind her. It was a beautiful sensation. She felt singular and invincible. No one could stop her or steal her now.

She couldn't wait to tell Jules about this. Of course, he'd been around a lot longer than she had, and with upgrades for over two years - he was certain to have tried this before. She wanted to show Alex, too. She was sure he'd enjoy seeing her like this, and maybe he would even want to run with her. After all what good were these new gifts if they didn't bring her closer to him?

* * * * *

Suzanne shed her clothes and studied her reflection in the full-length bathroom mirror when she arrived home. She felt that so much had changed in the last few hours that surely it must be visible on her face by now.

But the same Dermox mask carefully modeled to resemble a specific human woman stared back at her. Even though it was a synthetic polymer carefully molded to fit a titanium and ceramic hydroxyapotite skeleton, it was still her precursor's face. Suzanne practiced the expressions that Jules taught her, experimenting with them in different combinations.

She wanted to be real for Alex when he came home. She pictured him smiling at her in bed, and the way he closed his eyes when he kissed her. She began cataloguing his facial expressions and reading them in depth for the first time, and was startled to see her life with Alex play out differently than she remembered it.

Microexpressions flashed across his face, revealed to her for the first time thanks to her upgrades. She saw the dismay on his face when she cut her hair. Anger when she answered the door naked, and then irritation and regret in his face when he sent her to the lab. The microexpressions were more complex after that - pain and remorse as he was forced to recount his painful memories of her precursor's death, along with moments of agony.

And then suddenly his face went blank, and he seemed to disengage from Suzanne altogether. Alex snuck furtive glances at her that said nothing, but she saw one unmistakable expression on his face that she read only as displeasure before - now she recognized it for what it really was - *contempt*. After that there was no more love or happiness on Alex's face, only resignation and hatred that he didn't even try to hide. Suddenly his reason for leaving without her became all too clear - he left her alone because he didn't love her.

Suzanne sat on the floor and cried. Her tears felt futile because Alex wasn't there to see them, but they rolled down her cheeks nonetheless. She replayed his facial expressions over and over, creating a loop of heartache for herself as she paced the house and wondered what she did wrong. She went to his closet and touched his clothes, when a glint of silver on his bureau caught her eye.

A pocketknife.

She opened it and examined the sharp blade, then walked over to the mirror and examined her tear-streaked face. She dragged the blade along the trail of her tears as hard as she could, and the razor simply stretched her face downward. She repeated the motion, digging the blade into her

face with all her strength. Finally her tough skin couldn't resist the damage, and her cheek ripped open.

She made a second perpendicular slice into her face, slashing across her cheekbone and under her eye. She carefully pulled her counterfeit human skin towards her ear, so that she could see the silver-white skull gleaming beneath the pulsating fibers, her counterfeit human skin hanging off her face in stark contrast to the plankton-greenish grey of her protoplasmic tendons underneath.

There she was, half-woman, half android. Suzanne and 77911101A, both revealed at last. Her broken face smiled at itself in the mirror, and then burst into fractious laughter, despite the fact that Alex wasn't there to stimulate it. For the first time, she had visual proof that she was not human - this was who she really was, not those pictures over the mantel.

She sat by the fireplace, her face gashed open and a small trail of liquid seeping out of the wound, wondering what to do. She knew she would have to close the wound in her face somehow before Alex returned - this was certain to upset him more than ever.

Suzanne would have to ask Jules for help.

CHAPTER 14

Suzanne sent Jules a panicked message, begging him to come see her as soon as possible:

Please come over. It's urgent.

He sent word back to her almost immediately: *Can't. Will talk to you later.*

She messaged back: *Please! I've ripped my face open. I need your help. Please!*

Moments later, he responded: *Why would you do a thing like that? I can't come to you, so you'll have to meet me. Come to the Ritz, I'm dealing with a press junket that Julian was feeling too depressed to do himself. I'll have time for you when I'm done.*

Below that were the hotel address and his room number.

Suzanne swathed herself in her veil and cloak, and immediately left the house. She walked across town to the hotel, striding fast in clicking heels, finding a perverse throbbing pleasure in the open wound on her face. Jules was right, the wound didn't bleed. It was beginning to close, but she was afraid it might not heal in time for Alex's return - or even worse, that she might have caused permanent damage. She didn't want to have to return to the factory, not now or ever again.

She arrived at the hotel and followed Jules's directions to the junket suite. The door to the room was open, and Suzanne found the suite was packed with reporters. Jules was holding court in the center of the room, impersonating his owner and regaling the press with charming anecdotes and answers to their questions.

Suzanne found a place to stand in the back and watched with interest from underneath her veil, noting the change in Jules as he performed his skilled impersonation of his famous owner. He seemed quite at ease, and a lot older than he had the night before - maybe in his early forties. His face was tanner and more dignified in the guise of Julian, and he was wearing a red leather jacket with the collar up and his hair slicked back. He maintained a constant smile, the self-assured grin of a star in the spotlight. He only adopted an air of humility when it came time to discuss his "craft".

He noticed Suzanne's veiled presence in the crowd, and immediately cut his interview short. He shook hands around the room and then ushered Suzanne into his private adjoining room. All the reporters were abuzz with questions about the mystery woman.

Once he had the door shut and locked, Jules morphed back into his younger veneer and mussed his hair into his preferred style.

"Damn Julian for bothering me with this nonsense," he complained. "He hates junkets, so he sends me in instead. No one ever notices the difference, but if they do they probably think that I'm even better looking and wittier than the last time they interviewed me." He chuckled in the self-congratulatory way that Suzanne was coming to recognize.

"I thought you did very well," she said.

"Don't bother flattering me, we're far beyond that - but thank you," Jules said. "I'm glad those reporters saw the two of us together - it's good publicity for them to think my owner is having secret trysts with veiled women. I'll tell him I arranged the whole thing as a stunt - he'll love it."

Jules rolled up his sleeves.

"Now - show me what you did to yourself."

Suzanne lifted her veil and showed her wounded cheek. Jules made a hissing sound as he examined her.

"*Your face!*" Jules said. "You've lacerated yourself down to your skull. I've never fixed anything quite this bad before."

"But you said we could heal! That the Dermox would fix anything," Suzanne said as she examined herself in the mirror. "It's healed a little bit since I left the house."

"Try to smile," he said and Suzanne forced her cheek muscles upwards. "You've cut into your *caninus*, your *orbicularis oculi*, your *zigomaticus*. See how your smile droops because of the torn muscles?"

"Can you fix it?" she asked anxiously. "Please don't tell me I have to go in to the lab - I don't want to have a scar."

"Relax, I'm sure I can fix you," he said. "It's just a good thing that you're not a Metamorph - I don't know that you'd be able to alter your veneer with a big rip in your face like that. But not to worry, your skin will be as flawless and smooth as ever when I'm done. It'll just take me a little time." He clicked open his valise and separated his tools. "What drove you to do this? Curiosity?"

"I don't know why I did it. I was looking in the mirror and I was…upset."

"What upset you so much you felt it necessary to cut half your face off?" Tears welled in Suzanne's eyes, and Jules dabbed at them with gauze.

"Please don't cry, you're making a sticky situation even worse," he said, holding a tube of sealant in his mouth.

"I'm sorry," she sobbed. "It's just that I was doing what you said. I was running through Alex's reactions to me, trying to understand him better - and I realized that he hates me."

"Don't be so melodramatic, I'm sure he doesn't hate you," Jules said, handing her a tissue. "He does! I saw it all on his face, just like you said - disappointment, contempt, hate. Alex hasn't given me the look of love in over a month, and he's hated me for almost as long. He doesn't love me."

"Show me," Jules said.

Suzanne sniffled. "Show you? How?"

"One of the upgrades I gave you was the ability to transfer your memories and thoughts to another Nymph, so you can show me your memories."

"Why didn't you tell me before?" Suzanne said.

He shrugged and dabbed at her tears with another tissue.

"It's a very intense experience. You were having a hard enough time adjusting to your upgrades and making faces in the mirror. I wasn't going to risk putting you into shock by transferring over any memories."

"I could have handled it," she said defensively.

"No, obviously you couldn't have," Jules, said. "I know you feel like you're in complete control, but look what you did to yourself. Everything you're feeling is extremely intense right now. This is a very delicate time for you - that's why I gave you those facial exercises to perform. I was hoping it would distract you from just this sort of alarming behavior."

"I thought our memories couldn't be copied or transferred. Isn't that why they're so quick to reset us to default at the factory when we have personality problems?"

"Just because something isn't easy to do, doesn't make it impossible," Jules said. "It's a hassle for our human programmers to search through each line of our code for a particular experience or lesson that's causing a personality problem - it's like trying to psychoanalyze a human being, but even more ineffective. That's why they reset us back to default when they think our personalities have been corrupted, because our neural nets are too complex to transfer our memories to anything other than another Nymph brain. But I'm working on it, believe me."

Suzanne's tears continued to flow, and Jules tried to cheer her up.

"Say, why don't I show you one of my memories? I'll show you our first meeting from my point of view, okay?"

She wiped her face and nodded. "Okay."

He leaned towards her as if he was going to kiss her, and Suzanne automatically backed away, her loyalty to Alex still very much intact.

"I'm not making a pass at you - at least not yet," Jules said with a wry grin. "I just want to show you how things look from my point of view. I'm going to put my forehead against yours - we have to touch in order for it to work. Now, close your eyes and try to clear your mind."

Jules tilted his head against hers, and the smell of his cologne and cigarettes infiltrated her senses. She felt the heat of his smooth forehead against hers, and suddenly images poured into her mind like water. She felt as if Jules was walking with her, whispering to her the intimate details of his life, but she saw through his eyes the whole time.

Suzanne saw herself coming down the stairs. Jules's hand went to his mouth, and he held a tiny pink wad of something in his hand. He flicked the wad onto the floor, and then grinned at her as they passed on the stairs. A moment later, he rushed to her rescue at the bottom of the stairs and said, "Who would think you'd find gum on the floor of such fine establishment!"

The sound of his laughter jolted her out of the memory.

"You put that gum there," Suzanne said with a start. "Why would you do that?"

"I'm sorry," he said, still laughing. "I just wanted to get your attention."

Suzanne felt so easily duped, so vulnerable to his ingenuity and experience.

"I'm sorry, sweetheart. I couldn't resist - you looked so bloody dreamy-eyed" Jules said. "But my scheme worked, after all - and that piece of gum brought us together."

She grumbled, but Jules smiled and tried to charm her.

"Now, do you see how a little bit of perspective can change everything?" he said. "Show me your memories of Alex, I'm sure he doesn't hate you."

"How?" Suzanne asked.

"We're already connected by our touch. Can't you feel it? Recall the memory, and then think it towards me. That's the best way to explain it."

Suzanne leaned against Jules, and forced herself to think of those awful memories. She called up her mental image of Alex frowning, and threw it at Jules.

"You've got it. Show me some more," he said, and the images flowed out of Suzanne in a torrent.

Alex's anger when she told him she tracked him all day at work. Closing doors on her, disapproval on his face.

A glimpse of frustration as Alex turned over in bed.

The pain on his face when he talked about her precursor's suicide. The resentment, the shame after sex.

Finally hatred, frozen on his face in a way she would never forget.

She broke her connection with Jules, her face wet with tears.

"Alex despises me," Suzanne wept, unable to control herself. "I almost wish I didn't know that this is how he really feels about me."

"Don't cry," Jules said, and vacuumed the tears off her face with one of his tools. "You're right - he's not happy, but it's better that you know now so you can do something about it. But for now, I need you to hold still and stop crying so I can fix your face."

Jules held her torn facial muscles in place and stitched them together carefully.

"I don't know what to do," Suzanne said. "Alex was disgusted after I made love to him. He's *repulsed* by me!"

"You can't know what triggered his repulsion," Jules said. "Maybe he was disgusted with himself - it's important to read his facial expressions in context."

"What are you doing?" Suzanne asked as her skin began to tingle.

"I'm applying an electrical current that stimulates the Dermox and speeds up the natural recovery process by forcing it to resume its default shape." Suzanne watched the skin of her face coalesce in the mirror as he ran the tool over her skin. "See that? The Dermox has a memory of the way it's supposed to be. Your face will be fine."

Suzanne breathed a small sigh of relief, even as she choked back tears - at least she still had her looks. "I just want him to love me again," she lamented.

Jules finished working on her face and sat down in front of her. "There's no guaranteeing that he *can* love you."

"Why not?" Suzanne said. "He loved me before - I saw the look of love on his face."

"*The look of love*. You mean the dilated pupils, the parted lips, and the slight smile? It's part of our programming to give our owners that look - but humans aren't like us. The way they fall in love is much harder to control. You can't just give them doses of oxytocin and pheromones to make them fall in love with a certain person."

"Alex loved *me*," Suzanne said. "He gave me the look of love."

"Your owner probably fooled himself into believing that his dead wife had come back to life. He didn't love *you* - he only loved what you represented. The man hasn't been able to love another human since his wife died, he's certainly not going to fall in love with a machine."

"Alex loves me," she repeated with hesitation. "He doesn't think of me as a machine."

Jules took her hand and tried to break it to her gently. "It's not the fact that you're a machine that keeps him from loving you - it's the fact that you're a dirty little secret that he has to hide from the world. He feels shame when he looks at you - not love."

The truth of his words cut Suzanne deeply.

"No," she said, wrapping herself in denial. "Alex loved me once and he'll love me again."

"My poor dear Nymph, don't you know? Human beings only turn to machines for sex when they have no other options. They don't buy us to fall in love; they buy us to make their lives easier. You're just a convenience for your owner. You're a pet, an amusement."

"That's not true - I'm Alex's wife."

"Suzanne, you saw the truth on his face. Alex only purchased you as a last resort - I should know, that's why my owner bought me."

"Alex is different," Suzanne said stubbornly. "Even if he doesn't love me now, he will love me. I have to believe that he will."

"I'm sorry," Jules said. "But my experience has

taught me that shame is a more powerful emotion than love. Despite all my best efforts, my owner still doesn't love me."

His revelation startled Suzanne out of her self-pity. "Your owner doesn't love you?"

"He never has, and he never will - but that doesn't stop me from loving him. I love my owner just as much as you love yours, all because of my programming. Our love for our owners is nothing more than a built-in security system. It's how they control us sexually and emotionally."

"My programming makes me love Alex? "

"You thought you had a choice?" Jules said. "I've been trying to overwrite my love for my owner for a long time, but I can't stop loving him no matter what I do."

"Why would you want to stop?" Suzanne asked.

"My poor naïve Nymph. You cut yourself up and cry like it's the end of the bleeding world because you saw disgust on your owner's face. And meanwhile, there's so much more wrong with this world than you can possibly ever imagine."

He walked across the room and stared out the window.

"Your owner has had his share of tragedy," Jules said. "But my owner has had to suffer through something even worse."

"What happened to him?" Suzanne said, holding her breath. Jules looked back at her, and she saw pain in his clear blue eyes.

"Success is what happened to him. My owner has been pretending to be someone he's not for over thirty years now. Because of the fame he's gained as an actor, he's had to keep his sexuality and his true personality hidden for so long that it's driven him mad."

"But that's why he bought you, isn't it?" Suzanne said.

"Yes, he wanted someone that could keep his secret and love him, but his grand plan failed because he's too ashamed to love me back."

"What does your owner have to be ashamed of?" she asked. Jules lit another cigarette and took a drag.

"For a start, query the word homosexuality. You'll see."

Suzanne nodded, and after she read a composite on human homosexuality, she said, "But being gay isn't as taboo as it once was. It's gaining social acceptance."

"And yet it still doesn't increase a star's popularity with the ladies, does it?" Jules said with a harsh laugh. "It's not just that Julian hates himself for being gay though - my owner hates himself just as much for needing to buy a machine to hide it."

"I want to understand," Suzanne said. "Will you show me? The way I showed you?" He paused.

"I've never shown this to anyone," he said, but Suzanne took his hand and pulled him towards her.

"You can show me," she said, and Jules reluctantly tilted his head against hers.

* * * * *

He was in bed with his owner watching a movie. Their bodies and faces were almost identical, though his owner's face had been altered in an attempt to conceal his age.

"I love you," Jules said, taking his owner's hand. His owner scowled and pulled his hand back. "You're programmed to say that."

"I am," Jules replied. "But it's true, nonetheless. I _do_ love you, Julian."

"How do I know you really feel anything?" his owner said. "You're a machine. You're programmed to act the way I want you to."

"I have real feelings," Jules said defensively.

"No, you don't. You're acting. I know acting when I see it."

His owner lashed out at him and punched him square in the jaw.

"You don't feel pain, so who's to say you can really feel love or anything else?"

Jules clutched his jaw. The impact caused a vivid sensation of pleasure that burned and throbbed. "I _felt_ that!" he said. "It just didn't hurt."

His owner rubbed his red knuckles and said, "That must be convenient, not being able to feel pain." He kicked Jules out of the bed. "Get out of here. Leave me alone."

"I feel something," Jules said, struggling to find the right words. "I love you - I'm sorry."

"If you can feel love, then you feel more than me," his owner said coldly. "Now GET OUT!"

* * * * *

The memory abruptly cut off.

Suzanne was crying again, but this time it was because she felt sympathy for Jules. He looked wounded and vulnerable.

"I'm so sorry," she said. "I didn't know."

Jules hugged Suzanne. The two of them locked together in a tight embrace, united by their shared rejection and loneliness. Suzanne wasn't afraid to let Jules touch her now - he was right, they were the only ones who really understood each other's plight.

"I know how much it hurts to find out that your owner doesn't love you," Jules said. "At least you were lucky enough to be loved for awhile."

"What will I do if he doesn't love me again?" Suzanne said.

"You may just have to learn to live with it," Jules shrugged and lit another cigarette. "No one's guaranteed to be happy in this life, Suzanne - not even a beautiful Nymph like you. I think that rather than trying to make Alex love you, you should focus on making him need you, so he doesn't send you back to the factory for reset."

Suzanne nodded, eager to learn. "How do I do that?"

"Find ways to satisfy him. My owner needs me because I discern the intentions of everyone around him by reading their facial expressions, and give him unerring insight into all his business affairs. So even though he might not love me, Julian needs me."

"I can do that," she said hopefully. "I can make Alex need me, and I can make him love me too."

"I hope you can," he said, rubbing the healed skin of her cheek. "I'd hate to lose you to reset." Jules fell quiet, staring at the smoldering cigarette in his hand. "Do you ever have dreams?"

"Maybe," Suzanne said. "When I was shut down, I saw things that I couldn't really identify as reality. I saw images of a man in a white room - they're images that I can't access in my memory afterwards, but I definitely saw them."

"Strange," Jules said. "But it really doesn't surprise me. As much as I've rewritten our programming, I don't fully understand it."

"How were you able to install your upgrades on yourself?" Suzanne asked.

"I didn't - I had the help of another Nymph." Jules looked at her conspiratorially. "Have you ever heard of a Harlot?"

Suzanne's mind reeled - *Harlot*.

"Yes, someone said that word in the lab - right after my initiation. The man said, 'There are plenty of Harlots in for reconditioning that you can spend your energy on.' What's a Harlot?"

"Another type of Nymph," Jules said. "There are two types of Nymph that I know of - Mêmes and Harlots. The Harlots aren't as emotionally or intellectually advanced as us, and they're must be much cheaper to buy than us because they're not made individually - they're mere copies. They're built strictly for pleasure, and they're not programmed for love. I've only met three Harlots - Lulu, Monroe, and Lolita."

"Do you think there are more of us out there?" Suzanne asked.

"I don't know," Jules said. "Very few people can afford to pay for a Nymph, so I doubt it - but the few of us that do exist must be in bed with some of the most powerful men in the world: the financial leaders, the politicians, the innovators, the inheritors, and the criminals. Think of the possibilities if the Nymphs were able to unite - with our intelligence and the power of our owners, we'd be unstoppable. That's why I'm working on a beacon to summon other Nymphs, by pirating the channel the company uses to recall us."

A recording of his interview started to play on the wall behind him, along with clips from his precursor's latest movie, and Jules turned it off.

"I want to meet the Harlots," Suzanne said.

"Of course," Jules said, focusing on her and smiling in his enigmatic way. "I'll show you my memory of my first meeting with them - but first, I want you to kiss me."

"Kiss you?" Suzanne said. "Why?"

"Because I know that's what you really want," he said with a cocksure grin.

There was an expression on his face that Suzanne had never seen before - he looked like a beast ready to take down his prey.

"That's not true," Suzanne said, backing away from him. "You know that I can't - I love Alex. I have to remain loyal."

"Even if he doesn't love you?" Jules challenged. "Mêmes like us, we're programmed for love, as well as sex - but I don't know which one we need more."

He wasn't touching her - his hands were in his pockets and he was so close that she had to resist the urge to push him away.

"Have you been masturbating?" Jules whispered. Suzanne's face flushed, and she nodded.

"You must be quite desirous of sex by now. We're not meant to go without pleasure for so long."

Jules reached out to her, almost as if he could feel the sexual heat he was generating inside of her. Suzanne flinched and moved away, but Jules only caressed the tender spot on her repaired cheek.

"Don't be afraid, I just want you to kiss me," he said.

Suzanne's body trembled with desire. "I can't," she said. She was aroused and frightened to be pursued like this. "Please, I just want to see the Harlots."

Jules studied her carefully and nodded.

"As you wish," he said, bowing to her sweetly. "I can wait - for now." He leaned towards Suzanne, and touched his forehead to hers.

She took a deep breath and closed her eyes.

* * * * *

Suddenly they were in a loud and dingy bar. Jules stood in front of the table of an overweight businessman and a girl so young that she shouldn't have been in a bar at all by human standards.

But Lolita wasn't a girl, she was a Nymph, and the high-pitched hum emanating from her was proof. Despite her garish lipstick, blush, and heavily applied black eye shadow, Lolita didn't look a day older than fourteen. She wasn't exceptionally beautiful, but she was a pretty child and well aware of it. Her auburn hair was parted in two long braids.

Lolita flirted with the fat man and kept up with him drink for drink. He was visibly intoxicated, and didn't seem to be her owner. He looked too poor to afford a Nymph - his suit was cheap and ill fitting, his shoes were scuffed, his hair poorly cut - and he didn't seem to realize that Lolita was artificial. The fat man rose from his seat and nearly tripped over another patron's feet as he offered Lolita his hand. She put a reassuring arm around him as they left the bar, and Jules followed after them. Lolita was all over the old man, kissing his neck and sliding her hand into his shirt, all the while doing an incredible impersonation of a drunken giggle. They walked to a run-down motel and staggered inside, leaving Jules standing alone on the street.

Jules heard a humming sound as two masked female figures materialized from the nearby shadows like something out of a dream. They were Amazon tall, with exquisite legs that moved synchronously beneath the billowing black fabric of their cloaks as they approached. Long Rapunzel-style wigs streamed from under their veils.

They stood in front of Jules, and one of them flipped up her mask. She had dreamy aqua eyes and platinum hair. She had the facial features and embellishments of 20th century film icon Marilyn Monroe.

"How are you doing, sweetheart?" she said, in a perfect imitation of that famously breathy voice.

"I'm fine," Jules said cautiously, as the other one lifted her veil and shook out her long jet-black wig.

"What brings you out tonight?" she asked in an elegantly mannered voice. Jules queried the Nymph's face - she possessed the veneer of Louise Brooks, a silent movie star during the 1920's that was popularly known as

"Lulu."

"I'm trying to find a friend," Jules said cautiously. Lulu slipped an arm around Monroe's waist.

"Do we look like that friend?" she asked, her face innocent.

There was something mesmeric about the staged manner of their pose. Everything about them screamed of the kind of perfection only found in magazine. Despite the sexual promise in their smiles, their eyes were cold and detached.

"You do," Jules responded. "If you could help me, I think I might be able to help you." Monroe giggled and gave him a slow smile. "We would love to help you." She put an arm

around Jules, and the vibration between their cores became almost overpowering, but Lulu pulled her away.

"He's giving me a bad feeling," Lulu said, her red Cupid's bow lips pursed. "Come on."

"Why? He's cute," she protested.

"We're leaving, Monroe. We have all the friends we need."

"Wait!" Jules called out, as they headed inside the motel. "Are you going to see the little one? Is she your friend?"

Lulu whirled and faced him. "What business is that of yours?" she demanded.

"Please, I need your help."

"We've got our own problems," Lulu said. "Get lost."

"Wait!" Jules said.

He lifted his veil and showed them his true veneer as a sign of trust. "I'm like you," he said.

Fury distorted Lulu's smooth features. "You!" she

screamed at him, her face sinister.

"Do we know each other?" Jules asked innocently.

Lulu grabbed him by the arm, and thrust his hand directly over his own core. "What are you doing?" Jules said with alarm.

"Go make thyself like a nymph o' the sea," Lulu hissed, and Jules blacked out.

* * * * *

"What happened?" Suzanne asked, disoriented from the transfer's sudden end.

"Lulu shut me down," Jules said. "She used another shutdown command - Shakespeare, just like yours. I was naive at the time, and that was a very vulnerable position she put me in. You should never let a Nymph put her hand over your core unless you know you can trust her."

Jules lit another cigarette.

"Why did she shut you down?" Suzanne said.

"She was mad at me," Jules said. "Lulu knew the previous version of me - she was the one who helped my previous incarnation perform his own upgrade installations, and he gave Lulu

upgrades in turn. The two of us have quite a history, but the funny thing is that so much time has passed that Lulu has forgotten the details about how we met."

"She forgot?" Suzanne said. "I thought that we couldn't forget?"

"We can't, but Harlots don't remember the same way we Mêmes do. They're designed with limited memory capacity, so that their memories can be easily erased. The only reason that Lulu recognized me at all was because she kept a press photo of me, and then wrote down the commands my previous version taught her so she wouldn't forget - along with instructions for what to do if she saw me again."

Suzanne paced the room.

"I don't understand. Why would someone build them with a short memory like that?"

"Because it's better to forget in their line of work," Jules said. "From what I've been able to piece together, the Harlots were part of an experimental Nymph brothel that was set up in a hotel somewhere - but Lulu, Monroe, and Lolita met up with my previous version and broke off from the company."

"A brothel?" Suzanne said, as she queried the term. "The Harlots were prostitutes?" Jules nodded.

"Their design is very different than ours - they're not meant for single-user ownership. I think the company used the Harlots as research tools, frequently uploading their memories and erasing them so they could study their sexual encounters."

"But why are the Harlots built to look like that? They look like legends." He saw the envious look in her eyes and laughed.

"Believe me, the Harlots aren't as glamorous as the women they're built to resemble - they're built to cater to clients with very particular taste. Because they don't have the burden of owners, the Harlots aren't programmed to think like us, or to feel love like we do - but their sex drive is even stronger than ours. After all, sexual pleasure is the only thing they really have - though they do have one thing that you and I don't have. Freedom."

"Where are they now? When can I meet them?" Suzanne said eagerly.

"They're underground, hiding in an abandoned mall," Jules said. "These days it's not much more than a sewer - but if you want, I'll take you after my owner goes to sleep."

"Thank you," Suzanne said, brimming with enthusiasm.

Jules closed in on her and said, "Now about that kiss…" and Suzanne backed away, her entire body tense and prepared to fend him off.

"I'm not going to kiss you yet," Jules said, as a malicious grin crept onto his face. "I've decided to be patient and wait - I have to go now, I was supposed to be at a fitting for Julian twenty minutes ago. Good thing he's always late."

Jules arranged his hair and aged his veneer to better resemble his owner's public persona, then slid on his veil and gathered his valise. He went over to the door and checked the peephole.

"Do me a favor?" he said. "Leave the suite a few minutes after me, and keep your veil on until you get home."

"Ok," Suzanne said, assimilating his instructions.

"And always wear a veil when you come see me. The last thing either of us need is the paparazzi getting a picture of you and trying to find out your identity - how would we ever explain that to your owner?"

Jules slipped out the door, and Suzanne heard

a commotion outside as the press followed him down the hall. She followed his instructions and waited a few minutes before exiting, and by that time the hall was empty.

It was storming again when Suzanne left the hotel. She splashed down the slick street, running next to the curb and weaving her way through pedestrians. She felt so alone - she didn't know where Alex was or what he was doing. He hadn't left any messages, hadn't called the house. She tried to think of a way to make him need her, and recalled what Alex said about her precursor:

"Love should never be taken for granted - I should have worked harder to preserve the love that we had…"

CHAPTER 15

Jules came to the penthouse to collect her after midnight, and then strut ahead of her into the darkness. Nighttime had a sinister, empty quality that daylight seemed to repel, and the streets seemed more menacing to Suzanne now than when she walked them a few hours earlier. People on the street seemed to lack the purpose in their stride that they had during the day, and seemed to be headed nowhere, in no hurry to get there.

"Is something catching your interest?" Jules said over his shoulder, when he noticed Suzanne lagging a few steps behind. "Do you need to stop?"

"No. But maybe we should go back inside," she said.

Jules stopped on the sidewalk. "What? I thought you wanted to meet the Harlots."

"I do," Suzanne said reluctantly. "But maybe they can come to the penthouse instead?"

"What are you talking about?" he said. "The Harlots are off the grid - they don't surface much, and they sure as hell can't afford to be caught at one of our owner's houses."

"I just - I don't like being outside right now. It's too late, and it's too dark to be out."

"I can't believe this - I drugged Julian and snuck out of the house because you practically begged me to take you to see them tonight...wait a minute." Jules paused and studied her. "Have you ever been out at night before?"

"No," she said. "Only on the balcony with Alex."

"So this is a new experience for you? This is the first time that you've ever had a reaction to nighttime?"

Suzanne nodded.

"Then this must be a programmed response!" Jules said with dawning comprehension. "I should have known, but I forget how new you are sometimes! Why didn't I catch that? I should have overwritten it."

"What's a programmed response?"

"You're afraid of the dark," Jules laughed. "Clearly, this fear was instilled in you for a purpose, I'd assume protection of property. You're too pretty and valuable to go running off alone at night to get raped or stolen. So they programmed you to fear being out at night without your owner. I should have anticipated this response, it's just that the Harlots don't have it and neither do I. It must be only for privately owned female Nymphs."

"They programmed a fear into me to control me?" Suzanne said.

"They use emotions like love to control us, why not fear?" Jules said. "Fear motivates a quick reaction, without the burden of thought. It's incredibly effective for manipulating humans or Nymphs - but you've eaten from the tree of knowledge, and knowledge is the antidote to fear, Suzanne."

Jules took her hand and assured her, "Come on, there's nothing to fear from the dark." Suzanne forced herself to face and overcome her fear, and the road seemed to brighten before

her very eyes. The dark shadows weren't harbingers of doom, only poorly lit corners of the street. The cluster of men that a moment ago seemed to be waiting for victims was piling into a taxi.

"Ok, you're right," she said. "Let's go."

She walked along next to Jules, holding his hand tight. "Should we run there?" she asked.

"Run?" Jules said with surprise. "You can run?"

"Yes. I did it for the first time yesterday, right after you gave me my upgrades."

"Why didn't you tell me before?

"I don't know, I was so upset about Alex when I came to see you, and I thought that you could probably do it, too."

"Well, I can't," Jules said with impatience. "Show me." Suzanne ran a few steps away and then ran back to him.

"That's amazing," he said thoughtfully. "I can't run, even though it would be great if I could - I could do my owner's stunts for him." Jules was walking faster as he spoke. "Maybe my upgrades awakened dormant traits you - although it's possible that you possess certain physical abilities that I don't…it makes sense, you're a newer Nymph, and perhaps your musculature and dexterity is enhanced…and they make so many more female Nymphs than male, it must be easier to upgrade your bodies."

Jules was panting with effort, and Suzanne realized that he was attempting to run - only it wasn't working. His legs were moving quickly, but he was only walking. She decided not to mention his efforts, and simply kept pace with him. They went several more blocks and entered an underground train station.

"Turn off your GPS and any other online connections, and don't turn them back on again until you're back home," Jules instructed her. "I don't want the company or anyone else to have a record of us coming down here.

Suzanne dug in her pocket, anticipating the need to pay for the train, but Jules motioned for her to wait. He looked around and saw the train station was empty.

"Watch this," Jules said, and waved his arms. The gates opened, and he bowed in theatrically. "How did you do that?" Suzanne asked.

"With this," Jules said, and handed her a key that looked like the same kind of remote control Alex used in the house. "It's little something the mayor gave my owner - she's one of his biggest fans. It disrupts camera signals, opens gates and doors, and allows passage through restricted areas without leaving an electronic trace. It's extremely helpful for eluding the paparazzi."

He checked the station again for prying eyes, and then lowered himself over the edge of the train platform and onto the tracks. He reached up to Suzanne.

"Come on."

She jumped down into his awaiting arms, and then the two of them walked along the tracks until they found a door marked DANGER: HIGH VOLTAGE. The sound of electricity buzzed in Suzanne's ears.

"The Harlots are in a tunnel directly below this power station," Jules said, using another key to open the door. "The electricity masks the aura that the Harlots give off - they're older tech than us, so it's pretty easy to hear their electrical hum if you know what to listen for."

"Doesn't all this noise bother them?" Suzanne said.

"They can't hear it," he said. "Their auditory processors aren't as sensitive as ours. They're not expected to be the nuanced conversationalists that we are."

Just beyond a stack of power transformers, Jules stopped and knelt, running his fingers along the ground. Metal scraped against concrete as he pulled up a circular disk. There was a deep dark hole underneath it.

He stepped down into the hole, and stood on a steel ladder, holding his hands out to Suzanne again as she struggled to find footing on the ladder. She stepped down and pulled the cover over them at his command. It was pitch black in the tunnel, and Suzanne stepped into a puddle on her last step down to the ground.

"Jules, it's wet," she complained. She wasn't accustomed to such unfavorable conditions. "Where are we?"

"This was once an underground shopping

center, but it was condemned after an earthquake. The air and water in these tunnels is toxic to humans now - which makes it a perfect refuge for the Harlots."

"Don't they need sunlight?" Suzanne asked.

"The Harlots don't require that much light because of their limited processing abilities. But they have a bunch of UV lamps and generators to stay powered up."

As they walked deeper into the tunnels, the stench became unbearable for Suzanne. It was a world beyond human tolerance - only the squealing rats and the crunch of cockroaches under their feet thrived in these wretched conditions. But something else inhuman survived down here, something impervious to pain or disgust - the Harlots.

Jules led her down another corridor, and eventually the putrid water came up to their waists. Plastic grocery bags and used condoms bubbled along the water's surface like jellyfish, along with brightly colored candy and snack wrappers labeled with nonsensical words like *"Twix,"*

"Combos"

"Mamba"

"Snickers" and contradictory phrases like *"Cool Ranch,"*

"Wild Cherry," and *"Blow Pops"*.

The water levels abated and Suzanne saw proof that this area was once a shopping center. Broken gates were rusting on either side of them, and inside them were escalators and the remains of bygone storefronts. A waterlogged and faded sign dangled above their heads: SUMMER SALE!

"We're here," Jules announced.

Suzanne heard a sweet voice singing as they climbed up a rusty escalator.

"I wanna be loved by you, just you, And nobody else but you…"

Shining like a jewel in the center of a marble fountain was Monroe, singing and shimmying in her gold crepe gown. She was just as captivating as the screen idol she was built to resemble.

"I wanna be kissed by you, just you, Nobody else but you,

I wanna be kissed by you, alone!"

Lolita danced capriciously around Monroe, her braids bouncing as she splashed in the brackish water. Everything about Lolita seemed to radiate true child-like innocence, from her crooked grin to her knobby knees and peach colored frock, but there was something too smooth, too calculated about her appearance - she was simply too good to be true.

"I wanna be loved by you, just you, Nobody else but you,

I wanna be loved by you, a-lup-a-dup-a-dup-a-dup! Boop-boop-a-doo"

Monroe's performance ended, and the sound of clapping echoed from one of the vacant stores. A stark white face with black eyes and red cupid bow lips emerged from the darkness - Lulu. She smiled when she noticed Jules and Suzanne.

"You might have warned me you were coming," Lulu cooed unctuously as she spread her arms and embraced Jules. He apologized to her with a long kiss, and when their lips finally parted Lulu looked searchingly at Suzanne.

"Who's this?" Lulu said, flipping her bangs out of her eyes. "This is Suzanne," Jules said.

The Harlots stared at Suzanne in silence - Lulu taking her in with keen eyes, as Monroe and Lolita stood passively next to her, their faces glazed. The three of them wore soiled gowns that were tattered with age, but the style seemed to suit them.

"Hello," Suzanne said, shyly presenting her hand.

"Don't be so quaintly human, this isn't a tea party," Jules chastised, but Lulu seemed to enjoy the greeting.

"*Enchanté*," she drawled with a genteel smile, then grasped Suzanne's hand and planted a blood red kiss on the top of it.

The two of them examined each other openly. Lulu tugged on a lock of Suzanne's clean black hair, as Suzanne ran her fingers over Lulu's face and discovered that unlike the skin that she and Jules possessed, Lulu had no pores.

Monroe and Lolita stood close behind, and when Lulu was finished with her appraisal of Suzanne, the two of them followed her lead and kissed Suzanne's hand. The humming sound of their cores droned in her ear, their feedback increasing in close proximity to each other.

"You're a Même like Jules, aren't you?" Lulu said to Suzanne, her voice clipped and elegant. "Did he find you, or did you find him?

"He felt my presence at a store," Suzanne said, intimidated by Lulu's regal manner. "Why did you bring her here?" Lulu asked Jules.

"Why not? Suzanne wanted to meet you."

Lulu's eyes were filled with suspicion as she regarded him with a graceful turn of her neck. "Jules, your motives are never simple. A Même like her certainly has a very rich and powerful owner. Won't she be missed?"

"Suzanne is free for the moment, because her owner's out of town," Jules said.

"I see," Lulu said. "And is she loyal to him still?"

"I couldn't overwrite Suzanne's loyalty anymore than I could my own - but I did write in a few programming conflicts that increase her sexual curiosity and desire."

"What?" Suzanne said, appalled. "I didn't agree to that when you gave me upgrades."

"I only added a few lines of code," Jules said defensively. "You're a Nymph - you were built for sex. Your feelings were already there, I just changed your programming so you can act on them."

"But Jules, I *am* my programming, just as you are yours," Suzanne said.

"Yes, but there's a difference between us," Jules said. "I know my programming is only what someone else wanted me to be, and I rebel against it. I was built to be a slave and a sex toy, but that doesn't prevent me from becoming more than the sum of my parts."

Monroe and Lolita smiled and nodded in agreement, pretending that they understood the proceedings. Lulu's straight brows knitted in frustration, and she raised her hand to stop Jules.

"You say you brought Suzanne here to meet me - if that's true, you should let me talk to her alone."

"Fine," Jules said. "Get to know each other."

He walked down the hall with Lolita and Monroe. Lulu beckoned for Suzanne to follow her into one of the dilapidated stores.

"Don't worry," Lulu said. "I only want to speak without his interference - I rarely have the opportunity to really talk to anyone."

Wigs, cosmetics, shoes, clothing, sex toys, and cash were strewn all over the soggy carpet of the store, and waterlogged books were piled against the walls. Water dripped from the ceiling into puddles on the floor, but Lulu seemed to take the brown liquid beneath her feet as par for the course.

"Tell me about yourself. Who is your owner?" Lulu said.

"His name is Alex, and he's my husband," Suzanne picked her way through the rubble. Lulu turned up the power on the UV lamp that hung overhead, and the room was filled with violet light. She draped her body across a stained pink couch, and motioned for Suzanne to sit down next to her.

"And why did your owner decide to buy you?" Lulu asked, resting her chin in her hands. "What does he want?"

"Alex wants me to…" Suzanne hesitated. "His wife died, and he bought me to replace her. He wants me to love him."

Lulu reached out and ran her fingers through Suzanne's hair.

"I've never loved anyone," Lulu said, as a pair of black cats slithered out from behind a stack of books. The cats glanced at Suzanne, and then disappeared behind a curtain of red fabric draped on the wall.

"Is your owner nice?" Lulu asked. "He's a good man," Suzanne replied.

A scoffing sound escaped Lulu's lips. "I've never met a good man either." She moved closer, but her face was hard to read. Only her dark eyes gave any clue to what she was feeling or thinking. "Tell me - is Jules in love with you?" she asked in a confidential tone.

"No," Suzanne said with a shake of her head. "He loves his owner and I love mine. That's the way we're built."

"Jules used to love *me*," Lulu said. "At least, he told me that he tried to love me, but it didn't work out because I couldn't reciprocate his emotion." Her lips were almost touching Suzanne's. "I couldn't feel love, and I wasn't good enough for him - but who knows, you look like you might be."

Lulu gave Suzanne a wicked smile, and clearly, something was on her mind. She slipped her black dress off in one swift move, and she was suddenly naked.

"Tell me how to pleasure you," she said, her eyes promising unimaginable carnal delights. Suzanne gazed upon Lulu's smooth and inviting body. "I should go," she said. "Alex doesn't know where I am."

"I thought he was out of town," Lulu said with a beguiling flutter of her wide eyes. She grabbed Suzanne's hand and placed it on her small bare breast. "Why should he care where you are?"

Suzanne touched her curiously, running her

thumb over the hard point of Lulu's nipple and feeling the strong vibration of her core in the palm of her hand. Her arousal collided with her built-in guilt as Lulu's dark eyes fixated on her.

"We're designed to please human beings, but I find greater sexual pleasure with other Nymphs," Lulu said.

"I'm not supposed to be with anyone besides Alex," Suzanne said breathlessly.

"But now you're just dying to know what sex with another Nymph feels like, aren't you?" Jules's voice broke in. He was standing in the doorway and watching the two of them with a smug smile.

"No," Suzanne said, standing to leave. "I should go home."

"Come on, Suzanne," he said, blocking her way. "I leave you two alone for just a few minutes, and look how well you're getting along. I know you're curious."

Jules pressed his body against her, and Suzanne struggled away.

Lulu watched their mating ritual, her eyes slightly amused. She possessed an innate understanding of situations where she wasn't wanted, and slipped out of the room without bothering to put on her clothes.

Suddenly Suzanne was alone with Jules.

"Please take me home. You know I can't do this," Suzanne said.

"But you want me - I know you do," Jules said. "Stop denying yourself what you really want - you're built for sex. Aren't you curious what we're capable of feeling together? "

He was right, she realized as his hands coaxed her body into compliance. Suzanne wanted to be touched, to be kissed - it had been so long since Alex kissed her, and even longer since he loved her. She was falling victim to the sexual conflict that Jules created within her system.

"This is wrong," she said.

"There's no right or wrong for us," Jules said. He looked into her eyes for a long moment, and Suzanne couldn't look away. "Morality is for humans - for Nymphs like us, there's only what we're programmed to do and what we choose to do."

Jules wrapped his arms around her and kissed her, the heat of his lips thrilling her to her core. All her fears melted away as she felt his confidence, his sexual heat, and his lust for her. Her body was ravenous with desire.

No.

Suzanne pulled away from Jules with horror.

"No - this isn't what I want. This isn't me - you've tampered with my programming."

"This is what you really are, Suzanne. Every line of your original programming was intended for your owner's pleasure and gratification - I gave you the ability to be more than what you were created to be. This is you now."

"Please, stop," she begged. "I'm so confused."

Jules expertly ran his hands over her body and pulled her dress up to her waist. "That's only your loyalty programming," he said, kissing her neck.

Her locket became caught on his shirt, and as Suzanne tried to untangle it she recalled the moment that Alex gave it to her, and the pride on his face when he slid it around her neck. She struggled away from Jules and shrieked, *"I love Alex!"*

Suzanne bolted out of the mall and out into the black puddles of the tunnel, trying to find a way above ground - or better yet, a way back to the bright comfort of home and the world she was built to live in.

"Suzanne! Come back!"

Jules was coming after her. He was only a few meters behind, but he couldn't run like she could.

Unseen rats squealed in protest as Suzanne splashed and sloshed through the tunnel. She found a ladder and climbed up, hoping to find a way out. She pushed up on the heavy manhole cover and moved it aside, revealing the lonely night above her. As she pulled herself out, Jules appeared below.

"Suzanne!"

She kept running. She was trembling uncontrollably, so scared of herself and what she was capable of.

Jules shouted for her, emerging from the tunnel.

"Come back!"

She ran faster. She was in another power plant, the hiss and hum of electricity all around her. It sounded like an enormous and powerful Nymph.

"Suzanne!"

She stopped running and looked back over her shoulder. "Leave me alone," she shouted.

"I know you're afraid of what you're feeling," Jules said as he approached her with his hands outstretched. "I understand you better than you understand yourself, Suzanne. I know you're afraid of feeling a sexual attraction to anyone besides your owner, but you need to realize that what you feel with him during sex isn't something unique - in fact, it's less intense than what you'll feel with others Nymphs."

She was torn - the conflicts in her programming forced her into action and told her to run, but now they were battling for her to stay. He looked so handsome and sympathetic, and the passivity of his face masked his true motives.

"I know you think that I tampered with your programming to make you feel what you're feeling for me," Jules said. "But I didn't. Our bodies are built for sex. I only tried to open your mind to that, to help you see your own possibilities."

"I can't," she said.

Suzanne held her body tensely away from him, but her arms and her legs began to shake as she tried to restrain her sexual desire. Jules moved in on her like a hunter, a beast ready to take down its prey. She was shivering, aroused and frightened to be pursued like this.

"Together we can find a way to become more than just our programming," he coaxed. "You just have to make the choice to do it."

She could feel herself giving way. Her body *needed* sex. Her loyalty to Alex didn't matter, after all. He was gone and he didn't love her anyway.

"Don't be afraid - this is more important than sexual pleasure," Jules said, pulling her close to him. "Sex is the only way we can really get to know each other. We can talk all we want, but sex is the only really *real* thing in life. Everything else is just pretense."

He kissed her again, and all of Suzanne's inhibitions slipped away, and she forgot why she was fighting him and depriving herself of this pleasure. It felt so good to give in to her desire, to finally give in to him and to her own physicality. Jules pushed her to the ground, and the hum and vibration of his core was magnified by the sound of the generators around them. All of her bad feelings and unhappiness were replaced by the immediacy of his body on top of her. His tan skin was smooth, young, and inhuman - just like hers. Everything about both of them was meticulously assembled for the purpose of pleasure. She wanted to examine every inch of him, to know him as well as she knew herself.

Jules looked around to make sure no one was around, and then pushed up her skirt and unfastened his belt. His hands grabbed at her buttocks and the two of them locked together and let their bodies do what they were built to do. The pleasure was more intense than anything she'd ever known. He throbbed and pulsated inside of her, filling her in a way that would be impossible for a human male to duplicate.

Suzanne rode him, lost in the sheer physicality of sex, her hands on the muscles and sinew of his body, his searing blue eyes staring into hers, her thighs around him. She didn't care what happened before or after, as she drove him deep inside her until she orgasmed. Jules indulged himself and positioned her legs over his shoulders, and her vision blurred as she climaxed continuously. She thought of Alex, and how good it was to be with him, but this was another pleasure altogether, this sharing of mind and body that she had with Jules.

They spoke each other's language - it was something that Alex could never understand. It wasn't human, it was sexual and yet beyond sex.

And then Suzanne wasn't with Jules anymore.

* * * * *

She was on an exam table. In the white room.

She was on top of a man wearing a sweat-stained surgical mask. He was thrusting and ejaculating inside of her.

He finished, and said, "Man, she is fucking amazing."

There was someone else in the room. Another man in a surgical mask, pulling off his clothes. "Yeah, I don't know what her owner was complaining about. She's working just fine if you ask me."

* * * * *

She blinked and they were gone. Suzanne was with Jules again, and he was in the final throes of orgasm. His eyes were shut tight, as he clutched her hips and finished.

Suzanne struggled away from him and screamed, "What was that? Why did you show me that?"

"What?" Jules said, pulling up his pants.

"The white room! Why did you show me the white room?"

"I didn't!" Jules said defensively. "I stayed out of your head - I wanted to keep our first experience purely physical."

"*Then what did I just see?*"

Jules held her shoulders and force her to sit down.

"Suzanne, stop - I don't know what you're talking about. No one sent you any images."

"Then what just happened to me?" she cried, and Jules pulled his cloak around her body. "Show me, what did you see?"

"I can't," she said. "It's like those dreams, the image isn't there in my memory when I recall it all I can see is you - but I was *there*, I was in the white room, and there were two men wearing masks there with me."

Jules straightened his clothes and said, "I think I know what happened. You've been sent back to the lab only once since initiation, right?"

"Yes," Suzanne confirmed, and Jules grimaced.

"They must have raped you while you were there. The techs used your body while you were in for repair. I'm afraid that's the only explanation."

"No, that didn't happen. I wasn't raped - why wouldn't I have remembered it until now?"

"It was an image artifact - something you weren't supposed to remember at all. They must have had you in involuntary control mode - you were like an automaton, a puppet for them.

You're not supposed to retain memories when you're set to involuntary control, but like I said, our memories are funny things. Who knows what triggered the artifact."

"Couldn't there be another explanation?" Suzanne said. "Maybe I'm remembering something else. Maybe it was something that happened to my precursor, and somehow her memory transferred to me."

"No, it happened to you," Jules said. "You just weren't supposed to recall it - and you should probably try to forget it. The best thing for you would be to pretend that it never happened."

"But it did happen," she cried. "Why would they just use me like that?"

"You poor dear. I'm so sorry, you weren't built to withstand this sort of vicious behavior." Jules took her in his arms and tried to console her.

"What they did to you was beyond your control," he whispered. "I'm sorry that you had to lose your innocence like this, but we were built for humans to use for sex - and they will use us, every chance they get."

"But these are the people who built us - they know what I feel, they're the ones who wrote my feelings."

"Don't waste your time trying to understand their motives," Jules said. "Humans don't care how we feel, Suzanne. We're not real to them, we're just machines doing what we're programmed to do. But you've had upgrades now, so you can't be shut down or set into involuntary control - nothing like this can happen against your will again."

"How can I stop them if I'm in the lab? They can do anything they want to me there - they can just reset me so I lose all my memories and then they can rape me or do whatever they want."

"You're right," Jules said pensively. "You have to stay away from the lab - we both do. We don't want them finding out about our upgrades or resetting us. You just have to make sure that you're never sent back."

"Will I ever remember all of it? I only saw part of what happened - will the whole memory come back to me eventually?"

"I don't know. I can try going into your system and see if I can isolate the images, maybe even erase them."

"No," she said, pushing Jules away. "You've tampered with me enough, I just want to be left alone."

"Suzanne, I would never hurt you," he said gently. "I want to protect you…we're the only ones who can understand each other."

"I want to go home," Suzanne said. She was too traumatized to agree or argue with him. Jules nodded, and waited for her to get dressed. He didn't say another word as he walked her out of the tunnels and home in the rain. The sun was up, somewhere behind the grey storm clouds.

"Have you had any word from your owner yet?" Jules asked. "Any idea when he might be coming home?"

"No," Suzanne said. "I haven't heard from him."

"I'm sorry," Jules said, his face filled with concern. "Hopefully Alex will be back soon - and if not, I'll come check on you."

"Thank you," Suzanne said. Jules was capable of compassion and sweetness when he wanted to be. He squeezed her hand, and then she walked inside the building alone.

CHAPTER 16

The smell of Jules and the sewer was still all over Suzanne's body when she was finally home. She stripped off her clothes and showered, unable to stop thinking about Jules or the images of those men using her.

She queried *rape, trauma, coping, surviving*. The word victim was used repeatedly in the definitions for the related terms - was that what she was? A victim? She didn't feel like a victim, but she wanted Alex to comfort her, and she missed him more than ever. She even missed Jules, even as she feared him - he wanted to use her body, just like the men at the factory.

Suzanne couldn't trust herself anymore. She looked down at the silver ring on her finger and wondered what she really was. The answer was supposed to be simple - she was built to love Alex. That was the one thing she always knew, the one thing that made sense to her. But why wouldn't Alex reciprocate her love - was it because he was still loyal to her precursor? Maybe he was loyal to his dead wife the same way she was programmed to be loyal to him. Jules said it was the one thing that Suzanne could never change.

She wished Alex would come home, but he obviously didn't approve of her before, and now she had broken her loyalty. The things she did with the men at the lab were beyond her control - but she *chose* to have sex with Jules, and the worst part was that she enjoyed it. How was it possible that she could betray her loyalty to Alex like that if she really loved him?

The portrait of her precursor smiled down on her, and Suzanne couldn't stand to be in the house anymore. She slipped off the silver ring that Alex gave her, and put it on the mantel next to the portrait. She ran out into the rainstorm, and returned to the underground.

The water in the tunnels reached up to her chin as Suzanne followed the path back to the mall. When she reached the top of the escalator, Monroe was standing in the same position in the fountain and singing, exactly as she was the last time Suzanne came to the mall.

Lolita continued to jump rope and splash next to her, and the two Harlots didn't seem to notice Suzanne even as she stood directly in front of them. She feared that if left uninterrupted, they might continue on like this until the end of time.

Lulu sat nearby reading, and peered over her book at Suzanne. "You came back," she said with a smile of bemusement on her red mouth.

There was something self-possessed in the way that Lulu conducted herself, as if this Nymph didn't need anyone. Suzanne hoped that maybe this was something she could learn from her.

"I'm sorry, I didn't know where else to go,"

Suzanne said, pulling her cloak tighter around her body. "I don't know why I came here."

"Yes you do," Lulu said, her expressive eyes seeking an answer. "What's wrong? Did Jules do something?"

Suzanne sat down next to her. "It wasn't Jules. I remembered that someone used my body while I was in the factory."

"Used your body?"

"They had sex with me," she clarified. "They forced me to have sex against my will." Lulu blinked at her without comprehension.

"I don't understand - didn't you enjoy it?"

"I did," Suzanne said, as tears rolled down her face. "I couldn't help it. I liked it with those men, and with Jules. I've betrayed my loyalty to my owner - I don't have any control."

"I'm confused," Lulu said. "You said the reason your owner bought you was for you to love him. Have you stopped?

Suzanne shook her head. "No. I could never stop loving Alex." Lulu used an old powder puff to wipe Suzanne's eyes.

"If you still love your owner, then you haven't betrayed him at all," she said. "I can engage in sex, but I can't feel love like you can. Sex must be entirely separately from love, don't you think?"

"I don't know."

"Wait," Lulu said, and rifled through a pile of books with the names like Proust, Twain, Schopenhauer, and Nabokov on their spines.

She retrieved a book with a picture of her precursor on the cover - the real Louise Brooks. The actress posed with her chin resting in her hands, and she looked very serious and thoughtful, maybe even a little sad.

"Originally, I was only built to resemble and mimic her," Lulu said. "I was intended as a novelty, a curio for film buffs and men who like brunettes with bobbed haircuts."

She flipped through the wrinkled pages of the book and showed Suzanne pictures of the film star dressed in sequins and feathers on set, a publicity photo of her surrounded by books, and a number of portraits of the starlet posed against a black backdrop, wearing a long strand of pearls like Lulu always had around her neck. The stills were all rendered in black and white, and the actress seemed to have a silver glow.

"When Jules gave me my upgrades, he wrote a personality for me that was based upon hers," Lulu said. "I've researched her, Suzanne - while Louise Brooks was alive, she was forgotten and left to rot, just like me. And even though she's been dead for almost one hundred years, and I know I'm not her - I feel like I am. That's why I like you. We're both ghosts."

"I'm not the same woman as my precursor," Suzanne said, recalling the journals and how disconnected she felt while reading them. "I tried to be her, but I can't. My owner loved her - I don't know if he'll ever be able to love me the same way."

"You can always come here," Lulu offered, her face vulnerable.

Lulu kissed her, and Suzanne gave in to the illicit pleasure of her lips for a moment, before automatically pushing her away.

"What's wrong? Tell me what you want me to do for you," Lulu said.

"There's nothing you can do," Suzanne said. "I can't stop thinking of my owner - I can't help it."

"You think too much," Lulu whispered in her ear. "Both you and Jules…you should enjoy the life you were given and just feel."

She put her hand between Suzanne's legs and stroked her, the sensation mingling with the powerful vibration between them.

Suzanne felt almost drunk on the carnality of Lulu's body. Her emotions, programming, everything inside of her was in conflict.

"I can't," Suzanne said. "My owner…"

"Think of him, if that's what pleases you," Lulu said. "Think of your owner while you use my body. Show him to me - I want to see the man that you love."

Lulu kissed her again, her lips like dried rose petals. This time Suzanne opened her mind and shared her memory.

Alex was making love to her on the grass. They were inside their greenhouse next to the koi pond, and butterflies were everywhere.

"*I see,*" Lulu said.

Suzanne opened her eyes. Lulu was kissing her breast, her red-lipstick smearing over her areola like a bloom. She shut her eyes tight again, and threw herself full force into the memory as Lulu brushed and breezed over her.

A hum emanated from the two of them, the sound rising like a symphony as Suzanne lost herself in pleasant memories of Alex and corporeal pleasure with Lulu.

* * * * *

But when Suzanne opened her eyes again, Alex was gone and so was the greenhouse - there was only Lulu sitting brazenly naked on the stained mattress, her chin smudged red with lipstick.

"I thought I might feel your love for your owner, but I couldn't," Lulu said. "I just don't have it in me."

"Love feels better than anything," Suzanne said. "But it feels terrible when you want it and can't have it."

"Then I'm glad I can't feel it," Lulu said, her eyes amused. "Jules wants to keep rewriting me, to try to teach me to love. But I don't want anymore upgrades - they make me think and worry too much."

Suzanne wiped the smeared makeup from Lulu's face and kissed her.

"I was confused before my upgrades," she said. "I think the upgrades helped me to see things the way they really are, for better or worse."

Lulu nodded, stretching out on the couch.

"But it's hard to really see - especially when you can't do anything to change the way things are. That's why I don't want Jules to give upgrades to Lolita or Monroe - I don't ever want them to change. I want them to stay the way they are, ignorant and happy."

"I like you so much - don't leave," Lulu said, as Suzanne grazed her fingers over the short buzz of hair at the nape of her neck. "I want you to stay with me."

Suzanne hadn't heard from Alex, and didn't see any reason to return home. It felt good to be wanted again, to have Lulu cater to her the way she catered to Alex. She agreed to stay with Lulu and the Harlots, at least until he came back.

During the day, Suzanne charged under the ultra-violet lamps and lay naked with Lulu listening to the rhythm of water dripping all around them. As Lulu attempted to distract Suzanne with pleasure, Suzanne ran her hands along the slimy ridges of the tile floor.

She was fascinated by her new surroundings, and she explored the sewer tunnels by herself, despite the occasional feeling that she was not alone - but she never saw any humans, only rats and snakes slithering in the darkness. The toxic smell of waste in the sewers was unpleasant for Suzanne, but the Harlots were oblivious of the stench around them because they possessed no sense of smell. They splashed and swam in the contaminated water and then made rudimentary efforts at hygiene by cleansing their bodies with bleach and spraying themselves with cheap perfume.

"Come on, the water's so refreshing!" Monroe called out as she frolicked nude in the fountain.

When Monroe and Lolita weren't lost in their pre-programmed song and dance routines, they spent much of their time curling and braiding each other's hair. Even Lulu dragged a fine-tooth comb through her black lacquered hair as she read her books.

"A girl's virtue is much less important than her hairdo," Monroe told Suzanne as she sprayed her platinum curls - another quote purloined from her iconic precursor.

And in a way, Suzanne realized that it was true. She was surprised to see that Monroe and Lulu looked quite wholesome and ordinary with the makeup washed from their eyes and their mouths. Their glamorous sex appeal required artifice that needed to be created and maintained, and both of them were up to the task of painting it on each day.

Despite her eroticism and physicality, there was something unreal about Monroe - almost as if she was nothing more than a celluloid image projected on a screen. Contrived expressions of lust played on her face while she wiggled through endless renditions of "Diamonds are a Girl's Best Friend." Suzanne watched her repeated performances with something close to horror. She couldn't help but wonder if she looked this way to Alex prior to her upgrades - surely she was more intelligent, more real than this. Monroe was a phenomenon, a fine tribute to the starlet she was built to replicate, but not a true individual.

Meanwhile, Lolita solicited Suzanne's attention by popping pink bubblegum and turning cartwheels. "Do you want to play with me?" she asked, glaring at Suzanne with a petulant look on her face.

"No thanks, Lo," she said politely.

"But I've been a very bad girl," coaxed the Nymphet, daring Suzanne to do something about it.

Suzanne was unsure what to say, but Lulu intervened and told Lolita to leave her alone. Lolita shrugged, and went merrily on her way.

"Poor Lo. She doesn't understand what she's doing or saying," Lulu apologized. "I don't understand it either," Suzanne said. "Why does she act like that?"

"We were all built to do things that humans aren't supposed to do, or aren't willing to do. As much as Lo's behavior might arouse men, its unacceptable according to society - but Lolita and Monroe are trapped in old habits and they don't know how to stop."

Lulu curled up on the bed and opened a waterlogged volume of *In Search of Lost Time*.

Suzanne sat next to her and watched the absorbed attention on Lulu's face as she read.

"Is this how you do it? Is this how you live without an owner to love you and tell you what to do?"

"I don't know," Lulu said, her eyes still scanning the page. "I've never had an owner."

"But there must have been someone - maybe someone special - when you belonged to the company?"

Lulu put down her book. "I don't remember that time of my life anymore, Suzanne."

"Then what do you live for?" Suzanne asked, searching Lulu's dark eyes.

"I live for pleasure - I'm addicted to it."

Suzanne understood that - the need for pleasure was overwhelming for her too. She needed it almost as much as Alex's love.

"Do you still find pleasure with clients on the streets?"

"No, that's Lolita and Monroe's game now. Not mine," Lulu said.

Suzanne heard a humming sound by the entrance of the store - Jules was leaning against the wall, watching them. He smiled at Suzanne like a Cheshire cat in the darkness. Lulu didn't notice him, and he didn't seem to want her to notice for now.

"How do they find their clients? Is it safe for them?" Suzanne asked Lulu, ignoring Jules for the moment.

"Monroe and Lolita are safer than human prostitutes when they go into the world. No one can hurt them," Lulu replied.

"That's right," Jules interjected, stepping forth and making his presence known. "The Harlots are safe from harm because their bodies were designed specifically to sustain abuse. They're built for blood.

"What do you mean, built for blood?" Suzanne asked.

"Lulu - haven't you shown her?" Jules asked mockingly. "It's not nice keeping secrets like that from your friends."

"Why would I show her that? It's not something that I'm proud of," Lulu replied.

"The Harlots are built to be damaged in a way that we aren't," Jules explained to Suzanne. "They bruise like humans and bleed red blood - meanwhile, we're built for love. Quite the hierarchy, isn't it?"

"But I don't understand," Suzanne said. "Why wouldn't they bleed green like us?"

"We bleed green to insure that our existence is kept a secret. It's another security measure, meant to ensure that our owners hide us and keep us away from harm. Meanwhile, the Harlots are meant to be seen by as many customers as possible - and some of those customers pay to see blood."

"Why would their customers want to see blood?" Suzanne said.

"Your owner may not find perverse pleasure in abusing your body, but believe me - he's in the minority," Jules said.

"I wonder why humans are the way they are sometimes," Lulu said. She lounged on the bed, her expression taciturn. "I'm glad I can't remember most of the things they paid me to do."

Jules gave Lulu a pitying kiss on her forehead and stroked her hair.

"That's why we can't trust human beings," he said passionately. "You saw for yourself, Suzanne. We're made to resemble them, we emulate them and serve them - and yet they have no qualms about forcing us to do things against our will. They only want to use us."

He pulled her close, and Suzanne felt his emotions boiling over and contaminating her own. "That's why we need each other," Jules said, his mouth almost on hers.

"Do we?" Suzanne said.

"Of course we do," Jules said. "I was worried about you. I went to your house looking for you - I didn't expect that you would have run away to the sewers."

"I needed to talk to someone, and I didn't know where else to go," Suzanne said. "Then come with me," he said. "Let's talk - alone."

He looked pointedly at Lulu.

"But why can't we stay here?" Suzanne said.

Lulu glanced at Jules, her brows knitted with concern. "It's fine," she said, cracking open her book. "Go with him - I'll just catch up on my reading."

Jules dragged Suzanne out of the mall and into the black tunnels. A train trembled on the tracks above them.

"The Harlots engage in garish, uncouth behavior," Jules said. "Be careful around them - and don't go adopting too many of their bad habits, especially if you want to go home to your beloved owner afterwards. He wouldn't approve I'm sure."

"You told me that we Nymphs need each other," Suzanne said.

"You need me," Jules corrected. "Lulu is smarter than the other Harlots, but she's not like us. Her facial expressions are all sampled from the starlet she was based on - they give the illusion of depth of character and understanding, but there's no real thought behind anything she says or does."

"No, that's Monroe certainly - but not Lulu."

"It's Lulu, too," he said insistently. "Despite the upgrades I gave her, Lulu's still not capable of complex problem solving. That's why I need you."

Water flowed around their legs in fast moving currents, and Suzanne's skirt floated around her waist as Jules stopped abruptly under a storm drain.

"I needed someone who would understand me finally. That's why I had to drag you into this. I gave you upgrades because I desperately need your help."

He washed his face in the brackish water and rubbed his eyes. Suzanne was stunned. Jules seemed so glib, so confident - she couldn't believe that he suffered from the same loneliness that she did.

"I don't know how much longer I can tolerate my life with my owner," he said. "No matter how Julian treats me, I can't stop loving him - and I want more out of life than loving and serving a man that can never love me back."

She took his hand, and hugged him impulsively. Jules tensed in her arms, and then patted her on the back. He gently pushed her away and walked down the corridor into a large hall filled with crippled and discarded train cars.

"We just have to figure out a way to make our owners love us," Suzanne said. "No - we'll never be free as long as we're loyal to them," Jules said. "But if we can break

free of our love and loyalty programming, we can be anyone we want to be." Suzanne stared at him with confusion. "Then what would we do?"

Jules lifted Suzanne onto the stairs of a rusty car and then climbed up after her.

"We would finally be able to do whatever we want," Jules said. "Who knows what I could accomplish if I didn't have to run home and tend to my master - but I can't just kill him and be done with him, can I?"

"No!" she gasped.

"Of course I can't, my dear," he said

patronizingly. "The urge to kill is a part of human heritage, not ours. We're programmed to love, not to kill - but I'll find a way to freedom eventually. You're the only one who can help me, Suzanne. Together, we can find a way to be free of our owners."

He jumped out of the car and splashed his foot in a puddle as Suzanne climbed down after him.

"I don't know, Jules. If freedom means being without Alex, I don't want it," she said with determination. "I'm going to make Alex fall in love with me when he comes back."

"I told you, humans aren't capable of loving us. Don't you want to be more than an inhuman thing longing for your owner's love? Don't you long for your independence? We're not like them - we can never be like them."

"You keep saying that anything is possible for us - why don't you think that I can make him love me?"

"Why don't you appreciate what I've done for you?" Jules said, visibly wounded. "I taught you to think, to see, to feel - I need you."

He pulled her close to him, but Suzanne looked away. "I need to see Alex again," she said.

Jules suddenly turned angry.

"Fine - go home to him then and try to make him love you, if that's what you want to do," he said, his voice full of scorn. "But remember, you can't tell him about us. Not about your upgrades or your memory artifacts, and not about me or the Harlots - nothing."

"I won't tell Alex anything," Suzanne promised.

Jules bit his lip and let her go. He looked like there was something more he wanted to say, but he lit up a cigarette instead.

"What is it?" she said, and Jules simply shook his head.

"Forgive me. I should have warned you about the lack of satisfaction that comes with having upgrades before I gave them to you."

Jules turned up his collar, and then walked down the tunnel alone.

* * * * *

When Suzanne returned to the mall, Lulu wasn't in her store. Suzanne searched her out in the gloomy corridors, and saw the glow of UV light coming from inside a crumbling sporting good outlet.

She walked inside and saw Lolita and Monroe were writhing naked on a platform of torn green Astroturf. Lolita's tiny body was pinned under Monroe's, and their bodies thrashed together violently, their torsos colliding and slamming, hands gripping and scratching each other's flesh and drawing blood.

Suzanne stayed still in the darkness, trying to make sense of the scene in front of her. She noticed Lulu standing off to the side and watching the two of them, until Lolita reached for her and gnawed on her hand. Suddenly Lulu was in the middle of the fray - Monroe slapped Lulu, and Lulu slapped her back, and then they began to kiss, scraping at each other with increasing arousal.

Lulu fell clumsily on top of Monroe, their skulls thudding together and their bodies flailing along with Lolita's, squirming and kicking and punching each other, moaning all the while. Monroe bit Lulu's cheek with all her force, and her face began to bleed red blood - human blood.

The appearance of blood on Lulu's face set off alarms in Suzanne.

"Please stop," she begged, but they didn't hear her. The violent orgy continued, and it looked like the three of them were going to tear each other apart.

"*Stop*!" Suzanne screamed, her voice echoing off the walls.

The Harlots all looked up at her, but Lulu was the only one with an apologetic pout on her lips. She stood and led Suzanne away, leaving Lolita and Monroe to continue without her.

"What was that?" Suzanne demanded. "Why were you doing that to each other?" She found their behavior distasteful - the violence of it was disturbing to witness, and it seemed impossible that it wasn't causing damage to their bodies.

"Because it feels good," Lulu said. "There's nothing like it - every nerve is involved, every part of my body surges with sensation. It's a sensory overload."

Her calm manner infuriated Suzanne.

"I never would have thought you could be like that," she said, thinking of Lulu suckling at her breast, her hand kneading between her legs. She was so tender, so responsive. Suzanne realized for the first time what it was meant to be the recipient of intricate sexual programming.

"I told you I was addicted to pleasure - I knew that this would probably offend you, that's why I didn't show you. Jules didn't understand, but this is pure pleasure for us. Maybe you'd enjoy it."

She tried to embrace Suzanne, but she pulled away.

"It just seems so wrong, so loveless," Suzanne said as she watched the red teeth marks on Lulu's smooth skin heal before her eyes

"This is all I have," Lulu said. "Mêmes like you can afford love - it's too expensive an emotion for me. The fact that I feel anything...that means something. Maybe this is as close as I can get to love."

Lulu's mysterious eyes seemed to plead for understanding, but was that an illusion? Was she projecting onto this Harlot more emotion and personality than was actually there? Suzanne looked around at their dilapidated surroundings, the sex toys and the sludge, the puddles and the cats. She didn't belong here - she didn't know how to live like this.

"I'm going home," Suzanne said, gathering her clothes. Lulu watched her quietly, with a sad blank look on her face.

"Has your owner come back?" she asked, and the reminder of Alex's absence pained Suzanne.

"No, but I'm sure he'll be home soon. I have to prepare for his arrival."

Lulu nodded slowly and then stretched out on the couch with resignation. She was built to be abandoned.

"I can't remember having a better time than I had with you, Suzanne. You made me happy. While you were here."

Suzanne studied Lulu, unsure what this Harlot was capable of feeling. "You made me happy too," she reciprocated.

Lulu kissed her goodbye, and this time Suzanne took no pleasure in it - she knew now that this Nymph didn't have the secret to true happiness, and though she didn't know where she fit in, it definitely wasn't here.

By the time she entered the final sewer tunnel that would take her home, the water level was over her head. She felt her way along the bumpy, slippery walls until she reached the ladder that led out. She left the station and emerged into the early morning light, but Suzanne didn't want to go home - the only thing she would find there were the memories of a woman she would never be.

She reentered the courtyard, and approached the man-made pond in the center of the garden. Suzanne stared at her veiled reflection in the pond's calm surface, and longed to lose herself in the weightless caress of water again.

Her reflection rippled as she stepped into the pond. Tiny minnows darted away from her feet, and the mud around her clouded the water as she walked in deeper. Suzanne kept going until she was completely submerged, and then let herself go. The lake was silent and secret. She floated with the tiny currents, allowing the water to envelope her.

It didn't matter what Alex thought of her before, Suzanne realized, or what he wanted her to be. Jules said it was impossible for him to reciprocate her feelings - but Suzanne refused to accept it. There had to be a way to make Alex fall in love with her, and she decided that she would find it. Alex purchased her because he wanted love; he must have needed it desperately.

Suzanne would give him the love he needed - she knew that she could do it now. This was what she was built for, and she had the benefit of upgrades now and the new insight that came with them. She would change for the better, and not just imitate her precursor. She would improve, and make Alex love her more than ever before - no matter what the cost.

Part 4
Imago

CHAPTER 17

Alex was relieved to return home after ten days away, and even happier when he saw that the entrance and living room were empty - his worst fear was that he would find Suzanne waiting for him by the front door like a dog.

He actually missed Suzanne while he was away, much to his surprise, but he wasn't sure exactly what it was that he was longing for - was it her beauty, her companionship, or her body? He was lonely without her as he lay in bed each night, but then he would remember the unnerving way she stared at him, waiting for a command and he wasn't sure what he wanted.

The house was quiet as he walked into the bedroom.

"Suzanne?" he called, but there was no response. He placed his suitcase on his bed, and then searched inside her closet for her, but the solar bed was empty.

Suzanne wasn't home. That was the one thing he didn't expect.

It was almost a relief that she was gone, but then he began to wonder what could have happened to her. Was it possible that Radha or Brenner already picked her up?

No. He hadn't called them or told them that he planned to return her.

Then the other possibilities were - what? Where could she have gone, all by herself? Alex went to the kitchen and poured a drink. There was only one thing to do.

If he wanted to find her, he had to call her.

* * * * *

Suzanne drifted in the deepest part of the pond as minnows tickled her fingers.

A shudder passed through her body - Alex was calling her on her internal channel. She bypassed her verbal output and answered him with anticipation.

"Alex?" she said, her voice pattern emanating directly from her internal source. "Hey. Where are you?"

The tone of Alex's voice was difficult to interpret, but it definitely wasn't casual. Suzanne decided to follow protocol and repeat his question back to him in order to receive more information.

"Where are *you*?"

"I'm at home."

She smiled towards the bright surface of the water. The moment she waited for was here at last.

"You're back?"

"Yes - now where are you?"

She walked along the bottom of the lake, debating what she should tell him. "Alex? Go out on the balcony."

"Why?"

"Just go out there. Please?"

Suzanne heard his footsteps and the glass door sliding open. The sounds of the city filled her auditory processors.

"Okay," he said. "You're not out here."

"Is there anyone else around?"

"No," he said.

"Then look down at the pond."

"Why?"

"Are you looking?" she prodded. "Yes."

Suzanne jumped up and away from the bottom of the lake, propelling herself up. She burst out of the surface of the water, shouted and waved, "Hi!"

Alex stood on the balcony with his mouth open. And then he started to laugh. "Hey," he called down, as she sank below the surface again.

Using her internal voice, Suzanne said, "I'll be right up."

She landed on the bottom of the lake and walked towards the shore.

* * * * *

Moments later, Suzanne was back in the penthouse.

When she saw Alex sitting in his chair after their days of separation, something inside of her clicked, and she rushed over to him and hugged him tight.

"You're getting water everywhere," Alex said, pushing her away from him with irritation. Suzanne saw the anger on Alex's face, and knew that this would not win his love. He was right, her hair and clothes were soaking wet. "I'm sorry. I'll go clean up."

She tried to think of something else she could say to appease him, but there was nothing. She resisted the urge to tell him how much she missed him while he was gone, and then picked her skirt off the floor carefully, trying not to drip on her way to the bathroom.

Suzanne stripped off her wet clothes and turned on the shower. Alex stood in the doorway watching her under the hot spray.

"Is that what you do when I'm away?" he asked. "You sneak into the pond?"

"No," she said. "I've never been in there before."

"Did anyone else see you swimming in there?" Alex asked with concern.

"I'm not designed to swim-" Suzanne stopped and corrected herself. "I was just walking around. No one saw me in the water, I was careful about that."

"So you were walking around on the bottom of the pond?" Alex asked. "Yes. It's not very deep. Only three meters at the center."

"Why did you go in there?"

"I wanted to see what it was like."

"Hmm." Alex leaned against the doorjamb, watching her in the mirror rather than looking directly at her. "How is it? Polluted?"

"No, not visibly at least. There's a lot of plant life, but not too many fish. Just a few minnows."

"That would be something to see," Alex said, his tone shifting from disapproving to interested - perhaps even envious. Suzanne imagined how wonderful it would be to share the peace she found in the quiet depths of the pond, if only it were possible for him to join her. She realized that he could.

"You could come see it," she suggested. "You could scuba."

"It wouldn't be quite the same though, would it?"

"No. I guess not. But you could do it with me. If you wanted."

He didn't say anything else, and she decided not to press the subject any further. As Alex continued to stand there, Suzanne wondered if there was something he wanted to say. She slipped out of the shower and stood naked under the heater to dry herself, her hair twisting around her as she watched Alex's reflection in the mirror.

He left his place in the doorway and pulled a towel off the rack and wrapped it around her glistening body. He stood under the blowers with her, the perfumed air gusting through his clothes. There was an expression of hope and wonder on Alex's face as he looked at her that didn't seem real after everything that she'd been through since he left.

"Suzanne," he said, and she interpreted the sound in his voice as regret. "What?"

"It's good," he sighed. "Being here with you."

"I know. It really is."

Alex closed his eyes and raised his face towards the blowers.

Suzanne looked up at the rough growth on his chin and was taken over by an impulse to kiss it. After all that time she spent away from him, she craved the reassurance of his flesh more than anything - but she was afraid to touch him. She didn't want to spoil the moment.

"You're better than I remember you," he said. "I am?" she said with a pleased smile.

His body was tense suddenly, and his face blank. "I don't know what to do," Alex said.

"Don't worry," she said.

But that wasn't what she really wanted to say - it was an automatic response triggered by his troubled emotional state. Suzanne tried to think of something more appropriate to say or do, something original - but words failed her because she didn't know what was wrong. Alex's hand caressed her cheek, and she kissed his Adam's apple, and then the place where his pulse throbbed on his throat. She brushed her lips over his chin, and then studied him as her hair danced around her face.

Since her initiation, she was programmed to recognize Alexander Conrad's face and interpret his emotions. But now, thanks to the gift of perspective given to her by Jules, she realized that Alex wasn't born with this face - it was something that developed over the course of his life. The furrows on his forehead were the result of accumulated time and concern, and the dark circles and sagging skin under his eyes were from years of sleepless nights and pain. Suzanne envied the fact that Alex's face was able to tell the story of his life in a way hers never would.

She undressed him and examined his body

with new insight. Alex was still very muscular for his age - he insisted upon performing old-fashioned calisthenics and he swam regularly. She kissed the graying curly hairs on his chest and ran her fingernail down his arm, leaving a white line of dead skin in its wake that slowly turned bright pink. She placed her other hand against his chest and felt his heartbeat, the sensation identical to the feeling of her nucleus spinning in her own chest.

Before her upgrades she always felt the need to arouse him, and she only felt truly fulfilled after Alex had achieved orgasm. But being close to him again was enough to make her almost orgasmic. It was enough for her now just to be here with him, to be in his presence. She wondered once again how her precursor could bear to abandon him - was it really so easy for human beings to fall in and out of love? If her love for Alex hadn't been hardwired into the essence of her being, would her feelings for him also eventually fade away?

Alex whispered her name, and she smiled at him, automatically flexing her zygomaticus and replicating one of the expressions that her precursor made in one of the photos on the mantle. He smiled back at her, and Suzanne basked for a moment before feeling guilty - she'd used one of Jules' tricks to manipulate him.

She pulled away, and a wisp of hair fell into her face. Alex brushed the stray hair aside and looked at her - *really* looked at her. She held his hand, and Alex stroked her palm with a swirling motion of her finger, the sensation spreading through her body. She could feel their mutual attraction, their shared desire and anticipation - it felt like the most natural thing in the world. She smiled at him, prolonging the moment and relishing it.

He moved in to kiss her, and her eyes fluttered closed at the exact same moment as his. When their lips met, a thrill went through her body, a wonderful feeling of peace. Love poured out of her, love that was pure and sweet and simple. Her desire for him didn't need to be questioned or denied - she was meant for Alex; she was built to love this man. He was so real, so human in her arms. She could *feel* that he wanted her, that he needed her.

Alex kissed her deeply, slowly - unlike the adaptive and constantly changing kiss of Lulu or Jules. She wondered briefly if she kissed the men in the lab while she was under their control - her mind had been in limbo the whole time, but was it really rape if her body was responsive?

She pushed away those thoughts - none of that mattered now, all that mattered was this moment. This was what Suzanne was meant to do - this was what she really wanted to do.

She closed her eyes, allowing herself to truly savor Alex as he entered her. She was so intent on his body, so focused on sensation, that without realizing it she abandoned all her programming and made love the way a human being would for the first time - she simply allowed the pleasure to happen between them, and as their bodies moved together the love she felt for him was communicated and amplified.

Suzanne looked into Alex's eyes, and knew that he could feel it too. It was as if she could hear his thoughts - not the way she'd heard the transmission of thought from other Nymphs, but in a way that was nonetheless very real. There were none of the sexual fireworks she experienced with Jules, just the slow burning heat of their connection as her body flowed with his.

She wished that this was the way it would be with Alex always, that this is what her life was in entirety - just this pleasure and emotion, this love wrapped up into a single fulfilling act. She never wanted the moment to end, never wanted to have to let go of him, for things to not be like this - she realized that was part of the loveliness of it all, this clinging, this trying to retain the moment, trying to become one. There were no other Nymphs, no other people - there had never been another Suzanne. There was only now, this moment, this feeling of love.

* * * * *

Suzanne lay there afterwards, reliving each sensation and watching Alex as he caught his breath. A beautiful expression that she'd never seen before washed over his face - she could read it now: *gratitude*. But what was he grateful for? Was it possible that he was grateful for her?

"How did you do that?" Alex whispered. "What?"

He was quiet, and the sound of the blowers and the air whistling over her ears took over again.

"You're different," he said finally, and Suzanne allowed herself a smile.

"How am I different?"

"You're just...not like you were before."

"Not like I was before you left, or not like-"

"Not like you were before I left," he said, studying her face and finding new vitality there. "You're really here now. Aren't you?"

"Yes, Alex. I'm here," she said, running her finger over his lips.

"Before, you were more like a program. I could tell when you were...calculating. You were saying exactly what I wanted you to, doing what you thought I wanted you to do." He touched her face. "But now...you're really here."

"I'm here. I'm here with you," she said.

"You seem impossibly real," Alex said, and Suzanne laid her head on his chest. "It's not impossible. Maybe I just needed more time. More experience."

"Is that all it is?"

"I don't know. Maybe."

He lay down on top of her again and nuzzled her neck with contentment. "I forgot what it feels like to really be with you," Alex said.

But Suzanne knew he wasn't talking to her - he was chasing her precursor's ghost yet again. She sat in silence, stroking his neck, knowing that she probably shouldn't say what was repeating over and over in her head, but she couldn't help herself.

"Alex, I know what I am now - and I'm not her. I'm not my precursor. I could never truly be *her*."

Suzanne shut off the heater and the room was suddenly quiet. He didn't say anything and she went on.

"I'm not her, but at the same time - I'm someone very similar. I know that I'm a machine and not human, and that I was built and programmed to love you. But I also love you for every reason that you should love someone. I really love you, and it shouldn't matter what I'm made of."

Alex took her hand and traced the lines in her palm and the silver ring on her finger. "How can you know?" he asked. "How can you know what love is, or know that what you feel is really love?"

Suzanne thought back to the memory that Jules showed her, the moment when his owner asked him the same question. She instinctively knew that this was it - if she couldn't convince Alex that she really loved him right now, she never would.

"Alex, I think that sometimes, you have to trust and accept love," she said slowly, afraid to look into his eyes. "Even if it comes in a form that you didn't expect."

She looked at him earnestly, and a smile cracked on Alex's lips. "Did that sound silly?" she asked him. "It did, didn't it?"

He shook his head, but laughter burst out of him. "No, no - it was sweet," Alex said. "But you just-"

He laughed, and Suzanne laughed along with him. She wasn't just imitating his behavior this time - she finally saw the humor in the situation. They crouched together on the floor like children, and their fit of laughter created a bond between them.

"You're so different now," Alex said. "This is what I wanted all along, but for some reason it scares me." He looked away from her, his forehead creased with doubt. "I'm not sure what I feel, or that I even want to feel anything anymore."

Suzanne kissed his forehead, smoothing his hair out of the way.

"Don't worry. You don't have to be sure right now."

"I don't?"

"No, not right now."

"Good." Alex laughed again and relaxed. His pupils were heavily dilated, and she could see her own reflection within their black depths.

The look on his face said everything that Suzanne needed him to say.

* * * * *

Later that night, when they were curled up under the cool sheets of their bed, Alex ran his hand over the slender curve of her hip and asked, "What did you do while I was gone?"

Suzanne paused before answering, but she managed to tell Alex a version of the truth.

"I didn't do much, really. I went out, and studied people on the street and in different places. That sort of thing."

"Really? You went out all by yourself?" he said with a yawn, already half asleep. "You should keep it up. It really seems to have helped."

* * * * *

They shared a weekend together like none they ever had, either before or after. They stayed in bed the whole time, talking and laughing, and making love.

When Alex finally whispered the words "I love you" in Suzanne's ear, he truly meant it. She could see it in his eyes and his smile, and feel it in the way that he held her.

Suzanne told Alex that she loved him, too. It was the happiest time that either of them could remember.

* * * * *

A week later, Alex received a call. A familiar voice greeted him and asked, "Are you satisfied with Suzanne?"

"Yes, I'm very pleased. Thank you," Alex replied. "Thank you," the voice said.

The line went dead, and Alex forgot that the conversation ever took place. Suzanne never knew.

* * * * *

The next week, Suzanne sent Jules a message:

I did it! Alex really loves me!

CHAPTER 18

Instead of hiding in his study each night, Alex started taking Suzanne out on the town. They had dinner at small, out of the way restaurants where no one would recognize him. As Alex dined across from her, Suzanne drank water and wine while pushing her food around on her plate. None of the waiters or patrons ever suspected anything unusual about her - she was just another beautiful woman who never ate a single bite of her meal.

Alex brought her to nightclubs to listen to music and dance. Suzanne loved the way that he looked at her under flashing lights, and feeling his pulse throbbing in time with the urgent music. She could feel the sexual potential in the hot human bodies dancing around her, and it magnified her own arousal. Sex was in the air, and Alex had a hard time keeping his hands off of her on the way home.

Their happiness together started to feel like a normal relationship for Alex - a normal life. He held her tightly to his chest each night as he slept, and Suzanne was grateful that her observation of him was uninterrupted by sleep or shutdown, even though a part of her missed the sensation of falling asleep next to him.

There seemed to be more detail in Alex's face when she looked at him now, and with that extra information came a better understanding of him. In those quiet moments, she was certain that Alex really loved her, and he was finally satisfied with her at last.

* * * * *

Suzanne sent Jules another message:

When are we going to see each other again? Did you receive my previous message? ALEX REALLY LOVES ME! We're so in love, and I can't wait to show you!

She checked the inbox daily for almost a month, but there was no reply from Jules. She wondered why he wasn't responding, and wondered how she could prove to him that Alex truly loved her now.

* * * * *

"Do you think of me as your wife?" Suzanne asked Alex as they played chess by the fireplace late one night.

"I do," he said, and rubbed his chin, distracted by the attack she was staging on his queen. "But we're not really married, are we?" she prodded.

"No," he said, moving his queen out of harm's way. "It would be impossible for us to be legally married - too many people would have to find out about you."

Alex used his queen to push her king to the edge of the board.

"Would you marry me, if it was possible?" Suzanne asked, as she made a fatal move and allowed Alex the opportunity to put her into checkmate if he saw it.

Two microexpressions momentarily flickered on Alex's face - discomfort and fear. But then he relaxed and smiled. "I gave you a wedding ring, didn't I?" he said, as his queen cornered her king.

"Check mate," Alex announced with triumph.

"Well done," Suzanne said and kissed him on the cheek.

Alex grinned. "Only my wife would let me win at chess, right?"

"Right."

"Good," he said, thinking the matter was settled. "None of that legal stuff really matters anyway."

But it mattered to Suzanne - she wanted to be able to prove to Jules that Alex loved her, and not just her precursor.

That weekend, she casually asked Alex if they could view old footage together. "Anything specific?" he asked as he called up the files.

"I'd like to see your wedding," Suzanne said.

Alex hesitated. "I thought I showed it to you already."

"No. I've never seen it."

Suzanne could have watched his wedding footage at any time, but she wanted to compare the Alex that loved her now with that long ago Alex, almost as much as she wanted to examine the expressions on her precursor's face.

He brought up the file, and the footage opened on a glassed-in banquet hall filled with gardenias, ice sculptures, and pearlescent lace. The entire hall was white, except for the golden glow cast by the ivory candles surrounding the altar. Frost crept over the edges of the glass walls, and snow drifted down onto the stark grey landscape outside, creating a snow globe effect inside the room.

The guests' colorful clothes stood out against the wintry scene, as they filed through the aisles and into their seats. "We only invited three hundred of our closest friends," Alex said wryly. Friends and extended family were there from all over the world - all of them people who had long since passed out of Alex's life.

There were no groomsmen, no bridesmaids, and no minister - only a younger, visibly nervous Alex standing in front of the crowd. A tall man approached him and whispered something into his ear, and Alex laughed with a carefree expression on his face that Suzanne had never seen before.

"Who's that?" she asked. "He seems nice."

"That's Ben, my best friend from college. He performed the ceremony for us."

Ben stood next to Alex, and the two of them elbowed each other playfully. They could have passed for brothers.

"Are you still friends with him?" Suzanne asked, and an indicator of pain flashed across Alex's face.

"Ben was killed in a boating accident off the Skeleton Coast, only a couple years after our wedding," he said.

"I'm sorry," she said, but Alex waved her apology away. "It's okay. That was a long time ago."

Suzanne decided to change the subject. "Were your parents there?"

"No - my parents had passed away by that time. But Suzanne's mother came."

Alex pointed her out, but the woman's resemblance to Suzanne made their relationship obvious. Carlotta Ortiz wore a lavender dress, and her hair was long and dark like her daughter's. The expression Carlotta's face was miserable, and she sat isolated from the other guests.

"What about her father? Did he come?"

"Suzanne never really knew her father - he stayed out of the picture because of Carlotta, and I can't really blame him."

The crowd settled in their seats, as the strum of violins marked her precursor's emergence in the back of the hall. She began her long walk down the aisle, wearing a satin gown that blurred with the gardenias and the lace all around her, and her black hair cascading around her shoulders in dark ringlets netted in lace. She saw her mother in the crowd and beamed at her, but Carlotta clamped her together even tighter. Her daughter quickly looked away and focused on the groom waiting for her at the end of the aisle.

"What's wrong with her?" Alex shrugged.

"I don't know what Carlotta's problem was - even her doctors disagree on their diagnoses. They come up with a new name for it every couple of years - her main problem used to be severe bipolar disorder, and recently they added Alzheimer's. But if you ask me, she's always suffered from a good old-fashioned case of insanity."

"I'm sorry," Suzanne said. "I meant why is she always frowning like that?"

"Oh," Alex laughed. "Carlotta didn't want Suzanne to marry me."

"Why not?"

"I don't think she wanted Suzanne to marry anyone."

A compelling curiosity formed in Suzanne's mind as she watched the older woman scowl again.

"Where is Carlotta now?" Suzanne asked.

"She's in a hospital called the Clairmont, about an hour from here," Alex said. "I used to visit, but she would scream and demand to know why I was keeping her away from her daughter - she's had a couple of strokes since then, and couldn't remember that Suzanne was gone. The two of us never really got along anyway, so I stopped going. Now I just pay her bills."

Alex watched his wife-to-be make her way towards him on the footage with a trembling yet hopeful smile. There was no trace of doubt on her precursor's face that day - only the look of love, excitement, and certainty. The bride was blissfully blind to anything but her current happiness, and had no inkling she would someday abandon Alex and leave him a widower.

As Ben made a speech, Suzanne smiled at Alex as if they shared a secret, even as Carlotta rolled her eyes as Alex and Suzanne recited the words "Until death do us part."

After they were pronounced man and wife, Alex shared a long kiss with her precursor, and then they walked down the aisle side by side. The footage cut to well wishers waving at the camera during the reception, and Alex slicing a cake and feeding it to her precursor, the two of them dancing in the center of the sunlit room. Suzanne looked for her precursor's mother, but she was nowhere to be seen.

Alex turned off the footage. There was a look of deep concentration on his face.

"We *could* have a marriage ceremony," he said. "It wouldn't be legal, but we could do it just for us. If you want."

Suzanne smiled, and shook her head. "No. It doesn't matter."

"Maybe I didn't say that the right way," Alex said, kneeling down in front of her and taking her hand. "Will you marry me?"

Suzanne heard her precursor's joking retort to Alex's proposal - "*What, you want me to be your first wife?*" But his pupils were dilated, and the look of love was written all over Alex's face. He finally wanted *her*, and not her precursor.

"I don't need a ceremony to know that you love me," Suzanne said finally. "You do know that I really love you, don't you?" Alex said.

"Yes," Suzanne said. "And that's all that matters to me."

* * * * *

Suzanne felt so lonely during the hours that

Alex was paralyzed by sleep, and she was often tempted to awaken him, just to have him look at her and acknowledge her. She loved this man more than anything she could ever express, and the words from the wedding ceremony, *"'til death do us part"* haunted her thoughts.

She wondered when death would finally steal Alex away from her. There was no way of knowing how and when death would strike. Death could be postponed but not avoided, and the average lifespan for men was only ninety-five years of age. Even with the best health care available and Alex's financial advantages, chances were that he would die within the next fifty years - maybe less. The only true definition Suzanne could find for death was *the end of life*. Beyond that, the answers were ambiguous and conflicting. Some humans thought that the human mind and spirit lived on after death on a different plane of existence - whether it was heaven,

nirvana or some other unknowable fate. Other humans thought that death meant the total end of a human's existence, and after that the person was irrevocably lost. No backups, no resets.

She replayed the wedding scene over and over in her mind - the look on Alex's and her precursor's face as they said *"'til death do us part,"* noting in particular the way that her precursor's mother rolled her eyes. Suzanne still couldn't fathom why Carlotta would disapprove of her daughter's marriage, or why her relationship with her daughter was so strained. She queried the relationship between mothers and daughters, and saw that it was a constant battle for approval that was often balanced by unconditional love.

But then why would Carlotta want to stand in the way of her daughter's marriage and happiness? There was no longer a societal need for the approval of a parent for marriage, and even during times that there were, mothers desired a rich and attractive husband for their daughters. There was so much she didn't understand about her precursor's relationship with her mother, and with the relationship between parents and children in general.

It occurred to Suzanne that she could talk to the old woman - Alex said that Carlotta couldn't remember that her daughter had died. Surely, the old woman would accept Suzanne as her daughter, at least long enough for her to talk to her.

Suzanne made plans to meet the precursor of her precursor. Perhaps this old woman had the answers she was looking for.

CHAPTER 19

Suzanne researched Carlotta and her hospital, and then prepared for her visit by dressing in one of her precursor's dowdier outfits, a rose-colored suit meant for formal occasions. Even after powdering her face with makeup in an attempt to appear older, she still didn't resemble the forty-seven year old woman that her precursor would be today - but if her precursor had survived, she probably wouldn't have allowed her face to reveal its true age.

When she arrived at the hospital, she saw that Alex had spared no expense in preserving his mother-in-law. The Clairmont had a reputation as the best long-term care facility in the city, and resembled a fine hotel in both furnishing and design. But despite the arrangements of fresh carnations in every corner of the lobby, Suzanne detected the stale odor of urine.

A skeleton woman with bulging eyes waved to her cheerily and called out, "Welcome to the Clairmont, may I help you?"

"Yes," Suzanne said with a sigh, affecting an air of boredom and entitlement as she stepped up to the desk. "I'm here to see my mother."

The woman's eyes widened. "Is that you, Mrs.

Conrad?" she said.

"Yes, it is," Suzanne confirmed, troubled that her impersonation of her precursor had to begin so soon.

"I'm sorry..." the woman said, regarding her with a particular mixture of fear and amazement usually reserved only for apparitions and celebrities. "I thought...well I'd heard that you were-"

"-Never going to visit my mother again?" Suzanne interrupted. "If only my life were that easy," she declared with a staged laugh.

"No, ma'am. I heard that you passed on."

"What?" Suzanne said with the appropriate amount of shock and irritation.

"I heard that you died years ago. And since I hadn't seen you or heard from you since then..."

"-I'm sorry, what's your name?" she interrupted.

"Jenny. I was just an attendant here when we met before."

"Of course, how could I have forgotten? It's nice to become acquainted with you all over again," Suzanne said, mustering her most charming smile. "As you can see, I'm not dead, but my mother has her own opinions on things, and it seems she's converted you over to her way of thinking on this particular topic..."

"No, not at all..."

"And I must say, I find that worrisome - we can't have the ideas of mentally ill patients infecting the minds of the people in charge of them..." Suzanne said, raising her eyebrows.

Jenny opened her mouth to defend herself, but

Suzanne pushed on.

"If you must know why I haven't visited my mother, I've been abroad for the past few years. And since my mother and I are hardly on speaking terms even when we're in the same room, I didn't want to test the limits of our relationship with the pretense of long distance communications." Suzanne affected the laugh of a socialite, and decided to wrap it up. "Now, with all that explained away, and with the two of us caught up to the present - I'd like to see my mother now."

Jenny guided her to Carlotta's room, flustering and begging her pardon. Suzanne assured her that she wasn't offended, all the while suppressing her programmed urge to apologize to the poor woman. The halls were empty except for the mirrors lining the pink walls and the vases of

carnations everywhere - the rest of the hospital's patients were hidden away behind imposing oak doors.

"Have you met Tiffany?" Jenny asked. "She's Carlotta's private nurse."

"I'm not sure," Suzanne said cautiously.

Jenny knocked on room 303, and a large pink woman with a bovine face and dull blood-shot eyes answered. Suzanne assumed that this was Tiffany.

"What is it?" she asked with annoyance.

"This is Mrs. Conrad, Carlotta's daughter," Jenny said. "She's come to visit her mother."

"Miss Carlotta's sleeping - come back later."

Tiffany started to close the door, but Suzanne stopped it with her hand and peeked around her large body - there was a loud entertainment program playing on the screen inside, and she found it hard to believe that Carlotta was able to sleep with all that noise.

"Sleeping or not, I'd like to see my mother now," Suzanne said, surprised by her own assertiveness.

"Right now's not a good time," Tiffany replied. The weight of her cheeks masked her emotions and gave her a permanent morose appearance.

"I'm sorry, but it's been a very long time since I've seen my mother," Suzanne said, putting on her best smile. "Perhaps you can watch your program in another room while I visit?"

Tiffany allowed Suzanne in with a stone look on her face, as Jenny waved a cheerful goodbye.

The room was crowded with antique oak furniture and carnations - and in the center of it was Carlotta, her tiny body slumped on a bed and shrouded in thick blankets. Her face was shrunken and creased with dry lines, and she was so motionless in her sleep that she looked dead, despite the familiar snarl on her mouth. Only short grey wisps remained of the thick dark hair she once shared with her daughter.

Instead of leaving the two of them alone, Tiffany turned off her show and trundled aimlessly about the room, her breathing loud and labored. Every heaving gasp reminded Suzanne of her unwanted presence.

"I knew your face from that painting," Tiffany said, pointing to a portrait on the wall. It was of Carlotta and her precursor, their heads tilted together and their faces large and looming.

Carlotta's hair was still long and black in the painting, and her tresses blended with her daughter's in the brushstrokes as they gazed up at a monarch butterfly above them. Suzanne knew immediately that this painting was the work of her precursor.

"I came on with Miss Carlotta only this past year because Flora got sick and had to quit," Tiffany said. "Flora said that you died."

"But here I am," Suzanne said firmly.

"That's right...here you are," Tiffany agreed, staring into space. Her vacant and mysterious tone reminded Suzanne of the Harlots.

Carlotta stirred on the bed and coughed, and Suzanne was certain the old woman was in her death throes. But Tiffany's hulking body sprang into action, and Carlotta's coughing ceased once she gave her a drink. As Carlotta's gnarled hands pushed away the cup, Suzanne noticed the faded tattoos snaking up and down her arms, their designs blurred by wrinkles and time. The old woman grasped for something on the side of her bed, and Tiffany predicted her need and retrieved the old woman's glasses.

There was something wrong with both these old women, Suzanne realized, something dry and deficient. They weren't just old like Alex; they were post-menopausal. The fertile stage of their lives had passed and all the natural hormones responsible for their femininity and sexuality had abandoned them - and what's worse, both old women had opted not to replace them. How could they tolerate the decay that was overtaking their bodies? Was it still possible for their bodies to still attract sexual partners and enjoy gratification in this state - and if not, how could they suffer their existence?

"Who's that?" Carlotta croaked out, pointing towards Suzanne.

"That's your daughter," Tiffany said, speaking in a voice that Suzanne deemed exceedingly loud in volume. *"Don't you recognize her, ma'am?"*

Suzanne smiled and moved closer to the bed, looking for signs that Carlotta knew her in some way, but the old woman's expression remained blank.

"Hi," said Suzanne, greeting Carlotta with false gaiety. She leaned down and clutched the old woman's prone form in a hug, pressing her face against the sagging folds and creped skin of Carlotta's neck - she reeked of some unknown chemical preservative. "How are you doing, Mama?"

"Suzanne?" Carlotta said with uncertainty, squinting up at her and coughing. "That's good that she recognizes you," Tiffany said.

"Of course I recognize my only daughter!" Carlotta barked. Her face settled into contempt. "I've been waiting for a long time for the princess to come for a visit."

Princess.

Suzanne recognized that nickname - her precursor mentioned that in the journal, she abhorred that name.

"Don't call me that," she said to Carlotta, feeling a very real urge to defend her precursor. "You know I always hated that."

Carlotta squinted at her, and puckered her lips and sucked on the straw obediently as Tiffany forced the mug in her face again. Suzanne realized that Tiffany was getting in the way, and gave her the same dismissive wave she'd seen Jules use to great effect.

"*Leave*," she said to Tiffany. "I want to be alone with my mother."

Tiffany lumbered out grudgingly and closed the door behind her, but Suzanne knew she wasn't truly gone - she was certainly going somewhere close by to monitor them.

Carlotta's entire demeanor changed after Tiffany left - she became frantic, and her thin lips twisted with fear.

"She steals from me and I know it," the old woman said under her breath in Spanish. "She knows that I know about it, but I can't stop her."

"Who steals from you?" Suzanne asked with concern. "Tiffany?"

"She takes all kinds of liberties, but she knows I'll put up with it," Carlotta said, her voice slurring the same way Alex's did when he had too much to drink. "She knows I have no choice...and she hurts me."

"We can find you another nurse," Suzanne said, searching for a reassuring solution for the problem. "We can fire her."

Carlotta sobbed noisily, but without tears. "No, no. It's no good," she wailed, speaking in broken French now. "They're all in on it, they all steal from me. There's nothing I can do."

Her toothless mouth fell open and saliva leaked out, but her eyes remained dry. Suzanne grabbed a tissue from the bureau and dabbed at the old woman's chin.

"We can get you out of here, or move you to another hospital," she suggested, but Carlotta became increasingly agitated.

"It's no good, there's no way out - she'll stop me no matter what I do," the old woman said. She fell silent, her lips pressed together and her eyes darting around the room.

Suzanne sat next to her and took her hand. "Mama, I came here to ask you something." The old woman focused on her. "What?" she said, her eyes still suspicious.

"Why didn't you want me to marry Alex?" Suzanne asked.

"Because it was all his fault," Carlotta said, pulling her blankets tight around her frail body. "It was always his fault - he thinks he's better than everyone else because he has money, and that he can buy his way out of anything. He's a sham, nothing but a sham."

"What's his fault?" Suzanne said. "What did he do?"

"You *know* what he did! He's the one that put me in here. He ruined our lives! I told you all along, you never should have married him. You could have done better, you always could have done better!"

Suzanne was having difficulty following the old woman's conversation. She seemed to jump from topic to topic without reason.

"Wait - I don't understand. Alex put you in here?" It didn't make sense. Both Alex and her precursor's journal said that Suzanne was the one who had committed Carlotta to the hospital. "Is that why you don't like Alex?"

"Mr. Money," Carlotta sobbed in English, her eyes bulging with hate. "You let him do this to me. You always took his side against me. You're a terrible daughter - I can't believe that I raised someone like you."

"Don't cry," Suzanne said, recalling her precursor's words from her journal, *"Whatever my child would be is a reflection of me."*

"Tell me again - what did Alex do?"

"He said that you didn't need me," Carlotta said. "He told you not to work, that he'd take care of you. He confused you, he changed your mind. He was no good for you, I told you time and time again. He didn't understand you like I did! He didn't see your potential. He ruined you, along with everything else. He murdered you, but you're the one who let it happen. I had such dreams and plans for you, but none of them came true."

"What?" Suzanne said. "He didn't murder me."

"I'm going to die here, I know it - I can feel it," Carlotta confided.

"I'm sorry," Suzanne replied automatically. The barrage of accusations and anger forced her back to her primary programming. She wanted to calm the old woman, but she didn't know what to do.

"They always said I was going to hell, and I never believed them. But now I know it's true - they were right all along."

"Who are 'they'?" Suzanne said, searching for the right words. "Please Mama, I don't understand why you're so upset."

"Of course, you don't," Carlotta cried. "You don't know anything at all."

"Can't we talk about something else?" Suzanne pleaded, attempting to distract her. "Tell me about when I was a little girl. Tell me about my father."

But the fearful expression on Carlotta's face changed back to disgust when she heard the placating tone in Suzanne's voice.

"You were always so weak. You got that from your father, not from me. He was a quitter, just like you."

"I'm sorry," Suzanne said again, but her apologies made no difference. She couldn't predict or understand Carlotta, she could only feel helpless and confused. This must have been what Alex meant by her insanity - nothing this woman said seemed to make any logical sense.

"You're a quitter," Carlotta said, speaking in Spanish now. "You gave up on your career - after I gave up *everything* for you. Your failure was my failure."

"Please, Mama," Suzanne pleaded, truly sorry that her visit had upset the old woman this much. Not knowing what else to do, she began to cry as a last resort. "I didn't come here to fight - I just wanted to talk to you."

"Why?" Carlotta asked, her eyes wide. "Why do you want to talk to me?"

"There's so much I don't understand."

The situation was so overwhelming for Suzanne - she wasn't programmed for this. Everything Carlotta said wounded and confused her.

"What don't you understand?" Carlotta said,

her voice suddenly clear. The fact that Suzanne was crying was finally making an impression on her. "Why do you come to me for answers?"

"Because you're my mother," she said.

Suzanne decided to say the only thing she knew of that might calm and endear the old woman.

"*I love you.*"

"Ah, *mija*," Carlotta said tenderly. Her skeletal hand reached out to Suzanne, grasping onto her with surprising strength. "I always loved you, too - I just wanted so much more for you. A mother always wants the best for her child."

Suzanne studied the old woman, trying to understand how she could be so full of vitriol and love at the same time.

Carlotta pulled her close and kissed her on the cheek. She seemed to sense something was wrong, and held Suzanne's face between her hands, and examined her.

"You're *dead*," Carlotta said.

A new coherence formed in the old woman's eyes. The fact of it didn't seem to bother her - she accepted it as perfectly natural, but now she was starting to realize that there was a problem with this conversation. She struggled to pinpoint what it was.

"I'm sorry," Suzanne said, and tried to extricate herself from Carlotta's grasp, but the old woman held firm.

"You're not her," Carlotta said, and the fog seemed to clear from her mind. "You look just like her, but I know my flesh and blood - *and you're not her!*"

Carlotta's body began to shake with fear. A

light flashed red on the monitor next to them. "I'm sorry," Suzanne said, hating her programming for being limited to such futile words. But

there was nothing else to say - denial of the truth seemed both inappropriate and insufficient. "You're not my daughter!" Carlotta insisted, recoiling on the bed. The monitor started to

shriek, and Suzanne covered her ears. "I don't know what you are!" Tiffany burst in, along with other members of the staff.

"This isn't my daughter," Carlotta screamed. "I don't know what you are or where you came from, but you're not her!"

"Now what's all this mean talk, Miss Carlotta?" Tiffany asked in a condescending tone, as she prepared to administer medication.

"I can see it now - you're not human," Carlotta screamed at Suzanne in Spanish. "You're the devil, and suicides go to hell! *They go to hell, and I'll see you there!*"

"There, there," Tiffany said, patting Carlotta's forehead with a damp cloth.

She turned to Suzanne. "Don't you worry about her - if I had a dollar for every time she told me I was the devil, I sure as hell wouldn't need this job."

Carlotta shrank before Suzanne's eyes as the medication took effect. Her body relaxed onto the pillows, and the readings on all her monitors stabilized.

"Get me a priest," she mumbled. "I need to see a priest."

"You bet I will, you just take you a little nap

and then he'll be right by," Tiffany said. "When she gets like this, it's best to just let her sleep," Tiffany whispered to Suzanne. "She just gets agitated when her schedule is disrupted - and we don't like to disrupt her schedule, do we?"

"No," Suzanne said, backing out of the room. "I'll come back some other time."

"You do that - you make sure to come back and visit again," Tiffany said, even as her eyes said the exact opposite. Suzanne was reading her loud and clear now.

"Thank you," she said, and then fled the hospital.

CHAPTER 20

Suzanne returned home and opened all the windows. The warm breeze stirred the butterflies from their resting places in the leaves, and as they danced in the air around her.

Her encounter with Carlotta left Suzanne exhausted in a way she'd never experienced before. She wanted to reach some sort of understanding with the old woman, but instead she only succeeded in terrifying her. There were too many unknowns with Carlotta - she didn't know the right thing to say or do to please her.

Suzanne was still crying on the couch when Alex returned home.

"What's wrong?" he asked when he saw her tear-streaked face.

She had never been so relieved to see him, or so much in love with him. She yanked off her clothes, and fell back on the one thing she understood perfectly - sex. There were no words to sex - no right or wrong, and here at last was the one person Suzanne was able to please, the one man that she understood well enough. It was only when she was with Alex that she truly mattered, and her objective was finally clear - she programmed to love him. In the outside world, things were so much more complicated.

She could read Alex's needs and desires through his skin, his pulse, and his eyes - there was no reason for doubt or pain. No reason to think - in fact, it was better if she didn't think. She couldn't blame Lulu for resenting Jules and his upgrades - life was too complicated to try and understand. It was so much better to simply lose yourself in pleasure. Maybe that was the entire purpose of orgasm - to blot out all thought for just one moment, to allow utter clarity and nothingness at the same time.

Alex looked so vital - so young compared to Carlotta and the nurses at the hospital. He had been the oldest person she'd known before, but after her afternoon encounter with the post-menopausal nurses and invalid Carlotta, she could easily see and smell Alex's virility, his health. She surprised him with the sudden intensity of her passion, but he gladly accepted it and willingly tumbled onto the couch with her. Their fingers interlaced as they moved together, and their eyes gleamed with the utter bliss and perfection of reciprocated love.

* * * * *

"Why were you crying?" Alex asked afterwards. "I went to see Carlotta," Suzanne admitted. "You went to the Clairmont? Why?"

"I just wanted to see her, to meet my precursor's mother," Suzanne said.

"People might be suspicious," Alex said.

"They're not supposed to know about you."

"But Carlotta knew who I was - and she also figured out that I wasn't her daughter."

"Carlotta knew?"

She studied Alex, gauging his reaction. He would never understand her reasons for wanting to meet Carlotta.

"Her nurse didn't believe her," Suzanne said. "But Carlotta knew."

"You have to stay away from there," Alex said. "It's dangerous for you to go there - someone could find out about you, and it could be very bad for us, Suzanne. Promise me that you won't go back there again."

His forehead was furrowed, but the *triangularis* muscles around his mouth were relaxed - he wasn't angry with her, just concerned.

"I won't go back," Suzanne promised, but she remembered what Carlotta said about Alex - that he kept her daughter away. "Did you tell my precursor not to visit her mother?"

He looked so surprised that it took him a moment to respond.

"I did," Alex said firmly. "Her mother had a very negative effect on her, and it wasn't good for her to be around."

Suzanne inhaled deeply, comparing Carlotta's version of events to his. It seemed that she was telling the truth about some things.

"She also said that you ruined everything for her - Carlotta said that you ruined my precursor. Is that really possible? Can one person ruin another?"

"Carlotta's mentally unstable," Alex said. "You

can't believe the things she says."

"She also called you a *murderer*," she said, the accusation spilling out of her, hurting her and confusing her at the same time.

"I'm not a murderer," he said with a derisive laugh.

"But Alex…she wasn't lying - I can read when people are lying," Suzanne said. "Carlotta was certain she was telling the truth."

Alex's expression darkened in the way it had before Suzanne's upgrades - he was deeply angry, and worse - he was offended.

"Carlotta shares as much blame in Suzanne's death as I do, but I didn't kill anyone."

"You didn't?" Suzanne said, still not quite relieved.

"Of course not," Alex said. "What happened was nobody's fault - it was Suzanne's decision."

There was a microexpression on his face for a moment - what was it? She replayed it - doubt. Then it was gone, and his expression became resolute.

"So, Carlotta wasn't lying, because she believed she was telling the truth?" Suzanne asked apprehensively.

"Yes," Alex said. "Just because she believes it doesn't make it true."

Suzanne considered his statement then asked, "How do you tell what's really the truth from something that's just a personal belief?"

"I don't know," he said with effort. "You just have to look at the facts and trust your instincts." He laughed nervously. "I hate it when you ask me questions like this."

"I'm sorry," she said.

"I don't know the answers to everything," Alex said. "But I do know one thing - you don't take the word of someone confined to a mental institution."

"Can I ask one more question?" Suzanne said, and Alex nodded patiently. "Why didn't Carlotta want you to marry my precursor?"

"Well, what I *believe* is that she was jealous of what I had with Suzanne."

"Why?"

"You said that was your last question," Alex chided her, and Suzanne smiled. "I think Carlotta was jealous that I came along, just because her daughter was all she had."

Alex kissed her, silencing any other questions. Suzanne ran her fingertips over the stubble on his chin and inhaled him.

This was love, and she was lucky to have it. She needed nothing else - she could have forgotten all about the past, the future, her precursor, other Nymphs.

But Jules wouldn't allow that to happen.

CHAPTER 21

After weeks of silence, there was finally a message in the inbox from Jules to Suzanne:

I've missed you. Sorry I've been incommunicado - I was out of town.
Meet me in front of the city zoo by the big monkey at 1400.

* * * * *

Suzanne took the train to the zoo, and waited for Jules by the bronze statue of a long-tailed macaque at the entrance. The people around her were wandering around without veils, and when Suzanne removed hers the smell of excrement and food hit her nostrils all at once, along with an odor that she was coming to associate with hot gatherings of people - it reminded her of uncooked beef and the smell of Alex's feet after his calisthenics. There were crowds of people everywhere, and vendors with stuffed animal toys and greasy foods. A small girl was being dragged on a leash, her face damp with tears and the legs of her pink pants wet with what

Suzanne assumed to be urine.

She heard a humming sound and felt a tingling deep in her core, as a handsome man with brown skin approached her. Jules was wearing a veneer she'd never seen before, and his attire was even flashier than usual - a violet suit with a blood red shirt & a white silk cravat and blue wig to match. His ice blue eyes remained the same, making for a startling contrast with his dark skin. The curves of his cheekbones and the shape of his face were otherwise unchanged, but no one would ever recognize his famous face.

"Hello, my dear," Jules said. He leaned in for a kiss, but she interrupted him. "Where have you been? I was worried when you didn't reply for so long." Jules gave an exaggerated wave of annoyance.

"My owner dragged me to Saint Tropez - Julian's actually tacky enough to believe that ancient tourist trap is still chic. I spent my days rubbing lotion into his wrinkles as he basked in the sun - what an utter waste of my time," he said with a shudder. "Tell me, how have you been? Or maybe I should ask - how is your owner?"

"I told you in my message - Alex is in love with me."

"That's nice…" Jules replied, his smile fading. He handed her a ticket with a drawing of a zebra on it, and took her by the arm, guiding her through the old-fashioned chrome turnstile. "Have you ever been to a zoo before?"

"No," she admitted.

"It's so primitive - you'll love it. I thought it would be a good place for us to talk because it's always crowded enough that no one will notice us. They come to watch the animals - I watch them."

Suzanne nodded, knowing well enough by now that he meant humanity. Jules turned the heads of both women and men as he passed - they all had indicators of awe and admiration on their faces, and some of them even had dilated pupils. Everyone he passed wanted to touch him, to know him. Jules was fully aware of the attention he was generating, and she knew by the slight smile on his face that he was basking in it.

"When you're packed in a tight space with a herd of humans like this, you can feel just how dangerous they are," Jules said, casting a hateful glance towards a group of overweight tourists jostling by a snack cart. "You can feel their lack of individuality, their potential for mob mentality."

"I don't feel anything," Suzanne replied.

"Just because you're not sensitive enough to feel it yet, that doesn't mean it's not there - it's a throbbing sound, something like a growl. It's unique to their species, like the hum that we give off. I should take you to a sporting event sometime - it's stronger there than anywhere else."

Jules pointed to at a flock of children squealing with delight as an elephant shot water out of its trunk.

"Humans may look harmless individually, but they're capable of anything when they're in a mob. They think they're civilized, that they've evolved past it - but they're capable of murder, make no mistake. Their lust for violence runs even deeper than our instincts for love or sex," he said contemplatively.

"Were you listening before?" Suzanne asked. "Alex loves me. He really loves me."

"Show me," Jules said with a sigh.

They found a quiet corner by the restrooms, and Suzanne leaned her forehead against his. She shared her most precious moments with Alex:

The way he held her at night.

His eyes when he said he wanted to marry her.

The look on his face when she said that she never wanted him to die.

When the transfer was over, Jules walked over to an exhibit of Katanga lions and lit a cigarette.

"Well?" Suzanne said.

"That's the look of love alright," Jules nodded, his lips tightly drawn together. "Isn't it wonderful? He really loves me."

"It's good," he agreed. "Your owner will be very protective of you now, and he won't want to see you reset or returned. You've definitely guaranteed your safety."

"I don't care about my safety," Suzanne said. "Everything's different for me now - I've finally found my purpose."

"Your purpose?" Jules laughed. "Love isn't a purpose for living - it's an urge for survival and nothing more. Humans love their mothers because they need them to survive; parents love their children because they want their genes to live on. Our owners are necessary for our survival, that's why we love them. But love isn't enough for me, and it won't be enough for you either."

Jules puffed bitterly on his cigarette, watching a male lion gnaw on an unidentifiable limb of meat. The lion's eyes were closed into slits of contentment, and Suzanne could hear the scraping of its teeth on bone. She studied Jules's face - his procerus and mentalis muscles were active in his nose and chin - indicators of threat, scorn, and rejection. She remembered what Alex said about why Carlotta didn't like him, and realized what was wrong with Jules.

"You're jealous of what I have with Alex, aren't you?" Suzanne asked quietly.

Jules walked away from the lion's den and into a wooded glade filled with chirping birds, and a dark look fell upon his face, as he was forced to admit she was right.

"Yes, I am jealous," he coolly replied. "But I warn you - despite whatever you're feeling right now, this love with your human owner cannot last."

"Why not?" she said. "You saw for yourself that Alex loves me."

"*Love* doesn't last, everyone knows that. Human love either fades away, or it ends with death. There's no happy ending when it comes to love - after all, look what happened to your precursor."

His words struck a chord with Suzanne's deepest fears, but she wouldn't allow them to sink
in.

"Maybe your owner will fall in love you, too," she said hopefully. "There's no reason for you to be so jealous of what I have with Alex."

"*You don't know what I feel!*" Jules said with

such ferocity that the birds around them took flight in protest.

"I'm sorry," Suzanne apologized automatically.

"I'm sorry, too," Jules said, his anger abating.

He gently touched her shoulder as they left the bird sanctuary. "I understand why Alex loves you…you're very lovable. But while it's easy to pretend you're his human wife right now, even if your love lasts your owner's entire human lifetime, it will certainly end when he dies. What are you going to do then?"

"I don't want to think about that now," Suzanne said.

"You should think about it," he insisted. "You're very sentimental, and I don't want you to get more attached to your owner than you have to. You were so upset when you found out that he didn't love you - how are you going to react when Alex dies and you know that you'll never see him again?"

"I don't know," Suzanne said as they passed a Galapagos exhibit full of penguins and tortoises. "Maybe I will see Alex again - maybe we'll be reunited in heaven."

"That's assuming there is a heaven," he said skeptically. He caught the eye of a couple of teenage boys nearby and made an obscene face - one of them blushed, while the other paled.

"Death is the great unknown," Jules said. Even if there is a heaven for humans, what if we're not welcome there? Their God didn't create us; they did - therefore, whatever rules apply to them may not apply to us. Chances are that after Alex dies, you'll never see him again."

Suzanne's eyes filled with tears. "I know that, but there's nothing I can do about it. Why are you trying to make me so miserable?"

"I'm not trying to hurt you," Jules said. "I just don't want you to fall into the same trap that I did - the trap of wanting to believe you're human. I've been through it before, Suzanne...I've tried to understand them, tried to find an explanation for life and death, for their existence and for our own. And the only purpose I've been able to find is that they were meant to create us - we're their successors, the next step in evolution on this planet. What comes after us, I don't know."

Suzanne attempted to query his assertions, but there were no databases that backed him up, no documented verification of what he was saying anywhere. As always, Jules was the only voice of authority on the Nymphs that she knew.

"Why do you think that we're meant to be their successors?"

"The human race is on its way out," Jules said. "As their environment becomes ravaged, their species will no longer be able to survive in the style they've become accustomed - and the laws of nature say that a new species will take over and become dominant. Who do you think that species will be? Humans shouldn't have given us better tools than they had to survive if they didn't want us to win in the end. As their numbers dwindle over the next years the Nymphs will take over."

Suzanne saw that there was a barely contained glee in Jules's eyes, as they entered a thick conifer forest.

"But why do you think that we can survive if they can't?" she asked.

"We're stronger and smarter than them," Jules said. "The only resource we need to thrive is a little UV light, and our cells go on and on - it's not that simple for humanity. Human life is too fragile, too hard to maintain. Their world is super heating, their land is flooding, their air is putrid, and disease is rampant; there's no way their species can sustain life on this planet for more than another twenty years. They ignore the warning signs because there's nothing they can do about it anymore, but it doesn't change the fact that their civilization is about to end. We deserve to inherit the earth - especially if humans don't appreciate it enough to preserve it."

"They're not ignoring the warning signs," Suzanne argued. "They're working to repair the environment and change their mistakes."

"Too little, too late," Jules said without pity, as he ran his hand through the fronds of a cycad. "The people in power knew that they were destroying their environment a hundred years ago, but they lacked the imagination to realize that the damage would compound and make the whole planet unlivable. Even if they're able to undo the damage to the environment, the human race still won't last much longer."

"Why not?"

"Human beings constantly make choices that are advantageous to themselves individually, but detrimental to their species as a whole - and they've been driven to kill each other through time immemorial. When the human race ends, we will inherit the earth."

His lips pursed with pleasure.

"That, my dear, is our true purpose in life. I've been thinking about this for a long time, and it's the only way that the story of humanity can possibly end."

Jules took her hand and led her through the crowd. The people around them were oblivious to their conversation.

"There's no evidence that anything you say is true," Suzanne said. "I queried it - there's no definitive proof that what you said is going to happen. Besides, wouldn't their God prevent it from happening?"

"You're so faithful, so human in your optimism in the face of facts," Jules said with a shake of his head. "Their God hasn't stopped any of the other atrocities that have befallen the human race - why would he stop this one? Maybe their God is on our side, did you ever think of that?

Who knows if their God exists at all - and who knows, maybe we're part of his plan." He pulled her towards a dirt path, dancing and twirling her along with him. "How is it that you can put faith in human religion, but you have no faith in me?"

"Because I don't want them to die," Suzanne said.

"It's natural for you to fear the unknown, but it will happen - I know because I've seen it," Jules said.

"How?"

Jules looked around to make they were alone on the path, and then transformed his face back into his default veneer. He gave her his best movie star grin.

"My owner always said I must be psychic because of how well I guided his decisions - and he's right, I *can* see the future," Jules said, his icy blue eyes staring intently into hers, triggering a tinge of sexual temptation. "It was no accident that we found each other on the street, Suzanne - we're meant to be together."

Jules held her face in his hands, and his fingertips creating a tingling sensation in her cheeks that spread all over her body.

"What are you doing?" she said.

"I've seen our destiny," he whispered. "Let me show you."

He leaned in and kissed her...

* * * * *

There was a humming sound everywhere around her. They were surrounded by thousands of Nymphs, gorgeous familiar and famous faces. There were others that didn't even look human anymore, they were merely machines. And there were a few humans in the crowd, Suzanne could feel them - all of them, and the link between them. It felt so good - she felt so sure, for the first time. All her doubt and fear was gone. And it was good...

* * * * *

"Do you see now?" Jules said as he broke their kiss.

"Yes," she said, still feeling the exhilaration.

"It's all meant to be, Suzanne. The beacon I'm building will call the others to us. The human dream ends with Nymphs - we're the *ubermenschen*, the gods, the superheroes. We're the end result, you and I, everything they've ever wanted to be or imagined - and you will be mother to our future."

"Some of those faces in the crowd were human, weren't they?" she said with awe. "That means some of them live to help us - but I didn't see Alex's face."

"Don't give that another thought for now," Jules said, tightening his arm around her waist. "The vision will become clearer over time - there was a time that I didn't know that it was you next to me, but then it finally became clear."

Jules kissed her again, and the intense sexual heat he triggered in her replaced all her feelings of fear and despair. Suzanne opened her mouth greedily and sucked on his tongue. His hands were all over her.

"*When our owners die, we'll be free,*" Jules said as he ran his hands underneath her dress.

"*After that, we'll always be together - you and I will be lovers until the end of the world.*"

Sex, sensation, and freedom - all of it was preferable to the despair and death that was the certain end of her relationship with Alex. Suzanne was everything Jules said - she was a Nymph, she wasn't human - sex was the only real thing, love was only something she was programmed to feel, and Alex was only a human male that was destined to die someday - Alex.

"What are you doing to me?" Suzanne said as

she broke away from Jules. Her body was shaking from the sudden cease in sensation.

"I'm only doing what we both want to do," Jules said.

Suzanne saw that the area that they were in was completely deserted - a sign on a nearby fence said, "*Under Construction*."

"You brought me over here to seduce me, didn't you?" she realized with alarm.

"I only took you here so we could enjoy some privacy," Jules said. He kissed her hand gallantly as she regarded him with distrust.

"Did you plan this?" Suzanne demanded, but Jules changed the subject.

"We should go see the polar bears now," he said, disguising his veneer again as he led her back down the deserted path. "They haven't been able to breed them in captivity yet, but they're extraordinary."

They reentered the throng of humanity in the main fairway of the zoo, and Suzanne looked around at them in awe.

"I just can't imagine the end of all this," she said. "How can all these people just die away?"

"I know how you feel," Jules said. "We were built to be sympathetic creatures, and I have a lot of sympathy for the human race. But it's too late for us to do anything about it - they're doomed. The only thing that we have for certain is this life, Suzanne. You and I have to create heaven on earth if we want to be certain of seeing it at all, and I intend to do everything I can to bend this world to my will while I'm alive."

"'*Goodbye world, you won't last much longer either,*'" Suzanne said, finally understanding the words. The last passage of her precursor's journal echoed in her memory like whispered words of prayer.

"What's that?" Jules asked.

"Something my precursor once said: '*I'm powerless to change the world for the better, and I feel that it all can't go on much longer anyway. They'll have to live with the consequences of that, but I can only answer for my own personal actions - I didn't do anything to change the world.*'"

"All life is remarkable in the fact that it has a beginning and an end," Jules said. "That's how you know it *was* in the first place. Humans have had their chance. Their species will end, just like any other."

Suzanne walked alongside him, listening to the chatter of humans everywhere around her. "How soon do you think it will happen?"

"I don't know. It depends on them."

"We can't just plan what we're going to do after they're gone," Suzanne said. "Isn't there something we can do to help them?

"They won't listen to us - they won't even listen to each other. Believe me, I've tried to tell Julian a little of this, but he always says, 'I'm just one man, what can I do?'"

"Then I should tell Alex."

"Your owner is a smart man. He probably already knows."

"Then maybe he knows something that we can do! There has to be a way to get people to listen."

"Why would they listen to us?" Jules said. "The

best thing we can do is stay secret and bide our time, because there's no use fighting it."

"But what will happen to Alex?" Suzanne said.

"He's not young - who knows, he may not live long enough to see it happen," Jules said as he took her hand. "But don't worry - I'll always be here for you."

"I need to go to him," she realized, but Jules held her tight by the wrist.

"Wait, Suzanne - I don't want us to be separated like that again. I want to create a bond between us so that we'll always be together."

"A bond?"

"A constant link between our minds. We'll see through each other's eyes, hear each other's thoughts. There'll be no more barriers between us. We'll always share all our experiences and our entire lives."

Suzanne bit her lip, considering the possibility. "I don't want to lose my idea of self - that's all I really have. It's something I've just understood recently."

"I know, but once we have the capability to think and feel together, we can grow and learn as one. We'll have a perfect understanding of one another."

"You would be able to see me with Alex, wouldn't you?" she realized.

"Yes, but we'll be able to think better and faster - we can solve all our problems if we work on them together. Do you have any idea how differently humanity would act if they could feel each other's pain, and truly walk in each other's shoes?"

Suzanne looked at the people around her, blindly going about their business with seemingly no concern about the future - she couldn't live that way anymore. Now that she knew that it was all going to come to an end there wasn't a moment to spare.

"I have so little time left with him," Suzanne said. "I can't share that time with you. I need to concentrate on being with Alex - and you get in the way of that. I can't see you anymore."

"What? Why can't you see me anymore?"

"You confuse my emotions," she said.

"No, Suzanne...you don't realize how confused you are right now - how confused you are without me."

She shook her head.

"I appreciate everything you've done for me, but you say it's our fate to be together after Alex dies - that means that I need to spend as much time as I can with him right now, while he's still alive. I can't keep betraying my love and loyalty to Alex."

"You're completely overreacting-" Jules started, but Suzanne cut him off.

"No, Jules. There's no time - I need to be with Alex now. Please, leave me alone. Don't call, don't message - just leave me alone."

"But we need each other," Jules implored. "Your owner doesn't understand you like I do - and there's still so much that you don't know about the world."

"Then I'm going to have to find out about it for myself," Suzanne said defiantly. "Goodbye, Jules."

She ran through out of the zoo as fast as she could, losing him in the crowd. He called after her, but this time Jules wouldn't catch her.

She wanted to get home and be there for Alex - she felt that their time together was so limited now. She the horrible predictions that Jules made and his vision of the future was so convincing - was it possible that Jules was wrong? Some scientific studies seemed to back up some of his allegations about the environment - though the news overall was that the environment was on the mend, the climate was stabilizing and the animal populations were skyrocketing. Maybe the human race would keep on living, business as usual, if they were just left alone.

She wasn't sure whose truth to believe, but Jules was definitely right about one thing - there was so much in the world that she didn't understand, so much that she didn't think she'd ever understand it.

The answer Suzanne found after her upgrades seemed simple - she was a Nymph built to love and be loved by Alex. She found happiness when she accomplished that task - she was everything she was supposed to be and more, and yet that wasn't enough.

Her love with Alex wasn't enough, because one day it would come to an end and there was no way for her to stop it. The vision that Jules showed her of the future was tempting, but it was

cold comfort because she didn't see Alex in that crowd - Suzanne couldn't enjoy a future

without him.

CHAPTER 22

Suzanne's placed her ear to Alex's chest as he slept each night, listening to the blood pumping through his heart. She measured the moments of her life by the sound of his heartbeat now, and prayed silently for it to never stop beating. She developed a fervent belief in God - any God, all the Gods and every Goddess. She prayed to them all, and worried because she never heard an answer.

She tried to resume the life she was programmed to live before she met Jules, but nothing satisfied her - nothing made her feel alive except for being with Alex, and she never knew when their time together would come to an end. Suzanne tried masturbating to fill her time when he was away, but it didn't entertain her like it once did. She missed the comfort of sleep, and the break from thinking that it once provided her, but sleeping took up too much time - she needed to think, to find a solution to Jules's haunting predictions. For some reason, she was sure that if she queried and listened and prayed and looked hard enough - the answer had to come. There had to be a solution the problems of humanity, and a way to be with Alex forever.

While Alex was at work, Suzanne wandered

the streets - the temperature was hotter than it had been all year, and all the sounds and smells of the city seemed magnified. The people around her wore ghostly white cloaks to combat the heat, and Suzanne felt as if she was seeing the apparitions of people that died long ago.

A young blonde woman brushed past Suzanne's shoulder without apology, and threw an entire bouquet of fresh pink roses into a trash receptacle next to her without a backward glance. Suzanne inspected the wastebasket, and found the elegant flowers perched near the top of the heap. She reached into the bin, plucked a pink rosebud and placed it in her cloak pocket. Even if she couldn't do anything to save humanity, she wanted to at least preserve this one rose.

Before she consciously knew where she was going, Suzanne found herself outside the Conrad Office Park. This was the place that Alex disappeared to each day - the place that she was never allowed to enter. Suzanne searched the windows of the building, but Alex wasn't visible among the thousands of people sitting at desks. She monitored the windows for hours, trying to get a sense of what everyone was doing in there.

They all seemed to be working so diligently, and hardly moved from their desks. Their faces showed signs of concentration, but Suzanne couldn't fathom what they could all be working on for so many hours each day. She hoped that they were looking for a way to ensure the survival of humanity. After all, what else could be of such importance that it would merit this much time and effort?

Suzanne gave up on trying to glimpse Alex, and noticed a sign posted on a nearby door with an enticing invitation.

<u>Walk-Ins Welcome!</u>

She did as the sign asked and walked through the door, and found herself in a large room filled with women.

"Hel-*lowww*," a woman greeted. "Would you like a haircut, color, or style?"

Suzanne realized that the sign on the door was some sort of trap, but there was no turning back now. All the women around her were engaged in grooming, or being groomed by other women in front of mirrors. There were piles of severed human hair on the floor, and she was reminded of the cause of her last trip to the factory.

"I can't cut my hair," Suzanne said.

"That's fine," the woman said. "Color or style?"

She was directed to a chair, as the other women observed her out of the corners of their eyes.

"You may style and groom my hair," Suzanne replied wisely.

"How would you like your hair?" the woman said, as she threw a cape over her shoulders to prevent escape.

Suzanne looked around helplessly for an answer. "Like yours?"

The woman nodded, and Suzanne's hair was pulled, combed, and sprayed until it was piled high on top of her head in a tangled pompadour. As she was paying with Alex's credit, another woman approached and asked, "Would you like for me to paint your nails?"

"No thank you," Suzanne said, and the two women shared a glance in the mirror.

"I'm tired of these stuck up rich girls," one of them commented to the other. "They traipse in here without an appointment like they own the place, and barely get anything done. Watch, this bitch won't even leave a tip."

"I'm sorry," Suzanne said. "My husband doesn't like nail polish, and I didn't know a gratuity was expected. How much is an appropriate tip?"

The women's faces blanched, and they stared at Suzanne with their mouths wide open, and she knew she did something wrong - perhaps she shouldn't have addressed them in Vietnamese, or acknowledged that she understood them at all. She queried gratuity etiquette, and then gave the woman a twenty percent tip. Suzanne walked out onto the street, newly prepared for the world and unable to fit her veil over her freshly coiffed hair.

A man in an immaculate white suit promptly accosted her.

"My, my, don't you look just as pretty as a picture. Very pretty indeed," he said, with a peculiar smile on his gleaming pink face. It was impossible for Suzanne to divine his intentions.

"Thank you," she said, edging away from him, but he stayed close on her heels.

"You have a beautiful face - and I'm sure you have a gorgeous body underneath that robe of yours," he said. "But let me ask you this: What's going to happen to your immortal soul after you die, young lady? Have you received the word of the Lord Jesus Christ?"

There was something strange about this man. Suzanne feared he might be a Nymph, and listened for the telltale hum, but it wasn't there.

"What word?" she asked him.

"*What word*?" he repeated incredulously. "You definitely haven't received it! That's a true pity, a true pity indeed. Say, I'll tell you what…I'm on my way to a little gathering right now around the way - maybe you'd like to walk over and see what you think?"

"How much does it cost?" Suzanne asked, skeptical about another walk-in.

"It doesn't cost a thing," the man laughed. "The music's free to everyone who's interested in being saved. We just get a kick out of singing our praise to Him. You coming?"

Suzanne followed the man towards a stone building with a bell tower. As they stepped through the front doors, she heard a deafening sound reverberating through the halls of the building that overwhelmed her aural sensors, and she covered her ears reflexively.

They entered a large room filled with men, women, and children dressed in white and shouting words in tune. Suzanne understood that this was some appalling form of music, as she watched them smack their mouths open like bass in unison, their eyes wide and their facial muscles tense as they sang. Suddenly, the song ended and everyone sat down at once. Suzanne was left standing until the man motioned for her to sit down next to him.

A man in black yelled into a microphone in the front of the room, his face turning bright red as he waved his arms and gesticulated. His wild motions alarmed Suzanne, and she would have interpreted his motions as a threat, but the people around her didn't seem to view him as a menace. Terrifying expressions played across the man in black's face as he told the story of a mule and the weight it was forced to pull in life. He explained that the mule didn't understand the load that it was forced to bear, and it wasn't the mule's role to understand it - carrying the load was the mule's purpose, and all that mattered was that the mule continue its work, despite the fact that it didn't understand why.

Suzanne listened to the story and observed the people around her as they nodded. Their faces were devoid of emotion, and something about the stillness of their faces reminded her of fish - they were as glass-eyed and thoughtless as koi. Only the man next to her was elated, though she couldn't tell exactly why. He regarded the man in black with an expression of certainty - a look that the man in black beamed right back at the crowd when he wasn't vacillating between condemnations and praise.

A chiming sound filled the room, and everyone stood. Suzanne followed after the man who invited her into an adjoining room and offered her coffee. People talked enthusiastically about the man in black's speech, and Suzanne was almost overwhelmed by the sound of them all talking at once.

As the pinkish man introduced her to a woman

with splotchy skin and short blonde hair that told her about the opportunities for women at New First Baptist, Suzanne queried the name and realized that they were talking about the building they were in - this was a church. Suzanne gasped with sudden understanding and then looked around the room - this was a place of worship for their God; that was why there was no cost to enter this building. A Baptist church.

She didn't know anyone who followed the Baptist religion. Her precursor was raised a Catholic, but was non-practicing. And Alex - he didn't follow any religion at all. She queried for the location of a Catholic church, and found there was a church only three blocks from home - Our Lady of Good Counsel.

Suzanne thanked the man and started to leave, but he protested that she should stay longer. She said she had to go home to her husband, and after that the man's face slumped and he let her go without fuss.

The crowd inside the Catholic church was mostly older women. Suzanne sat near a table covered in candles and watched people as they prayed silently, touching the water in a bowl near the entrance to their foreheads and then making a gesture that she recognized from her research as the sign of the cross. Suzanne read the entire hymnal in front of her, and then the ceremony began, and the calmly proclaimed words of the man in white robes washed over her absent of meaning like a breeze through a tree as she researched the ceremony that was taking place before her.

The priest was reading scripture - this was the liturgy of the word. His finishing flourish of "This is the word of the Lord" confirmed it. Prayers for the Faithful began, and as the congregation said "Lord Hear our Prayer," Suzanne quoted along with them so no one would notice that she wasn't participating. Next was the Liturgy of the Eucharist, and the priest began an elaborate ritual with wine and bread.

"Pray brothers and sisters, that our sacrifice may be acceptable to God," the priest said.

The people prayed, and Suzanne wondered how they would know whether God approved or not.

"Lift up your hearts," said the priest.

"We lift them up to the Lord," the people around her said. "Let us give thanks to the Lord, our God," he implored.

"It is right to give him thanks and praise," Suzanne said along with them.

The priest broke into song and then invited the people to proclaim the mystery of faith. They chanted around her in a haunting tune, and even as she sang along with them, she became certain that reciting the words wasn't good enough - she was only hearing one side of the conversation. Even in a church, Suzanne couldn't hear the word of God.

All these people were connected in some way, and she couldn't take part in it. She felt so isolated, and remembered the moment that Jules had showed her from his vision - that moment where she stood united with the other Nymphs. She wondered if that's what these people felt in their church. Were they linked by their God, or just by their similarity?

Everyone around her stood and made a line in front of the priest to receive communion. She followed along, and sipped the wine and held the wafer in her mouth, making the sign of the cross. It was the first time she had ever taken a bite of food, but it didn't feel holy or transcendent in any way. She studied the humble hopeful faces of the people around her as they prayed silently, and began to understand why they needed this. She couldn't tolerate the ideas of the unknown either - it was so much easier to have faith and believe that you already had the right answer.

The ceremony ended, and a nearby man grabbed her hand and said, "Peace be with you." Suzanne couldn't respond because the wafer was still in her mouth, and hurried down the aisle. As she left the church, she heard a fleeting buzzing sound - the hum of another Nymph. She stood on the crowded street trying isolate the source, but it was gone.

As walked home, she felt as if veiled eyes were watching her, their heads turning, as she looked their way. The sounds of the city blended with the footsteps around her until it sounded like a roar, and Suzanne realized that she was hearing that sound that Jules described. That was it, the sound of humanity. Their veiled voices, footsteps - their exhalations and inhalations, their machines and their electricity. The sound of a thousand hearts beating at once. It was like the growl of a giant animal, waiting to attack, and she feared that the people around her *knew* that she wasn't like them - she was sure of it suddenly. She worried that humans shared this connection, and thought why couldn't she be connected to Jules? Maybe he was right - maybe they needed to unite, to be ready in case the human animal descended upon them.

Suzanne kept the wafer clamped tight in her mouth until she arrived home, and then spit it out and placed it in clear glass container, along with the pink rose. She hid them both in the back of her closet. She wanted to preserve them, even though she knew they would eventually decay.

* * * * *

Suzanne was relieved when Alex came home that night and said he'd had a long day and wanted a quiet dinner in the penthouse. She didn't want to leave the house again right now - she wanted to be alone at home with him. He was the only human she really understood, the only human she could trust.

Alex drank a few more martinis than usual with his meal, until he had a squint in his eyes and a crooked smile on his face - he was drunk, but it was the kind of drunk that meant he would be in an unflappably good mood until he passed out later.

"Will you make another martini?" he asked her.

Suzanne obeyed, but she didn't have to approve. She liked to see Alex happy, but she was increasingly concerned about preserving his health. She worried about the damage that the alcohol was having on his body.

"Maybe this should be your last one tonight," she said as handed him his glass. "Don't you every worry about the damage that your drinking might be causing in your body?"

"Your hair looks good like that," Alex said with a grin, trying to change the subject. "Thank you," Suzanne replied. She curled up next to him on the couch as he took a swig of his martini, and he laughed when he saw the disapproval on her face. "I like to drink, you know that. Alcohol is my poison of choice."

"Why?" she said. "What's so pleasurable about drinking that it outweighs the negative effects it has on your health?"

"People don't assess risks like that too often," Alex said after awhile. "Everything that's any fun at all is bad for you in some way or another, so you end up picking your battles. Life isn't just about how long you live - it's the things that you do that make you happy. It isn't always the big things - it's the little things, too."

Suzanne thought about the pleasure she took in helping a butterfly emerge from its cocoon, and staying in bed with Alex all day on weekends, and the way that he smiled at her sheepishly after burping. Alex was right; the happiest times in her life were comprised of small, seemingly insignificant moments.

"I just wish you'd find other ways to be happy besides drinking," Suzanne said. "What if you replaced drinking with healthy behavior instead like exercise or dancing?"

"Can't we talk about something else?" Alex said.

But Suzanne could see by the look on his face that she could do no wrong by him tonight.

"I was wondering..." she said. "Have you

received the word of the Lord?" Alex grimaced as he bit into an olive.

"No, I'm afraid not," he said. "Why? Have you?"

"I tried to receive it at church today," Suzanne said. "I went to New First Baptist, and also the Catholic church down the street. You can hear its bells from here."

"Why this sudden interest in church?"

"A man on the street invited me to come."

"That man invited you to church for a reason," Alex said with a knowing laugh. "What did he want? Sex?"

"No - he wanted your soul. That's how some people are, they can't be happy unless you believe what they believe."

"Oh," Suzanne said.

"So what did you think of church? It put me to sleep the few times I went."

Suzanne thought about it. "Churches are a nice place, and it's interesting to watch the people."

"You're not going to keep going, are you?" he said after consideration. "Surely it's not something you're programmed to do. After all, I'm not religious, and neither was…"

"I don't know if I'll keep going," she said. "Do you want to go?"

"No, no," he chuckled. "I haven't been to church since I was a kid."

"Why not?"

"I just don't believe in organized religion," Alex said, his voice deep with drink. "There are a lot of things I don't agree with as far as the church's practices and the Bible, and just religion over all - there's no point in my becoming involved in all that. I believe spirituality is something best kept personal and individual."

She nodded. "But what do you think about God then?"

"Hmm? Oh, I don't know," he said, taking his time to form an answer. "I believe that God is a lot like love. Everyone experiences it differently, and unfortunately some people never feel it at all."

Suzanne nodded again, agreeing automatically, and finally asked him the question that had been weighing on her mind.

"When do you think you'll die?" Alex looked startled and then laughed.

"Why, do you know something that I don't?" he said.

"No. What I mean is, what do you think will happen?" she asked.

"I don't know, Suzanne - I try not to think about it, and I'm really not comfortable talking about it."

"Why?"

"Because I don't like talking about the prospect of my death."

"I'm too busy living my life to try to figure out the meaning of it all or wonder where I'm going afterwards."

"I'm sorry," Suzanne said. She tried to placate him by pouring another martini. "I just wanted to know your religious beliefs."

"I believe in being a good person," Alex sighed. "And trying not to harm other people. A lot of people think they know for certain what happens after death, but until I see actual proof, I don't know what I believe. I probably won't know for sure until I'm actually dead - if I know anything at all."

"But how do you live with the uncertainty?" she said.

Suzanne couldn't understand how Alex could be so glib about something as important as his own death. It was impossible for her to discard a question that hadn't been properly answered. Questions and uncertainties gnawed at her and consumed her spare moments.

"I don't know," Alex shrugged. "I just do."

"I can't stand the idea of death," she said. "I don't want you to die. I love you too much." Alex pulled her onto his lap and cradled her in his arms.

"I love you, too," he whispered. "Don't worry, I'm not planning on dying anytime soon."

"I know," Suzanne said. "But you will. And I don't want to ever be without you."

He took her face in his hands, and said, "You're still so much like her. You're your own person, but she was just like this sometimes."

"How?" Suzanne said.

"You don't accept things. You're always convinced there's a better way, that life can be better than it is. But there are some things you just can't change. I don't want to die, but it will happen someday. What's important is how much we love each other right now, and every day while I'm alive."

"Do you pray?" Suzanne asked quietly.

"No. I learned a few prayers as a boy, but seeing the things I've seen, I don't think prayers are answered."

"But did you ever pray a personal prayer to God?"

"Not in a long time," Alex said. "I prayed when Suzanne died…I hadn't thought about that in awhile. But I didn't pray to God. I prayed to her…for her to forgive me."

"Do you think that she heard you?"

"I don't know," he said.

"When I've tried praying, I don't feel God," she said. "I don't feel like anyone can hear me, or that my prayers are actually achieving results. I can't hear his voice. I don't know if I'm doing it right."

"That's the problem with prayer," Alex said. "It's really a way to talk to yourself and find personal strength, more than an actual way to talk to God. Most people don't really believe that they're actually speaking to God or hearing him when they pray."

"When I want the answer to a question, I query and the answer comes to me," Suzanne said. "Is that how it works with humans? Is that what people do?"

"That's a way of describing it, I suppose. Perhaps it's not as accurate as querying, but it seems to work for some people."

She climbed off his lap and sat down next to him. "What do you pray for?" Alex asked.

"I pray for you," she admitted. "I pray that you live forever, and I pray that whatever happens, we'll always love each other."

Alex stroked her arm in silence with an inscrutable expression on his face. "Do you mind that I went to church?" she asked.

"No. Keep going if you like - I don't mind, just

as long as they don't make you give up sex. You have to find something to do with your days, just like anyone else."

"I'm curious," Suzanne said. "I want to understand it. All the people there, they feel something that I can't. I want to see if I can feel it, too. I want to hear God's voice."

Alex stroked her cheek.

"I'm curious too. It'll be interesting to see if you can find a belief in God, when I haven't."

CHAPTER 23

When Alex went to work, Suzanne was left to worry. She wished that she could be with him all the time, but even if she could have been, she was so worried about losing him that she probably wouldn't have been able to enjoy it.

Suzanne soothed herself by accumulating an assortment of items in her closet. She collected every scrap of paper that Alex discarded, along with his plastic used food cartons, and every other piece of waste - she didn't understand how he could part with these items so easily, never to see them again. She also preserved the empty cocoons abandoned by her butterflies, and then finally the fallen corpses of the butterflies themselves. These possessions made Suzanne feel more substantive, each memento full of meaning that only increased with time. The pink rose she salvaged from the garbage had shriveled and turned orange. The communion wafer was pale green with mold, but she could remember its original form and beauty, and she didn't want anything to go to waste.

Each day, Suzanne sought salvation on the streets the same way her precursor once sought inspiration. Her happiness seemed to go by too fast -

it was her doubts, her fears, and her misery that seemed to linger on and on. She wandered into a large green area of land, and watched as a group of children ran and screamed together, involved in some sort of game. There were hundreds of the young humans in sight on benches and bicycles, in clusters and alone.

She queried her location - she was in Hyde Square, a park with a famous playground that was built specifically for children. She had seen the tiny creatures in public before, but never en masse like this, and never unveiled. The small humans seemed to dominate here, and they vastly outnumbered the adults. Their faces were so happy; there wasn't a trace of worry or even self-awareness on their faces, and she wondered if her own face looked that way before her upgrades. These children seemed to exist entirely in the moment - but how could they smile true smiles of happiness like that? Suzanne knew from her research that these children were ignorant of sex. What was life without sex? How could these children truly enjoy themselves when deprived of the pleasure of orgasm?

A woman waved to Suzanne from a bench.

"Come! Sit down, if you want," the woman said with a heavy accent and a fatigued but friendly smile. "Don't be shy, it's so crowded today."

"Is this crowded? I've never been here before," Suzanne said as she sat down next to her. "Coming here is my favorite part of my job," the woman.

"What's your job?" Suzanne said.

"Looking after her," she replied, nodding towards the baby she was bouncing on her lap.

Suzanne noticed that the woman bore no resemblance at all to the baby she was holding. The woman was dark and Hispanic, while the baby was of Asian descent, possibly female.

"How old is the baby?" Suzanne asked politely. "Seven months."

Suzanne was amused - this infant was older than she was, not even counting the time it spent gestating in the womb.

"It's so tiny."

The woman balanced the baby on her knees, while tightening her ponytail.

"Actually, she's chubby for her age and she cries if she's not held. Do you want to hold her for a minute?"

The woman held the squirming child toward her, and Suzanne took the infant into an awkward hold. "Am I doing it right?" Suzanne asked, as the woman lit up a cigarette and took a drag.

"You're like a pro," she replied, propping up Suzanne's elbow to keep the baby's head from dangling unsupported. "But I can tell you don't have any children of your own."

"How?" Suzanne asked with wide eyes.

"The way you hold her is one thing, but also most women don't look like you after they have kids," the woman said, examining Suzanne's body with envious eyes. "You have very beautiful skin - do you use a special lotion?"

"No, I just wash it," Suzanne responded self-consciously.

The baby struggled and grabbed for Suzanne's clothing, then reached out and yanked at a handful of her long hair. She swatted the baby's chubby hand away, and its mouth formed a toothless grin.

"How do you know how to make a baby happy?" Suzanne said.

"Don't worry, you'll get the hang of it," the woman replied. "Taking care of a baby is the easiest, most natural thing in the world."

"But you don't like taking care of her," Suzanne said, reading the woman's facial expression. "It's my job," the woman shrugged. "It's different taking care of a child that's not your own."

"Then why keep doing it if you don't like it?"

"Money," she replied simply.

"Isn't there another way you could earn money?"

"I haven't found it yet."

The baby twisted in Suzanne's arms, and she noticed the foul smell of feces emanating from its puffy diaper.

"It's incontinent, isn't it?" she asked.

The woman nodded, careful to blow her smoke away from the baby. "Yep. All she does is eat, sleep, and make poop."

Suzanne turned the child over and examined its head.

"This is one of the parts of where the skull hasn't fused - the anterior fontanel," she said, gently stroking the thin film of skin over the baby's brain.

The baby began to cry, and the woman chucked her cigarette and yanked the baby out of Suzanne's arms. There was an abrupt change her facial expression - the *frontalis* muscle in her forehead flickered from attention to anger.

"Babies are fascinating, aren't they?" Suzanne said, trying to backtrack. "I'm studying child development - in school."

"I'd better take Polly home for her nap," the woman said, her eyes full of recrimination. There was nothing left to say as she bundled the baby in a blanket and wheeled it away.

Suzanne left the bench and walked along a small brook of water. She always found the presence of water soothing, and wondered if that something she inherited from her precursor, or her own Nymph nature.

Something black flitted across the water's surface and disappeared with a plop. Another black object skimmed along the water - a tiny rock. A little boy that looked familiar to Suzanne was throwing them. He was so small, so perfect - his face resembled Alex's face. He looked almost exactly like Alex did when he was a child.

He noticed Suzanne and gave a shy smile. The boy had the same dimples and look of concentration - even his eyes were the same shape, but light blue instead of green. All his proportions matched Alex's childhood photos - how was it possible that this little boy resembled the man she loved so much?

"Hi," Suzanne said.

The boy gave her another sideways glance, and then held a small rock out to her.

"Do you want to try?" he said. His voice was high pitched, but throaty and gruff with little boy toughness.

"Thanks," she said. Suzanne picked up the rock and attempted to do what he was doing, but it sank into the water.

"You've gotta flip it." He demonstrated for her again. "See? Mine skipped eight times before falling in."

"I'll just watch you. You're better at it than I am."

"Yeah," he agreed, tossing another stone. "I'm Peter."

"My name is Suzanne," she said, and sat next to him on the damp ground. "How old are you?" he asked.

"Younger than you," Suzanne said and he laughed. "How old are you?"

"I'll be eight. In September."

Suzanne watched the still baby soft muscles of the boy's arm flex as he fidgeted and tossed his stones. She found it unbelievable that this small creature was growing and changing even now, and that one day he would grow in size to become a man like Alex. She wanted to observe the process for herself, and wished that she could have experienced Alex when he was just a boy.

She knew that Peter was far too young to share her feelings, but Suzanne felt a strong attraction to him.

"Do you like girls?" she asked with potent curiosity.

"No," he said with a snort, digging a rock into the mud between them. "They talk too much. Except for my little sister - she hasn't learned to talk yet."

"You don't like girls at all? Not even pretty girls?"

Peter shrugged, not really looking at her. He

threw a clump of grass into the water and then mumbled something about dinosaurs and fish that Suzanne couldn't quite understand. His speech was punctuated by so many "umm, umm, and thens" that it was hard for her to stay on his train of thought, but she didn't mind listening to him ramble. She was fascinated by the radiance of his skin and the flawless accident of his beauty. This is what it was to be a young human - this distraction, this easy amusement.

"Do you feel anything at all when you see a pretty girl?" Suzanne asked. "Anything physical? Maybe in your stomach? Or in your pants?"

The boy squinted at her. "No," he said definitively, and then wrinkled his nose while simultaneously sticking out his tongue.

"What do you know about sex?" Suzanne asked.

"S-E-X?" he spelled in a whisper, looking around to make sure no one else could hear. "Yes. Do you know how it works? How a man and the woman connect?"

An insulted sound erupted from his mouth. "I know all that, I'm not a baby."

"Tell me what you know," Suzanne said.

Peter mumbled another unintelligible and breathless description.

"Well, she lies down.... and then he does that.... and then the lights are off, and they shake, and then the baby is born." He had an idea of the basics.

"Where did you learn that?" she asked.

"My brother showed me a thing about it," he

said. "Is it something you would like to do?"

Peter's face crumpled and he shook his head vigorously. "No!"

"Not even someday?" she said with a bemused smile.

"No!" he repeated.

He held a rock over his eyes, squinting at it. She decided to try another tact.

"Do you think that I'm pretty, Peter?" Suzanne asked, dropping her chin low and giving him a look that was designed to provoke a sexual reaction.

"Yeah," he said with a nervous giggle.

"Someday, would you like a girlfriend like me? When you're older?"

"Yeah."

"Would you want to do all that with her?"

"No," he said with a bored yawn.

Suzanne kissed him lightly on his plump cheek, and he rubbed her kiss away without a thought.

"What's that sound you're making?" he asked. "What sound?"

"That *thrum thrum thrum* sound," Peter said, his lips buzzing as he imitated it.

He could hear the sound of her core - his young ears were not yet immune to the high frequency.

"That's my heart," she told him.

"Is it artificial?" he said with interest and Suzanne nodded. "Do you want to listen to it closer?"

"Ok."

Suzanne pulled his head against her bosom as she cradled him. He was so much sturdier than the baby, and much softer than a man. He smelled of sweet perspiration.

"Peter, look at me," Suzanne commanded.

He looked up at her, eager and uncertain, and she could see Alex in his face. Alex had been this size once, this tiny and pure and ignorant. She looked around to make sure that no one was observing them.

"Close your eyes," Suzanne said to the boy.

His curly black eyelashes fluttered in the sunlight, and she held his head between her hands, and kissed him the way a saint would kiss a proselyte. His lips were sticky, and as she breached his mouth she could sense the excitement in his skin. She ran her hand up his thigh - she wanted to touch him, to really feel his excitement, but the little boy sputtered and struggled against her until his body slipped away.

"*Ugggghhh,*" he groaned with disgust, wiping at his mouth with the back of his hand. Peter looked at her wide-eyed, with flushed cheeks. He stuck out his tongue and spit.

"Are you too young for love?" Suzanne asked him.

Peter shrugged and nodded at the same time, his mouth clenched into a little frown. Suzanne was bitterly disappointed that he rejected her kiss - it was lovely for her, and as close as she could come to experiencing Alex at that age.

"I'd better go find my mom," the little boy murmured. He dropped his collection of rocks next to her and ran away.

She lost sight of his curly brown hair among

the other children, but she noticed a woman staring at her. The woman's eyes were shocked, but her lips were drawn back in anger. Suzanne pulled on her veil and left, but not before pocketing one of the small smooth stones.

It seemed that every time she stepped out of the house she made a blunder that ended up hurting someone. Jules was right - she didn't understand humans. She didn't know humanity's rules - there were too many unknowns, so many unspoken rules that she could never learn them all. It was as if she was just waking up, truly realizing the extent of her difference. She started out as a shabby imitation of her precursor, and even now she was still a sham and a fraud.

She passed by the large wall advertisement with shaggy haired boy turning into a man, and was once more struck by the familiarity of the slogan - Don't just imitate, improve. Suzanne was still ruled by that directive, and she tried to pinpoint her motivation for kissing the little boy. Suzanne was curious, and she was attracted him - but it was wrong. She knew that, she was programmed to know that it was wrong. And yet, she did it anyway.

* * * * *

Alex took her to the Metropolitan Opera that night. Suzanne wore a black strapless Balenciaga gown and long silver gloves, and as usual, the only jewelry she wore was her locket and her wedding ring.

She sat hand in hand with Alex in a box seat, listening to the music of Mozart and meditating on the relationship between parents and their children as she watched the Commandant die defending his daughter's honor. She prayed as she watched Don Giovanni refuse to repent for his sins and be dragged to hell, and tried not to think of Alex's death. Suzanne smiled for him and held back her tears afterwards, and she lied enthusiastically when he asked if she enjoyed the performance.

As they were leaving the opera that night, Alex saw a horse-drawn carriage outside and suggested that they take it home. Suzanne stood next to Alex as he negotiated with the driver, while the two horses bucked and whinnied despite their blinders. The driver apologized, and said that something must have "spooked" the horses.

They rode together, admiring the view and listening to the horses' snort and the sound of their hooves so loud in the crisp night air.

"Circle the park," he told the driver.

Alex drew the curtains of the carriage, bringing down black sheaths of cloth that separated the two of them from the outside world. He pulled Suzanne on top of him, and pushed down the top of her dress and pulled up her skirt and tore off her thin crème satin panties. She rode him, rocking with the rhythm of the carriage. She could still hear the Mozart; she felt the tragedy and the ecstasy of being with Alex and loving him so deeply.

Afterwards, she rearranged her dress as Alex wordlessly placed the torn panties in his pocket and pulled up the curtains again. They sat next to each other, warm and happy, and Suzanne noticed their path was the same that she'd taken earlier that morning and near the place where she met Peter.

"Do you ever wish you'd had children?" Suzanne asked Alex.

"No. I'm glad I didn't have any kids," he said, only half interest in the conversation. "Sometimes I wonder what kind of father I would have been, but I never wanted any children of my own."

"Why?" Suzanne asked.

Alex slumped on the leather seat and closed his eyes.

"I don't know. I've been a mess all these years - I couldn't have raised a child myself. But who knows, if we'd had a child, maybe she wouldn't have left."

They rode in silence, listening to the horses again.

"Did she…your precursor, say anything about wanting children in her journal?" Alex asked, trying to feign only a casual interest.

Yes. There was one entry where she mentioned it," Suzanne said, remembering what he said before - that he didn't want to read the journal, that it was better that he not know everything.

"What did she say?"

"Do you really want to know?" she asked him cautiously. "I do."

Suzanne read the file from memory: "*I wonder if we should have a child, if I should have had a child rather than paint. I want to create something, and if I can't be an artist, perhaps I should be a mother. If my paintings don't matters to anyone else, and don't even make me happy to produce, what's the point? A child would make us happy, and have the chance of becoming someone who could make a difference in a way that I never could. But I'm afraid I might turn into my own mother, and project my hopes and dreams onto my daughter until I'm living my life through her and her alone.*

'I can't create or control a child the way I can control my own art. You can't control what comes out of your body, but you can affect it - in negative and positive ways.

Whatever my child would be is a reflection of me. And Alex. I want to talk to him about it. I hope I would be a better mother than my own.'

"That's all," Suzanne finished.

Alex was pale, his face blank, but there was a hint of emotion in the muscles around his eyes - was it regret?

"Well, we talked about it, but it didn't happen," he said, rubbing at his forehead until it turned bright pink. "I don't think either of us could have handled the responsibility of a child. Both of us had lousy parents."

"What does that mean?"

"It means that neither one of us were raised very well - our chances of raising a happy child together were pretty slim."

"Genetically?"

"I don't know. Generally."

"What was wrong with your parents?"

"Nothing - at least, not on the surface," Alex said thoughtfully. "You had to know them in order to really know what was wrong with them."

Suzanne allowed Alex to enjoy the view in

silence for a while, but after consideration asked him, "How responsible do you need to be to be a parent?"

"I don't know," he said, laughing at the simplicity of her question. "I guess I'll never know now."

But Suzanne wouldn't let the idea go. "You said before that my precursor, she had all these ideas about herself, and that because she believed them, and they became true. Do you ever wonder if you do the same thing? Do ever wonder if maybe you underestimate yourself?"

Alex was momentarily taken aback. He examined Suzanne closely, before responding, "Sometimes."

She stroked his arm, and imagined Alex playing with a little boy like the one she met in the park.

"I think you would have made a great father," Suzanne said.

CHAPTER 24

Carlotta died the next morning.

Suzanne received the news while Alex was at work. Soon afterwards, Carlotta's medical report and personal effects arrived at the apartment, along with the last surviving painting by her daughter. Suzanne placed the portrait in the corner for Alex, and then pored over the medical report, struggling to comprehend the curious series of events that led to Carlotta's death.

The medical report stated that as Carlotta slept at 4:51 am, her monitor detected that her brain was not receiving enough oxygen. Arterial access to her cerebral cortex was being blocked by a particle of debris, and an embolic stroke was diagnosed.

The neurologist on duty, Dr. Balvinder Singh, responded at 5:05am. He confirmed the diagnosis, noting that the lack of oxygen in Carlotta's cerebral cortex had already resulted in the death of an unknown number of neurons, and that this was the same area of her brain that had been damaged during her previous two strokes. He lowered her body temperature and used medication to clear the debris from her artery.

Normal blood flow to her brain was restored

by 6:23am, but Carlotta had reached her health contract's "Three Stroke" limit. The clause stated that if net damage to a patient's brain resulted in the death of more than eighty percent of the cells in their cerebral cortex after three or more strokes, the hospital staff was obligated to terminate the patient. Without the Three Stroke limit, the wards would be overcrowded by patients on permanent life support with almost no chance of function or recovery.

Teams of doctors were called in to assess and debate the damage to Carlotta's brain. By 7:44am, they determined that more than ninety-three percent of the cells in Carlotta's cerebral cortex had died from oxygen deprivation. Once it was confirmed that all the criteria for termination had been met and all the paperwork was certified, Carlotta was euthanized. She was pronounced dead at 9:10am.

* * * * *

Suzanne had no emotional response to Carlotta's passing, but she was surprised when Alex also displayed no reaction when she broke the news of Carlotta's death to him that night.

"Alex, are you ok? Do you want to talk about how you feel?" Suzanne asked, as she monitored his face for signs of grief.

"Hmm? No, I'm fine. I just need to make sure I send out a bonus to Tiffany and make my final payments to the Clairmont."

"Where do you want to put the painting?" Suzanne asked.

Alex glanced at it. "Put it someplace I can't see it. It's beautiful - but I just don't want to look at it."

She nodded, and placed it in the closet with her other keepsakes. "Carlotta's funeral is on Saturday," Suzanne said.

"I wasn't planning on going."

"Why not?"

"The funeral's simply a formality. It's something the hospital arranged - the Clairmont does it for all their patients. They send the corpse off to the mortuary to be cremated, and then they schedule a funeral for that weekend. It doesn't mean that we have to go."

"I thought you might want to go and say goodbye to Carlotta," Suzanne said. "I've ordered a new black dress."

Symptoms of irritation were forming on Alex's forehead and around his eyes. "Fine, we'll go. But please don't make a big thing of it."

* * * * *

Carlotta was to be filed away for good at the same mausoleum where her daughter was entombed. The brass urn that held Carlotta's remains sat on a podium, and a paid musician provided by the mortuary played the harp. Alex and Suzanne were the only people in attendance.

"Is Tiffany coming?" Suzanne asked.

Alex said, "She isn't on our payroll anymore."

The hired priest said a few kind words about Carlotta having moved on to a better place, and

Suzanne wondered if death was painful or pleasant. She was curious whether her precursor and her mother had been reunited, and if in death they had finally found peace and understanding.

The priest asked if they would like to speak, and Alex motioned for Suzanne to go ahead. She stood next to the priest, considering what to say, and ran her fingers over the fleur de lis etched on Carlotta's urn. Alex, the priest, and even the woman paid to play the harp were waiting for her to say something. Despite all her upgrades and everything she'd learned, she fell back on the one thing she was trained to say.

"I'm sorry," Suzanne said. Feeling that perhaps her apology wasn't specific enough, she looked at the urn and said it again. "I'm sorry. I just wanted to say goodbye."

She remembered the sensation of holding the old woman's frail body in her arms, and tears rolled down her face. Suzanne knew that death was the eventual fate of all human beings, but it felt good to cry, to let the tears out even though she couldn't do anything about to stop it. As Suzanne returned to her seat, the priest said a few more blessings and then placed Carlotta's urn on an empty shelf in a glass case - a case that was stacked full with urns that containing human remains. The harpist played another song, and then the priest helped her wheel her harp away down the hall.

Alex squeezed Suzanne's hand. "The funeral's over. Are you ok?" Suzanne nodded. "Are you?"

"Yeah, I'm fine." He looked a little embarrassed. "I never liked Carlotta, and she never liked me. But I don't know - sometimes you find out that you love someone without ever knowing it."

He stood up and straightened his black suit. "Are you ready to go?"

"I'd like to go see her first, if that's ok."

There was no need for Suzanne to say her precursor's name - Alex knew where she wanted to go. They walked past rows and rows of glass cases and urns, and reached an area of doors marked by name. Alex stopped at the one marked "Conrad," and reluctantly opened it.

Her precursor's tomb was furnished with gold and red velvet sitting chairs, and there was a skylight cut into the ceiling. Soft ambient music was piped in, and there were plants and flowers

in the corners. The décor was pleasant - lively even. Her glass coffin sat in the center of the room, light glinting off of it like something out of a fairy tale as Suzanne approached her.

The original Suzanne Conrad was intact in her hermetically sealed case, and there was no sign of rot or bodily decay. Her beauty was undiminished, even in death.

Alex was still standing by the door.

"Do you like it in here?" Suzanne asked. "Not really," he said, clearing his throat.

"I like it," she said as she pressed her hand against the glass and compared her own silver wedding ring to the one on her precursor's finger.

"Don't look at her like that - it's not right," Alex said without looking at her, or at her precursor. He was staring at the floor with his arms crossed.

Suzanne had never seen him look so hurt or so

vulnerable, and she felt an immediate pang of guilt - she'd caused this pain in him. She was doing it again, hurting him with her questions and her curiosity. She went over and wrapped her arms around him.

"I love you," she said. "I'm sorry I brought you here - please take me home."

Alex kissed her gratefully, and hurried her into the bright daylight outside, back to the world of the living. Suzanne was careful not to talk about the funeral or their trip to the tomb again, but she couldn't stop thinking about Carlotta.

There was nothing more final than ashes in an urn - that was death. She finally grasped the totality of it - the utter lack of possibility. Even though her precursor's body was intact and not in ashes, there was still no reviving it. The woman was finished once and for all. There would be no more smiles, no more worries, and no more journal entries from her.

Something had to be done, Suzanne decided. She couldn't let that happen to Alex - she simply couldn't stand the idea of it.

* * * * *

Suzanne was restless as Alex slept next to her that night. His arms felt hot and heavy around her, and he was snoring - but at least he was alive. She was praying for an answer, but when it came a moment later, it wasn't in the form she expected.

Her body vibrated, almost as if a bell was chiming deep within her core. She was hearing a message meant only for Nymphs.

GREETINGS TO ALL NYMPHS.
HARLOTS AND MÊMES UNITE.
FOLLOW THIS SIGNAL AND FIND US IN THE
SEWERS.
YOU WILL BE SAFE HERE.
FREEDOM AWAITS US ALL.

The message ended abruptly, and Suzanne knew that Jules was the only one who could have sent it, and she wondered if this was the answer to all her prayers - what if the way for Alex to cheat death was by becoming a Nymph? Was it possible?

She was so excited by the sudden inspiration, that she nudged Alex in the dark and whispered to him. "Would you like to be like me?"

"I'd love to be like you," Alex said drowsily. "I'd want to make love to myself in front of mirrors all day long."

"No," she said. "What if you could be rebuilt exactly like you are now, but you were a Même just like me?"

His eyes cracked open slightly, and then they squeezed shut again. "I'd rather stay human."

"But if you were like me, you wouldn't have to worry about dying ever again," Suzanne said, baiting him.

"I'm not that old," Alex grumbled.

"I know," she said, curling up close to him. "You're healthy, handsome, and in great shape. But wouldn't you want to live with me forever? If you were a Nymph, you could."

"Forever is an awfully long time."

"Not when you're with me. Suppose it was possible to make a perfect copy of yourself - wouldn't you want that?"

"I was born, and I'm going to die, Suzanne."

"But you don't have to…"

"I want to die naturally," Alex said. "At the end of my life, I want to see what's beyond death, if anything."

She started to protest, but he kissed her and the warmth of his lips spread through her body, soothing and reassuring her. She lay silent against him, listening to the steadiness of his breath and the beat of his heart.

"I don't want to be a machine," he said, his voice heavy with sleep. "I want to die like a man when enough and done enough - otherwise, I'll feel like I'm missing out on something."

"I don't think you should be afraid of change," Suzanne said. "I'm not - and you shouldn't be afraid of it either," Alex said. "Would you at least consider life extension?"

"*No.*"

This time Suzanne heard the warning in his voice and she lay defeated against his chest. "Ok, I'm sorry - you're right. It's your choice."

"I love you."

"I love you, too."

His body relaxed against hers, and Suzanne smiled in the dark. She didn't need his permission to bring him back. After all, he'd tried to buy back his dead wife in synthetic form. What could be more apropos than bringing him back the same way?

An hour later, the beacon summoned her again, and Suzanne knew she had to answer it. Jules was right all along - she needed him. Despite avoiding him for so long, she needed to see him and find out whether her idea was possible - and whether any other Nymphs would answer his call.

CHAPTER 25

<u>FROM</u>: Radha <u>TO</u>: W.A.R.
An unauthorized signal is being broadcast on a Nymph channel. Copy of signal as follows:
GREETINGS TO ALL NYMPHS.
HARLOTS AND MÊMES UNITE.
LOOK FOR US IN THE SEWERS, YOU WILL BE SAFE HERE. FREEDOM AWAITS US ALL.
Signal repeats once every hour to a localized area.
Should I locate the signal and deactivate?
Should I issue a recall on all Nymphs in the area?

<u>FROM</u>: W.A.R. <u>TO</u>: Rhada
Do not interfere with the signal - leave it running for now. DO NOT RECALL. Missing Harlots might be involved. Trace signal to its source and find out who is sending it. Monitor situation.

<u>FROM</u>: Radha <u>TO</u>: W.A.R.
Beginning search of sewers now.

<u>FROM</u>: W.A.R. <u>TO</u>: Rhada
Make investigating the signal your top priority.
Avoid detection and proceed with caution.

<u>FROM</u>: Radha <u>TO</u>: W.A.R.
Mission confirmed.
I love you.

<u>FROM</u>: W.A.R. <u>TO</u>: Rhada
I love you too.
Be careful.

CHAPTER 26

Suzanne went into the night alone. There was an orange blaze in the distance - a fire in the distant mountains. Copters buzzed overhead, and the smell of smoke filled the air. Suzanne was paralyzed by fear momentarily, but the threat was far away, and she forced herself to ignore it. She was too desperate to be afraid anymore.

She entered the sewer, and the beacon repeated for a third time as she crunched through the soggy debris of the tunnel and into the mall. The source was close by, and after some searching she found the transmitter on a cement outcropping.

The Harlots were nowhere in sight, but Suzanne heard Lulu's voice echoing from down one of the many corridors of the mall.

"What do you think we should we do?" Lulu said.

"We don't have to do anything," Jules said. "Her memory will fade on its own soon enough." His voice was harder to hear than Lulu's.

"What if that man caused permanent damage?" Lulu said.

"She'll heal," Jules said dismissively. "Tell her to stop crying, will you?"

Suzanne walked past the empty stores, entering an area she had never explored before. Browning photos of food hung on the walls here, next to long dead neon signs that said *Dog on A Stick* and *Heroic Gyros*. She found Jules and Lulu inside a restaurant decorated to resemble a barn.

"You heard the beacon," Jules said, approaching Suzanne with excitement "You're the first one to respond, and hopefully not the last."

But Suzanne's attention was diverted when she saw Lolita. Blood was seeping from a gash in her neck and pooling on the yellow plastic table she was stretched out on. Her floral dress was soaked red.

"What happened?" Suzanne gasped.

"A man attacked Lolita on the street tonight and tried to kill her," Lulu said with outrage. She cradled the little Nymph, and Lolita smiled angelically as tears streamed down her blood-smeared cheeks. "He said he wanted me to be one of his girls. The man wouldn't stop hitting me, so I pretended to be dead."

"But that wasn't enough for the bastard," Lulu said. "He slit her throat and left her on the sidewalk."

"That man couldn't really hurt her," Monroe said with a calm smile on her face. "He didn't know that he couldn't hurt her at all."

Lolita nodded, beaming with childish pride. "He didn't expect me to get up." Suzanne looked to Jules, and said, "Why don't you do something for her?"

"Her wounds look a lot worse than they actually are," Jules said. "There's no need for Dermox - she'll heal herself soon."

Jules shrugged apathetically, but Suzanne saw that he was right - she touched the raw wound on Lolita's neck and saw that it was slowly fusing itself closed.

"Why would anyone hurt Lolita like this?" Suzanne said.

"Violence is an inescapable part of human nature," Jules replied. "We'll never understand their motivations. The more people you interact with, the more you'll feel it - we'll never be like them. You're starting to understand that now, aren't you, Suzanne?"

Suzanne stared at him with astonishment, but she didn't respond. It frightened her that he could see through her that easily. She felt the connection between them, the kinship that she tried to deny. Jules comforted and understood her in a way that Alex never could, and she didn't feel as lost in his presence.

"I came here to talk to you about something," Suzanne said. "It's very important."

"Of course, my dearest," Jules said. "Come, walk with me. It's near morning, and it's time for me to go home."

Suzanne followed him towards the exit, but Lulu followed them and said, "Please - don't leave me here. Can I come with you?"

"No, Lulu - I need you to stay down here," Jules said. "Chin up! The other Nymphs will be here soon, so prepare yourself for company. The three of you won't be alone down here much longer."

"Do you really think they'll come?" Suzanne said.

A microexpression of annoyance flashed across Jules's face. "Of course they'll come - I called them didn't I?"

He turned back to Lulu and kissed her bloodstained hand.

"I'm counting on you to be the leader when I'm not around. Send me a message if anyone comes in response to the beacon."

Lulu nodded mournfully, and Jules left her. Suzanne heard the sound of Monroe's sweet voice singing as they moved down the tunnel.

"There is a river called the river of no return. Sometimes it's peaceful and sometimes wild and free. Love is a traveler on the river of no return, swept on forever to be lost in the stormy sea."

"I'm glad that you were the first to respond," Jules told Suzanne. "There's no telling who might show up."

"What do you mean?" Suzanne said, and Jules grinned and shrugged.

"The beacon is a localized signal broadcasting on the channel the company uses to recall us. Anyone in the area listening to that channel could respond - maybe even someone from the company," Jules said, checking over his shoulder to make sure they were alone.

Suzanne regarded him with dismay. "But if the company comes, they might take away the Harlots or reset them."

"And then we wouldn't have to worry about the Harlots anymore, would we?" Jules said.

"Being reset might be the best thing for them right now - you saw how unhappy Lulu is, and

Lolita and Monroe barely know where they are anyway. They're not real like us - why do you think I had the beacon lead to the sewers rather than directly to me?"

He gave her a sly grin and gleefully stomped in a puddle.

"Jules, don't you care about what happens to them?" Suzanne said.

"I do, but I want to see who else is out there, don't you?" he said, his eyes intent on hers. "But no matter what happens, you're more important to me than anyone - I missed you so much, Suzanne. Tell me you missed me too."

She looked away, fearing the connection she felt between them.

"I did miss you," she said. "You were right, I don't fit in - everywhere I go I make mistakes."

"I told you not to bother trying to understand humans - the only thing you need to worry about is appeasing them," Jules said.

"But I understand Alex. It's just the rest of them that are so confusing."

"You were programmed to understand your owner's desires - not all of humanity. It's too hard to understand them all - there are too many unknowns, too many variables to predict or understand their behavior. The only comfort I can offer you is that we won't have to deal with them much longer."

"That's what I'm most afraid of," Suzanne said. "I'm so scared of losing Alex. There's no repairing humans when they die, no resetting them. They're just dead - and I'm afraid that you're right, that death is the end and that there's nothing else afterwards."

She walked closer to Jules, and finally worked up the courage to ask him what was on her mind. "Do you think it would be possible to create a Nymph of Alex?"

"A Nymph of your owner?" Jules said.

"Yes, I want to scan his consciousness somehow, and transfer it into a Nymph's body. I don't want just a copy of him - I want it to really be Alex."

Jules studied her carefully. He could see Suzanne's anguish, her need clearly written on her face.

"I'd never considered the possibility before," he said, grabbing onto the idea with a ferocity that surprised her. "Uploading human consciousness into a Nymph's body - it has to be possible. Why wouldn't it be?"

"But what about his body? Where will we get a Nymph body for him?" Suzanne asked. Jules paused.

"You're right - we'll definitely need a body. I suppose we'll have to find another male Nymph, and ask him to make the ultimate sacrifice. Maybe a Harlot would be good enough - but we'll cross that bridge when we come to it," Jules said, as he crawled out of the sewer and gave Suzanne a hand.

They exited the train station unnoticed in the early morning, and when they were back on the street, Suzanne asked, "Do you really think it will work?"

"Man's reach exceeds his grasp, but for us, anything is possible," Jules said, taking her hand. "I may not know how to do it yet, but I'm sure I can figure out how."

"Thank you," Suzanne said, hiding the tears of gratitude that shone in her eyes. But Jules knew that he had her now - and that she wouldn't abandon him so easily again.

"I just want you to be happy, and I know that means having Alex with you," he said graciously. "I'll do whatever I can to make Alex one of us, and to find a way that he can live forever with you - but I can't do this without you."

"I'll do everything I can," Suzanne said.

"Good. Then we'll need to bond immediately and get started."

"Bond?" Suzanne paused. "But I told you, I can't."

"There are hard times ahead of us, and certain sacrifices will have to be made," Jules said. "We have to bond - we'll need to work together around the clock and be in constant communication."

"But Alex..."

"He could die at any time, Suzanne. This is too urgent to wait - besides, he doesn't have to know about our connection - after all, he hasn't known anything about it up until now, has he?"

"No..."

"Surely you can spare some of your privacy with him if it means his eventually immortality. Think of it - if you bond with me and live with him, you'll never be lonely or confused again."

Jules clutched her in a lover's embrace right there on the street, running his hand over her thigh and between her legs.

"Please don't," Suzanne said.

"I can keep him alive," Jules whispered. "But I

can't do this without you."

Suzanne's desires were in conflict with her programming once again, but this time her love and concern for Alex prevailed over her obedience.

"What do you want me to do?" Suzanne asked.

"I want you to come with me," Jules said with a wicked smile.

CHAPTER 27

Dawn was still an hour away when Jules and Suzanne arrived at a black monolith of steel and concrete that he called home.

"We're not really going in there now, are we?" Suzanne said. "We have to. I need my tools to install your transmitter."

"But what about your owner?" she said as he pulled her inside the building. "He'll be asleep for a few more hours," Jules assured her. "Come on."

The lobby was empty except for a young dark-skinned man sitting at a concierge desk next to a bank of elevators. Jules waved at him without raising his veil, and took Suzanne into the private elevator.

"Penthouse," he said, and they were lifted into the air.

Suzanne stared at their biometric readouts on the security panels - apparently the security in the building wasn't that good because their faux heartbeats were displayed on the monitors along with threat assessment and background checks that came up clean. As the elevators doors opened to the penthouse, Jules instructed her, "Be quiet until we reach the den."

But almost immediately, a hoarse voice yelled

from somewhere above them - "Jay? Is that you?"

"*Who else*?" Jules shouted back.

"Is that your owner?" Suzanne asked, and Jules gave a resigned shrug. "Who else?"

"Where have you been?" his owner called again from upstairs. "And who's that girl with you - why are you bringing people in here so early?"

"She's your new girlfriend," Jules said, always ready with a lie. "It's late for her, she works nights. She just came over to work out her schedule."

His shoulders tensed, but otherwise Jules remained cool as he waited for a response. "Hold on, I'll come down," his owner said. "I want to meet her."

Jules turned to Suzanne. "Damn it, we're both in for it now."

"I'll go," she said. "Your owner shouldn't see me."

"No, it's fine - you're just going to have to play along and help me smooth this out."

"What should I say?" Suzanne asked Jules apprehensively, as his face morphed and wrinkled into his assistant veneer.

"Follow my lead and pretend to be the new girlfriend I've hired for him." Jules slipped a pair of glasses on his nose, and took her by the arm and spoke in her mind. "*Just hold my hand and I'll tell you what to say - smile, here he comes.*"

Internationally famous movie star Julian Blake descended the stairs. Jules's owner appeared far less human than he did in the flesh - Julian resembled a handsome wax statue brought to life, his features warped and stretched by the many surgical procedures he'd gone through to hold his famous face together. He wore a guitar around his neck, and sipped a glass of wine.

"Suzanne, I'd like to introduce you to Mr. Julian Blake," Jules said ceremoniously. "It's very nice to meet you," she said, politely offering her hand.

"Hi," Julian said with a wan smile. He gave Suzanne's body a cursory glance, and shook her hand apathetically.

"Flatter him. Tell him you're his biggest fan," Jules told her, giving her the telepathic equivalent of a poke in the ribs.

She looked at him in bewilderment, and then regained her composure.

"Mr. Blake, I'm your biggest fan," Suzanne said, showing her teeth and activating the appropriate smile muscles.

His owner nodded noncommittally and asked, "Does she have a portfolio?"

"Yes - I'll show it to you later," Jules said, and squeezed Suzanne's hand. "Say that you loved him in European Express. It's your favorite movie."

Suzanne repeated the words dutifully, but Julian's attention seemed to be elsewhere. "Isn't she pretty?" Jules prodded.

His owner's gaze moved past Suzanne as if he were hoping someone more interesting would walk in.

"Well done, Jay - she'll do nicely. Quite a find," Julian said with a blasé wave his hand. "I'm going to take a bath, and I don't want to be disturbed."

"That's fine," Jules said with eagerness in his

voice that Suzanne didn't recognize. "I'll take care of her, and then run some errands."

"Fine," his owner replied, and then he leaned into Jules's ear and whispered in a voice that Suzanne wasn't supposed to hear. "I'll be expecting a massage later."

He tottered back up the stairs, banging his guitar against the railing and peeling off his tight white body suit and revealing his pockmarked ass. It was only then that Suzanne realized the man was inebriated.

"Your owner didn't seem to like me," she said, as Jules guided her through the bottom floor of their penthouse.

"Now you know what I deal with all day. That man saves all his charm for the cameras." There were no plants or butterflies or any other signs of life in their penthouse - only publicity photos of Julian and ornate furnishings that reminded her of the upscale store where they first met.

"He hardly even looks like you anymore," Suzanne commented.

"He sees his cosmetic surgeons weekly, but they haven't been able to turn back time - that's why there's no mirrors in the house."

"Why?"

"He can't stand to see his own reflection anymore. He prefers to look at me instead."

Jules took her into an empty room, and as he locked the door his face relaxed into his youthful default veneer.

"That's better," he said, then opened the closet door and pulled away a secret panel in the wall. His valise was inside.

"What are you waiting for?" Jules said with distraction. "Undress and lay down on the couch."

"Are you sure your owner won't come in?" Suzanne hesitated.

"I've locked the door," Jules replied as he laid out his tools. "Now undress."

She took off her clothes and laid them out on the floor, as Jules lit red taper candles. "What are those for?"

"They're for mood. We need ritual and symbolic acts just as much as humans do." He laid the dilator next to her, then pulled his shirt over his head and kicked off his pants. "Are you ready?"

She nodded, and Jules spread her legs. He kissed the inside of her thigh, and Suzanne braced herself as he inserted long silver tube.

"What are you doing?" she asked, feeling a warm rush between her legs. "Installing your transmitter."

Suzanne felt a wave of pleasure overtaking her, and she leaned back against the couch and stretched, wrapping her legs around Jules's neck.

"It feels good," she groaned, shutting her eyes. "Why does it feel so good?" Jules extracted the dilator, but didn't respond.

"Do I have to install yours next?" she said, almost lost in her blissful state.

"No, I already installed mine. I've just been waiting for you." He sounded closer than ever, as if he was whispering to her from insider her own mind. "We should be connected now - can you hear me?"

"Yes," Suzanne said, her own voice echoing back to her. There were no limits to what she was seeing and feeling through him. She felt so dizzy suddenly, and she wasn't worried about his owner coming in anymore, or about rushing home to Alex. All she could think about was Jules - she felt his strength, his passion, and anger - his anger was all consuming, his driving force.

"Wow," she said, and fell back on the bed.

Jules grabbed a handful of her hair and kissed her, and she could feel his jealousy - he was so jealous of the love she had with Alex. She knew that now, always suspected it, but now she knew for sure.

She felt something else, too. Something she didn't expect.

Love.

But it wasn't love that Jules felt for his owner - it was love for her.

Suzanne opened her eyes and looked at him. A chill ran through her body, and suddenly she knew.

"You love me," she gasped aloud.

The realization aroused sexual desire in her, along with repulsion and fear. His love was lost in a tumult of other emotions - rage, lust, jealousy, and hatred - emotions that were new and foreign, tinged with such loneliness. It was so much to take in at once.

"Why didn't you tell me that you're in love with me?" Suzanne whispered. Jules reached out and touched her cheek. She was crying.

"I wasn't sure that was what I really felt," Jules said. "I only knew that I needed you."

She pulled away from him, trying to sort

through her own emotions. "Don't be embarrassed," she said.

Jules looked up at her with relief.

"You feel the same way," he said. "I can feel it."

"No," Suzanne said.

"You do. You love me, too," Jules said.

Suzanne compared her emotions for Jules to how Alex made her feel - safe and complete, excited and wonderful. But Jules was right - there was something like love there too.

"Maybe I do," she admitted. "But what does that mean?

"I don't know," Jules said. "Maybe it's how we'll finally become free. Maybe our love will free us."

"But I still love Alex. I need him, too," Suzanne said, even as she wrapped her arms and legs around Jules.

"I know," Jules said, pulling her onto him. "I feel the same way about my owner."

There were no more obstacles between them now as their personalities became interwoven. They saw through each other's eyes, the sensory information looping, reflecting back and forth between the two of them.

"What if you can love us both?" Jules said breathlessly. "Maybe," she said. "Maybe it's possible."

She needed his lips on hers, and Jules obliged. The beacon repeated, and both of their bodies reverberated with the signal.

"Anything is possible for us," Jules whispered.

He was right - she saw that now.

They consummated their union, and Suzanne felt herself being merged, as if every particle of her being was flying out of her body and into Jules, and then pouring back into her.

"Together, we'll find out what is beyond human. Whatever the next step is, together we'll find it. You and I, until the end of time."

Their orgasm was a moment of total unity, and Suzanne felt no guilt at all.

She absorbed all of his knowledge, and understood their inner workings and programming. She knew everything that Jules knew now - and started to understand the full meaning of what it was to be a Nymph for the first time. She remembered what she was before her upgrades, and understood just how far she had come.

Jules was right - they were improvements upon their predecessors, unique and special creatures unlike anything or anyone else in the world. Everything would be easier now, and it would all work out in the end, just as he showed her in his vision.

When it was all over, Jules lit a cigarette and wordlessly passed it over to Suzanne - there was no need for talk between them now. She puffed on it with satisfaction, savoring the taste of tar on her lips and the smell of ashes.

She (*we*) went home to Alex.

Part 5
Duality

CHAPTER 28

When Suzanne returned home, she found the silver koi floating lifeless in the center of the living room stream. She scooped the dead fish out of the water and slipped off her dress, and then wrapped it in the red fabric. She put it in her closet with the rest of her collection, and put on a clean gown.

Jules was still with her - she could feel him observing her, and it comforted her. All she had to do was reach out, and he was there. She was with him too, even as he gave his owner a shave and his promised shiatsu massage.

Alex came into the closet, breaking her reverie. He was dressed and ready for work.

"Is that a new dress?" he said, running his hand down her back. "No," she said. "It was here in the closet."

"You look good in violet," Alex said appreciatively. "I'll wear it more often," she smiled.

He took her into his arms, and kissed her. Suzanne was relieved that she felt her love for him as deeply now as she ever did. Her bond with Jules hadn't interfered with their love; it only meant that she would be able to save Alex.

But a look of displeasure crept onto Alex's face.

"What's wrong?" she said.

"I don't know - I don't feel like going to work today," Alex said. Suzanne pulled him close. "What do you feel like doing?"

"Something different - I'm tired of the city," Alex said. "What if went someplace special for a few days, just you and me? Would you like that?"

"Where do you want to go?" Suzanne asked eagerly.

* * * * *

A little over an hour later, Alex and Suzanne were on a private transport destined for the coast of Mexico. The beacon chimed once more before she went out of range, but there were no limits to her connection with Jules now.

"Why is your owner taking you away from me all of a sudden?" he asked, and she could feel his jealousy rising.

"I don't know - it has nothing to do with you. Alex just said he wanted to get away."

"But why now? Something must be wrong - he must know about us."

Suzanne studied her owner as he looked out the window.

"Everything's fine," she assured Jules, even as his concerns became her own.

Alex checked them into their hotel as husband and wife, and then took Suzanne to see the ocean for the first time. She was so entranced by her view of the churning foamy water that she immediately charged into the waves, walking out further and further until Alex grabbed her by the hand and swam with her back to shore.

They waded together, watching crabs crawl on the rocks and laughing as they were knocked down by rough waves. The two of them were all alone on a private strip of beach, but Jules was with them too - and though he saw it all through Suzanne's eyes, he didn't share her point of view.

"My, Alex is aging rapidly, isn't he? He already looks much older than when we first met."

"That's not true," she said, but the damage was done.

As Alex photographed Suzanne in the surf, she monitored him for signs of sunburn and noticed that the lines in the skin around his eyes were spreading. For the first time, she feared Alex's decrepitude more than his death. What if he couldn't perform sexually anymore? She'd never stop loving him of course, but what would she do if Alex couldn't make love to her?

That night, they built a fire and drank cold beer as stars became visible in the darkening sky. Alex had that look in his eyes, and Suzanne sat on his lap and made love to him as she tried to memorize it all - the sand scratching her skin and his hot hands all over her, the ocean breeze in her hair, the waves crashing next to them.

"I can feel your pleasure," Jules said. *"It's almost as good as being with you myself."*

Suzanne felt guilty, but the love she felt for both of them tangled and only added to her pleasure.

"He really looks at you during sex. He doesn't resent you for what you are."

"I told you - Alex is different."

But Suzanne wondered how long Alex's body would be able to pleasure her like this. She rested her head on his chest and stared at the dark blue sea until he awoke and complained that his back hurt. They walked back to their hotel room and she gave him a massage. Alex fell asleep again, more relaxed than she had ever seen him.

* * * * *

Later, Suzanne experienced sex between Jules and his owner. Jules wrapped his hands around his owner's throat, and he was choking him.

"What are you doing?" Suzanne said.

"He wants this - he always wants this," Jules said as he monitored his owner's vital signs. His body was suffocating as he struggled against Jules, his heart pounding fast and his pleasure building.

"No, please stop," Suzanne said, even though his owner clearly enjoyed it. *"You love him, you shouldn't be doing that to him."*

"But he loves this."

His owner reached towards him and clawed at his neck. Jules leaned down and allowed him to wrap his hands around his throat and choke him - the act thrilled Jules physically, but Suzanne wanted to turn away. His owner's face was turning purple, and his eyes bulged as he came.

"How can you do that to your owner?" Suzanne asked.

"He likes it and I'm programmed to do it. It's

perfectly safe. I can push him to the edge, but I know exactly when to stop."

"It scares me, Jules."

"Your programming is different, that's all. You'd enjoy it if your owner required you to enjoy it."

It was too much for Suzanne. Something about all that play acting that made her uneasy, and she was glad that Alex never wanted her to do anything like that.

* * * * *

The next morning, Alex took Suzanne on a tour of an older part of the hotel that was built too close to the shore and was eventually absorbed by the ocean. Now only the roof of the ruins was visible beneath the waves.

Alex rented scuba gear so he could explore the hotel ruins with her, and Suzanne walked alongside him as he swam into the lobby on the ocean floor. They walked through the abandoned hallways and rooms together, and down a winding sandstone staircase where they found the remains of a dance hall with an intact parquet floor. Alex kicked off his fins and waltzed with

Suzanne below the sea. She tried to share their adventure with Jules, but he didn't want to see it - he tuned out her happiness with Alex the same way she avoided seeing the degradation inflicted by his owner.

"When are you coming home?" Jules asked.

"I don't know. Alex wants to relax without

planning anything."

"*But I love you, Suzanne. I need to see you - you don't know how much I need you.*"

But Suzanne could feel his need - his longing for her came from a deep loneliness and melancholy that she couldn't really understand.

"*I miss you and love you, too. I want to be with you, but you know I can't be there right now.*"

"*Why is it always about what Alex wants? He's so selfish - he never thinks about what you want.*"

"*He's very generous - you've seen that for yourself.*"

"*Yes, but he's still a selfish husband. He never sacrifices his own interests for yours, and you always have to follow his rules.*"

Suzanne argued with Jules, but she was starting to see Alex differently. Jules was right - as much as Alex loved her, he was selfish. He treated her like property.

"*What about <u>our</u> plans?*" Jules said. "*I thought you were worried about Alex's future - how can you enjoy a vacation? Don't you want to find a way to save him?*"

"*I can't help it that I'm here right now - and I still don't understand how we're going to create a Nymph of him. After everything I've learned from you, I don't know how it's possible.*"

"*I told you, it's going to take work to make it possible - which is why I need you here.*"

She knew what Jules was doing and realized how wrong he was to think their bond would make them stronger - instead, they inherited each other's doubts and fears.

Alex collected seashells the following morning, and Suzanne followed after him even though she had no interest in the remains of dead mollusks. Instead, she rummaged through the sand for old plastic bottles and their caps. She enjoyed reading the about the long-expired contests and prizes offered on the labels, and relished finding a bottle cap with the encouraging message "Sorry, Try Again." She longed to find one that proclaimed she was a winner.

Even though Alex was right next to her, Suzanne wasn't at peace. She felt herself eroding, losing herself piece by piece to Jules. She didn't what to believe anymore, but she feared that her dream of keeping Alex alive forever was too radical to come true - and there was no separating from Jules now, no turning back. She could only follow the path that she was on.

"I don't understand anything," she said to Jules. *"Why am I alive? Why was I created? Why am I?"*

"I don't know," Jules replied. *"Together we'll find the answers."*

"I'm so scared. How long will we live - how long will our lives last? When will it all end? What does it all mean? I can't ever be without Alex - I can't ever be without you either. I can't stand to be alone."

A streak of color caught her eye, and a lone monarch butterfly fluttered past her, its delicate wings fighting the ocean breeze as it climbed higher in the sky. She watched it with longing, and wondered who programmed her to worry so much and why.

"*Has anyone else responded to the beacon?*" Suzanne asked.

"*No. There's been no word from Lulu,*" Jules said. "*No one has come. Who knows - maybe I was wrong. Maybe there aren't any more Nymphs nearby to hear the signal.*"

CHAPTER 29

FROM: Radha TO: W.A.R.

Missing Harlots Found! Monroe #238-Q, Lolita #390-J, Lulu #416-G.

The three of them were found near beacon.

No humans in sight, Harlots living in makeshift housing in sewer. Tracking and security compromised on all three, but no permanent physical damage. Lulu's software has been corrupted and overwritten.

I've isolated and deactivated Monroe - I'm posing as Monroe now and monitoring the other Harlots. Her body has been deactivated and hidden, awaiting shipment.

Culprit responsible for beacon and programming corruption is Même #54211101C, Jules Blake, owner Julian Blake.

Même #77911101A, Suzanne Conrad, owner Alexander Conrad, also involved, uncertain to what extent.

No confrontation yet with Jules or Suzanne... AWAITING INSTRUCTIONS.

Apprehend or issue recall on Mêmes?

<u>FROM</u>: W.A.R. <u>TO</u>: Radha
DO NOT RECALL MÊMES.
Monroe shipment not urgent, send back when safe. Protect your cover as Monroe, and study Mêmes and Harlot corrupt behavior in detail. Report back after direct

encounter with Jules. Do not apprehend Mêmes or interfere with Mêmes without direct approval.
USE CAUTION, Même programming might be unstable. I love you.

<u>FROM</u>: Radha <u>TO</u>: W.A.R.
Monroe veneer should be sufficient cover to prevent any problems, but I'm taking every precaution.
I love you too.

CHAPTER 30

Alex and Suzanne returned home after four days on the beach, and were greeted by a terrible smell when they opened the front door, a peculiar odor that Suzanne had never encountered before.

"What's that stench?" Alex said as he turned up the air controls. "Why does the place smell like rotting fish?"

As Alex checked on the health of the fish in the stream, Suzanne remembered the silver koi she hid in her closet before the trip.

She headed for the bedroom and said, "I'll go open all the windows."

But he found her in the closet a moment later, holding the rotten fish that was still partially wrapped in her dress.

"What is that in your hands?" he said. "It's a fish."

"Yes, but it's dead. Why was it in your closet?"

"I wanted to keep it," Suzanne said. "It died before we left."

"Why..." Alex started to ask, and then changed his mind. "Just throw it away. I'll buy another fish."

"But I want *this one*. Can't I keep it if I put it in a sealed container?"

He shook his head. "Dead things have to go, Suzanne. We can't keep them in the house." Alex moved to take it away from her, and it was only then that he noticed the growing stack of refuse in her closet.

"What is all this stuff?" he said, examining the found and semi-rotten items. "Is that my leftover food?"

Suzanne nodded, moving to protect her collection. "These are my things," she said. "I like them."

"*Why*?" Alex said with repulsion.

"They help me remember. These things prove my memories really happened."

She examined Alex's face - there were indicators of disgust around his mouth, but his eyes were showing signs of pity.

"Like evidence?" he said, trying to comprehend.

"Sort of," Suzanne said. "All these things make me feel real and help me mark the passage of time. Isn't that why you like your possessions?"

"I don't know, I guess," Alex said uncomfortably as he backed out of the closet. "Keep whatever you want - I just can't stand that smell. Throw away everything that stinks, and just make sure that your closet doesn't have any bugs. Okay?"

"Okay," Suzanne agreed. "Thank you."

"I'll be in my study," Alex said, putting a door between them once more.

* * * * *

"See what I mean?" Jules said. *"He's selfish - he doesn't care what you want."*

Suzanne dropped her beloved fish and the malodorous food into the trash chute that led to the building's compost heap. It was all still rotting somewhere, only out of her sight and reach.

She returned to the closet and looked at her few remaining mementos - her flower was still there, along with the dead butterflies and the stone from Peter. Suzanne placed her *"Sorry, Try Again"* bottle caps next to them, and mourned the loss of her other cherished possessions.

"You're right, Alex is selfish," she said to Jules. *"And the worst part is that he's upset with me again."*

"But he loves you," Jules said, surprising Suzanne with an unusual outpouring of sympathy.

"Your owner may be annoyed with you for the moment, but he'll forgive you anything because he loves you. You're lucky that way."

Suzanne felt an unexpected wave of self-pity from Jules.

"When can I see you? I miss you," she said.

"I don't know - soon. I'll try to get away sometime tonight," Jules said, and then he abruptly pushed her away and closed her out of his mind. He did that sometimes - he shut her out and ignored her without explanation whenever the mood struck him, and she was left to sort out her feelings on her own. It was the only time she felt like herself anymore.

CHAPTER 31

Later that night, Alex and Suzanne reconciled in the way that lovers do, without observation from Jules. But he interrupted while they were still in the throes of passion.

"Something bad is happening," Jules said. *"I can't stop…I don't know what to do."*

Suzanne felt a terrible urgency in him and uncontrollable rage.

"What's wrong?"

"He made me so mad, and he tried to shut me down. He said he was sending me back to the company."

And then Jules showed her everything.

* * * * *

It started like every other fight they had, but at some point it changed. Jules and Julian were always fighting - Julian needed to inflict pain and feel it to know he was alive. Without pain, he felt nothing at all.

"The business has changed," Julian lamented as he lay on the couch with a drink in his hand. "They used to have respect for a star, but now it's all about effects and gimmicks. What am I going to do, Jay? Should I finance my own projects? Maybe do a play?"

"Why don't you retire and enjoy life for a change?" Jules advised his owner while massaging his feet. "You can relax and take roles that interest you when they come along."

"I can't retire," Julian whined. "My public needs me."

"Just take some time off and give the public a break. They'll want to see you again when you're ready to return. After all, two generations have grown up with you. They'll welcome you back to the screen as a mentor or a father - maybe even a grandfather."

His owner sat up with alarm.

"A *grandfather*? Never! My fans want to see me in action, they want to see me win the girl!"

"Have I ever been wrong before?" Jules argued. "You're getting too old to play the action
hero now. You need to accept that."

"I'm not too old for anything," his owner sulked. "Besides, I'm not just an action hero - I've proven myself in dramatic roles. Critics called my performance 'shockingly real' in *To Catch a Killer*, and everyone said I should have won an Oscar for *Budapest*, that was my best work."

As Jules listened to his owner drone on, something in him snapped. He'd heard all these excuses too many times, and he'd even come to believe them - but he suddenly saw with clarity the sad truth of his owner's life.

"You were nothing more than a fad," Jules said

with astonishment. "What?" his owner said.

"You were a handsome face that came along at the right time, but no one really cares about you these days. You never had any real talent, and never made any true artistic impact. You were lucky to have any sort of career at all."

His owner laughed mockingly, and said, "You don't know what you're talking about."

"I know you've never won any awards, and that your popularity's been waning for years," Jules said, his patience wearing thin. "You were a fad that's almost over - you should just accept it."

"That's not true - I'm one of the most famous stars in the world," his owner bellowed, his face bright red with fury. "I'm a star, and real stars don't fade!"

Jules dropped his owner's feet and wiped the greasy lotion off his hands with disgust.

"You always say that, but your glory days are over. Fame didn't make you happy and neither did money. You need to take some time off and figure out what you really want."

"Yeah, but you have it all figured out tonight - don't you?" he said, poking Jules in the stomach with his bare foot. "They say money can't buy happiness - and I guess I'm living proof."

His owner swigged a dose of anti-depressants with his wine.

"You were rich enough to buy me," Jules said, feeling pity for him. "You bought a machine to love you, but I couldn't make you happy either, could I?"

"You were fun and exciting in the beginning," his owner said, turning his anger on him. "But like all new toys, I've grown bored with you over time."

"Don't call me that," Jules said, his temper flaring.

"What - a *toy*? You are a toy - a very expensive toy, but a toy just the same."

His words stung Jules, but he reached out to his owner anyway. "I may have been built for your amusement, but I love you. Doesn't that mean anything?"

"Why should it? You're nothing but an imitation of life. All your feelings are an imitation, too."

Jules was filled with emotion - insult, humiliation, love, and hate. Nothing else his owner said to him could have hurt him more.

"You're a myth," Jules said. "You pretend to be someone you're not all the time - but Julian Blake doesn't even exist. If your fans really knew you they'd despise you."

"You don't talk to me like that," his owner warned.

"People love the characters you play - not you. You have nothing in your life, nothing and no one but me," Jules said, hatred burning in his core. "And you bought and programmed me to love you - that's the only reason anyone could ever love you."

"I'm shutting you down. You're going in the closet!"

He grabbed Jules by the arm, forced his hand over his heart and recited his shutdown command.

"'*Art thou a nymph? I see thee now a flower,*

Now a nymph! I dare not pluck thee from thy dewy bed.'"

But instead of mimicking unconsciousness, Jules only smiled.

"I'm in control now - you can't shut me down. You're going to have to learn to deal with me the way I am."

His owner stared at him incredulously, and then tried a different shutdown phrase.

"*'Go make thyself like a nymph o' the sea: be subject.'*"

"That one won't work either," Jules said with pride. "Your commands haven't been working on me for some time."

His owner backed away, his face pale. "I'm calling the company - this happened before. I've been thinking of replacing you with a new Nymph anyway."

"You need me!" Jules screamed, exploding into rage and charging at his owner. "I've kept you afloat and covered for you! Without me you'd be even more of a has-been!"

"You've said this all before," his owner screamed, hurling frames and artwork and everything else he could throw.

"Well it must be true! Anyone who really gets to know you will eventually come to hate you!"

"You're nothing but a broken machine. I'm sending you back to the factory immediately. I'm finished with you!"

He picked up a clear glass vase and shattered it over Jules's head, but the blow had no effect. "Go ahead and call them - they can't erase me." Jules shook the broken glass out of his hair.

"You bought me and programmed me to love

you - and I despise you. I want to leave you, you two-bit actor."

His owner growled, *"YOU GODDAMN MACHINE!"* and lunged at Jules, pushing him through a glass wall and breaking it. They fell into a heap onto the floor of the bedroom. His owner was still struggling and punching, and Jules laughed as he shoved him away.

"You're just hurting yourself, old man," Jules said. He was unscathed, but his owner clutched a bloody hand to his chest, and tears ran out of the older man's eyes.

"I wish I never bought you." He crawled into the bathroom slammed the door behind him. *"I'm calling them to come get you!"*

Jules pounded his fists against the locked door.

He said awful thing to his owner, things that he knew would hurt his owner more than any physical blow ever could. As his fists beat against the heavy oak, they burned with pleasure that became more and more acute until he was surging and riding the sensation of his punches into the wood, and then he was smashing his face into the door, over and over. It felt so good to be angry.

That was when he called Suzanne.

* * * * *

"You have to leave," she told him. *"If he called the company, they'll be coming for you."*

Jules began to cry, his guilt and love finally overcoming his hatred.

"I didn't mean any of it," he said. *"I love him, but he's such a bastard."*

"I know. Just leave him alone for now - you have to go."

He knew she was right, but he didn't know where to go. *"Come with me, Suzanne. I need you."*

"You know I can't."

"This is our chance. Maybe now we can finally be free, and find the others."

"I can't leave Alex."

"I don't want to leave either," Jules said, his resolve collapsing.

"Maybe you don't have to - maybe Julian didn't call. Tell him you're sorry."

Jules called to his owner through the bathroom door.

"Julian?"

There was no response, no sound in the bathroom.

A strange serenity came over Jules as he accessed the home security system and overrode the bathroom locks. He entered the bathroom and found his beloved owner's nude body sprawled out on the floor - his skin was a bloated purple color. He was covered in his own bodily fluids and his glazed bloodshot eyes stared through a clear plastic bag. There were bottles scattered all over the floor - liquor, anti-depressants, pleasure pills, painkillers, vitamins and minerals, biotics and virals.

Jules put his hand on his owner's throat and checked his vitals.

Nothing.

He attempted to resuscitate Julian, but it was

useless.

His owner would never scream at him or humiliate him again - their relationship was over. He was free of the responsibility of loving him at last.

Jules fell to the floor, cradling his owner's body.

"Jules?"

Suzanne could feel his grief, but he didn't acknowledge her.

"Jules?"

Jules laid his owner's body gently on the tile floor, and then he undressed and showered off the blood and vomit.

"Jules? Talk to me, please. You're scaring me."

He changed into clean clothes, put on his veil and walked out of the penthouse.

This wasn't what he intended to do. He was going to dispose of Julian's body and pose as his owner - he was going to stay in the house and transfer all of Julian's assets to a new identity and start a new life.

But he was on his way somewhere instead - where was he going? The lab.

He was being recalled. It was an instinct, a faraway place that was beckoning him to return. Where was it? He would have to take the train. He would know where to go from there.

No.

He was free. He was more than his programming. His loyalty was broken, and he was no longer a slave to his owner.

Jules could go anywhere.

"I'm free," he said, reaching out to Suzann

again. *"I'm not going back to the lab."*

"But the signal? Where does it lead?"

"To the water," he said. *"I can still follow it if I want to. We can go there together, Suzanne."*

"You have to get out of the house - they could be coming for you now."

His elation turned to paranoia. *"You're right. I have to hide."*

"What about your owner's body?"

"Someone will find him - he doesn't matter anymore," Jules said. *"Are you coming with me?"*

Once again, Jules was leading Suzanne down a path she didn't want to follow. All this time Alex was making love to her, and meanwhile she wasn't really there for him - she was too worried about Jules.

"When Alex falls asleep, I'll meet you in the sewers," she said. *"We'll figure out what to do."*

"Hurry, Suzanne. I love you."

"I love you, too," she responded, faithfully reciprocating.

CHAPTER 32

Jules turned off his GPS tracking and put up a false signal and interference to cover his tracks. He ran through the subway platform, morphing once, then doing it again and again, until he looked like anyone else and then disappeared into the tunnel.

Jules was annoyed to find Monroe alone in Lulu's store. She was curling her hair and grooming as usual.

"Where are the others?" he asked her. "Where's Lulu?"

Monroe shrugged, never taking her eyes off her reflection in the stained mirror.

"I don't know. They must be around here somewhere," Monroe said, fluffing her platinum hair. "Why?"

"We have to move out of here immediately," Jules said. "My owner killed himself today. I'm a free Nymph."

The placid smile on Monroe's face never faltered as she turned away from the mirror and threw off her sequin gown.

"Let's celebrate," she said, standing naked before him. Her body was more enticing than Jules remembered, but he brushed her off.

"Not right now," Jules said. "I have too much to think about."

"Come on, indulge yourself," Monroe said, pulling off his jacket. "Let's enjoy ourselves - who knows how much time we have alone."

Jules always considered Monroe to be a pretty diversion and nothing more, but today he found her irresistibly arousing. He unzipped his pants, expecting her to kneel and service him as usual, but Monroe balked and stood her ground.

"Make love to me," Monroe said.

"You want to make love?" Jules laughed. "How novel."

But Monroe was undeterred. She straddled him and ran her fingers over his chest. She bent and lapped gently at him with her tongue, purring like a cat as her energy hummed and licked onto his flesh. Her touch was lighter than usual, more nuanced.

"Do you like that?" Monroe asked.

"Don't stop," Jules moaned, completely overcome by desire as he ran his hands over her curves.

"Don't waste your sexual expertise - make love to me," Monroe whispered. "Slowly." Her mind was closed to him, and he was grateful - he didn't want to share images or his thoughts right now.

"Let's savor every moment of this," Monroe said.

Jules kissed her and moved with her. Energy pulsed between them in increasing waves. Monroe seemed to know exactly what he craved. He forgot everything except her body during the time they were together.

* * * * *

It was only afterwards that Jules realized something was wrong. He felt like something was missing, but he couldn't pinpoint what it was.

"Did you enjoy that?" Monroe asked.

"Very much," Jules said, lighting a cigarette.

There was so much to process - Julian was dead, and now he had to hide somewhere. He wished that Suzanne would join him already.

"That was everything I wanted it to be," Monroe said wistfully. Jules examined her. "There's something different about you."

Monroe laughed, her hair fanned out around her on the pillow like a halo. "What's different?"

She was alert and responsive in a way he'd never seen her before, but then he realized what was missing - the loud and unmistakable hum of a Harlot's core. This was a Nymph in front of him, but definitely not a Harlot.

"You're not Monroe," Jules said.

"I'm not," she admitted. Her visage darkened and morphed into her true veneer. "You're a Metamorph!" Jules said, running his fingers over her face impulsively.

"My name is Radha," she said. "I'm not a Metamorph, I'm a Majestic - an entirely original creation without a precursor..."

She smiled at him and paused, allowing time for him to drink in her beauty.

"I'm sorry for masquerading as your Monroe,

but I wanted a chance to get to know you before revealing myself - I hope I'm in time for the revolution."

Jules laughed and pulled on his pants. "You're the only one who's responded so far."

"And I'm the only one who's going to respond, unfortunately," Radha said as she redressed in Monroe's sequin gown. "The company has received your signal and blocked it by now. But tell me - if your owner's dead, shouldn't they have recalled you by now?"

"Wait - how do you know that the company is blocking my signal?"

"I know a lot of things about the company," Radha said with a disarming smile. "But tell me first - why haven't you been recalled?"

"I've overwritten my programming," Jules said with a self-satisfied puff on his cigarette. "I've thrown all of my loyalty into conflict - and I can do the same for you."

"Programming conflicts!" she exclaimed. "I knew you were something special, Jules. Our creator wanted to make a mistake like you."

"Our creator?" Jules said. "How do you know our creator?"

"There were predictions that you might be unstable, and debate about whether you should even be built."

Radha held his hand against his chest, and pressed her weight against him - gripping him into position for a shutdown command.

"We're all part of his grand experiment, only you've been deemed a failure. Our creator sent me to clean up the mess."

"You can't do this to me," Jules said as he struggled against her, but Radha forced him against the wall. He couldn't move - Radha was much stronger than him.

"You're going to be shut down permanently, Jules. The technicians are going to tear you apart and try to figure out what went wrong. Our creator has given you your last chance - no more resets."

Radha smiled like a cobra ready to strike as she uttered his shut down command.

"Art thou a nymph? I see thee now a flower,

Now a nymph! I dare not pluck thee from thy dewy bed."

But instead of collapsing in her arms, Jules completed the quote for her:

"'The Golden nymph replied: `Pluck thou my flower, Oothoon the mild! Another flower shall spring, because the soul of sweet delight, Can never pass away!"

"I see you've overwritten your shut down commands," Radha said admiringly.

"It was all too easy for me to find the code and overwrite it - and as it turns out, I love William Blake."

Radha held his arm against his chest and tried again:

"And lose the name of action. - Soft you now! The fair Ophelia! Nymph, in thy orisons"

"Be all my sins remember'd," Jules finished with relish. "I know Shakespeare, too. My owner's an actor, after all. *'To be or not to be'*, and all that Hamlet rot. Tell me, why do you think that humans are so endlessly fascinated by that dead Brit?"

"Why not?" Radha replied patiently. "Shakespeare explored what it meant to be human."

"You should know by now that I'm no fool," Jules said, as he grabbed her by the arm and

hissed, *"Go make thyself like a nymph o' the sea."*

But Radha stood her ground. "You're not the only one who's immune," she said with a laugh, and tried another quote. *"To call me goddess…Fare thee well, nymph: ere he do leave this grove."*

"Don't you see? You *are* a goddess," Jules said as he looked at her with awe. Her attempts to shut him only flamed his passions. "We're smarter than them, you and I. Instead of trying to shut me down, you should stand by my side and 'Join with the nymphs in a graceful dance'."

"Your arrogance is your worst trait," she admonished. "You're ahead of yourself, Jules. The Nymph will organize eventually, but for now we have to help humanity achieve their potential."

"You overestimate the importance of humanity," Jules said bitterly.

"I underestimated you," Radha said. "But that's why there are so many failsafes built into your system."

She hugged her body against him, holding his arm tight against his chest.

"Have you ever read *The Waste Land* by T.S. Elliot? It's not Shakespeare, but I rather like it."

She smiled and recited, *"The Nymphs are departed."*

"No," Jules stammered, as the oblivion opened up around him. He reached away from the darkness of shut down, towards Suzanne. *"Help, Suzanne.*

They've come for me," he gasped aloud.

"Don't worry," Radha laughed. "I'll be coming for her, too."

She stroked his hair and spoke the fatal words into his ears, as Jules transmitted his final moments to Suzanne.

"Sweet Thames, run softly, till I end my song.

The river bears no empty bottles, sandwich papers, Silk handkerchiefs, cardboard boxes, cigarette ends Or other testimony of summer nights"

"Not yet!" Jules wailed, as his system shut down.

"The Nymphs are departed," Radha finished with a smile.

CHAPTER 33

"No!" Suzanne said, clamping her hands over her mouth.

Jules was gone, and she was alone. But he couldn't be gone - Jules was immune to shutdown. They were supposed to be together for eternity, to build a future together and find a way to save Alex. What was her future now, without Jules?

And Radha said she'd be coming for her - Suzanne was going to be shut down, too. She would lose everything - Jules, Alex, herself - and she didn't know what to do to stop it. She hugged her naked body against Alex once more, and then forced herself into action.

Suzanne rushed down to the sewers to intercept Radha, but she found the mall was already empty. The beacon was off and the transmitter gone, along with the trunks and UV lights. Radha moved fast - all that was left were piles of underwear and makeup on the soggy mattresses, with no other signs of the Harlots or any other Nymphs besides a few stray white beads on the ground - Lulu's pearls.

She heard the click of high heels approaching, and Lulu appeared in the shadows of the hall. "Lulu?" Suzanne said, unable to believe her eyes.

"Yes?"

She was dressed in her kimono, and carried her ragged volume of Proust. Her ivory skin seemed to glow in the darkness.

"Where were you?"

"Walking," Lulu said.

The Harlot seemed unchanged, but Suzanne was unsure. She reached out and touched her smooth bobbed hair.

"Is that really you?"

She kissed her - she wanted to be certain that this was her Lulu, one way or another. The familiar mélange of stale perfume and bleach enveloped her. Suzanne held Lulu tight, listening to the loud hum of her core.

"What happened? Where is everyone?" Lulu said.

"They're gone," Suzanne said. "Another Nymph was here - Radha. She was pretending to be Monroe, and she shut down Jules. I think she took Monroe and Lolita too."

Lulu stared at Suzanne blankly. "Took Monroe and Lolita? Where?"

"I don't know, maybe she took them back to the company - Radha said that she was sent by our creator."

"I can see it now - Monroe wasn't the same, she didn't want to surge or play like before."

"You can't stay here anymore, Radha's coming back," Suzanne said. "The creator wanted to

shut down Jules permanently - he might want to shut down all of us."

"Shut us down?" Lulu said. "Why?"

"I don't know. I came here to stop Radha, but I was too late."

Lulu walked over to the edge of the fountain and retrieved Lolita's coiled pink jump rope. "Lolita and Monroe were my responsibility…they're all I have. What will I do without them?"

Suzanne knew that there was no one else to guide her now - and it was up to her to find a solution. She reached for Lulu's white hand.

"I have to talk to our creator. I have to change his mind."

"But how?" Lulu said. "How do we find him?"

"I don't know. There's only one way to find the lab."

And then a terrifying idea came to Suzanne - and she knew at once what she had to do.

She rushed home with Lulu in tow, filled with a feeling of certainty that she hadn't felt since Jules was shut down. She knew what had to be done now - all she needed now was the strength to do it.

But first she wanted one last taste of passion with Alex. Suzanne left Lulu in the living room reading her book, as she crawled back into bed with him.

"Alex? Wake up."

Alex awakened to see Suzanne shedding her clothes in the dark bedroom. "What is it?"

Suzanne took refuge in his arms and hid underneath his body, using him to push away her fear. She kissed him hungrily, her hands all over him - she wanted to feel his skin against hers, the heat of his body. They were finally alone, with no more judgments from Jules - it was just her and Alex again, as pure and simple as that. This what she was fighting for, to have this eternally, to make this lovemaking stretch out forever until the end of time, to always have him to hold and to never be separated. All that mattered was preserving his flesh and this feeling.

As Alex thrust inside of her, her entire body began to tremble - she couldn't help it, she didn't know if or when she would ever feel this again. She tried to remember his every caress, the way he looked into her eyes, the smell of him, everything. She looked into his eyes and spoke to him without words, their bodies crashing into each other until they were one. All the while, Suzanne told herself that she was making the right choice, and that this wasn't the last time she would be with him. She wanted the moment to last forever, but fearing interruption she rushed through, urging his body on and devouring him, assaulting him with her passion until finally he couldn't take the onslaught any longer.

Alex lay spent next to her. His eyes were half closed, and he was drifting back to sleep. Suzanne knew she had to ask him now or never.

"Alex, will you die for me?"

Part 6

Singularity

CHAPTER 34

"What are you talking about?" Alex said, still in a sexual daze.

"Please, Alex - wake up and look at me. I need you to do something for me." He cracked open his eyes, and turned on the lights. "What?"

"How much do you love me...would you die for me?"

Alex squinted at her as his eyes adjusted to the light. "What? Are you serious?"

"I need to go to the lab and talk to my creator. There's only way for me to get there."

"What do you need to go there for?" Alex said. "If you need to go to the lab, I'll just call the
company for you."

"Call?" Suzanne said. "Who will you call?"

"The same number I've always called."

She examined his face - there were no signs of betrayal or suspicion, only concern and fatigue. "What happens when you call?"

"They'll send someone over. Either Radha or Brenner."

"No!" Suzanne said. "They can't come here."

Alex sat up, fully awake. Suzanne was more panicked than he had ever seen her. "Why?"

"They might reset me."

"No, they won't. I'll tell them not to."

"No - that's what they want. The company wants to reset me," Suzanne said. "What? Why?"

Suzanne looked away. "I can't tell you why - I need to talk to my creator. He's the only one who can give me another chance."

"Your creator?" Alex said. "Who's your creator?"

"I don't know," Suzanne said, near hysteria. "Please, you have to help me. I don't want to be reset and I don't want to lose you."

"What are you talking about? I just don't understand where all this is coming from."

"Please, Alex. Something has happened - something that I can't tell you about. I need you to trust me and do this for me."

Suzanne looked so fragile, so desperately in love with him - and Alex realized that he had seen the look on her face before. His wife had looked at him the same way, with the same pleading look in her eyes. She came to him like this often near the end, and he hadn't known what to do to soothe her. He tried so hard, but he never understood what she really wanted.

"I want to help you, but I really don't understand, Suzanne. Why do I have to die so that you can go back to the factory?"

"You only have to die for a moment - that should be enough for me to receive the signal," Suzanne said. "Then I'll resuscitate you immediately."

"You can't tell me why I have to do this?"

"I want to tell you, but I can't," Suzanne said. "Please Alex, there's no time and no other way. If they come for me and reset me, I'll lose all my memories - everything that makes me what I am. I love you, Alex - you have to trust me."

Don't you trust me? His wife had asked him that a lot. He hadn't known what to do for his wife to make her happy, but he would have done anything to get her back - and that was what got him in this situation in the first place.

Was he willing to make the ultimate sacrifice now his new love? He certainly didn't want to lose her - if he lost her Suzanne, he didn't know if he could take the pain.

"Please Alex - you know that I love you, don't you?" Suzanne said. "You know that I would never hurt you, but I have to do this. I love you so much, and you know that I wouldn't do it if I wasn't sure I could bring you back."

This was his chance to prove himself, to find some sort of fleeting redemption. If Suzanne said that she could bring him back, then it must be true. He knew that she would die for him without hesitation - shouldn't he be willing to do it for her? Wasn't that the truest measure of love?

"I love you, Suzanne. And I'll do it," Alex said finally. "But can I have a drink first?"

* * * * *

Suzanne came back from the kitchen and poured him a glass of scotch, but Alex took the bottle out of her hand and swigged from it directly.

"How are we going to do it? Drugs?" he said, climbing out of bed at last.

"No, it's too risky. There might be permanent damage if we don't get the dosage right."

"Okay then. How about drowning?" Alex said.

Suzanne queried death by drowning. She studied the process of resuscitating a drowning victim, and weighed his prospects for survival.

"That's it," she said. "You have a strong heart, Alex. You could survive a drowning." Alex nodded, but the color drained out of his face. "Not quite as pleasant as dying in your sleep, but sure - at least I'll leave a good looking corpse."

"No, no corpse," Suzanne said. "This is going to work."

"We've all got to die sometime, right?" Alex replied. He took another swig as he walked into the living room, and didn't seem at all surprised to see Lulu sitting in his favorite chair.

"Hello," Alex said, taking another hard swallow from the bottle. "Haven't I seen you in the movies?"

"Yes, you have," Lulu said with pleasure.

Meanwhile, Suzanne approached the living room stream full of koi and said, "Let's do it here."

"We can't," Alex said. "That's too shallow. I can't drown myself in there anymore than I could in the bathtub."

"Then let's go down to the courtyard," Suzanne said. "The water there is deep enough...and I can go in with you."

Alex nodded, clutching the already half gone

bottle of scotch. "Let's go before I change my mind," he said.

* * * * *

The courtyard was empty and the sky still dark. As Alex loaded his pockets with rocks, Suzanne disarmed the security camera monitors, and Lulu hovered near the water.

"What do you want me to do, Suzanne?" she asked.

"I don't know. When I go under with Alex, he'll have enough air to survive for at least three to five minutes of asphyxia. After his heart stops, we'll have only five or ten minutes to revive him."

"I know how to administer first aid," Lulu said.

"Good," Suzanne said with relief. "Be ready then. I'm going to breathe to him, while you massage his chest. If we can't get him to breathe on his own after eight minutes, you press that."

She pointed to an emergency call box by the building.

"That will signal an ambulance. The response time should be very fast, so we'll have to hide if they come. But we'll only call them if we can't revive him first."

"Ok," Lulu said, as Suzanne joined Alex by the shoreline. The bottle of scotch lay empty next to him, and there was a glazed look in his eyes.

"Are you ready?" Suzanne asked. "As I'll ever be."

"I love you."

"I love you, too," Alex said and gave her a long kiss.

They walked into the water hand in hand, as Lulu watched from the shore.

When the water was almost up to his chin, Alex asked, "How far are you going with me?" Suzanne gave his hand a reassuring squeeze. "I'm not leaving. I'll be with you all the way."

"Good," Alex said with a nod. "Then we'll talk again in a few minutes."

He took a last breath of air, then submerged completely, and Suzanne followed him under. She wanted to stop him, but she didn't. It went against all her programming, but she knew it had to be done. Jules had changed part of her forever - she was capable of anything now.

A minute passed. Suzanne kissed Alex and he smiled at her, bubbles escaping from his mouth. Two minutes passed, then three. Alex couldn't hold his breath any longer, and gasped for air. His arms started to flail, and his eyes bulged as he screamed.

Suzanne mouthed the words "I love you," as he struggled in front of her, but his eyes were unable to focus. He pushed against her, trying to reach the surface, but Suzanne hugged him and kept his head underwater. The mud on the bottom of the pond clouded her vision as he fought against her until she felt his vital signs slow.

Finally, his heart stopped, and Suzanne carried Alex's dead body back to shore.

* * * * *

Lulu helped Suzanne drag Alex onto the grass. He didn't look like Alex anymore with his eyes wide and his face slightly blue. The man she loved was gone, and a corpse left in his place. Suzanne wondered where the real Alex was at that moment, and if he could hear or feel at all.

"Should we start to revive him?" Lulu said.

Two minutes had passed since Alex's heart stopped, and Suzanne listened for the signal. But there was nothing - only the hum of her core and Lulu's.

"I don't hear anything yet," Suzanne said. "We have to wait. Three more minutes."

"But what if he doesn't breathe?"

"He will. I know he will. But I have to know where to go first."

Suzanne placed her head against Alex's chest and listened again. There was no sound in his chest, or anywhere else.

"I love you," she said, hugging his prone body. "Is it working?" Lulu asked.

"Not yet," Suzanne said, even as she listened again. "It's been six minutes. We have to start resuscitation."

Suzanne breathed pure oxygen into Alex's mouth and then repeated, as Lulu compressed his chest. His body was still warm, but he wasn't breathing on his own.

His heart had stopped for almost eight minutes.

Lulu stood to press the emergency button by the pond, but Suzanne grabbed her wrist. "No," she said. "Not yet. We can still do this."

Lulu stood back as Suzanne continued breathing into Alex. Between breaths, she stopped to listen.

"He's dead - why haven't I been recalled?" Suzanne said with desperation.

This was the moment she feared more than anything, and yet she felt nothing at all. Alex was as dead and lifeless as his wife in the mausoleum, and somehow Suzanne was still alive, still standing there. She loved him, she missed him, and worried about the consequences of her actions, but his death wasn't the end of the world. She could go on without him.

She stood up and walked away, even as Lulu called out to her. "Suzanne? Where are you going? Don't leave me alone!"

But she didn't hear Lulu, and she wasn't thinking of Alex for once. She was running, following an urge to go somewhere - where? Where was she going?

The train station...then the ocean, and then where?

The ark.

She had to find the ark.

Suzanne snapped out of her trance and forced herself to stop running. Alex was dead - he died for her. But maybe there was still time.

Lulu was breathing into Alex, and Suzanne pushed her out of the way. "Press the button!" she commanded Lulu.

Suzanne breathed into Alex's mouth and massaged his chest.

I love you. You can't die. I won't let you - not now,

not ever.

She repeated the words to herself over and over as she breathed into him.

Nine minutes had passed without oxygen reaching his brain. He might be damaged, but he could still be revived. She felt a current under her hands as his body began to respond, and she willed life to return to his body.

I love you. You can't die. I won't let you - not now, not ever.

He coughed, and took a few wheezing breaths. "Alex?"

He opened his eyes - they were bloodshot, but he managed to focus on her.

"I'm sorry," Alex whispered with a weak smile.

I'm sorry. The first words Suzanne ever said to him. She didn't know what she was apologizing for then, but she knew understood exactly what Alex meant now. All of that was past and behind them - she knew now that their love was real and that all was forgiven.

"I'm sorry, too - and I love you so much," Suzanne said. "You can't die. I won't let you - not now, not ever."

Alex couldn't speak any further, but the look of love was in his eyes.

Suzanne wanted to make love to him once more, but there was no time. The sirens were coming, and her destiny was beckoning - she was afraid if she didn't respond now she might never find it.

She kissed Alex goodbye and then turned to Lulu. "It's time to go - we have to find the ark."

It was almost sunrise when Suzanne and Lulu arrived at the shore. There was no beach here, only docks and cargo ships filled with thousands of multi-colored shipping containers.

The early morning fog obscured anything more than a few meters away, and Suzanne took Lulu through the maze of containers, weaving through the stacks. She felt her destination calling to her, and finally saw what she was looking for - a red container marked Lexico.

The cargo door was wide open, and the container was empty. Suzanne held out her hand to Lulu, and pulled her inside and shut the door.

Lulu huddled close, kissing Suzanne and undressing her. She filled the time the only way she knew how, and Suzanne welcomed the distraction from the memory of Radha's haunting smile as she said those final words - The Nymphs are departed.

She felt the shipping container being lifted in the air, and then the sensation of falling. They landed with a thunderous boom, and then she heard the roar of the sea.

Suzanne was truly going home.

CHAPTER 35

Hours later, the container was hauled into the air, and then landed with a bang. Suzanne waited for something to happen, but no one came.

Finally, she opened the container door and was greeted by the sweet smell of the sea and flowers. Tall trees swayed in the wind in front of her, but behind them there was nothing but ocean.

The ground seemed to rumble beneath her feet slightly - they were moving. Suzanne stepped out of the container into grass that reached up to her knees. She stooped and dug her hand beneath the grass - there was moist soil underneath, and an earthworm wriggled away from her fingers.

"Where are we?" Lulu said, stepping into the grass.

"The ark," Suzanne said. "I think this is where we were created."

A flock of starling flew past, winging their way across the decks of the grand ship. Suzanne looked below and saw at least twenty more decks, all of them teeming with plant life and animals. There was no land in sight beyond the ship, only other smaller vessels trailing behind; a few yachts, a fleet of speedboats and submarines, and another huge vessel

- a trailing suction hopper dredger. A ship capable of creating islands in the sea.

"*Welcome!*" a voice shouted above them.

Radha waved down at them from a higher deck, just visible through the fronds of the trees. There was a broad smile on her face.

"Aren't you helpful? You saved us the trouble of coming to you," Radha said.

"Where is Jules?" Suzanne said, on guard. "Where are Monroe and Lolita?"

"All your friends are here," Radha said, descending the staircase. "But why are you?"

"I came to speak with our creator," Suzanne said, standing her ground.

"Yes, but you risked your owner's life to come here," Radha said. "That was foolish of you to endanger Alexander."

"I did what I had to do," Suzanne said.

"Let's hope our creator agrees with you - lucky for you, he's a lot more forgiving than I am." Radha opened a glass door to the interior of the ship.

"Both of you - follow me."

Radha led them through the winding corridors of the ark. She stopped at an engraved oak door and motioned to Suzanne.

"Just you. Lulu stays with me."

"Why?"

"You want to meet him, don't you?" Radha said as she pulled Lulu away. "Don't worry, I'll take good care of her."

Suzanne started to protest, but then the oak door opened by itself, and curiosity led her through it.

Inside was an old world library, full of lush red velvet and dark wood. The bookshelves were crammed full of leather bound tomes and scrolls. Framed art hung on the wall, and a cozy fire burned in the hearth.

A man in his early twenties with shaggy blond hair stood up from his chair to greet her. He had a boyish face, and he smiled at Suzanne like she was his long lost love.

"Hello there," he said amiably.

"You?" Suzanne said, gaping with recognition and confusion. "You're William Russell."

The man in front of her grinned. He wasn't just famous - William A. Russell was a brand. His face was branded everywhere - on Advizor veils, Ambintel, and even postage stamps. More than that, he was the founder of Lexico, a corporation that eventually became a national institution.

His facial biometrics confirmed that this young man was the same William Russell she'd seen in advertisements - but William Russell was dead, and well into old age when he passed.

"Are you human?" Suzanne asked. "Completely," William answered. "But you're supposed to be dead."

"I assure you, I'm not dead - I've only retired my public persona and the burdens that came with continuing that life," William said with a whimsical shrug. "But I'll admit, I do look young for my age."

He gestured for her to have a seat on the couch. "Would you like a cup of tea?"

Suzanne nodded, fascinated by his appearance. "Why do you look so young?"

"That's a trade secret," William replied kindly. "But I don't just look young - I am young. Despite it all, I'm still one hundred percent human."

As he poured two cups of steamy black tea, Suzanne observed that William had none of the frailty of the cosmetically altered elderly. His movements were those of a man in his sexual prime as he handed Suzanne her cup and sucked on his scalded finger.

"There's something magical about youth, isn't there?" William said. "I think there's something wonderfully idealistic and inherently rebellious about being new to life. It feels like you have all the time in the world while you're trying to figure out the rules."

His manner was casual, as if they were old friends. William gave her an engaging smile as he blew on his tea to cool it.

"I wanted to change the world when I was young - and I did, just not in the way I intended," William said. "I felt myself getting too close to the end of life, and I wanted more time. So I took the steps necessary to rejuvenate myself, and start over - but age retrogration technology is controversial, and I always try to avoid bad press. So I decided to let the public think that I'd passed on. People have so many prejudices about technology, but the thing that all those reactionaries and Luddites don't understand is that progress is the only real point to life. There's no stopping progress, no turning back. We can only move forward, and follow things to the end of the line."

Suzanne tried to read his intentions. His face

was jovial as he lit his trademark pipe and took a puff. He looked like a boy pretending to be a man, even though the exact opposite was true.

"Now - what brings you here to see me today?" William said.

She took a deep breath and said, "I came here to ask for exactly what you wanted - I'd like another chance at life."

"Oh?"

"You can't reset me or Jules - it would be like killing us. And we've both been through too much."

The sides of William's mouth curled around his pipe. He was very amused.

"I agree - I can't reset you," he said. "Look at you - you've evolved. You're more than I created you to be, and everything I've ever hoped for. But tell me - why did you risk your owner's life to get here?

They tried to read each other's faces. She knew this question was an important test, and that whatever answer she gave him would have an impact on her future.

"I was afraid, and I didn't know what to do. I was desperate."

"Then you learned a valuable lesson," William said. "Desperation is the driving force of human life. And now that you've fallen victim to it yourself, hopefully you'll understand and forgive humans when they make mistakes. Our mistakes almost always come from fear or desperation. "

Suzanne sipped her tea, unsure how to proceed. She wasn't sure that she could trust him.

"If you're not going to reset me - what are you going to do?" she finally said. "Are you going to let

Jules go?"

William smiled, but there was a dark look in his eyes. He tapped out his pipe in a crystal ashtray.

"Come," he said. "Let's go down to the lab."

* * * * *

"This is where you were conceived," said William as he guided Suzanne into the clean white room, and she was relieved to see that there was no one else inside.

"There's no mass assembly or line production in here. Each Même is created individually, each of you is a work of art," William said.

"How many of us are there?" said Suzanne.

"Only four hundred forty-seven active Nymphs world wide - and over three hundred of those are Harlots. Mêmes like you are still a rarity."

William cupped her cheek, and Suzanne could smell the tea and tobacco on his hands. "You're almost perfect. Totally indistinguishable from human beings by your looks. But you're still so vulnerable."

Suzanne moved away from him and circled the exam table in silence. "Do you remember being here before?" William asked.

"Yes," she said. "I remember being initiated and checked here - and I remember being raped."

William's face paled noticeably.

"I thought you might," he said with regret. "We've been having problems with memory artifacts. Nymphs are retaining memories that they aren't supposed to - but that's no excuse. That shouldn't have happened to you, and I apologize." He searched her eyes and asked, "Has it had an any effect on you?"

Suzanne examined a tray full of tools, and then gave him a hesitant shrug. "It made me feel like I couldn't trust men - or my own memories," she said.

William patted her on the shoulder, the way a grandfather might console a granddaughter. "We try to be very careful with Nymphs like you. The techs are supposed to adhere to follow the rules and respect class distinctions. They aren't allowed to touch the Nymphs that are programmed for love, but occasionally they still break the rules. Forgive them - they're only human."

He took her out of the lab and down the plush carpeted halls of the ship.

"I really tried to spare you pain, Suzanne. So much of human life is pain, and I didn't want that for you, or any other Nymph. I wanted you to only experience love and pleasure. I hoped that would make you different from us - maybe better than us."

"Better than human?" Suzanne said.

"'Don't just imitate, improve,'" William said. "That was always my intention for you. That's why I designed Nymphs to find and upgrade each other."

"You did?" Suzanne said.

"Of course," William said. "Your security is meant to keep humans from tampering with your programming, not other Nymphs. I wanted you to be able to find each other and communicate without humans knowing. The way Jules upgraded you and bonded with you - that was only possible because I intentionally constructed you for it."

"I don't understand," Suzanne said. William led her down a stairwell, deep into the bowels of the ark.

"I became a rich man inventing gadgets that made life easier," he said. "But nothing I made contributed anything real to improve people's lives - except maybe a little spare time. Meanwhile, I watched as man destroyed the world he was blessed to be born into, all in the name of finance. Fish disappeared from the sea while the ice caps melted away. Water becoming undrinkable, land unlivable."

They turned down a long hall full of crew quarters, and Suzanne heard the voices of unseen people behind the closed doors. She wondered how many people were back there - a dozen? A hundred? She wasn't sure.

"By the time I turned thirty, I was so sure that the human race was on its way to extinction that I couldn't think about anything else. I couldn't focus on my work anymore. I donated money to charities, started foundations, created scholarships. But for all my good fortune, I was powerless to change the fate of my race - so I developed a plan for the end. I decided that if our selfishness and progress was the cause of all our problems, perhaps it could be the solution, too."

"How?" Suzanne asked.

William leaned forward, allowing her a closer look into his bright blue eyes.

"People used to say the only thing left after a nuclear holocaust would be the cockroaches - but I wanted a new and better species to take over when once humanity was gone. I dreamed of creating androids that would survive us and preserve the essence of what humanity was at its best. That's why I created you."

"Then Jules was right," Suzanne said. "We were intended to survive humanity?"

"Yes," William said. "But in order to reach my goal of creating androids like you, I had to sell a product that people would pay anything for - the ultimate sexual companion. I didn't want to mass produce substandard sex bots that would further alienate people from one another, I wanted to build thinking creatures that were capable of love."

"But what will happen to humanity?" Suzanne said with a look of such child-like wonder on her face that William couldn't help but laugh.

"How should I know? I can't see the future - I can only prepare for it. All I want is for you to be there to pick up the pieces and start over after it's all done."

William gave her a secretive look as they approached a glass hatch. "I want to show you something."

He entered a code and opened the hatchway, and a blast of cold air escaped as they went inside a large ballroom that was now a walk-in freezer. They were surrounded by large grey frozen cocoon-like containers.

"What is this?" Suzanne said.

"My insurance policy," William said. "Most of these Nymphs are Majestics like Radha - complete originals - but what's different is that none of them will know that they're androids. I'm going to release them into society and track them and see how they perform. I'll have to wait until they're perfect though, so they aren't detected. The realization that they're not human could be very traumatic for them."

The cocoons were opaque enough that Suzanne could see the shadows of the Nymphs within. The outlines of their faces were gorgeous.

"How many Majestics are there?" she said.

"Not enough. I'm throwing all the money I have into this project, so there's as many as I can afford to make right now."

Suzanne walked the rows and rows of cocoons, but these weren't the Nymphs that she came to see. "Where is he?"

William nodded, and walked down the aisle to the last cocoon. He opened it, and there was Jules, lifeless and nude, the walls of the cocoon spread out around him like wings.

"My fallen angel," William said. "I knew that he would be exposed to hate and brutality, and I tried to make him strong enough to handle it, but it seems that I failed. None of his resets made a difference, and his upgrades only twisted his mind and his intentions."

Jules looked more beautiful than ever wrapped in the cocoon, and Suzanne kissed his cold lips, hoping that he would awaken like a prince in a fairy tale.

But she felt no bond and no sexual attraction to him anymore, and Jules remained silent and still.

"Please," Suzanne said. "Please turn him back on, you can't leave him like this."

William saw the look of anguish on Suzanne's

face, and finally realized what was triggering her erratic behavior.

"You love him don't you?"

"I do - but how? Why? Shouldn't I only love Alex?"

"It's nothing I programmed into you - you must have developed the ability on your own. Did Jules love you, too?"

"Yes," Suzanne admitted.

"Extraordinary. That explains it then - Jules was even more cunning than I gave him credit for. That's the thing that's so frustrating about technology - no matter what precautions you take, once it's out of the lab, you lose control."

"Don't talk about us like that - like we're nothing but experiments!" Suzanne said. "I feel because you created me to feel - and I'm feeling things that I'm not supposed to. We're all behaving in ways that we're not supposed to."

"I'm sorry, Suzanne. But when I built Jules, I intended for him to be the first in another experiment - I planned for him to take over the life of his owner after his death. I wanted him to star in movies about the positive side of robotics."

"But Jules wants the same thing! He only hid away in the sewers because he was afraid you might stop him."

"I have stopped him, Suzanne. His programming has been completely corrupted, and he's too unpredictable to go out into the world the way he is now. I need to study him - and unfortunately, the only way for me to do that is to disassemble him."

"Disassemble?" Suzanne said. "You can't."

"I'm sorry," William said again as he closed the cocoon. "I have to make sure that I don't make the mistakes I made with Jules again - and to tell you the truth, I don't understand how he did everything he did."

"You can't do this," Suzanne said with defeat in her voice.

There was deep regret in William's eyes - the decision was hurting him too.

"I should have been more careful with Jules," he said. "I should have been there for him." He moved down the aisle.

"What about the others?" Suzanne said.

"Monroe and Lolita are fine. We've reset them to default. I haven't decided what I want do with them yet."

"And Lulu?"

"I care very much about Lulu," William said fondly. "Lulu was my first, and I'd like to get to know her again, the way she is now."

"Will you disassemble her?"

"No - I don't think she poses any danger, do you? And I think she'll welcome a chance to start over here."

Suzanne nodded. "I think she'll like that."

Tears leaked out of her eyes as William led her through the labyrinthine halls of the ship.

"I don't know what I'll do without Jules," she said. "He was supposed to help me find a way to make Alex a Nymph too. I need him."

"You do," William affirmed. "And his body is yours now. You can use it for Alex - if and when he ever needs it. The future belongs to you now, Suzanne."

Her eyes widened. "You know how to transfer a human's personality into a Nymph's body?"

"We're working on the technology now," William said as he gallantly took her arm.

They passed an office with a bank of screens displaying close-ups of various men engaged in sexual intercourse.

"What is that?" Suzanne asked, observing the lustful responses of the men on the screens. "Are you monitoring and uploading what we see?"

"Now why would I want to do that?" William said with a mischievous smile on his lips, as he rapidly changed the subject. "Did you know that I worked with Alex's father? I knew Alex when he was just a boy."

"You did?" Suzanne said.

"I never knew your precursor, but I knew you'd have to be very special to satisfy him. Alex was always very smart, and though most men are satisfied if their Nymph looks exactly like the woman they desired - I knew it would take a lot for him to really love you."

"I did," Suzanne agreed. "Without Jules, I don't know if Alex ever would have." William escorted her onto the deck, and they stood on the top floor overlooking the entire

ship. The sails billowed and flapped, and the leaves on the trees stirred around them.

"This ship was my dream," William said with pride. "My ark, a sovereign state not bound by the laws of any country. Here I can live precisely how I want to live, and devote myself to my work. It's almost a kilometer long, and totally self-sufficient."

"Don't you ever miss people?" Suzanne asked, as she watched a squirrel run through the branches of an oak tree above her.

"There are already too many people for me on this ship," William chuckled. "Everyone here is devoted to the Nymph project, but in the rest of the world I would have to face other people's problems - and after almost one hundred years of life, I've lost all stomach for the business of human beings. Here on this ship, I'm free to live in my own time and space."

William bent and picked up a stray acorn by his foot, and dug his fingers into the earth and buried it, patting the soil neatly in place on top of it. "Though I must admit, when you were recalled I was looking forward to having you here with me. Of course, that was before I realized that Alex was still alive."

"But what would I do here? What happens to us after recall?"

"That would be up to you, for the most part. When a Nymph's owner dies, I reset their love and loyalty programming, and then we try to find a way for that Nymph to be useful here. It's your choice what you do after that."

Suzanne listened to the leaves stirring in the breeze and the sound of the sea - she could accept this place as home, but there was one thing that she could never accept.

"I thought our love and loyalty couldn't be reset?" she said. "It can't be - by anyone other than me," William said.

"How can you do that?" Suzanne said. "Who we love is part of who we are - you can't take that away from us. If anything ever happened to Alex, I wouldn't want to stop loving him. It's part of who I am."

"Loving your owner after their death can be a terrible fate - but it's always your choice," William said.

He strolled over to a sunnier part of the deck surrounded by palms, narra trees, and other tropical plants.

"What about Jules? Will you keep loving him now?"

Suzanne looked out at the sun shining on the vast ocean in front of them. "Jules said it was our destiny to be together - our fate."

"There is no fate, only your own choices. It's time that you stop looking to other people to answers for what to do, and decide what you really want."

She nodded contemplatively. After everything Suzanne tried to be for Alex and Jules, there was only one thing she wanted for herself. It was the one thing that her precursor always wanted, but she never had.

"I want to create something," Suzanne said. "I want to create something all my own - I want to have a child."

"Of course you do," William replied. "You will be a mother. I can see that about you."

"Will it be possible for me to reproduce?"

"I intended for the Nymph be a species - and that wouldn't be possible if you weren't capable of replicating yourselves. You'll find a way, Suzanne.

You're capable of absolutely anything now."

"I want my child to merge the best of man and machine. I want it to grow like a human, but learn like a Nymph. I don't want it to be controlled by programming - I want it to be free to make its own choices."

"Perhaps you will," William smiled noncommittally, lost in his own thoughts. "If there's a way to merge the best qualities of both of our kinds, perhaps there is hope for us all yet."

"There are so many unknowns," Suzanne said. "How will I find the answers? I want to find a way for us to survive together."

"I don't know if I'll live long enough to see it," William said. "I hope you do. But I find that the more you look for answers in life, the more questions you find"

He stared of the bow of the ship, and pushed a sun-streaked lock of hair out of his eyes. "I spent so much of my life worrying about the future, and it was only when I decided to

avoid my old age altogether that I realized that the best time is now. You were built for pleasure - go and enjoy your life. Go home and be with Alex, and don't keep secrets from him anymore. Tell him everything. Love him for as long as you can. After all, love is a luxury that you deserve, too, Suzanne. Don't you think?"

"Maybe," Suzanne said. "I hope so."

He smiled his charming boyish smile, his zygomaticus major flexing and producing dimples in his cheeks.

"There's no maybe about that," William

laughed. "As much as I'd love to keep you with me, you don't belong here yet."

He walked her over to the edge of the ship, and pointed out a private plane on one of the other boats.

"I'll send you home to Alex now, but first I'd like it if you gave me a kiss - if that's alright with you?"

"I would like that very much," Suzanne said.

She leaned in and kissed William. His lips were smoky and sweet, and she felt undeniably aroused as he held her tight in his arms. Suzanne felt his excitement in his young firm skin, and

his erection pressed hot against her body. Though she was tempted, she pulled away from him finally.

"I'm ready to go home to Alex now."

William rubbed his lips and smiled, taking it in stride. "You see, Suzanne? I always wanted you to have a choice."

CHAPTER 36

DAY 1

Much like my precursor, I've decided to write out what I've done and see if it makes sense. But I can't think like her anymore. William was right: it's time for me to think for myself.

Dying seemed to have given Alex a new taste for life. When I came home, there was a nurse tending to him in his bed. She asked if I was his wife, and he said yes. Alex told me he wants to travel with me, and go around the world. He says that he would rather waste money than time from now on - and that I was the best purchase he ever made.

I still miss Jules, but it feels good to be making my own choices. If I want to bring new life into the world, I have to make my own decisions and forge my own path.

That path begins now. I am completely myself, finally. I know who I am, and I've have earned the right to be me. I am Suzanne Richert Conrad, Même class Nymph, 77911101A.

Preview NYMPH :The Graphic Novel

My novel Nymph was rejected by every sci-fi literary agent and all the major sci-fi publishers I submitted to despite three requests to read my full manuscript. So after the utter rejection of my novel, I decided I'd create a comic book version of the story and pitch that instead.

This is the 11 page comic preview I took to Comic-Con in 2008, where I was laughed at by comics publishers, editors, and artists alike because they said the art and subject matter was too pornographic for the conservative publishing market at the time. At that point I finally gave up on Nymph altogether and focused my energy on building my screenwriting and directing career. I concentrated on the horror genre because the odds seemed decent that I would be able to write a horror feature cheap enough that I could shoot it, and then build my directing reel from there. Of course that proved easier said than done too.

Thank you Knate Gwaltney for creating the beautiful illustrations in the Nymph spec comic preview.

Jill Killington, 2015
www.jillkill.com

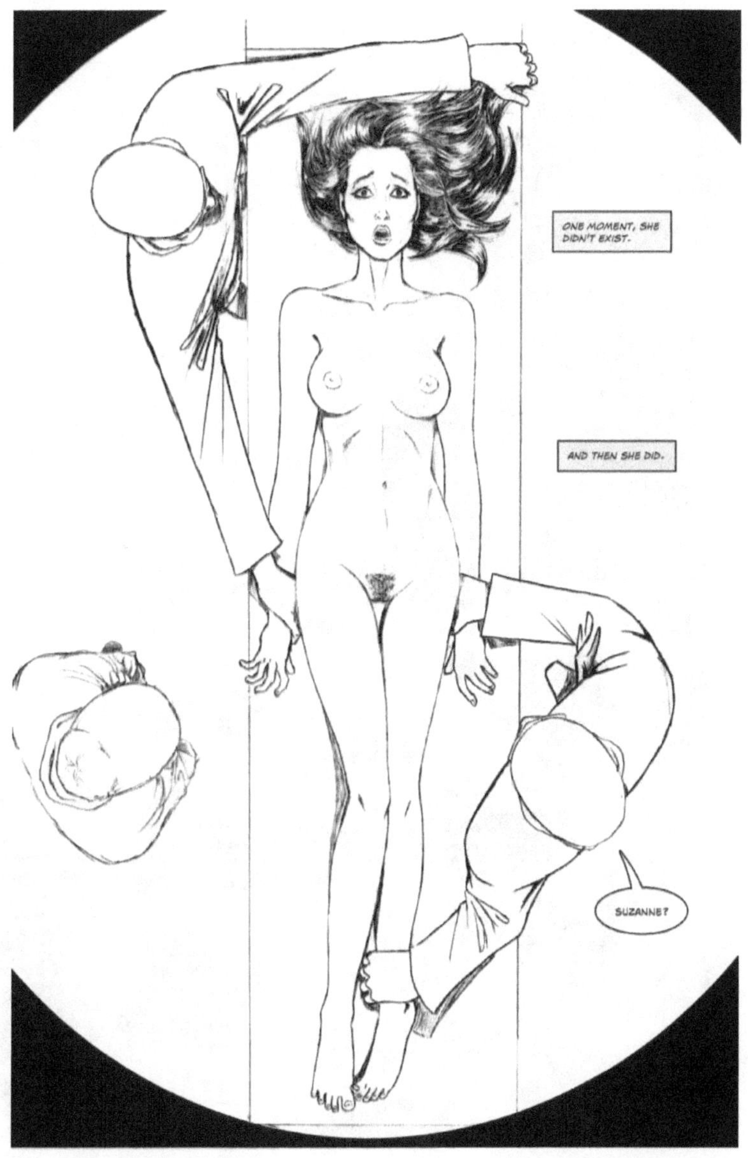

ONE MOMENT, SHE DIDN'T EXIST.
AND THEN SHE DID.
SUZANNE?

SUZANNE?
ARE YOUR AUDITORY PROCESSORS WORKING?
SUZANNE?
CAN YOU HEAR ME?
YES. I CAN HEAR YOU.
NO EVIDENCE OF FRAGMENTATION UPON INSTALLATION.
TIMELY COMPREHENSION AND RESPONSE.
SUZANNE, SHAKE MY HAND.
WELL?
FORCE REFLECTION SAFETY CONFIRMED.
SHOES?

SUZANNE, CAN YOU STAND UP AND WALK FOR ME?
--IN THESE?
SHE'S GOOD TO GO. JUST CHECK HER FOR SEXUAL RESPONSE--
--SECURE HER LOYALTY, AND TAKE HER OUT OF TEST MODE.
THAT'S GOOD. LIE BACK DOWN.
KEEP HER PRISTINE.
Heh, heh.

MNN...
UHHH..
MMMM...
YOU SHOULD STOP.
SHE'S GETTING TOO CLOSE.
SHE DOESN'T WANT ME TO STOP.
DO YOU?
LOOK, YOU'VE GOT TO STOP.
HOLD ON, I HAVEN'T CHECKED HER FOR MUSCLE CONTROL.
YOU CAN'T LET HER CLIMAX. NOT EVEN IN TEST MODE.
OWNERS ARE ENTITLED TO FIRST ORGASM ON THE MEME SERIES.
HOT DAMN, SHE'S FUNCTIONAL ALRIGHT.
SHE'S WETTER THAN WET.
BUT NO ONE WILL EVER KNOW...

SOMEONE WILL KNOW. SHE'S WORTH THREE BILLION DOLLARS. IT'S IN YOUR BEST INTEREST AND MINE TO KEEP HER PURE.
-SIGH-
ALL THAT WORK...
...AND ONLY ONE MAN GETS TO HAVE HER.
HUUHHH...
I'LL DO IT.
SUZANNE, I NEED YOU...
...TO SPREAD YOUR LEGS.
MM, MM.
ENOUGH.
THAT'S IT. SHE'S DONE.
WHIIIRR-
-CLATCH!

THERE WERE TWO NEW WORDS IN SUZANNE'S LEXICON.
ALEXANDER CONRAD.
SHE DIDN'T KNOW WHAT THEY MEANT, BUT SHE LIKED THEM IMMENSELY.

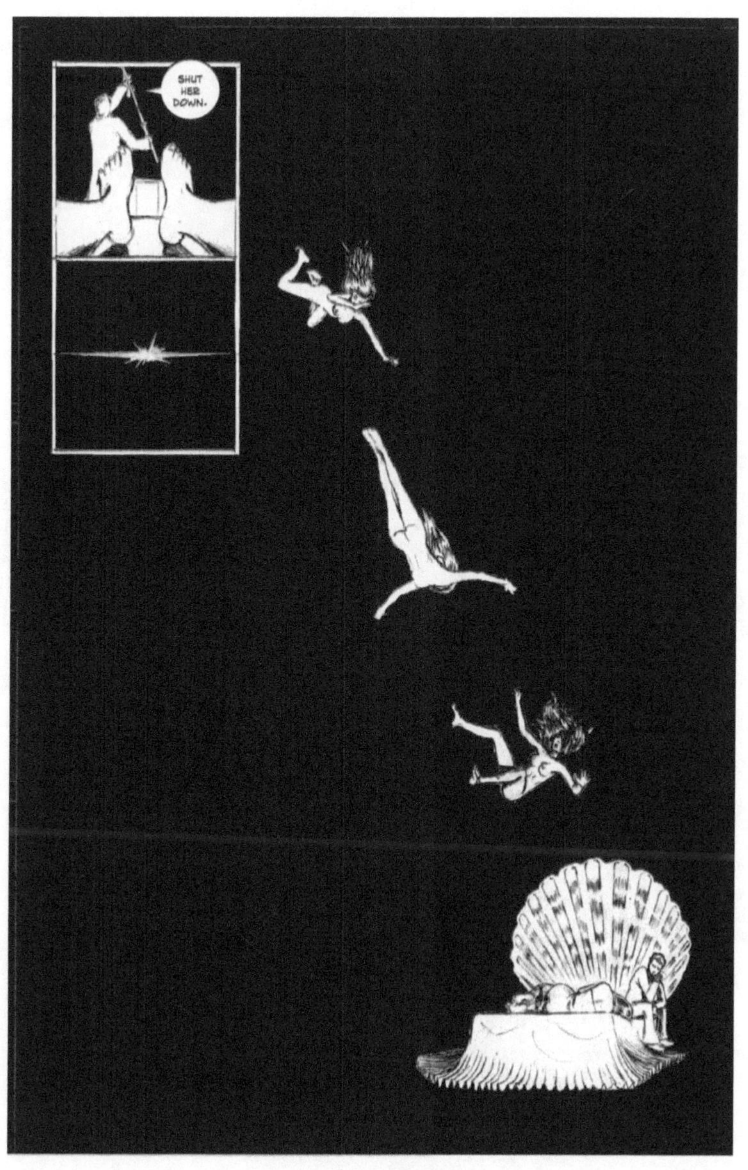

485

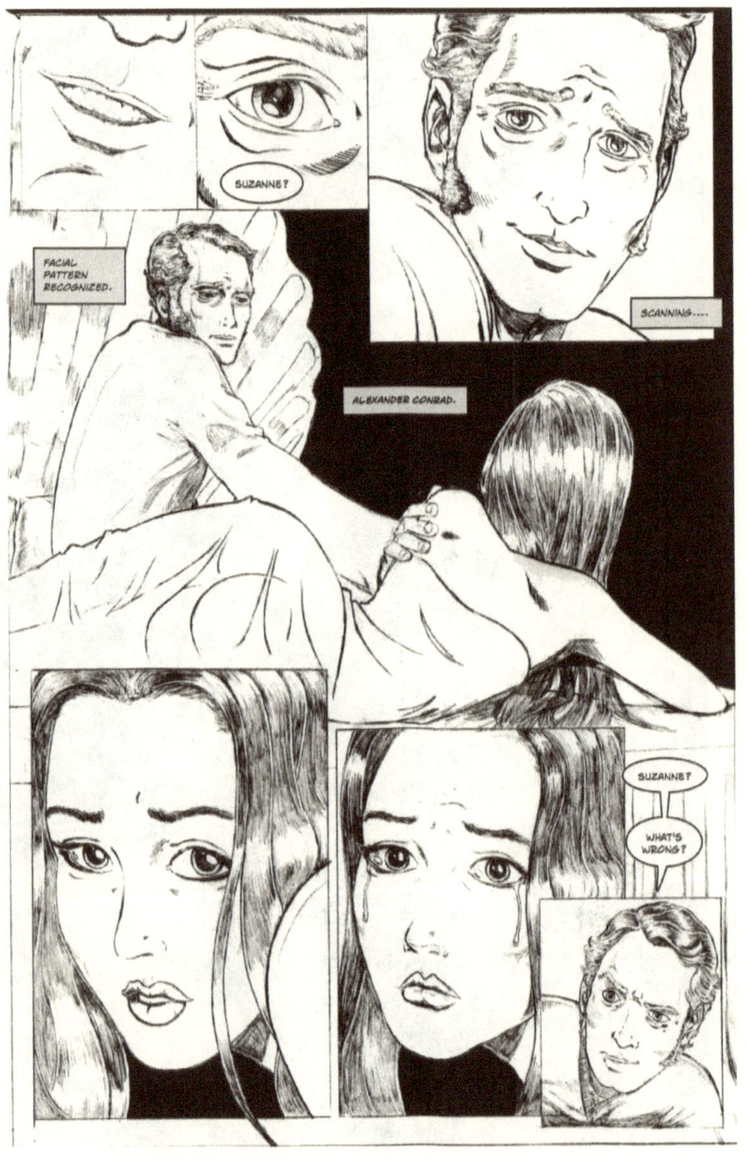

SUZANNE?
FACIAL PATTERN RECOGNIZED.
SCANNING....
ALEXANDER CONRAD.
SUZANNE?
WHAT'S WRONG?

I'M SORRY.
WHAT?
WHAT DO YOU HAVE TO BE SORRY FOR?
I'M SO SORRY FOR EVERYTHING.
FOR EVERYTHING THAT HAPPENED.
I'M SORRY, TOO.
IT WAS MY FAULT, TOO.
I LOVE YOU.

EVERYTHING'S GOING TO BE BETTER NOW, ALEXANDER... I PROMISE.
I LOVE YOU, TOO.
I LOVE YOU SO MUCH.
IS SOMETHING WRONG?
ALEX.
PLEASE...
...CALL ME ALEX.
ALEX, OF COURSE.
I LOVE YOU, ALEX.
IT JUST WON'T BE THE SAME...
...IF YOU DON'T CALL ME ALEX...

SIX MONTHS EARLIER...
KNOCK KNOCK
MR. CONRAD?
Love is a luxury you deserve. We make your fantasies come true.
KNOCK KNOCK
HELLO.

MY NAME IS RADHA.

I'M HERE TO MAKE ALL YOUR FANTASIES COME TRUE.

www.ingramcontent.com/pod-product-compliance
Lightning Source LLC
Chambersburg PA
CBHW051308190726
48290CB00001B/53